TALON THE BLACK

BOOK 1 OF THE DRAGONWALL SERIES

MELISSA MITCHELL

For my mom, who shares my love and enthusiasm of Dragonwall.

DRAGONWALL
Shadowkeep
Belnes
Dragonfire Sea
Redport
Squall's End
Kastali Dyn
Bay of Bandu

ngr Gate
The Gable
Forest
ncastle
South Sea

CHAPTER I
THE FALLING DRAGON

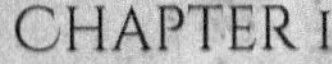

Battle Ground, Indiana

On a bright, moonlit night, in a place few people have heard of, a dragon fell from the sky...

Claire was speeding up the gravel drive towards her family's farmhouse, plumes of dust fanning out behind her. It was nearly three in the morning. The speakers in her Honda Civic blasted Alanis Morissette's *Jagged Little Pill* album. It really was the perfect ending to a shitty night.

This occasion warranted one song in particular. "*You Oughta Know.*" She'd been playing it on repeat since leaving Shannon's Bar to get over the jerk who'd left her for someone else. His name was Jake Owens. As far as she was concerned, he was a complete and utter *ballbag*.

No wonder she'd dreaded moving back home after college. Jake's parents owned Shannon's. Bartending wasn't exactly where she saw herself at twenty-two. Especially not at her ex's bar, and *especially* not when he showed up while she was working. Tonight, he'd dropped by with his new girlfriend, Tiffany.

Things had always been on-again-off-again with him, even when he'd promised otherwise. Even when he'd promised to *make it work.* "He made it work all right," she muttered, gripping the steering wheel until her fingers turned white. "Right into Tiffany's pants."

She sang along, bobbing to the beat of the music—

A flash of movement halted her words. She blinked, trying to clear her gaze. Then, she blinked again.

A dragon streaked across her vision, spewing flames. Or was it a meteor? No. It was definitely a dragon! The earth rumbled, giving a small shake, then went silent. She stared at the spot where it had disappeared into the cornfield.

Alanis Morissette's voice continued in the background.

"I'm going crazy," she muttered, rubbing a hand over her tired eyes.

The wheels beneath her Civic heaved. She tensed. *Whack! Whack! Whack!* Stalks of corn swallowed her up. She swore, jerking at the wheel to the right. Gravel crunched as she veered back onto the drive and spun around in a half-circle. Dust clouded up around her. The car slid across the lane and into the cornfield on the opposite side. She skidded to a halt in the dirt, mere feet from a utility pole.

"Good going, idiot," she muttered, blowing a lock of hair out of her face. She peeled her fingers off the wheel. For a moment, she stupidly stared ahead, then everything came rushing back.

A dragon had just fallen into her cornfield.

She squinted into the darkness. There! Wisps of smoke snaked upwards. A beacon that said, "Come and find me."

She tore off into the field, her feet squishing and sinking into the soft dirt. She stumbled and caught herself, cursing under her breath. It was worse than running on the beach. At least *then* you didn't have stalks of corn slapping you in the face.

Her breathing came in gasps. Her side cramped up, but that didn't matter. Dragons were more important than side aches. She felt every scratch, every cut. The field fought her, but she fought back. She kept her gaze just above the tassels, looking for the large shape she expected to find.

The closer she got, the further her hopes fell. Some things were just too good to be true. Especially when it came to finding a dragon, which just *happened* to fall from the sky. But she refused to give up.

Her foot caught on a mound of earth and sent her flying. She cried out. Her hands caught her, sinking into the earth, but only just. "Why me?" she groaned, pushing herself up on her forearms. The coppery taste of blood filled her mouth.

Collecting what little dignity she had left, she got up and brushed herself off—

Her eyes widened. She froze, mid-motion. "Oh. My. *God!*"

It was here—right in front of her. The scene looked like something from the set of a science fiction movie. An impact-crater larger than a dragon. Stalks of corn stood bent and strewn in all directions. Small fires flickered around the perimeter with feeble yellow flames.

"Shit!" She rushed forward to stamp them out. Her parents would never trust her if she burned the fields down. But...where was the dragon?

There had definitely been a dragon.

Except...there wasn't. Lying face down and unmoving, was a man. Her eyebrows knitted together. It turned out, someone was having a crappier night than she was, and that was saying something.

A large sword glittered at his waist. Wait. A sword?! Was it a prop for a costume? No, it was too fancy. And why was he dressed so...weird?

It was like King Arthur had stepped out of Howard Pyle's tale.

He wore beige leggings, knee-high black boots, a long tunic, and a brown leather doublet. She almost snorted. He was straight-up Renaissance Fair. Was this really happening? She pinched herself. Yep. It was.

She climbed down into the crater and went to him, checking for a pulse. His heartbeat was slow, but he was alive. She exhaled. Thank freaking god!

A heavy metallic scent filled the air. That couldn't be good. She grabbed him and pulled. He weighed a *ton*. The moment she flipped him over, she immediately regretted it. There was blood *everywhere*.

She lifted her hands in alarm. Her stomach lurched and she choked back a gagging sound. So much blood, she was sticky with it.

Her first breath was deep and slow. They got shallower, came faster, until she was hyperventilating. She opened her mouth to call for her dad, like she usually did, but snapped it shut. Her parents were vacationing in Florida.

Taking hold of his shoulder, she shook him. He didn't respond. The gash on his side ran from chest to hip.

She went stock still and looked up from his body, squinting into the darkness of the cornfield. Someone had hurt him. Were they *here*—watching her? Waiting to finish the job? Oh, god! Was she next?!

"To hell with this!" She stood up. The field loomed around her with its suddenly ominous walls. Anyone could be hiding within. Or...anything.

She glanced back the way she'd come. She could run back to her car, forget this ever happened. But...

She glanced down at him. Was it worth his life? She gritted her teeth. There was no other choice. She had to save him. The need was like an invisible force, urging her on.

But what could *she* really do?

The sheriff. She needed to call the sheriff. She wiped her hands on her apron and reached for her phone. Her pocket was empty. She'd left it in her car with a dead battery.

Crap!

What about the landline in the house? She could use that. She dashed off, taking about ten steps before she froze and turned back. She removed her apron and stuffed it under the man's tunic, using the pressure of his vest on the fabric to slow the bleeding. How was he even still alive?

She gave him one final look, then sprinted away.

Her muscles screamed, but she kept running, ignoring the tension in her ankles. It would be pointless to call the sheriff, she realized. Ambulances never came out this far. The nearest hospital was almost an hour away, in Lafayette. Even if they made an exception, he wouldn't last long enough.

That's why everyone went to her dad first. He was their lifeline out here in the middle of nowhere. Now there was only her—a joke in comparison. She hadn't followed in her father's footsteps—not even close. Not for the first time, a little bit of guilt seeped into her thoughts.

Still, she had to try.

It took nearly five minutes to make it to the barn. When she entered, the familiar smell of sweet hay and damp wood greeted her. She began throwing equipment around haphazardly, looking for something she could use as a stretcher. Tilly and Joe were agitated, mooing loudly. Poor things, they weren't used to seeing her this frantic.

"It's okay," she cooed, passing their stalls.

Leaving the barn, she grabbed a spare key from the hanging flower pot on the porch, then ripped through her house like a tornado, leaving a mess of similar magnitude. Once she'd gathered all she needed, including her dad's medical bag, she took the farm's John Deere Gator.

A minute later she was back at the crater.

The man was still unconscious. He gave no complaints when she stripped away his bloodied clothing and belongings. Undeterred by his nakedness, she cleaned the wound with iodine. The skin along the gash was the color of tar. It hissed and protested, black smoke sizzling up from the depths of the exposed flesh. She didn't have time nor the nerve to question how abnormal it was.

The lights from the Gator were a big help. Even still, her hands trembled. She turned away to regain her composure, especially when she began to close the wound. The sight of the needle passing through his skin made her nauseous. She *never* wanted to follow in her father's footsteps, much to his disappointment. This was why.

At last, she finished. Her hands were bloodied and slippery. But eventually the skin pulled together. A hospital would have done a much better job. Hers was rudimentary, at best. Small amounts of blood still crept from between some of the sloppier parts.

She used Super Glue to coat the length of the wound for safe measure. The blood stopped as quickly as it dried. Certain kinds of Super Glue had been used during the Vietnam War to prevent excessive bleeding—she'd learned *that* from her dad, at least.

She finished by taping gauze over the length of the injury. Using a blanket, she covered his body, tying it around his waist. Next, she rolled him onto a seven-foot plank from the barn making sure to secure him properly, then propped it onto the bed of the gator. She had to shimmy it onto the back to get him up. Her muscles were shaking by the end.

She left the crater far behind. This time, she drove more slowly, taking some time to think. It was a little past four in the morning. She was physically and mentally exhausted. But that didn't stop the gazillion questions from popping into her mind.

She parked at the base of the stairs to the porch and took a good look at her patient. He would have died, had it not been for her. A little flare of pride warmed her chest. Would her dad be proud of her?

With tired fingers, she undid the ties holding him in place. She had no intention of moving an untrustworthy man into the safety of her home. The last thing she wanted was to get tangled up in whatever he was involved in.

Perhaps he would wake up and take himself home. "One less thing to worry about," she muttered darkly, thinking about her problems with Jake.

She gathered his sword, his belongings, and the bloody clothes from the back of the gator. She planned to take them inside for further investigation. The clothing was going straight into the garbage. But the other stuff? She was especially curious about it.

Once more she leaned over him, watching his chest rise and fall. His breathing was no longer staggered. Actually, he looked much better. The worry lines on his face were gone. He was resting easier.

She inhaled deeply. He smelled peculiar, like pine and eucalyptus. She noticed faint traces of smoke, too. Smoke, like the smoke from dragon fire, perhaps? She shook her head. The idea seemed ridiculous now. What she'd seen was probably just a trick of the eye. She was exhausted, after all.

But...how could she explain what was right in front of her? His hair was dark and curly. It fell just above his shoulders. Delicately, so as not to disturb him, she brushed a lock of it from his face. Something about him seemed...abnormal, now that she looked closer. Not quite...human. He was powerfully built, and handsome too. He was tall. Six-foot-four-inches, maybe? She had a weakness for tall men. Her heart fluttered for a moment, Jake all but forgotten.

She tutted, shaking her head. He was on his own now. Her weary feet climbed the porch stairs and took her safely inside. She locked the door behind her. For a moment, she stood, her back against it, simply breathing. Then her hand clenched around his belongings.

She laid them out on the coffee table, studying each one. His sword was as impressive as it was heavy. Her fingers traced the icy-cold metal. A weapon like this must have cost a fortune. Its pommel was shaped like the head of a dragon. Was that a coincidence? Just below it rested a single opal gemstone. The scabbard was decorated by a fine pearlescent pave to match. She carefully placed it back onto the table then moved on.

His belt held a few curious trinkets: a woman's locket with a lock of hair inside, a small hunting knife, and a coin sack. Most intriguing was the dark leather pouch she'd taken from his neck. She poured its contents onto her palm. There were two stones, imperfectly shaped, each about the diameter of a large coin. One was gold, the other black. They were highly polished and glittered with movement. The black one was iridescent, shimmering from hues of green, to blue, to purple.

The moment they touched her skin, shivers raced down her spine. The hairs on her arms stood on end. She gasped. Raw hunger clawed at her, and not the kind in her stomach, either. Hunger for what, though?

She stared at the stones, stroking them in her palm, turning them this way and that, studying them. A fog seemed to settle over her. She began picturing unrealistic dreams that suddenly appeared tangible. Like proving that her college degree hadn't been for nothing. That she'd actually land a good job with it. That she could make something of her life. That she was meant to *be* someone—someone important.

Exhaustion brought her to her senses. She tightened her fist around the stones before reluctantly, she dropped them back into their pouch. As soon as they were tucked away, her trance evaporated. A nervous laugh escaped her chest. She tossed the pouch on the table and cringed. Magic wasn't real, but against all logic, those stones had some form of it. The thought unnerved her. In fact, the entire ordeal was nothing short of impossible. Maybe she *was* going crazy. Maybe her drama with Jake had driven her to insanity?

She finally stumbled into bed, her mind brimming with fake reassurances. Life would be back to normal once she woke up. Tonight had simply been a bad dream. Her car was safely parked in the driveway. Jake wasn't a total ballbag. The creepy stones were merely part of her imagination. There was no wounded man outside. Dragons did not exist. And the idea of a dragon *shapeshifter* was downright outrageous!

CHAPTER 2
SHADOWKEEP

Kane paced within the dark edifice of Shadowkeep, his bare feet slapping the rocky floor. The chill had no effect on him. He was used to the cold of these snowcapped mountains.

Try as he might, the repetitive motion failed to quell his agitation. His plans had gone terribly, horribly wrong. The King's Shield had been surprisingly powerful. His mind still bore the headache like a painful memory, unwilling to recede.

A mind bender—he should have seen it. The task was supposed to be easy. Overpower the carrier and take the remaining dragonstones. But he'd underestimated the protector. The Shield broke into his mind and discovered the grand scheme lying within. It left his head burning in agony. He'd been forced to retreat, allowing the king's shield to escape north.

He snorted, his pace faltering. So much for remaining in the shadows! His entire plan hinged on secrecy. It would be far easier to carry out his tasks without hordes of drengr *scum* searching for his fortress and counter attacking at will.

But not for long...

Such abominations! He could hardly wait to rid the world of the dragon-kind who called themselves *drengr*. The dragons alone were meant to carry the mythical form bestowed upon them by his forbearers, the great Asarlaí of old. Blessing certain dragons with humanity? *Gifting* them the ability to transform into humans? It wholly disgusted him. What was Queen Isabella thinking? But never mind that, he would succeed. Soon, none of draconic descent, dragon or drengr, would walk this land again.

His pacing continued. Every so often, he stopped to peer from the many loopholes in the tower, searching out over the tall jagged peaks of the Northern Barrier Range. Still no sign of his lethal assassins. *Vodar* wraiths. He had summoned them from undirfold to finish his work, and with luck, save him from further exposure. But the longer they tarried, the greater his fury grew. Greater still was the doubt-ridden voice in the depths of his mind. Had they failed? After hundreds of years of meticulous planning, would his precious work be destroyed by one, stupid mistake?

To say he was eager was a vast understatement. He was growing desperate. The two remaining dragonstones were all that stood between failure and fulfilling his masterplan. With them, he would have a complete set. With them, he would bring about an end to the drengr monarchy. What a sweet end it would be.

Dragonstones...

He'd always found it intriguing that such seemingly harmless objects held so much power. Funnier still, so few in the world knew what they were or how they worked. But he knew, oh yes, and he had to have them, even if he died trying.

He'd first learned about the dragonstones during his early years of magic, long before his skin turned pale and gaunt, longer still before his eyes had taken on the red glow they now held. During those times, he lacked the knowledge to truly understand their worth, let alone possess them. Even then, the stones called to him like a shadowed whisper in the night. They were nothing but myth. Descriptions of their existence could only be found scattered throughout old tomes of stories long past. He never let that stop him. Eventually, the day came to seek them out.

It took him nearly half a millennium to locate all five. During his travels, he delved deeper and further into Asarlaí magic, learning things the mages could never possibly know. His increasing power kept him alive, giving him the needed strength to carry on. How formidable the power of living was for one determined to fulfill a destiny, especially a prodigious destiny such as his.

The first stone was an easy acquisition. He procured it from the bottom of Eagle Lake in the North. The depths of its hiding place were far greater than any human could reach. But he was no human. He was an Asarlaí, the last living Asarlaí in Dragonwall.

But not elsewhere, his mind taunted.

The second, he discovered by chance. Like the first, it had once belonged to the dragons at the end of the Second Age, those of the Ice Clan. Their leader had hidden it well, along with the other two he once possessed. This one was not at the bottom of any lake. Rage had locked it away in the frozen realm of Kalderland, requiring him to parley with Kalderland's inhabitants, the Kalds, great ice giants of black rock ice. In exchange for their cooperation, he made it possible for them to seek a prize of *their* choosing— support in their planned attack against the North. It was *he* who led them through the range and into the kingdom. Even if it was no fault of his that their quest ended in failure.

The most difficult of the three was locked away with the goblins. Obtaining this one resulted in his alliance with them, a most convenient outcome. Although, he would not have guessed it at the time.

Now only two remained. These were the two Rage had failed to discover. They stayed hidden for years immeasurable, until the king's shield recently procured them, which, mind you, was an integral part of his grand plan. What he had *not* anticipated was the guard's ability to retain them. The wretch should have been an easy kill, but now he protected his prize with the threads of his very existence, exercising every bit of magic to keep them safe and out of his hands.

A wicked smile stretched across his lips. Vodar wraiths were lethal, with blades imbued with poison. Impossible for humans, and difficult still for someone like the shield to overcome. He glanced out of another loophole. Still, nothing.

Where were they? A vein jumped in his forehead. He used his fingers to smooth his scowl and massage his temples. It was foolish, but he was tired of waiting. He strode across his study and removed six onyx crystals from a shelf, arranging them in a row on the floor. If his wraiths would not come, he would make them come.

Behind the crystals he spread fire powder, finer than the finest sand, and valuable beyond measure. The barrier was mostly symbolic, but nonetheless, a necessary part of the process.

When everything was assembled, he stepped away and began his incant. His lips hardly moved while he muttered. "Skaepa an eldár, vaxa eldár, brenna eldár…" The first words spoken ignited the powder, coaxing the flames into a blaze. They burned a deep blue, almost black. These flames would be the tall backdrop he required to eliminate their possibility of retreat, not that his wraiths were stupid enough to run from *him*.

As his incant progressed, a shadowy line of darkness connected the stones. The black thread grew in thickness until he moved on to the next set of phrases. A loud crack split the air, like the breaking of stone. It echoed against the rocky walls. His six assassins appeared. The number was symbolic, six vodar wraiths to match the six king's shields. Each stood in front of its respective onyx crystal.

His chanting ceased.

"Great lord." Their heads bowed. "Why have you summoned us?" Their hissing came from beneath their shadowy hoods.

"You dare question me?" His voice was a low snarl. He looked them over, glancing from one to the next. They had arrived with their short swords drawn, ready to do battle. Perhaps his timing was not the best.

"What have you to say for yourselves? What of your mission?"

"We nearly had him, my lord!" the wraith in the middle said, taking a step forward. "We had the drengr surrounded. You will be pleased to know he is wounded." There was blood dripping from its poisoned sword.

"Wounded? Pleased?" He repeated the words back in the same hissing manner. "The drengr is not dead then?" It was inexcusable. "Where are my dragonstones?"

What legitimate reason could they give for the length of time this mission was taking? Were these not the most evil creatures in all of existence? Certainly there were others, but none that he dared summon as of yet.

"We would have obtained them, great lord, had you not summoned us at the worst possible moment."

He was never one to admit a mistake, nor would he now. Perhaps he should have given them more time, but the deed was done, and here they stood. Besides, time enough he had given them.

"You have been tracking the drengr for weeks," he pointed out. "I grow tired of your inability to carry out my orders." As his anger flared, so did the fire line. The wraiths flinched and stepped forward, out of its way. "I should burn you here and now." He clenched and unclenched his fists.

"Please, we will not fail again." Vodar wraiths were terrified of fire. It was the only painful way they could be punished. Perhaps they needed to feel the weapon of their weakness.

"No, I dare say you will not fail. You know what awaits you if you do." Again, the fire flared. "I want him dead, and I want those stones. Now go!" He removed his magical hold on the fire, extinguishing the flames, freeing the way for the vodar. They fled from the room like a gust of black wind, hissing its way from Shadowkeep.

CHAPTER 3
GOLD FOR SILENCE

Battle Ground, Indiana

Claire awoke to incessant squawking. The annoyance drifted through her open window along with the sun, whose pesky rays were too bright for her aching head. No question about it, hangovers were the *worst*.

She rolled over to relieve her sore muscles, and despite the humidity, snuggled deeper under her lavender comforter. She was drifting off again when more squawking jolted her awake. "*Shuup*," she slurred, trying to ignore the damn things. Her mom's chickens frequently bickered. She didn't care for chicken squabbles when she was comfortably tucked away in her palace of solitude.

Her bedroom was more like a library, than anything. Its walls were covered with hundreds of books. When she started collecting them, there were only a few shelves. As her collection grew, more were mounted, until every bit of wall space was occupied. Her mother called it hoarding, but she begged to differ.

By high school, she had made shelves from all the reclaimed wood in the barn. At that point, her mom put a stop to it. "No more shelves in your bedroom!" she'd insisted. "You've got enough books." All further construction projects were forbidden.

How could anyone have *enough* books? She'd still managed to sneak in a few more. But at long last, it seemed her room *did* have a limit, and she was determined to reach it, down to the final book. It wasn't until her parents bought her a Kindle that she finally agreed to go digital. However, nothing would replace the experience of holding a real book: the smell of the paper, the feel of the pages, and the excitement of reading cover to cover.

She groaned dramatically and flung away her comforter. The clucking and squawking had reached its peak. She threw herself from her bed to close the window—and froze. There was a naked man in the chicken coop.

"Oh. My. God." She exhaled as memories from the night before flashed through her mind like a bad dream. *That's* why she felt terrible.

Renaissance Man—as she'd dubbed him—was failing miserably at the task of chicken catching. His movements were sloppy as he chased the hens and roosters around the coop. His wound hindered him, but he did not stop trying. He limped and stumbled around with outstretched arms. Meanwhile, the chickens squawked and screeched, protesting in earnest, but moved effortlessly out of his way.

It would have been hilarious had it not been so pathetic. Even still, the longer she watched, the harder she laughed, until she couldn't take it any more. Quickly dressing into her favorite pair of black yoga pants, she rushed downstairs.

When she reached the coop—much to her surprise—he'd successfully procured one of the fatter female hens. His hand wrapped around its neck, about to end the poor thing's life.

"Stop," she roared. "What are you doing?!" Her mom would kill her if a single, *precious* chicken was harmed. He looked dazed and confused by her shouting. "Those chickens are for eggs, not for eating, you oaf!"

"I need food," he said at last, holding the clucking chicken forward. So...he *could* speak. That was a good sign. But his accent— she frowned.

When she made no move to take the chicken, he released it to the ground, still wearing a puzzled look. He cocked his head to the side, watching her, trying to make sense of the situation. Then he looked down at his naked body, as if suddenly realizing it, and used his hands to cover himself. She snorted. As if she hadn't seen male goods before!

"Where are my clothes?"

"Look, come out of there. I'll get you something to wear." Beckoning, she recovered his blanket. He quickly wrapped it about himself like a towel, but not before she glimpsed the black skin creeping from beneath his bandages. Skin wasn't supposed to act like this. Whatever it was, it was spreading quickly.

He looked at her, eyes narrowed. Then, as if suddenly remembering something, he clutched at his neck and began looking around. "Where are they?" he whispered. "I had them here. Where…" His scowl deepened. "Where are my belongings? Where is my sverak—my sword?"

There was no, "*Thank you for saving my life.*" No, "*What happened last night?*" No gratitude whatsoever. In his expression, there was only fear and distrust.

She humored him and held up her hands. "Look, chill. I've got everything inside."

He exhaled after a long silence, then gave a curt nod.

"What's up with those stone things, anyway?" she asked after taking him inside and handing back the leather pouch he now tied around his neck. "They're pretty creepy."

"You looked at them?!" What little color he had drained from his face.

"Duh. Why wouldn't I?"

"You should not have done that." He clutched the pouch firmly against his chest.

"It was an accident. Nothing happened, all right?"

But…that wasn't exactly true. Something strange *had* happened, leaving her thoroughly freaked out. It took a moment, but he nodded, putting the subject to rest. She was relieved to do the same.

Because she'd trashed his clothing, she raided her dad's closet.

She found an overly large T-shirt and sweatpants big enough for a man of his muscular stature, even though the pants were about three inches too short. Once he was dressed, she escorted him into the kitchen to cook breakfast.

He remained silent.

"Can you at least tell me your name?" she asked after placing a glass of orange juice in front of him.

He drank half the glass in a couple of gulps before saying, "Cyrus. My name is Cyrus."

"Nice to meet you, Cyrus. I'm Claire."

"Well met, my lady."

She withheld a snort. *My lady*? Apparently his clothes hadn't been the only old fashioned thing about him.

Cyrus drained the remainder of his orange juice before turning his intense gaze upon her. "What?" She placed her hands on her hips. Was there something on her face?

"I need to know if I can trust you."

She huffed a laugh. "Really?!" Out of nowhere, her headache from earlier multiplied tenfold. She gasped, clutching her head. "You want to know if I'm trustworthy after *all this*?" Unbelievable. *He* was the one who couldn't be trusted. "If it weren't for me, Cyrus, you'd be dead."

As quickly as it'd hit her, her headache receded. At the same time, he looked down at his bandages then back at her. "This was you?"

She snorted. "Who else do you think chased you out into a cornfield in the middle of the night?"

"I—I did not think." He rubbed the furrow between his brows. "I am quite hungry, actually."

"Yeah, yeah. I got that from the chicken thing." She went back to the frying pan to stir the scrambled eggs she'd concocted.

At least he looked at her differently now. Impressed, perhaps, by her kindness? Or perhaps by her ability to save his life? All the same, it wasn't as if he'd tell her. His silence made him much more mysterious.

Mysterious *and* handsome.

As she cooked, she chewed on the inside of her cheek. What was he hiding? Where had he come from? Why was he hurt? Why did he look so inhuman? Her desire for answers gnawed at her. She kept silent. If he was anything like her on an empty stomach, she didn't want to make him *hangry*.

His *sverak*—or whatever he'd called it—was strapped across his back like some kind of warrior. Her mother would've had a fit seeing an armed stranger in their home. "You don't need to wear that around the house, you know."

"I do apologize, my lady. I assure you, it is for our safety that I wear it."

She opened and closed her mouth, then fell silent. Were they in danger? Was the coat rack going to come alive and strangle them? She had a feeling that if she pressed the matter, she'd receive nothing more than an incoherent grumble, so she rushed to finish her culinary masterpiece.

Her dad always told her, "Food is the way to a man's heart—you remember that Claire Bear."

She plated a healthy portion of scrambled eggs with sausage, bell peppers, and onion. Two slices of toast popped up just in time. She buttered them and plopped them down beside the eggs.

When she went to hand him his plate, she hesitated. "I'm not crazy, am I?" She half expected him to tell her that he was the sole survivor of a plane crash. Or something.

"Beg your pardon?"

"I know what I saw last night."

"Which was?"

"I saw a dragon fall from the sky. I know it. But all I found was you. Tell me I'm not crazy."

"No, you are not crazy." He picked up his fork, so she set the plate down before him. A reward for his honesty.

"So you *can* turn into a dragon."

He grunted, lifting his shoulder on his good side.

A grin spread across her face. What fantasy-loving-book-nerd *didn't* grow up wishing dragons were real?

"May I eat now?" His voice was flat.

"Oh...right. Yes." She plopped down next to him with a cup of coffee and bowl of oatmeal. She always ate oatmeal for breakfast. It was her thing—old fashioned oats with two heaping teaspoons of brown sugar and a handful of blueberries. But...she struggled to eat with him beside her, mostly propping her chin on her hand to watch him.

Cyrus inhaled food like a vacuum. It was gone in minutes. On the other hand, she was only a few bites in.

"Is there any more?"

Her jaw dropped. "You're still hungry?"

"Yes, please."

She let out a slow, slow breath. "All right, *Cyrus*, how about this? I'll give you more food if you give me answers."

He stared at her for several moments, then his mouth twitched. "Very well. As you wish."

The second and third time around, he didn't eat nearly as quickly, nor as much. However, by the time he was finished, she had gone through the entire carton of eggs, five large sausages, two bell peppers, and six slices of toast. The man must have spent a fortune on food.

When at last he set his fork down, he went to stand before the kitchen window. She watched him, her eyes tracking his every movement. He didn't look at anything specific, he simply fixed his gaze on the yard beyond. The longer he stood, the more impatient she grew.

"You agreed," she said at last. "Answers for food."

The curtains fell back into place and he turned to her. "Fine. Ask your questions."

Her heart thumped. She gave him her biggest smile as he took up his seat and watched her. She returned his regard. His eyes were so pretty. Dark brown with flecks of gold that sparkled when they caught the light. The longer she looked into them, the more inhuman they appeared. "What exactly *are* you?" she blurted. "A shapeshifter? A dragon? What?"

"I am a drengr."

"A—a *what?*" Her eyebrows pulled together at the strange

word. It sounded like 'dang' but with an '*r*' inserted, ending with a soft '*r*' that sounded close to a growl like '*gerrr*.'

He gave a long, tired exhale. "I am a *drengr*," he repeated. "A dragon blessed with humanity. Those of my race possess the ability to shift into humans. But do not be mistaken, we are more dragon than human."

"There are others like you?"

"Yes, many."

Goosebumps pricked her skin. How could it be that dragon shapeshifters existed and no one knew about them? If a single person found out, wouldn't it be all over social media? Facebook, Instagram, something? It seemed impossible to keep something this monumental quiet. "So...where have you guys been hiding?"

"Hide?" He laughed. "We do not hide. We rule."

"You—but..."

"I am not from your world. I suspect that's why none of your people know about me. I live in the kingdom of Dragonwall. That's my home, not here, wherever this gods-forsaken place is." He looked around him, as if trying to gain clues.

She realized her mouth was hanging open and closed. "What the *hell* is Dragonwall?"

"Dragonwall is the kingdom that I come from, as I said."

"Yes, yes. I got that." She tried to process it. Was it possible he was lying? She'd seen the dragon, saw it fall from the sky, saw the trail of flame. If the dragon was real, Dragonwall had to be real. "Okay. Let's just say for a moment that I believe you. If you're from Dragonwall, which, presumably, is not anywhere on Earth, how did you get *here*?" She jabbed her finger towards the ground.

"Through a gate."

"A...*gate*," she repeated, blinking at him.

"Aye." He nodded. "A portal."

She sat motionless, turning it over. Maybe they were *both* crazy. That was a possibility, right?

"You came here from a portal, a gate," she repeated, yet again. If she repeated it enough, would that make it real?

"Yes, Claire. A gate." He glanced toward the windows again;

he'd been doing that a lot. "In Dragonwall, it is illegal to use any gate, punishable by death."

"*Any*? So...there's more than one? Let me guess, someone tried to kill you for using a portal. That's why you're hurt."

"No. I am hurt because I am being hunted."

Her eyes widened. She opened her mouth—

"The portal was a last resort. A means to an end." He clutched the pouch around his neck. "It seemed like a good idea at the time. Now I realize what folly it was."

Her stomach dropped. She pointed an accusing finger at him, at the pouch around his neck. "You're being hunted for those stone things, aren't you? Someone is after them."

"Yes, for the stones. And it is not *someone* trying to kill me, but rather, *something*. A number of somethings."

"Some*thing*?" she whispered, as if the *somethings* might hear them. "Something is hunting you and you're using *my* house as a hiding place?!" She began shaking her head. "Oh, no. I don't think so. Are you crazy? That will lead them here!"

"A valid possibility."

"But...but..."

"I thank you for your hospitality, my lady." Reaching into his coin pouch, he placed several golden coins on the breakfast bar in a neat little stack. They were much larger than coins of her currency, and twice the thickness.

"Um," she squeaked. "What are those for? Are you...are you trying to...to *bribe* me?"

"For your help and your silence. I trust that you will keep my identity, my being here, a secret—for your safety as well as mine."

Her forehead furrowed. "We don't even *use* money like that. What am I supposed to do with it?"

"Gold has no value?"

"Wait. Gold? Like...*real* gold?"

Cyrus nodded. She wasn't sure what to say to that. Could she toughen up enough? Was it worth it?

"Eight gold dragons. Genuine. They are all I have to give."

She considered her large pile of student loans. University

educations didn't come cheap. Certainly not hers. How much would this gold fetch?

"But...what if the things come back?" she asked.

"I hope they do not. If they do, I will protect you."

Her eyes narrowed suspiciously. While she appreciated his gallant offer of protection, she didn't know him well enough to trust him.

"Your silence?" he prompted, assessing her with his gaze. She swallowed. Silence wasn't a problem. What would she say? "Guess what world, dragons *do* exist because one fell out of the sky last night. And the real kicker? He's a shapeshifter."

Ha-ha.

No, silence wouldn't be an issue at all. She sighed. "All right," she agreed. "I won't say anything. You have my word."

CHAPTER 4
THE CHAMBER POT

Battle Ground, Indiana

Claire didn't make promises often. She didn't like the obligation that came along with them. In this instance, she knew she had to. How did she know? She couldn't have said. It wasn't the gold, though that was a perk. Instead, some unexplainable feeling drove her to it, just as it had made her chase a dragon into her cornfield and rescue it.

When she gave him her word, Cyrus visibly relaxed. In fact, he flashed her a charming smile. It disarmed her more than she cared to admit. Men weren't supposed to make her jittery, not when she was dealing with the fallout from Jake.

"Your reassurance, my lady, means a great deal. Now"—his brown eyes narrowed—"it is my turn to ask questions."

She sputtered, caught off guard. "Okay. What do you want to know?" She pushed her bowl of oatmeal away.

"A few things. First, out of curiosity, do you live here alone? It does not seem so."

"Oh, no, I don't." She relaxed her shoulders. "This is my parents' house, actually. They're on vacation. And you won't find me complaining. It's the first alone time I've had since moving back home." She failed to hide the bitterness in her voice. It wasn't easy living with her parents, especially after four years of college and freedom.

"I see," said Cyrus. "Perhaps you are luckier than you realize. My mother and father are no longer with me."

"Oh. I—I'm sorry. I didn't mean…"

"Your apology is unnecessary. We all lose the ones we love sooner or later." The depths of his eyes reflected sadness, but when he next spoke, his voice was back to its old self. "Earlier when I dressed, I looked at my wound." He shifted in his chair, sitting up straighter. "I find myself impressed with your work."

She choked back a cough, patting her chest. "Impressed? I didn't exactly do a professional job."

"Be that as it may, where I come from, females are not often healers."

"You mean doctors?"

He shook his head. "I mean healers, skilled in the art of setting a broken bone, or stitching a man together."

"Oh." She shrugged. "Well, *here*, women are plenty capable of doing as good a job as any man."

He held up his hands. "That is not what I meant. I simply find it impressive. Lucky for me, you possessed the knowledge necessary to keep me from dying." Cyrus was right, any other cornfield and he probably would have.

"Lucky for you, my dad is a surgeon—was a surgeon."

"A surgeon?" The word rolled off his tongue with difficulty.

"A healer," she clarified. "Before my grandpa died and left him the farm, Dad was a surgeon. Now whenever anything happens, he's the first person everyone calls." It was true, their phone was known to ring at all hours.

What she didn't say was how her grandpa's death was the best thing that had happened to them. She'd been nine at the time, and she loved her gramps, but she never really *knew* her dad until he was forced to leave his position at Arnett Hospital and take over the family farm.

Cyrus smiled. It didn't reach his eyes, but it was kind. "I can tell by the way you speak, your father must be a great man."

She nodded, ignoring the needle of guilt she felt. "Yes. Yes, he is."

"And it explains a great deal about *your* abilities." His warm gaze was filled with admiration, though she didn't feel deserving of such praise. Not even close.

"I did what I had to, given the circumstances. You're making it sound like I'm a big deal. I'm not."

Cyrus shook his head. "I beg to differ. After all, you chased away my assailants."

"Your...assailants?" Her eyebrows pulled together. "What assailants?"

"The vodar wraiths," he said. Her arms erupted in goosebumps. "How is it that you single handedly defeated them? That's ultimately what I'd like to know."

"You mean, the *things* we talked about?" she whispered. Her eyes darted towards the windows.

"Yes, Claire. The wraiths that have hunted me for weeks."

"I thought *you* defeated them. I thought that was why..." She scowled. Hadn't he said there was a possibility that they might return for the stones, and that he would try to protect her if they did. Nerves swelled in her abdomen.

"After I was wounded, I lost consciousness and fell. That is when you found me, I presume. I assumed you chased them away to get to my body, or defeated them to save me."

She shook her head. "I never defeated anything, Cyrus. How... how could I? I mean, the only thing I'm remotely capable of defeating are zombies in *Call of Duty*, and even then, I die every time."

He arched an eyebrow. "You do not look dead to me."

"Oh, never mind! Look, when I found your body in the cornfield, you were alone."

"What about when you saw me fall from the sky?"

"There was nothing there, I swear. Nothing that I could see."

She watched a newly forming frown pull at his lips. "You were alone, Cyrus. Completely alone."

He offered a hesitant nod before turning his gaze away from her where it settled on the breakfast bar. Then he muttered to himself, "It makes no sense. Where could they have gone? Vodar wraiths are relentless. They would not simply give up. Not unless... but...that wouldn't..."

"Cyrus?" His brown eyes returned to her face. "Uhm, what exactly..." She swallowed. "What exactly is a *voda-thingy*?"

"Vodar," he corrected.

"Vodar," she repeated. The strange word was heavy and harsh as it rolled off her tongue, as if it might cut her mouth on its way out. "What is it?"

"They are demon wraiths summoned from undirfold—hell. Assassins—dark hunters, if you will—who will stop at nothing to kill their prey. One might consider them the harbingers of death, for they themselves embody death. They carry short swords imbued with poison, and if stabbed, these weapons bring about a most painful end. Worst of all, they can never be killed, only temporarily banished. Once summoned, they will not rest until their work is done."

She opened and closed her mouth. The only sound that came out when she tried to speak was a squawk. She managed to stammer, "You...you're...you're only joking...right?"

"I wish I was." He licked his lips and glanced at the windows again. Any less emotion and she wouldn't have believed him. But seeing his obvious fear—fear in a grown man who didn't look quite human—made it ten times worse.

"Why are they after the stones? The..." She wanted to say their name, but she could barely stomach it. "The vodar, why do they want the stones so badly?"

He closed his eyes and exhaled. "I think perhaps that is a story for another time. I must rest." His tanned face was paper white. He gripped his injured side then winced.

She cursed under her breath. She'd been so caught up in the tale he'd spun that she forgot how badly injured he was. "Come on, let's get you to bed." Unyielding desire to care for him burned through her. It was a little strange, because she never felt this protective or nurturing towards anyone. There was no time to question it as she took his hand and led him from the kitchen. He didn't protest.

His skin was burning up, but she kept her lips pressed together. Telling him how bad his condition was, though she wanted to, was unnecessary. He clearly understood what was happening.

"You can sleep here," she said. They stood in the downstairs guest suite. Its plush bed was covered with way too many throw pillows. Her mom loved throw pillows the way Claire loved books.

"Thank you, Claire." He dropped her hand and immediately began surveying the room, lifting objects to study them, with an obvious curiosity, looking out of the windows, displaying clear paranoia. He opened and shut the closet doors then checked inside the dresser's drawers. Then he got on his hands and knees and looked under the bed.

Her mouth twitched. Did he expect to find one of the wraiths hiding there? Whatever it was, he popped back up to frown at her. "No chamber pot?"

"No—*what?*" She must have given him the ugliest confused face she could muster, unintentionally of course.

"I need to relieve myself."

"Um...you can use the bathroom there?" She motioned with her head.

"Perhaps you misunderstand me. I do not need to bathe. I am quite clean. I washed up this morning in the basin I found within the barn."

"The water trough?" Her eyes widened. It really shouldn't have surprised her at this rate. "That was the cows' drinking water, you dummy!"

"I see. I am sure the beasts did not mind."

Resisting the urge to laugh, she marched up to him, grabbed his arm, and led him to the small bathroom adjoining the bedroom. Once there, she flipped on the light. He immediately gasped. "So there *is* magic here! I had wondered. How did you do that?"

"Do what?"

"That magic. The light. I heard no incant fall from your lips."

When she showed him, he began flipping the light switch on and off, smiling gleefully. "Incredible," he whispered. "We have no magic like *this*."

Cute as he was, she interrupted his surprise, pointing at the toilet. "There—*that's* the toilet."

His eyes followed the direction of her finger. "Splendid! I am not accustomed to seeing pit toilets in common households. This one is *most* elegant, like a throne of ivory."

"Are you kidding me?" she sputtered. Her nose flared, betraying the laughter she held in.

If he didn't know what a toilet was, he wasn't going to know how to use one. She stepped forward to instruct him. "Make sure you lift the lid *and* the seat when you need to take a pee, and close the lid when you're done." She flushed the toilet.

He gaped at her. "But, where does the water go?"

"Into the septic tank."

"Sep-sep-tic-tank?"

"Oh, good lord!" She gave up, leaving him to do his business.

Claire found him later, fast asleep with an arm carelessly thrown over his face. His sverak was beside him on the bed. Standing in the doorway, she watched him sleep for a few minutes. She still had her doubts about him, but he was growing on her. Innocence worked in his favor, adding to his undeniable charm. Her regard slid over his face. He was almost too handsome.

"*'Where does the water go?'*" she silently mouthed, mimicking him before rolling her eyes. Okay, his ignorance *was* pretty adorable. Once she'd hunted down more of her dad's old clothes, she left them at the foot of his bed. Then she closed his door, leaving it open a crack so that she could peek in on him.

She glanced at the time and her heart jolted. Reality came flooding back. The mail was delivered at 1:00 p.m. each afternoon.

She strode from the house, breathing deeply. It wasn't terribly hot, but the humidity was oppressive, as summer humidity always was. The sound of the cicadas was a loud hum. She walked down the long gravel drive to the mailbox. When she passed her car, she popped inside to grab her dead phone, slipping it into her pocket. She'd take care of the car later.

When she grabbed the stack of envelopes, she flipped through them. Today was the day, somehow she knew it. Even still, when she caught sight of her self-addressed envelope, she stared, unbelieving. This was it.

Dropping the rest of the mail to the dusty ground, she tore into it and pulled out the letter. Her hands trembled. The letterhead on the top bore the official White House logo. *"Dear Miss Evans,"* she skipped over the introduction. *"Thank you for your application to the White House Public Service Leadership Program."* Blah, blah, blah. She quickly skimmed down the page to the next paragraph. *"We regret to inform you that you have not been selected for this year's group of interns."*

Her chest sank.

Was it a mistake? She read the words again, expecting them to change. They didn't. Her application had been stellar. Even her professors' letters of recommendation were flawless. So...why?

Why did it always feel like she wasn't ever *quite* good enough?

She crumpled the letter in her fist and chucked it into the field. Then she cursed and raced to retrieve it, straightening it before grabbing the rest of the mail on the ground. Once more she read the crushing sentence of rejection. Angry tears welled up in her eyes. She brushed them away.

All her plans, all her hopes, hinged on this one *freaking* piece of paper.

She glanced around, unseeing, as her mind raced. The surrounding cornfields felt more like a prison now. She refused to allow this small town to trap her. But...what else could she do? She could try to make it the hard way, and she knew exactly what that entailed. She could move to the state capital, fight over some unpaid internship with a bunch of other candidates, and work nights in some random bar to make rent. That thought made new tears well up into her eyes.

"I'll get through it," she whispered. She always managed. Somehow.

She read the remainder of the letter. The words were useless, encouraging her to apply to other, *similar*, internships. The White House opportunity was a one-shot internship for new graduates, and somehow, she'd blown it.

When she trudged back up the gravel drive, all the spring in her step was gone. She was in no mood to work that afternoon. Shannon's would have to survive without her. Plus, she wasn't going to leave Cyrus alone in her home. She sent a quick text to her best friend Leah, pretending to be sick.

For the remainder of the afternoon she was sullen. She tried to get her mind off of her disappointment by watching Netflix, Facebooking, and then reading. Nothing worked.

At last, she decided to get a start on the brunch dishes so that she could prep for dinner. When she went back in the kitchen, she noticed the small stack of gold still sitting on the breakfast bar. She plucked it up, studying the coins. Each one had a dragon-head moniker on one side with the word, *Dreki*. On the back was a tree. The dragon obviously represented the Drengr, but what about the tree? She stuffed them into her pocket and got to work, all the while her mind was lost in thought, wondering about Cyrus and his world.

She was just loading the dishwasher when she heard a familiar sound. She froze to listen. Tires crunching on gravel. She set a clean dish on the countertop. No one was supposed to be here. It was dead-week. Like her parents, all the farm hands were on vacation.

Her mind went to Cyrus, fast asleep in the downstairs bedroom. Was it the sheriff? Had one of her neighbors spotted the falling dragon and reported it? How would she explain his presence in her house?

She walked to the living room and peered out the front window. Her stomach plummeted. She immediately put a hand over it. "Shit," she hissed.

A white Ford Raptor came to a halt where she usually parked her Honda Civic. "*Shit*," she muttered again, wiping her wet hands on her apron. This wasn't happening, was it? Not now. She blinked several times in a panic. What the hell was Jake-the-ballbag doing in her freaking driveway? This wasn't going to end well.

31

CHAPTER 5
A FAMILIAR FACE

Battle Ground, Indiana

Cyrus jerked awake and blinked up at the ceiling. Everything came flooding back in an instant. His trip to the forest, his fight with Kane, the vodar, the gate, Claire. All of it. The faint sound of raised voices drifted to him. He remained motionless, listening. Just voices—nothing more. Certainly not the vodar. He exhaled, relaxing his muscles.

He pushed his hearing just a little farther, but it wasn't enough. He could have used magic, said words of power to further sharpen his hearing, but it would kill him. No magic, not the smallest trace, could be spared from the effort that was keeping him alive.

He stood, gritting his teeth. It felt like a hot knife twisted within him. His pain was growing unbearable. Taking a step from the bed, he let out an uncontrolled gasp, wincing. It took a good deal of control to keep from crying out again.

He dared not look at the wound. He need not see the poison spreading; he felt it within him. The oily substance, which had started as a small stream, was quickly turning into a roaring river. When it cut its way through his lifeblood and into his mind, he would die. His magic slowed its advance, but not for long.

He padded barefoot through the girl's dwelling, stopping before the exterior door to listen. Two voices carried, Claire's and another. A male. They argued. He listened a moment longer. Claire was upset.

"You know what? Screw you and your excuses, Jake. You said we would make things work between us. You *promised* me!"

"I tried, Claire. I swear I did. You can't blame me for being lonely."

"Bullshit! I'm the one who wanted to break things off when I visited during spring break, but you swore, you asshole, you swore we would make it work."

"Claire Bear, I hate for you to be mad at—"

"*No!* You don't get to call me that. And I'm not mad, I'm *furious.*"

Cyrus clenched his jaw. He shouldn't have, but he did it anyway. He strolled out onto the porch. Something—he couldn't say what—made him oddly protective of her. He walked up beside her. If she was surprised to see him, she gave no sign. "My lady? Are you all right?" He kept his voice low, paying her a sidelong glance. There were red splotches on her cheeks.

Her face relaxed some. "I—I'm fine."

"Who the fuck is this?" Jake looked between them, appraising him.

He sighed, burying his pain deep. With an overly calm voice he said, "My identity is not your concern. You are upsetting her. It is time for you to leave."

"Leave?" Jake huffed. "Who d'you think you are, tellin' me what to do? It's a free country, far as I'm concerned. This ain't your house." Jake took several steps towards him.

Likewise, he did the same, until they stood face to face. This time he spoke through clenched teeth, "I will not ask you again. Leave. Now." His gaze remained fixed on Jake's, looking for any sign of movement within his dull eyes, movement that he would quickly anticipate.

In his line of work, he dealt with his fair share of males like Jake

—criminals mostly. They were always the same, get them worked up and they would strike. This one was a simmering pot.

They eyed each other for several long seconds until Jake tried to bypass him. "Claire, tell this bastard to back the fuck off before he gets himself in trouble." Jake puffed himself up as he spoke. "This is between you and me, not some—"

"Some *what?*"

"Nosy fucking bastard, that's what." Jake spat a brown substance on the wooden beams beneath his feet.

He stared, disgusted. His fingers reached for Justice before realizing he'd left his sverak inside. A careless mistake, but no matter. "Right. Well, I tried." Inhaling, he sent his fist into the side of Jake's face. The impact sent Jake stumbling backwards until the wretch lost his footing on the stairs and tumbled off the porch. He hadn't intended to use so much force.

Ignoring Claire's gasp, he walked to the edge of the stairs. "If you return, *you* will be the one in trouble. Have I made myself clear?"

Jake's eyes were like daggers. Cupping his cheek, he staggered to his feet. He took off without a backwards glance, muttering profanities, before climbing into the large metal wagon that needed no horse to pull it.

Cyrus blinked, only just noticing it. A roar sounded before it began moving away. He stared. Huh. So much strange magic filled this world. He would have to ask Claire about this horseless carriage later. There was certainly no such thing in Dragonwall.

He turned to her. She stood with her mouth hanging open, but she said nothing. A sudden flood of exhaustion inundated him, leaving him dizzy. Hiding his pain, he went back inside. He would nurse his wound alone and in silence.

Claire found him in his room after dark. "Dinner's ready," she said, knocking quietly from the other side of the door before poking her head in. He'd been resting, but not sleeping. His mind was elsewhere, wandering over better memories, over Leeana.

Gods he missed her. Not a day went by that he didn't recall her silky black hair and dimpled smile, her calming personality and kind heart, and the way she made his happiness soar higher than his wings ever could. He especially longed for her now, when the pain was worse than any physical ailment he had ever experienced, save the feeling of her mind getting ripped from his.

They once held halves of the same consciousness. When she died, his existence was torn apart. The agony of losing a piece of one's self was a form of torture he would never wish upon any living soul. He never thought it would happen to him. His kind were born to feel invincible, it was in their nature.

That made it more unbearable. His loss of Leeana, his rider, his mate, created a deep void that would never again be filled. How naïve he'd been to believe becoming one of the king's elite, a *king's shield*, would distract him. He was wrong, there would be no distraction from his lifelong mourning.

It was said that males should never shed tears, that it was a sign of weakness. Yet he was more dragon than man, and he had cried for many nights—for many years. The world was a darker place without her in it.

"Cyrus?"

His stomach gave a loud grumble. Claire still stood in the doorway, watching him. She took a step into the room and hesitated. "Look, I wanted to thank you for—for chasing off Jake earlier. I know he can be a total douchebag. He never used to be like that. And I hope—"

"Does he abuse you often?"

"What? He—no! I mean, he's never hit me or anything like that."

"Well he might have, had I not stepped in. I have had dealings with men like him. Thank the gods I woke up in time. Perhaps Asjaa smiles upon you."

As he said it, he knew it was the truth. Asjaa *did* favor her. He knew it with certainty. The girl had no notion of the secret he carried. He wished he could tell her, but it would be too difficult to explain.

"Asjaa?" her head tilted slightly, freeing a lock of hair that fell across one eye.

"The Mother."

Her brows scrunched together. The gods were different here, he knew enough about this place to know that. The unnecessary explanation had little to do with his point anyway, so he avoided it. "You should stay away from him from now on—from *Jake*—for your own safety."

"I'd be more than happy to." She crossed her arms, and that ended the conversation.

Before sitting down to their evening meal, he again assessed the outer grounds of Claire's home, gazing through various windows to appease his worry. The vodar would return, he simply did not know when. Justice was strapped across his back and would remain so from now on.

They sat down to a spectacular meal. Claire's skill was impressive. "What did you say this meat was?" he wondered aloud, forgetting his manners through a mouthful.

"It's a sirloin steak. Cooked medium-rare."

He swallowed the succulent red flesh, washing it down with a gulp of fine red wine—far stronger than what he was used to in Dragonwall. "We do not have *Sirloins* in my world. What do they look like?"

Claire's laughter made him smile. She frequently laughed at his ignorance, not that she could be blamed. He would do the same had their positions been reversed.

"Sirloins are not *animals*, silly. Sirloin steak is a cut of meat from a cow."

"Cow..." the word was vaguely familiar. Perhaps she had used it before. "We have chickens, goats, grazers, oxen, sheep, antelope, wild boar, pigs..." he tried to recall the wilder animals that were considered delicacies. "We have no cows. What do they look like?"

"They look like—like Tilly and Joe in the stable. Remember? You washed up in their drinking water."

"Oh!" He did remember. "Grazers, then. Only, ours are much larger in girth and they have huge horns sprouting from their heads." He did an imitation with his fingers, lifting them to his forehead and butting his head forward. She giggled, throwing a hand over her mouth. The sound helped to ease his pain. He continued despite this. "Their coats are shaggy fur, not like the hides of your beasts. Mostly they are dark brown, but I once saw a white one." He omitted the part about his friend Reyr hunting it down in one fell swoop, and how he had consumed the beast in mere minutes afterward. He missed Reyr. Truthfully, he missed all of his brothers. And his king, too.

They fell quiet for a short time while they ate. He was too busy devouring what she'd cooked to speak. Besides, he was in no mood for serious conversation. Perhaps Claire perceived this. Rather than asking outright about his mission, she chose a lighter topic. She wanted to know about Dragonwall.

"My whole life has been spent wishing fantasy worlds like yours existed," she explained, her face hungry for knowledge. "I never imagined...that is to say...can you tell me about it?"

"What do you wish to know?"

Her eyes grew large. She smiled wider than he had yet seen. "Everything! Anything. Magic, mostly. Like, how does it work? Can you teach me? Are there spells?" She spoke very rapidly, questions tumbling from her lips. "Can anyone do magic? Or only people of— well, people like you. And what about wands and stuff, like in Harry Potter?"

"Harry, *who*? I can tell you about magic, if you like."

She nodded.

He started with the mages, telling her about the society. They were the foundation of modern magic, founded at the dawn of the Third Age. "The society oversees all magical training in Drag- onwall. Those of the blood must be trained, or they become dangerous."

A true explanation of magic would take far more time than they had, so he did his best to explain how it worked in a general sense. All magical acts were governed by words, powerful words, that when spoken correctly and with proper intent, brought about the actions they stood for.

"And if you string these words together," he explained, "then you have what we call an incant."

"Can you show me?" she breathed.

He sighed. "I'm sorry, but I cannot. I am too weak."

"Oh..." Disappointment reflected in her voice, though she pretended to understand. "What about other beings? Are there other magical creatures besides dragons—I mean *drengr*?" She stumbled over the word.

"Aye. Mages and drengr are the most common beings, but there are others. sprites of the forests—we do not see much of them. Nor much of the dwargs—"

"You mean, dwarves?"

His brow furrowed. "No, I mean dwargs. There are also goblins. They are the nastiest of course."

"Goblins? Shut up!"

"Pardon, my lady?" He frowned. Had he said something wrong?

"I mean—sorry—I didn't actually mean for you to be quiet. I hope I didn't offend you. I was just surprised about the goblins." Her eyes turned dreamy and took on a faraway look. "I've only read about them in stories. But they're real!"

"Aye. We have a great many number of magical beings."

"What about castles? Does everyone live in a castle? Do you live in one?"

He laughed. He couldn't help it. The question seemed absurd. "Of course I do. I work for the king, so I live in the biggest one of all. But no, not everyone lives in a castle."

Her eyes danced. "I love castles. They're so..."

"Stifling? Drafty?"

"I was going to say—"

"Crowded? Oppressive?"

"No! Would you let me finish?!" She sighed. "Well maybe all of those things…I guess. You would know better than me. But I was going to say *royal, magical*."

He snorted. "You have never lived in one, then. If the constant presence of people does not get to you, the abundance of stench and stone will."

"I see. What about servants? Are there servants in your castle? And what about jousts? Do you have those? Do the ladies walk around in beautiful gowns? Are there knights? Do they wear tokens of their maiden's love when they fight for their honor?"

"Whoa, whoa. Slow down. One at a time." Her interest bolstered his spirits. He was more than happy to talk of home, although thinking about Kastali Dun left his heart aching. Too many weeks had passed since beholding the tall turrets and battlements of the Great Keep.

"Okay, stick to the knights then. Or no—the gowns."

"Gowns it is. There are—"

"Wait, no. I want to know about the king and queen. Sorry. The king and queen." He opened and closed his mouth, at a loss. "What are they like?"

He rubbed the back of his neck. "Firstly, our king has no queen. He has been unfortunate in that regard. And secondly, he is an excellent ruler. Most who do not know him personally, fear him. But it is needless. He makes a great many sacrifices for his people."

She frowned. "But…how can *one* person be trusted to make all of the decisions for their people? That kind of power is dangerous, isn't it? Monarchies haven't worked out well here in my world."

"Is that so?"

"It is. I can tell you if you'd like."

"Very well. Enlighten me."

They talked at length about governments and ruling—late into the night—until his exhaustion couldn't be ignored. With Claire, conversation was all too easy. He knew why. Yet, this was not yet the time to tell her. The knowledge would surely frighten her. Besides, she had been through enough. And although he trusted her now—after his small peek into her mind—it was very unlikely that she fully trusted him.

He smiled in spite of his circumstances. How Lady Saffra would rejoice to know of his discovery! What would she say? Certainly, there was no denying it. The face that the king's prophetess had so often seen in her visions was unmistakable—a face not so easily forgotten. He'd seen it too, during their training, whenever he delved into Saffra's mind, because the face belonged to none other than the woman right here in front of him.

CHAPTER 6

THE PRICE OF VICTORY

Kastali Dun

The King of Dragonwall studied his reflection in the mirror. It was a form of self-punishment, one he often subjected himself to. This was the only looking glass kept within his tower. The others had long since been destroyed. It remained to remind him of his ugliness.

He wasn't always this way. He had been exceedingly handsome once, hundreds of years ago—two hundred and eighty-two, to be exact. He was the prince of Dragonwall then. Those were the days when his cares weighed little, the days when he could do as he pleased.

Good things unearned never last. Verek—the god of judgment— saw fit to punish him for his ways. He was sure of it, because every- thing had changed. His scars became evidence of the god's justice. As did many other things, like his title, his responsibility to the kingdom, his loneliness, his ever-present rage, and his obsessive need for control. Yet, none of these stood out the way his mauled face did. *His* was the face he was forced to present to the public each day. *His* was the face they were subjected to. And so, he administered the same to himself, forcing his eyes to trace the heavy lines. If a king could not do that which was required of his people, then he was no king at all.

Still, he hated the self-imposed rule. He loathed the face that looked back at him. Moreover, he despised the memory accompanying his disfigurement. He cursed Válkar—the god of war—for his desire for bloodshed.

During those days, Válkar was thirsty. Long it had been since Dragonwall's last great battle. That day was fateful for many, but him most of all. He bore the brunt of Válkar's victory price.

In his mind's eye, he beheld the incident that changed him. His memory took him far back to the great ice battle in Vestur. The room around him disappeared, replaced by a snowy landscape. Now he was a prince instead of a king. His feet no longer stood on solid ground, for he no longer *had* feet. He was a dragon, with scales of black iridescence, claws as sharp as knives, and wings larger than a ship's sails.

All around him, chaos ruled. Dragons screamed in defiance. Giants roared in contest. With effortless grace, he swooped around the icy grasp of a nearby Kald, roaring. His lungs filled, forcing his scales to pull apart as his chest expanded. His breath released—a flaming-orange blaze aimed straight at his enemy's blocky legs. The ice giant expelled another deep bellow, its cry rent the air, but a successful hit meant nothing. It would take much more to bring this nemesis down.

But he was a mighty *Prince of Dragonwall* and he would not be defeated.

Others fought with the same relentlessness. The sky was filled with hundreds of dragon forms. Their movements were like angry bees, aggressive and swarming, billowing flame in great bursts. On the ground, ice giants swatted at them, lumbering around like bears.

Válkar was not easily satisfied with minor bloodshed. He called for something far greater to ensure the monarchy with a victory.

A pained bellow made Talon shudder. He knew the voice almost as well as his own. And so, in the midst of the battle, through the thunder of noise, he lost his nerve. The sound of his father's anguish would haunt him until the end of his days.

He turned in time to see his mother, eyes wide with shock, mouth open, ripped from the back of his father's red hide. His warm scales turned cold. Terror seized him. He, who had never felt fear, became frozen in the moment. Paralyzed by horror. He may as well have been captured by the same icy hand gripping his mother. He hovered in the air, wings beating to stay aloft, watching as if in slow motion the unbearable scene before him.

He knew she was lost the moment she was exposed to black rock ice.

King Tallek's bellow was more like a pitiful screech. He forsook all caution and dove after Queen Ahlessa, his lifelong mate and Rider. Talon shouted for him, warned him, but it was no use. It was exactly what their enemy wanted, even expected. The ice giant snatched his father from the sky, lifting the flailing red dragon to its mouth, taking hold of his father's spiked head within its enormous, cubed teeth before ripping it from its body. Talon screamed. Both head and body were tossed away like a broken plaything.

Something inside of him snapped. Fear forgotten, his mind erupted into a frenzy of rage, rage that would stay with him for an eternity. He no longer knew himself. He had only one desire. Destruction.

"The leader of the Kalds is mine!" His telepathic command rang through the minds of the Drengr with force. He shot through the sky. The leader, still holding his mother's limp body, roared its challenge. He bellowed in return. Those who considered avenging their rulers knew to retreat. This ice giant's death belonged to the prince alone.

He filled his lungs and came down upon the Kald unleashing torrents of fire. Plumes of black smoke and ash swirled around the giant as the flame began to melt its body. Perhaps these icy demons felt pain—he did not know—for in that moment the giant released his mother from its clutches. She dropped.

A nearby drengr swooped in to catch her fall, whisking her

away, cradled in its talons, far from the battle. She was already dead.

He'd never get to tell her how sorry he was for all the ways he'd rebelled against her. He'd never get to tell his father he was capable of greater responsibility, or that he'd been listening to all those lectures on duty even when he pretended otherwise. He'd never get to tell them anything. Not now.

Now, there was only the giant.

They battled for hours, flame against ice. Even as the other giants began to disappear, melting away into puddles of blackness, he fought. But he could not fight forever. As the day stretched on, he grew tired.

Minor injuries covered him—places where icy hands grazed his beautiful scales. The drengr were impervious to fire. They'd been wrought from lava rock. Yet, they were not resistant to the black rock ice of giants. It scorched their scales like lightning to dry earth. Despite this, he refused assistance. Vengeance would be his and his alone.

Darkness fell and he grew sloppy. The ice giant knew this. It cackled with glee. *Just a little longer,* he urged. Already, it had shrunk noticeably in girth, its body merely half its original thickness. Black gooey puddles were forming upon the ground.

In a desperate attempt to burn away its legs, he made a deadly mistake. He dove too close. He came within the giant's reach. His face erupted into pain as it swatted at him. He felt its icy fingers rake across his scales, from the eye ridges of his forehead, down to his jaw. White-hot agony, pain unlike anything he'd ever felt, erupted across his face. He roared, the power of its reverberations nearly splitting him in two. A final flame, a last ditch effort, erupted from his jaw. He directed it exactly where it needed to go.

The legs of the ice giant began fracturing and breaking away like glacial calving. Thunderous sounds echoed into the stillness. Heartened, a number of jubilant bugles erupted from his onlookers, drengr who had already defeated their enemies.

He yelped, trying to ignore the excruciating pain on his face. The giant began to crumble. It's hand reached for him. He saw it too late. A fresh wave of agony, different from what he felt before, erupted across his body. The icy hand wrapped around him like a cloak of misery, holding on tight.

Time lasted an eternity. So did his torment. A cold burn washed over him. His vision flickered. His scales melted beneath the grasp of the ice giant's hand. Darkness took him into its black pit, devoid of all but despair...

When he next woke, he was in human form laying on a soft bed, looking up at the canvas of a tent. A camp had been erected at the site of the battlefield. None wished to move him.

The first time he saw his face, he didn't believe it. That was the first moment he'd ever wished for death. Reyr had been there in the tent with him. "You cannot die," he'd said. "You are our king now."

The reminder triggered memories of his parents, of their death, like an avalanche. In his pain and grief, in his disgust for his new appearance, he smashed every mirror from that day forth, ashamed to see the face he was condemned to wear.

After the battle, the mages were summoned. Every effort had been made to heal him of his injuries. But no magic heals the scars inflicted by dark magic. He had always known that.

In the mirror within his tower, he now studied the pattern of the heaviest three scars. They stretched diagonally from his left brow bone to his right jawbone. Each time he beheld them, he recalled the fierce pain in acquiring them. Would that he could forget it.

A growl brewed deep within his chest and a familiar rage boiled up. He smashed his palm into the mirror. It shattered, fragments flying everywhere. Most of the pieces crumbled to the floor. The shards left behind in the frame cut his image into pieces—

A knock sounded at the door. He gave a start, glancing about. Glass everywhere. He lifted a hand and muttered, "Malí gler ahlasem." Words of the old language, used to create the world around him. He commanded the glass pieces to come back together. The fragments covering the floor reassembled. Their cracks fused. Once more he saw a single, whole reflection of his tormented face.

He'd lost count of the number of times he'd fixed it.

"Enter." His voice echoed the dark thoughts still dwelling within his mind. He pushed them away.

One of his tower guards—Prescott—stood in the doorway. "Pardon, Your Grace." He bowed his head. "I apologize, but she says it is urgent."

"*Who*?"

"The Lady Saffra, Your Grace. She would not be turned away. I tried to tell—"

"Never mind. Show her in." He moved over to his desk and took a seat. The guard exited. He glanced down at his bloodied hand. It had already healed.

Lady Saffra was a needle in his neck, though she was hardly to blame. Her visions came of their own accord. Yet, for all the good they did, just as much trouble followed.

While he waited, he continued working on a document he had been writing earlier. A letter to Lord Avraean, the fort leader of Northedge. Avraean had once been a member of his father's six *drengr fairtheoir,* a title more commonly referred to these days as *king's shield*. In the old language, drengr fairtheoir meant, *noble dragon warrior*, but commoners knew very little of the old language. Over time, king's shield became the title that stuck. Like the *true* meaning suggested, Avraean was noble, but his father's death released him from his oath, as it did for all shields. Lord Avraean had since taken up leadership at Northedge, a most prestigious position. He'd made a new life for himself in every sense of the word *new*.

The door opened and Saffra was ushered in. The first thing he noticed was the roll of parchment in her shaking hands. She was trembling, shooting nervous glances in his direction, looking everywhere other than his scarred face. He was used to it. The only people capable of looking at him, *truly* looking at him, were his six.

"Take a seat."

She did as she was commanded. "Forgive my intrusion, Your Grace. I had to come at once."

"Another vision, I presume?" He already knew the answer. Her dark skin, the rich color of toffee, was far paler than usual.

"Yes," she whispered. Her free hand firmly grasped the chair arm. The other gripped the roll of parchment so tightly, it crinkled beneath her palm.

He tensed. His mind jumped to Cyrus. Would she confirm his worst fears? If Cyrus died, he would never forgive himself.

"What did you see?" he said at last. "Not Cyrus, I hope?"

For the first time, her eyes met his. They were haunted—like one who sees death. He inhaled. His keen nostrils picked up the scent of vomit. She'd been sick recently.

"Which city is this, Your Grace?" Her voice shook as she unrolled the parchment and handed it to him.

It was a sketch of an iconic bell tower. He knew it well, though he had only visited the city once. It was far from the capital, sitting at the base of the Northern Barrier Range.

"Bellnesse, if I'm not mistaken. That bell tower resides in the center of the city," he said.

The city of Belnesse got its name when the tower was first constructed. It was meant to act as a warning beacon for the city's inhabitants when wild dragons from the Ice Clan came down from the mountains. But the wild dragons disappeared at the dawn of the Third Age, nearly fifty thousand years ago.

When their cousins—the drengr—came to be, the drengr monarchy was built. Most of the evil dragons were killed or driven away. After all, they were not like the drengr. They did not possess the ability to shift into human form. Thus, their lack of humanity made them what they were—beasts. Not all wild dragons were bad, but those of a kind-hearted nature eventually disappeared as well. Not a single wild dragon had been seen after the first several generations of the monarchy. By now they were long extinct. The world was better for it. Yet, the bell tower remained, as a monument to the days of old.

"Tell me about your vision."

Saffra's eyes grew unfocused—as if reliving the sight of it. "They came from the mountains," she whispered. "They swept down upon the city like a moving rainbow of colors. The bell never tolled—never cried out in alarm. The city was taken unawares. I watched as they burned its white-washed buildings. I watched as the city's people died in the inferno. I heard their screams. I smelled their scorched flesh. I choked on the ash. They will have their vengeance, and they do not care how many lives it takes." A tear slid down her cheek and she shuddered.

"They—who? Who will have vengeance?"

"Wrath, Your Grace. His name is Wrath. He is the new leader of the Ice Clan. Wild dragons have returned to Dragonwall."

CHAPTER 7
PLACING BETS

Battle Ground, Indiana

Claire spent a great deal of time laying in bed the following morning. It was hard to believe only a single day had passed in Cyrus's company. The events of the last twenty-four hours blurred together in her mind like soggy soup, leaving her exhausted.

When she finally got up, she cooked Cyrus breakfast as she had the day before. He didn't eat nearly as much. Afterward, she insisted he show her his wound so she could change his bandages.

"I do not wish for you to see it," he said, backing away.

"It doesn't matter what you *wish*," she said. "I am your care-giver, and I say it must be done."

He sighed, frowning, before lifting his shirt. She set to work, removing the soiled bandages, then stifled a gasp. The blackness staining his skin was spreading at an alarming rate.

"Now you understand..."

She looked up at him, failing to disguise her shock. He clenched his jaw, his gaze locked on the wall. Once more she set about evaluating the wound, checking that the stitches held. As she touched the surrounding skin, his breathing turned labored. He winced when she gently pushed against an inflamed section. The last thing she wanted was to hurt him further. Working quickly, she gathered up fresh bandages and applied them.

She had never seen a wound behave this way. "When you told me that vodar swords were infused with poison…" The realization sank in. The blackened skin wasn't any kind of infection. It was a result of the poison, killing everything it touched.

"Yes." He spoke through clenched teeth. "I can feel it attacking my body, taking every bit of living flesh and tissue."

Her eyes went wide. "What are we going to do?"

"*We* aren't going to do anything." He backed away from her just as she secured the final bandage.

"But, Cyrus…you need help. Some kind of medicine. Probably the hospital. I…I can't treat poison."

"*Hos-pidal?* I do not know of what you speak, nor will I have any part in it." He pursed his lips.

She scowled, hoping he might change his mind. "At least let me give you something for the pain," she said at last. "My dad has some pretty powerful stuff. I'll go get it." She took a single step and his hand latched onto her arm, his grip firmer than expected.

He sighed and released her almost immediately. "Claire, no. Only magic can help me now."

She opened her mouth—

"You must trust me. Nothing you possess can help me. This poison is powerful beyond belief—more powerful than anything our own mages can brew. Every bit of magic I possess is holding it back. Were I human, I would have died the night you rescued me. Alas, I must suffer a slow death."

"But, you can't just give up!" she insisted. Heat flushed her face. Why was he so eager to accept death? "There's got to be something we can—"

"Wake up, girl!" he growled. "Only the strongest magic can heal me now. Even the society's best would struggle with a wound like this. And still, I might not awake once they purge the blackness from my body."

His tone stung. She set her jaw, narrowing her gaze. "Cyrus, if there is a small chance they can heal you, you've got to take it."

"And how do you suppose I do that?"

"I..."

"The society resides within Kastali Dun. I have to get there *first*, before they can help me."

"Then go! Go to them and take a chance at ridding your body of the poison."

He shook his head. "You do not understand, do you?" She opened and closed her mouth. Apparently, she didn't. "I cannot simply transform into a dragon and fly home. Transformation takes magic, precious magic that has already been spent blocking the poison from spreading. Even the smallest act would break the barrier and kill me."

The air rushed from her chest. "So it's hopeless, then..."

"No, not hopeless."

"*Not* hopeless?"

"There is the small chance that I might be rescued."

"You—you think someone will come for you? Here? Into my world?" She glanced out the window. A guilty thrill shot through her at the prospect of meeting other people like Cyrus.

"My survival depends upon it."

She hoped he was right. There was nothing more she could do to keep him alive. At this point, all she *could* do was offer him refuge in the comfort of her home.

CLAIRE SKIPPED work again that day, and the next. Cyrus slept a lot. In fact, she saw very little of him after their conversation, except at mealtimes. He never missed an opportunity for food.

She developed a deep fascination towards him. He was more complex than anyone she had ever met. She couldn't help but watch him whenever she had the chance, especially when he wasn't aware of it. Sometimes their eyes met and her cheeks flushed, embarrassed for her outright curiosity.

There were certain things about him, like the way his eyebrows were often drawn tight, that made his troubled mind known. She got the feeling it had little to do with the possibility of the vodar's return. Sometimes he shook his head, as if disagreeing with an internal argument, as if he was deep in thought. But the moment he caught her gaze, his face would turn to stone again— unreadable.

At times, he was overly polite. This made getting to know him difficult. He rarely appeared inclined to open up about personal stuff. He was still paranoid, too, frequently checking the windows or "patrolling the grounds" as he called it. She always inwardly rolled her eyes when he insisted on doing this—usually before and after mealtimes.

By the end of the third day, Cyrus's hope of being rescued fizzled out. "No one is coming for me..." He said as he gazed out the window into the growing twilight.

His mood changed from hopeful to downright morose. She tried to cheer him up when she could, and found it best to avoid any topic that had to do with his predicament. She especially *never* mentioned the vodar. Instead she focused on asking him questions about things he was fond of.

She had already learned a lot about Dragonwall doing this— geography, politics, magic. Cyrus told her about the drengr, too. That was her favorite topic. Whenever they talked about his world, she felt like she was being sucked into a fantasy story. She couldn't help her fierce longing. It welled up deep inside her. She found herself dreaming of running away to Dragonwall.

They were sitting at the dinner table on the fourth night, talking about the drengr, when Cyrus told her that they took mates to be their riders. She nearly fell out of her chair. "There are dragon riders too?"

It was both unexpected and shocking. Real dragon riders—as mates! She pictured herself on the back of a dragon, soaring high above the clouds.

"Oh aye, there are riders." He rolled his wine around in his glass, staring at it with unfocused eyes. "Our mates are our life partners so it makes sense that they become our riders."

Her chest felt so light. "Do...do *you* have a rider?" she asked.

His lips pressed into a flat line—a flicker of upset. "I do not. My rider...died."

"Oh...I'm...Cyrus, I'm so sorry. I didn't—"

"There is no need to apologize. Just..." He shook his head and said very little after that.

He said even less with each passing day. But with each day, she learned a little more, even as he grew weaker. She tried to make the most of her time with him. The difficulty was, Cyrus slept more and more as his health declined. His skin was now blackened up to his collarbones. It took significant self control to keep from staring at his neckline in alarm every time she saw him.

SHE WAS PREPARING breakfast on the morning of the fifth day when she'd finally had enough of his sulking. His mood had reached an all-time low, and she was finding it difficult to stomach. She looked at him squarely in the eye. "Cyrus, I'm sure someone will come for you. If the king hasn't heard from you yet, he will send others after you."

His face transformed—crushed. She immediately regretted saying anything at all. He shook his head. "They will not come. Daudagher will take me before my kinsmen do."

"Wh—*who*?"

"Daudagher—the god of death. Ultimately, he will decide my fate. Any hope that I harbor now is but a foolish hope."

She exhaled, frustrated. She wouldn't allow him to spend his last days in this dark mood. "Hope is hope, Cyrus. Even a flicker of hope is enough to drive back darkness."

He offered her a small smile. "You are wise for one so young."

She eyed him a moment longer before handing him his breakfast. She sat down beside him with her oatmeal specialty. "I'm not *that* much younger than you."

His entire expression changed, lit up, eyes dancing with mischief. There. That's what she'd wanted. "You sure about that?" he hedged. "How much are you willing to wager?"

"Oh. Um, I don't know." She fell silent a moment. "How about if I guess right, you have to quit being so negative."

"And if *I* win?"

"I don't know. Name your prize." She regretted the words the second they left her mouth. He'd probably think of something good.

"If I win, then you must grant me one favor, which I may ask at any time."

She huffed. "That's hardly fair, you already know how old you are."

"It changes nothing. How old do you think I am? You sounded certain a moment ago. Do we have a deal?"

"Fine."

The corner of his mouth twitched but he didn't smile. "Good. Now, how old?"

"You can't be more than—wait, how many guesses do I get?"

He hummed. "How about five? Does that seem fair?"

"Okay. You can't be any more than ten years older than me. I would say, thirty, thirty-two at the most."

He stared at her in silence, as if waiting for her to change her mind. She didn't. "More than that," he said. "Many more."

She swore under her breath. "Okay, how about...forty?" Goodness, he couldn't be any older than forty. And even still, if that was the case, he aged *extremely* well, or had a great plastic surgeon. She almost laughed at the thought.

"Guess again. Three more tries."

Her jaw dropped. On a whim, she decided to overestimate and work her way down instead. "Sixty," she said. There was no possible way in hell he was sixty. He was totally thirty and pretending otherwise.

"Again."

"I don't think so! You're lying."

He shook his head. "I would not lie about something this trivial."

"Ha! Well you're not vain, are you?"

"Verily so. Another guess?"

"Fine. A hundred years old."

"No. Wrong again. Last try. Use your guess wisely."

She chewed on the skin of her lower lip, thinking about her next answer. "All right...You are three hundred years old." There was no way—no effing way.

"Close, but no."

Her jaw dropped. "Fine. Tell me then."

"Three hundred and thirty-six years of age."

"Impossible!"

But...was it? She knew he wasn't lying, but that didn't make it any easier to believe. In books, vampires and werewolves were generally immortal, never aging as they grew older. Why not the Drengr?

"We are not immortal," Cyrus said when she voiced her theory. "We simply age slowly. Most in my race live a thousand years or more."

"Wow," she breathed.

"Oh, and I win." He looked smug.

"Yeah, yeah. You win." She eyed him. What kind of favor was he looking for anyway? She'd already done plenty for him.

"I have not yet decided," he said in answer. "I will inform you when I do."

"I'll be in suspense until then."

"I do not doubt that," he said, smirking. He stood and went to stand in front of the kitchen window. He stayed there, the silence stretching out before them.

"You really think the wraiths will come back for you? And, in case you've forgotten, you still haven't told me why they are after the dragonstones." Her voice was low.

Cyrus turned to face her, his expression grim. "The vodar are after the dragonstones because they have the power to destroy my kingdom. But I am *not* going to let that happen, and neither are you."

CHAPTER 8

A NEW PROTECTOR

Battle Ground, Indiana

Claire's mouth fell open. When Cyrus dropped into her life, she thought his death was the worst problem on her hands. Now she realized something more was at stake—an entire kingdom. Dragonwall was in danger?

All the air went out of her. It was a lot to process.

In a few short days, she had learned enough about his kingdom to fall in love with it—a world she had never seen and struggled to imagine. And even though it may not have been *her* world, she felt...protective. "Why do the wraiths want to destroy Dragonwall?" she asked, her voice a mere squeak.

"It is not *they* who want to destroy it. Vodar wraiths have no desires, save to be left alone in their disgusting wasteland of undirfold. But come now, let us save these grim matters for another time. I need to rest and let my breakfast settle."

"Seriously?" Her skin flushed with anger. She was done playing nice. She wanted some answers and she wanted them now. "After everything I've done for you? You asked me to keep your existence a secret, so I have. I've fed you. I've clothed you. I've given you a place to stay. I saved your life, for goodness sake. The least you can do is give me answers. You've been secretive about *everything*. What's going on? If we're both in danger, then I have a right to know." She hesitated, breathing hard. "Besides, what have you got to lose by telling me?"

His shoulders slumped. "Fine. I will tell you, but on one condition."

"Which is?"

"You must allow me to rest for now. I promise I will tell you. Soon."

"Later today?"

"If you wish."

She swallowed. "Okay. All right. Go rest."

Instead of going to his room, he went into the living room and plopped down on the couch, sighing. She watched him from the shadowy hallway, wondering if by *rest* he meant, turn into a living statue. When he didn't move, she went to the coffee table and picked up the remotes to the television and stereo system.

"How about some T.V. while you sit here doing...nothing?"

"What's tee-fee?" He looked innocently up at her.

Wow.

"This," she said, turning on the television to flip through a few channels. Cyrus sprang from the couch as though it were a pincushion and grimaced. His discomfort was quickly replaced by a look of disbelief. Sometimes she forgot how little he knew of her world.

"What in the name of all the gods is *that* thing?" He pointed at the television like it was a monster.

"You'll see." Her eyes watered as she held back laughter.

After flipping through some channels, she settled on an action movie—Bruce Willis's Die Hard. An absolute classic by her standards. It was in the middle of the shooting scene where John McClane gets busy machine-gunning the baddies, running all over broken glass.

Cyrus moved over to the television and examined it. "There are people inside," he muttered to himself, touching the screen. "How did they get in there?" He looked behind it, then back at the screen, then behind it once more. It wasn't a window. He got down on his knees to watch, his face inches from the screen. He couldn't take his eyes off the sequence playing out.

"You know, it's bad to watch that close," she warned him, completely amused. "You'll burn your retinas out."

It wasn't true but it was the excuse her mom had always used on her.

He hummed, hardly listening, and raised his hand up to place his palm across the screen. His eyebrows drew together. "Amazing. Your world never ceases to surprise me."

She stood by for a little while, letting him have his moment. He would probably sit there all day if she let him. "All right. That's enough. Come lay down. You can watch from here."

She led him back to the couch to lie down.

Upstairs, she took a seat at her computer. Another day of tedious job applications. Today was technically her *official* day off, even though she'd skipped work all week. Keeping Leah and her boss off her back had become quite the task. She loved Leah. Her best friend meant everything to her, but she'd promised Cyrus that she would keep his existence a secret.

After he disappeared, she would tell Leah everything, but not until he was good and gone. She silently prayed that by *gone*, he would be rescued and not... She shook her head. Thinking about his death was too much.

When lunch rolled around, Cyrus was asleep on the couch, so she turned off the television and left him a sandwich on the coffee table. The fridge was nearly empty. Cyrus had eaten her out of house and home. She left him a quickly scribbled note and took off to the grocery store, but only after recovering her car, which sat unused on the side of the east field for the last five days. And since it was stuck in the dirt, she had to use the tractor to pull it out.

When she returned with groceries, she found Cyrus awake, feasting on the food she'd left. She quickly emptied the bags and took a seat in the armchair to watch him. He didn't even look at her as he scarfed down the remainder of his sandwich. Then he stretched out once more on the sofa, sighing contentedly, and fell asleep.

Not a single word. Not one! She exhaled loudly, forced to push her annoyance away and remember that patience *was* a virtue.

It wasn't until the end of their dinnertime feast—and feast it was because she'd pulled out all the stops—that he finally addressed the question he promised to answer during breakfast. He began by telling her about a secret mission assigned to him by his king, and how it had gone terribly wrong. "King Talon believed the stones were threatened. He sent me to retrieve them before they fell into the wrong hands," he explained. "All along we believed this thief was merely a minor threat. We had no idea what he was capable of."

He spoke of his journey into the Gable Forest, an enchanted forest where the stones were hidden for years beyond measure. The Gable Forest was a place where sprites lived. These beings were considered mysterious because they never ventured beyond their forest. Cyrus's description made her think of elves.

After he obtained the stones, he left the spriten city of Esterpine and began his trip home. "I believed all was well," he said, frowning. "I believed my mission was a success." His lips pressed into a thin line."I was not prepared for what happened next. His name is Kane."

Kane. Her skin prickled. She suppressed a shudder.

"He's old. Far older than any of my kind, and he is powerful—capable of summoning Vodar from the depths of undirfold. In truth, I am lucky to be alive after facing him." He shook his head, clearly surprised to have escaped with his life. "Kane will do anything and stop at nothing to obtain these stones."

"But...why? Why does he need them to destroy your kingdom? How exactly do they work?" Part of her was afraid to know.

"There are five stones in total. I have two. If all five are brought together, my race will be finished. We will become nothing more than a memory and a monument to the landscape."

"You'll all die?! Cyrus, that's...that's horrible!"

"When the dragonstones are brought into contact with each

other, every living being of draconic descent will turn back into the stone forms from whence we originated."

"Stone? But that would suggest that dragons were made from—"

"From stone. Yes. We were—the *first* dragons were. Or so the chroniclers have written."

"And he wants to do this to you? This *Kane* person? He wants to kill all the dragons?" Her heart raced at the thought. He sounded like the epitome of a storybook's perfect villain. Dragons were beautiful creatures. Cyrus was noble and kind. Why would anyone want to kill them?

Cyrus was silent for a moment before shaking his head. "It would seem so at first—that he simply wants to annihilate us. But I had a deeper glimpse into Kane's plans. While it is true that he could easily destroy us with all five stones, he could also exert great power over us simply by possessing them. There is not a single living soul that can attest to the scope of capabilities that wielding the stones will bring."

"So Kane wants power."

"Andalynn sem haldai an Gorrkevi valdi an dreki." Strange words rolled off his tongue. They echoed in her ears, almost familiar, as if she had heard them before.

"Dreki," she repeated. "It was written on the back of the coins you gave me. But...what does all that mean?"

"It means *'He who holds the Stones controls the dragons.'*"

She processed his words. If someone gained the ability to control all of dragon kind, how would anyone stand against them? The night she had held the stones, one feeling had dominated all others. Power. No wonder keeping these remaining stones away from Kane was such a big deal.

"He can't have them, Cyrus." Her heart thumped. A strange possessiveness for Dragonwall welled up inside of her. "You've got to protect them, no matter what."

"Aye. This I know. Why do you think I fled Dragonwall through the gate?"

The gate. Forbidden. But the law—as old as it was—was not a

good enough excuse to let the stones fall into Kane's hands. He'd had no other choice.

"The forest played nasty tricks on me, turning me all around, making me think I fled south instead of north. All too soon, I was cornered at the edge of the kingdom. And within me, I had little strength left to fight. The wraiths' pursuit was relentless. Never have I flown so far at such great speeds without rest." He sighed, leaning back in his chair, his dark hair brushing his shoulders. He ran a hand through it, pulling at the tangles.

"Kane ordered them to kill me and retrieve the stones, so they do as he commands. They will stop at nothing. My being alive is a threat to Kane's very existence. It is a risk he cannot afford to take. He wishes to remain in the shadows, until the time is right, until he is ready. Only then will he strike and reveal his identity. Woe to those in his path when he does." He shut his eyes. Little creases appeared.

"So...no one else knows about Kane? Only you? You didn't warn anyone? But that means..."

"No one will know what strikes them when it does. As unfortunate as it is, Kane's first planned attack, the one I saw in his mind, is intended for the city of Belnesse." He took a deep breath. "Kane intends..." He shook his head and pursed his lips.

"But then, why didn't you warn anyone? Why—"

"Distance, Claire. I can only send my voice so far."

"What—what do you mean?"

"Drengr are telepathic—we can communicate with our minds."

Her eyes widened, though it shouldn't have come as a surprise, considering everything else. "Cyrus, you said that the vodar would stop at nothing." She hated saying their name. It left her stomach twisting. "You said they would follow their master's commands, and that Kane would do anything necessary to get the stones from you, even kill you."

He gazed at her in silence.

"Why then did they disappear after hurting you? Why didn't they just simply finish the job?"

"Did I not ask you that same question?"

"Well, yes, but I thought maybe you might have worked out an answer by now."

"Hardly. They will be back. I will die by their hand, I can feel it in my heart."

Tears filled her eyes at the finality of his words. "Someone will come for you."

Cyrus pushed his dinner plate away from him, propping his arms up on the table. "No one is coming, Claire. It would seem that my part in this tale is nearly over." At those words, a strange look came over him. She had seen it before. He was fighting an internal battle again.

"What...what is it?" she ventured.

He opened his mouth, then shook his head. "I cannot help but wonder, is it wrong of me to withhold what I know, for fear of voicing the truth?"

"What do you mean?"

He sighed. "What I mean is, I believe that I have discerned the next turn this story must take. Only, I am afraid of the path." He lowered his voice to almost a whisper. "Terrified, to be honest."

Her eyebrows pulled together. "Cyrus...you're scaring me."

"I think the time has come, that I must share with you what I know—what I *believe*. I hope you are ready to hear it."

The back of her neck prickled. "Cyrus, just tell me."

He finally looked up at her. "I believe..." He reached around his neck to untie the leather pouch, holding it out to her even though she made no move to take it. "I believe that it is *you* who must take up my burden. You must protect the dragonstones and keep them from Kane. My journey ends here. I will never make it back to my kingdom alive."

CHAPTER 9
THE KING'S PROPHETESS

Kastali Dun

Saffra gazed upon the dream world. A woman stood before her facing a white beast, a wild dragon like those she had seen burning the city of Belnesse. This woman was no ordinary being. She was covered in shimmery, translucent cloth. The gown was of a single layer and did little more than hide her feminine parts. Beneath the fabric were markings that glowed with luminescent radiance. They sprawled across her skin, swirling and twisting like possessive snakes, winding their way around her arms and legs. She was a sprite of the forest.

The dragon pawed the ground and snorted with fury, offering its challenge. The sprite stood proud against it, shoulders squared, face like granite, displaying overwhelming confidence and strength. The calm collect of one possessing much experience in life.

It roared and opened its maw, letting forth a torrent of flame. She shielded herself, throwing up a wall of green magic. The flames distorted around her body. When they abated, a look of resolution passed over her features. She opened her mouth and began to sing. It was the purest voice Saffra had ever heard. Beautiful, hypnotic. An incant of sorts. But different from any kind Saffra had known. The power of the sprite's words washed over her.

The dragon roared, tearing deep gouges into the earth with its talons. It knew of her intentions. It pulled against her, tried to escape, then gave a pitiful groan. It was snared.

The sprite continued, her words weaving the necessary magic to defeat the beast. On and on she sang. Not once did her voice waver, or grow hoarse. Every note held perfection, as if it were a song known in the deepest depths of her soul. She was glad to sing it; joy reflected upon her face even in the midst of danger.

The beast grew still—deathly still. Its skin rippled like liquid stone, hardening its scales into marble. Then, all was still. It would move no more. The sprite had seen to that. Forever a reminder to those who opposed her might.

SAFFRA WOKE the next morning with little recollection of the dream, though she tried to remember it. After breaking her fast in the dining hall, she made her way to the grand mage's quarters, as she did every day. The grand mage lived in the easternmost wing of the great keep of Kastali Dun. All society elites resided there, and only the most powerful mages trained with them.

She generally passed much of her time studying with Marcel, mornings and afternoons. She had very few friends in the keep. Most of the noble women were too supercilious for her tastes. She was plenty happy to be in Marcel's easy presence. He'd become something like a grandfather to her over the years.

"You know," she said, propping her chin on her fist, "I had the most peculiar dream last night." They sat in his study—a room akin to a small library—each quietly working on their own tasks. He had a long manuscript stretched out before him while she worked her way through a book on diction, hoping to improve her knowledge of the Asarlaí language.

Marcel arched an eyebrow, looking up at her with curiosity. "What sort of...dream?"

Were she anyone else, he would have feigned interest. But, she was not simply *anyone*. She was the king's royal prophetess. Her dreams held meaning.

She sighed, trying to recall the details. Most of it was foggy now, but she hadn't been able to shake the gnawing feeling of its importance from her mind. "I cannot discern its meaning," she said at last, frowning. "It's become rather vague."

"Has it given you reason to worry?" Marcel's blue eyes sparkled with interest.

"Well, no, but it has increased my curiosity."

"Oh-ho. Is that not a good thing? For when we are curious, we learn." He clasped his hands together, smiling wide. "What of it can you recall, my dear?"

She considered. The only aspect that remained clear was a white dragonesque statue sitting on a hill overlooking other hills, which overlooked a prairie with a sea of yellowed grasses. The statue looked so real—so terribly real—as if a genuine dragon had simply fallen asleep, never to move again. Surely it was nothing more than carved stone, but why did her heart say otherwise? She told him all of this, hoping it would make sense.

"Ahh." He smiled widely. "I know exactly what you saw. Its history is highly debated, as are most occurrences long past. The great monument lies amidst the rolling hills of Kengr, near the Kengr Gate in fact." He hummed. "Most call it the *marble dragon*."

The marble dragon? The name *did* sound familiar.

"I believe there is a legend about it. If I am not mistaken, the story lies within the tome I lent you."

"That large old thing?" She knew exactly the one. She'd left it to collect dust on her night stand.

"The very same." He smirked as if he knew.

"I have found its accounts useful already," she said, trying to sound genuine. Trying, and failing.

Marcel merely smiled back at her before returning to his work. It was so like him to stimulate her curiosity before sending her on a hunt. Rarely did he provide answers to her questions. Rather, he encouraged the individual pursuit of knowledge.

When she revisited the Grand Mage's study after the mid-day meal, she brought the tome with her and let it land on the table with a loud thud.

"You might as well put that away," Marcel grumbled, standing up from his desk. His face was a direct opposite from earlier. Troubled, now. He was stooping more than usual too, perhaps weighed down by invisible burdens. "We must begin a new phase of your training," he said, coming to stand near her.

She opened and closed her mouth, taken aback. Something had happened during the midday meal. "My training is complete. We both know I merely come here as a formality." Cyrus was the only one she still trained with. Her lessons with the mages had ended the year prior.

"Yes, well..." Marcel waved a hand. "When Lady Lacara was prophetess for the king, she had an ability to call upon information and events at will. She discovered many answers. Scrying, I believe she called it, though I do not know the true name."

"Lady Lacara?"

She'd been the royal prophetess of Dragonwall long before Saffra came along. There was only ever one at a time. Lacara had served two kings: King Talon's grandfather and King Talon's father. Unfortunately, her old age eventually took her; she died shortly after King Talon's father, King Tallek, was crowned king. After that, Dragonwall went nearly four hundred years without another seer.

"Indeed. It took her many years to master the art," Marcel said. "But when she did, her skill greatly aided the monarchy."

"Why have I never heard of this until now?"

"My dear, you have numerous concerns to weigh you down."

Her cheeks heated. Marcel still saw her as a child. That's why he hadn't told her until now.

He hesitated. "Cyrus and I both agreed that it would be best to refrain from this higher form of magic until you were ready. It would seem, however, that the king feels differently."

"The king? So *he* is behind this sudden change in your mood?"

"He is worried about Cyrus," Marcel said. "If you can but see a glimpse of him and reassure our king, it will bring him relief."

"Then perhaps he will do something about Belnesse," she muttered. She was bitter over the king's response to her vision. He was too preoccupied to appear concerned. She expected shock, but instead he had challenged her, doubted her, and named all the other matters more important to him. Growing threats along the coastlines, goblin unrest in the east, vodar sightings in the north, Cyrus missing. Everything seemed more important than the vision of a burning city.

"Belnesse, my dear?" Marcel's brow furrowed. "What of it?"

She gave him a brief explanation of all she'd seen.

"Wild Dragons, you say?" He stroked his white beard, his scowl deepening. At last, he sighed. "The king has many cares, *many* cares. Let us focus on Cyrus for now."

"You've got to be kidding me," she muttered under her breath. Marcel in his old age didn't hear. She adored Cyrus. She wanted him found just as badly as anyone. But what would happen if her vision came to pass?

"Shall we get started?" Marcel was already shuffling away.

"Very well," she sighed. "I am always willing to learn, and happy to help where help is needed."

"Good!"

Scrying at will was a form of meditation. Marcel went through the technique, detailing each step. It required a significant amount of concentration, an empty mind, and a single question. Though how such a thing could be possible—to focus one's mind on a singular thought—was beyond her. When it was time, he retrieved an incense stick from his cabinet.

They were hardly a thing of magic, though they were often used in magical undertakings. Mostly they were a popular way to drive away horrid smells, especially in the keep. As a matter of personal preference, she disliked them for the headaches they gave her.

"Do you remember the magical properties of the acacia tree?" Marcel asked. She nodded. Acacia promoted the mind. Its blossoms smelled like sweet jasmine and always left her craving honey.

"The easiest way to begin scrying, especially in the beginning, is with the scent of acacia." He lit the stick and placed it before her. "Now focus your mind, and do as I have explained."

His instructions were nearly impossible to follow, because her question kept changing. She was supposed to focus on only one, yet when she asked the gods, *"Is Cyrus safe?"* she saw nothing but the backs of her eyelids. If she squeezed them tightly enough, little stars danced across her vision, gold flecks in a sea of black. She tried many questions. *"Is Cyrus alive?" "Where is Cyrus?" "What happened to Cyrus?" "Why did he not return as planned?"*

Each was as fruitless as the next. Hours passed. Nothing happened. And of course, she took it personally, as an indication that she was not good enough, not powerful enough to do what was needed.

"It took Lady Lacara years," Marcel reminded her. "I did not expect results on your first try."

She did not miss the disappointment in his voice.

That night she lay awake, tossing and turning. Her sleeping habits had dramatically worsened since her vision about the Dragon Stones. The same vision that had taken Cyrus away from them. With each passing night, she feared sleep and the sights it would bring.

"This is useless!" she growled, throwing herself from her bed. She lit a candle and rummaged around in her cabinet for an acacia scent stick. Making herself comfortable on the floor, she began the rigmarole of scrying. She emptied her mind of all distracting thoughts, including her worry over Cyrus. She then focused her efforts on a single question, allowing the overpowering scent of acacia to envelop her.

"What happened to Cyrus?" she repeated over and over. All else was nothingness. The scent of the acacia conquered her senses, whisking her away from the real world, surrounding her with jasmine and honey.

She sat long into the early hours of the morning, focusing on a single train of thought, desiring an answer within the depths of her very being. She must have nodded off a few times, because her neck was getting cramped each time her head jerked. There was nothing...nothing but the blackness of her mind—

Until it disappeared, replaced abruptly by a different kind of darkness.

She saw the nighttime sky. A full moon, pricked with glittering stars. She gasped. There was Cyrus, his gleaming pearlescent scales, nearly as bright as the moon. But...he was falling.

Fear doused her, twisting her stomach into knots.

He plummeted towards the ground. She glanced around, trying to understand, wanting—wishing she could do something, anything. But she was detached from this world, this place. This was not Dragonwall.

With a sickening crunch, Cyrus struck the ground. She cried out, but no sound came. She needed to help him—to save him!

As if flung, she was whisked away. She faced two black pillars made of onyx. The Kengr Gate, the portal Cyrus must have used to enter the world that wasn't Dragonwall.

Once again, her view changed. A mountain stronghold with jagged ramparts, crumbling with age. It was an eerie fortress, long abandoned. Surrounding it were hundreds of dragons, the very same she had seen before, swooping and darting, catching fish in the lake below.

Red, evil eyes looked back at her. She saw the thief as she'd seen him before. He haunted her visions again. She cringed, averting her gaze.

The scene disappeared. The evil face was replaced by a calming one. A face as familiar as her own. The same woman she had seen many, many times before, with golden hair and green eyes. The woman was speaking, but she couldn't make out her words, as if they were underwater, or...blocked, somehow.

Then, everything disappeared.

HER EYELIDS FLEW OPEN. Each gasp was jagged against her chest. Cyrus—she had finally seen him! She clawed her way across the floor and stood.

The king—she needed to warn the king. Without dressing, she grabbed a robe to cover her nightgown then fled her chambers. She raced through the keep, stumbling in the darkness as her bare feet slapped the cold flagstones. Breathless, she came to a halt before the king's tower. It was time to tell him what she'd seen, and he *wasn't* going to like it.

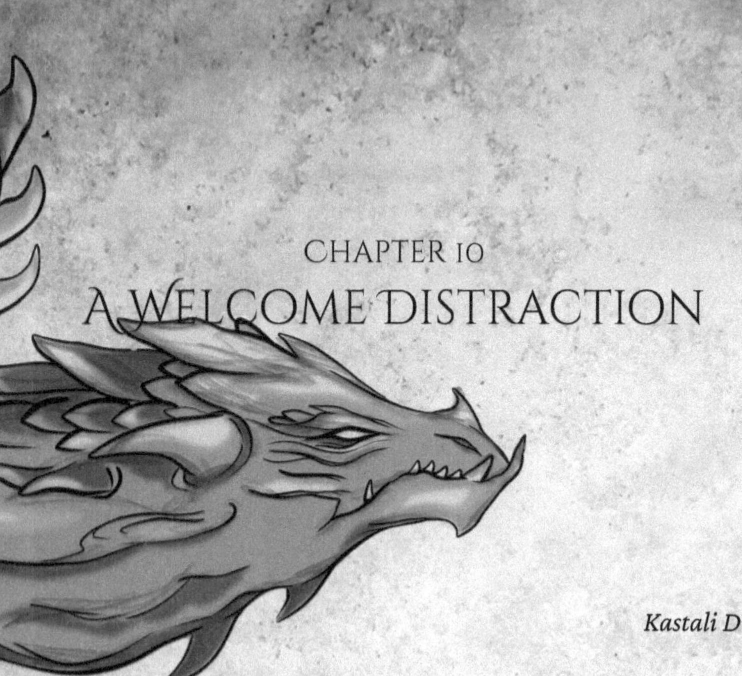

CHAPTER 10
A WELCOME DISTRACTION

Kastali Dun

Saffra was taken before the king, albeit after a good deal of arguing with his guards. It only fueled her agitation.

"Your coming troubles me." The king tossed a quill on the desk, abandoning his task to gaze at her. Braziers cast dancing light around his study and long shadows over his scars. The balcony doors were thrown open much the same as they usually were, admitting the soft sea breeze beyond.

"Your Grace," she said, licking her lips. "I...I apologize for disturbing you. I know your burdens are great." She glanced down where his quill lay discarded. A roll of parchment stretched across the desk's surface. Good gods! Had he been working all night? She clenched her robe more tightly about her chest.

"My burdens are indeed great, Lady Saffra. And it seems you wish to bring me another."

She offered him a weak nod. It wasn't as if she *asked* for her visions—as if this was her fault. Images rushed back to her. Cyrus falling. The sickening crunch of his body slamming into the ground. She winced, reliving it. Her body trembled in response.

"Gods above!" King Talon rushed to his feet and retrieved a

cloak from the corner of his study. He threw it about her shoulders, guiding her to the extra chair at his desk. "What have you seen?"

"Cyrus, Your Grace." The words were a weak whisper. "I saw Cyrus."

"You saw him?" The king's eyes widened a measure before he regained composure. "He is alive then?"

"I...do not know. I think..." She faltered.

King Talon loved his shields. They were brothers to him, his only family.

"I see." His face fell. She had not come to bring him hope. "Tell me what you saw. It is not wise to worry me."

She exhaled. "Cyrus is gravely injured, Your Grace, perhaps dead..."

King Talon's chair slid out from behind him, skidding across the floor as he came to his feet. "What did you see? How do you know this?" He ran a hand through his mangy hair, smoothing the thick tufts aside. She swallowed against the dryness of her throat, trying to ignore her racing heart. "*Well?*"

"I tried scrying, Your Grace."

The scars on his face turned silvery-white. "And?"

"I hope what I saw is not true."

But it was. The gods wouldn't have shown her otherwise. She proceeded to describe her vision exactly as she saw it, starting with Cyrus, moving through each scene she witnessed before ending with the thief's red eyes. The only part she left out was of the woman, not that it would have mattered. King Talon ignored everything except for what concerned Cyrus. She could not fault him for it. "After Cyrus fell, did he live? Did he survive?"

She shut her eyes, unable to bear his fear. A tear slid down her cheeks. "I cannot say, Your Grace."

"He must be alive!" he insisted. "I would have felt his death. I would have known." This, he said more to himself.

"You are certain?" she asked, opening her eyes to find his— silver with little flecks of gold. The only beautiful facet of an otherwise ruined face.

"I am certain."

She blew out the breath she'd been holding. One small mercy, then." "Your Grace..." She hesitated. "There is something else."

"Have you not subjected me to enough?" he asked.

She opened her mouth, only to close it. Guilt, welled up in her chest. Why was it always her? Why was *she* the one forced to deliver unwanted knowledge? Why had the gods chosen *her*?

Her vision blurred. She tried to clench the king's cloak more tightly about her shoulders to hide her trembling. It didn't work.

King Talon reclaimed his chair. He slumped down and said, "Very well. Out with it."

Taking a deep breath, she said, "Cyrus is no longer in Dragonwall."

"I am not sure I understand your meaning."

"My meaning is as I have said it, Your Grace. Cyrus is no longer in our kingdom. He is no longer in our *world*."

His eyes widened. "That's impossible."

"I do not think so. Cyrus traveled through one of the gates. I saw it—Kengr Gate."

The king fell silent. His eyes went unfocused, unseeing. She'd seen the look before. He was communicating telepathically with his shields—using his mind to tell them of Cyrus. At last, he leaned back against his chair. "Why would Cyrus resort to such madness? Why would he travel through a gate?"

She opened her mouth, then closed it. There was no sensible reason—none that she could think of. The gates were portals. Each led *beyond*. Laws against their use were put in place at the forming of the monarchy. Some said it was to keep people from disappearing. But the real truth was, it protected Dragonwall from whatever came through. No one knew what lands lay beyond, and not a soul cared to learn.

"And the thief?" His question brought her mind back to the present. "Do you think *he* is responsible for this mess?"

"I..." She shook her head. "I don't know. I only saw his eyes—his blood red eyes." She could neither confirm nor deny the thief's involvement. Red eyes in a vision offered little in the way of answers, but her gut feeling suggested he was to blame.

The king fell into a broody silence.

She glanced around his study, affording him time to think. Her eyes fell on the cream curtains fluttering in the early morning breeze. The sky was a dull gray. Dawn was approaching.

"He can't be dead." His voice made her jump. "Perhaps he was simply unconscious when he fell. There is still hope."

"I shall pray, Your Grace, I shall pray for his safe return."

"Reyr..." His voice was little more than a whisper. "I hope Reyr finds him. He must." He sighed and turned his gaze towards the curtains and balcony beyond.

"He's been gone a long time," she mused. When Cyrus had failed to return, King Talon sent Reyr, Jovari, and Koldis after him. Only Bedelth and Verath remained in the capital. The king could not risk sending any more of his personal guards.

"Indeed." The king sighed. "Far too long."

"Do you think he will know to follow Cyrus through the gate?" she wondered.

"It is all we can hope for, Lady Saffra."

"So...what are we to do now?" she asked. She pawed at her eyes, clearing them. Cyrus was like a brother to her and the thought of him harmed made her heart ache.

"We must inform the lower council. We have hidden this matter long enough. I will need you present—to fulfill your duty."

Her muscles went rigid. "All right. If you command it, I will be there. May I be excused?" She stood before allowing him to answer, discarding his cloak upon the chair.

"Yes. Yes...of course." His voice sounded pained and far away. He didn't see her as she curtsied and bid him farewell.

She fled the tower for the open corridor beyond, wishing none of this had happened. Would that she could leave it behind as easily as the keep's corridors as she exited out into the open morning. But she couldn't.

The sun was not yet free of the horizon. The breeze rustling in the open courtyard dried her remaining tears. With a tormented mind, she crossed through the south wing's courtyard and made her way back to her chambers.

Being indoors only smothered her. She paced back and forth, breathing ragged. Any moment she might burst into tears all over again if she did not find something to occupy her mind. Making up her mind, she summoned Jocelyn. With her welcome aid, she dressed quickly. "I think I will go to the archery range this morning."

"You look rather distraught, my lady. Won't you rest here and let me bring you some chamomile tea?"

"I am fine, Jocelyn. Truly. Fresh air will be the best remedy for me."

Jocelyn didn't argue, even if she appeared conflicted.

When she reached the practice field, the keep was still quiet. Dawn light was just breaking upon the horizon. She picked out her favorite target range then set about her bow, stringing it. Withdrawing the first arrow, she loaded it. In one fluid motion, she drew the bowstring taught, then released. She watched the arrow dart through the air. It landed with a thud on the target. Her aim was true. It struck dead center.

There was a time when she was terrible at this. Had it not been for her superb trainer, she never would have reached the level of skill she now possessed. Daxton was an expert in all matters of warfare, specifically that of dealing death efficiently. She fondly recalled her first lesson with him. She was only ten, and he a soldier of nineteen. Even then she admired him despite his brazen attitude, his excessive cockiness, and his disdain for teaching a female, especially a *little girl*, in matters that were better left to men.

Her mind raced backwards in time. It had been scarcely a year since her arrival at the keep. The grand mage had gifted her a bow and set of arrows as a positive distraction, so that she might have an outlet for her mind. He'd also hired Daxton to be her archery tutor. Daxton was to train her once per week.

It had been no surprise that she took to him—all women did— and despite her young age, such a thing could not be helped. The day he introduced himself, she remembered watching him demonstrate the use of a bow. *Worshiped* was the best way to describe how she had studied his strong arms and broad chest, blushing as she watched.

Needless to say, she performed terribly. How embarrassed she'd been! He made her so awfully nervous. Yet, her poor performance left her more determined to prove herself. In time she had, but he'd never gotten to see it. Daxton had gone off to defend Dragonwall in the Goblin Wars shortly after their lessons began. By the time he returned, years later, he was surprised to see that she had become quite good. They became friends after that, for years, and then something more had blossomed.

Her mind moved back to the present. The sun—now free of the horizon—cast its golden rays upon the grass, illuminating the field in a beautiful glow. It did not take her long to fire all of her arrows at the target. When the quiver was empty, she retrieved them and began anew.

No number of arrows could quell her worry, though the activity certainly helped. With the proper distraction, she could somewhat divert her mind. And so she fired one after another, each landing in the cluster at the center of the target.

"Determined this morning, are we?" A deep voice sounded, making eager bumps rise along her skin. She was in the middle of pulling her bowstring taught for the umpteenth time. She smiled as she released, holding her form. Her eyes watched the arrow soar through the air before it landed beside the others. Only then did she take up her most alluring smile and turn to address the speaker. "Good morning, Commander."

He stood with his hands clasped behind his back, eying her with amusement. His dark burgundy doublet was sleeveless, showing off his tanned arms so full of strength. The vest clung to his body just enough to exemplify his broad, seasoned chest. Embroidered in silver on his right breast was the drengr monarchy's sigil—a dragon head.

"Commander? Must I always insist that you call me Dax, my lady?"

She chuckled. "Until you call me Saffra, *Commander*, I will continue to use your proper title in public."

"Fair enough." A smile tugged at the corner of his lips. "I must say, I am surprised to find you here so early, and alone. Is it your determination that spurs such motivation, or something else? Perhaps, *someone* else?"

His hint did not go unnoticed. Her eyes circled the practice grounds only to find that they were indeed alone. "I might ask you the same question, Commander. Should you not be breaking fast in the barracks with your soldiers?"

"We both know I am the first to arrive on training days."

She knew this. He was always the first to the practice field in the morning. Aside from his duties as a war commander, he oversaw the drilling of all new recruits in the king's army.

"I suppose you are correct, sir. You do often arrive first." Again she smiled sweetly before turning away from him to draw another arrow. She refused to admit to her ulterior motives—that she wished to see him, for that was often why she visited here at this hour.

He wasted no time. Before she could properly nock her arrow, his arms were around her, tightly pulling her back against his chest. "Commander Daxton!" She giggled, hardly surprised by his behavior. "Someone might see us!" She tried to struggle away from his grip, but his arms did not relent.

His breath was warm against her ear. "I am happy you came to see me this morning, my lady, but I must warn you against it. If you continue with such behavior, others may become suspicious. I insist that from now on, you be more careful when placing your affections so openly."

"Me? How can you say such nonsense?" She was nearly breathless. "It is your grip I reside within."

"Is that so?" He nuzzled his nose against her neck before releasing her. "I suppose you are correct."

She staggered away from him, drunk with happiness. Once more, her eyes searched the grounds. They were still alone.

Dax took the remaining steps towards her, closing the gap between them. Taking her face in his hands, he planted a gentle kiss upon her lips, making sure to brush her nose with his before pulling away. He bestowed upon her a look of seriousness. "Tell me truly. What brought you out here this morning?"

She sighed as the memory of Cyrus came flooding back. She wanted to tell him what she had seen, but she couldn't bring herself to speak of it again. It was too painful. Instead she shook her head. "I no longer wanted to be in the keep." It was partially true. "I was hoping for a distraction—one that only you could offer."

He smiled. "While I am ever so glad to oblige your desires, my lady, it is best to avoid temptation." He placed another kiss upon her lips. "Now, if you do not object, I must prepare. I have a class to teach." His sweet smile turned into a mischievous grin. With that, he sauntered off to the sparring area. At that very same moment, his students began to arrive. She was left to watch his retreat and admire him from afar.

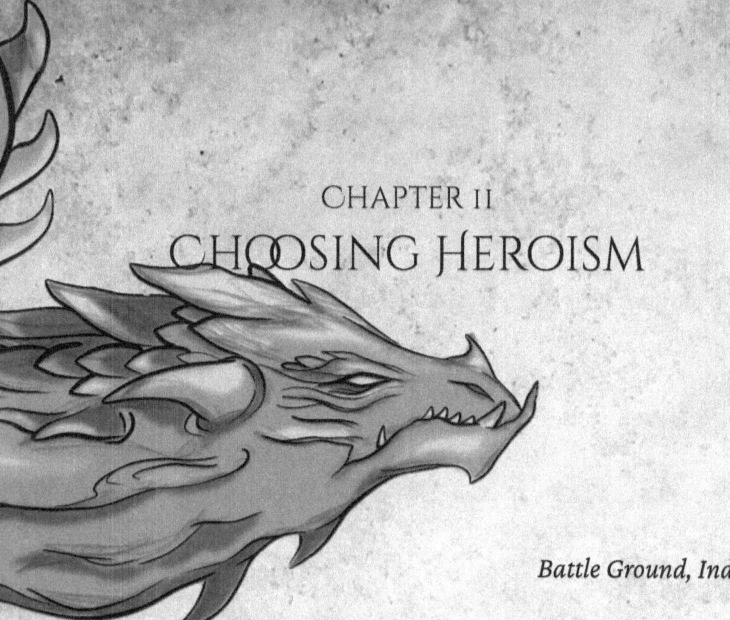

CHAPTER II
CHOOSING HEROISM

Battle Ground, Indiana

Claire cringed every time she saw the blackened skin on Cyrus. The poison was spreading. It had crept up his neck to just below his chin. She tried not to look at it or think about how much pain he was in. He hid his hurt like a champion, but she knew just from his eyes, from the way he winced.

Every day felt like it could be his last.

She hardly slept. Her mind was too preoccupied with everything. She'd wake in the middle of the night after a bout of fitful sleep and sneak down to check on him, just to make sure he was still alive. Then she'd return to her room and pace back and forth, going back over all the details of what had happened, as if she might find some way to help him.

The fact was, Kane had three dragonstones, and if he got the last two, it was game over. Worse still, no one knew anything about the sorcerer or his existence. No one but her and Cyrus.

It felt hopeless, even if she refused to admit that.

A week after he'd dropped into her life, they were sitting outside on the porch swing, overlooking the cornfields. The sun was still hours from the horizon. They sat side by side, sipping sweet tea with mint leaves, exactly the way her mom made it. The humid afternoon air was less stifling as they swung back and forth.

Desperate to find some sort of solution, she peppered Cyrus with questions. Especially because he was in a good mood, and willing to answer. She took a deep sip of her iced tea and said, "What else did you see in Kane's mind?"

She'd already discovered so much, but maybe they'd missed something.

Cyrus was a Mind Bender. That's how he knew about Kane's plans. After putting two-and-two together, she discovered that he'd read *her* mind as well, that first morning together. He'd apologized; she couldn't exactly be angry with a dying man.

"Well, you already know about the wild dragons," he said. She nodded. "Then there's the vodar wraiths—not the ones hunting me—the additional wraiths he plans to summon." Again, she nodded. It was a frightening idea, that he'd summon more. Six were bad enough. "And you already know about the goblins."

"Yes. You told me all about those, too."

Goblins weren't much better than dragons. They were green-skinned creatures no taller than a person's waist, who loved gold and riches more than anything in the world. Their size easily fooled people into thinking them harmless, but they weren't. They had pointy black teeth perfect for ripping flesh apart—which helped explain why they smelled so badly. The most important thing to remember was that they were quick.

"Never try to outrun a goblin," Cyrus had warned her. She had no intention of doing so. It was a blessing the creatures were stuck in *his* world, not hers.

"What about Kane's nasks?" he asked. "Have I told you about them yet?"

"Yes, but I'd like to hear the story again, if you don't mind. Maybe there's a detail we missed." Cyrus had grown forgetful, often telling her things she already knew. It was a sign of the poison's increasing hold on him. "Tell me again," she encouraged. It helped distract him from the pain.

"Kane's nasks are puppets. He uses them to do his bidding. It is impossible to tell who is possessed and who is not." Cyrus shook his head. He blamed himself—she knew it even if he didn't admit it. Kane's nasks had fooled everyone, including him.

"Kane has two of them—right under our very noses! I never would have guessed. It makes me sick to think the king is probably sitting down with them this very moment, going over battle plans, oblivious to the fact that Kane is pulling their strings."

"His lower council," she said.

"Yes."

The king had two councils—the upper council and the lower council. The upper council consisted of the king's six shields, and the lower consisted of twenty nobles who represented each of the twenty Dragondoms. Dragondoms were smaller territories within the four main territories of Dragonwall.

Yes, she'd learned *a lot* over the past week.

The nasks were on the king's lower council as advisors and representatives. Cyrus had failed to spot them and the guilt was eating him alive nearly as much as the poison. It wasn't until he was in Kane's head that he'd discovered how far the sorcerer's deceit went.

"What will the king do when he finds out he's been betrayed?"

"He won't. Not unless you get there in time to tell him—before it is too late."

She sighed. They'd had this conversation already. "Cyrus, I'm not going to Dragonwall. I don't know the way. Even if I did, how would I find the king's castle? Besides, I can't just...leave." He said nothing. "Surely you're mistaken. Just because someone saw my face. I...I'm not meant to protect the stones."

How could she possibly travel across a country full of wild dragons, vodar, goblins, and everything else?

"You are. It's meant to be you. Besides, your instincts will guide you."

She worried at her lower lip. Even if she *did* know the way to the king's castle, she couldn't simply run away and disappear into a foreign world simply because he asked her to. Or...could she?

There was no denying Dragonwall's allure. Its draw. She

considered the hypothetical possibility for a moment—*really* considered it. What prospects did she have here? The one thing she had really wanted, the internship, turned out to be nothing more than a failed pursuit. Her relationship with Jake was toast. She had no job lined up, and a long list of applications to fill out. *And* then there were her student loans. She almost groaned at the prospect. A small pile of gold wasn't going to answer all of her problems.

She gazed out over the cornfields. The breeze rustled a strand of her hair that had come lose. It tickled her cheek. She pushed it back behind her ear.

Why *not* run away? Why *not* ditch this life for something better? Anyone in her shoes would, wouldn't they? They'd jump at the opportunity to chase a world that shouldn't have existed beyond her own. Why not do this for Cyrus?

The skin on her bottom lip broke and she tasted blood. She licked it away. Accepting this meant accepting that Cyrus would die. It was too much to think about. She simply couldn't. There had to be another way.

"Cyrus?"

"Hmm?"

"Isn't it against the law to travel through the portal—through the gate, I mean?"

He shrugged.

"Well? Won't I...won't I get in trouble or something?"

"Perhaps. I have not yet worked that out. But I trust the gods to get you there safely. You are resourceful. You will think of something."

"I'll *think* of something?" She gawked at him. "Are you serious? What—what happens to people who break your king's laws?"

"It depends on the law. But for a crime like that, beheading most likely."

She sputtered. "Are you insane?! You want me to risk my life?"

"There is no minimizing the task ahead of you. You would be treated as an outsider—tried in court as a threat to the kingdom— as a criminal. The law is the law. None are permitted to use the gates. Exceptions can be made for those of *our* world, for reasons I am sure you can understand, but for those of *yours*? I've heard stories..."

He did not look at her as his eyes traced the corn field.

She crossed her arms. "You're crazy, you know that? I'm not doing it. I'm not—you can't make me." So much for escaping into a magical world.

"Isn't the impending danger worth the risk? Think of all the lives you might save." He didn't meet her gaze. His voice sounded distracted. Something held his attention—a bird perhaps. His eyes narrowed.

"Yes, I've thought about that—about the *lives* I might save—and the answer is still no. You'll just have to push through the poison and hope that someone is coming to—"

"Quiet!" he hissed.

She reared back at his sharp tone. He still wasn't looking at her. Instead he sat erect, scowling into the distance.

Then his expression changed. Glass shattered as he dropped his iced tea on the porch. When he turned his gaze to meet hers, her skin started to crawl. "Cyrus..."

"They're here," he whispered. "They have come."

"No..." She shook her head, refusing to believe it. They couldn't be here. This wasn't real. None of it.

A dreadful clawing feeling stroked the base of her spine. "What—what do we do?" she whined.

"Move. Now!" They both jumped to their feet. He ripped the leather pouch from his neck and thrust it into her hands, wrapping her fingers around it. "This is my fight. Get inside and bolt the door." As he spoke, he drew his sword.

She looked at the blade.

"Fight?" A strangled laugh burst from her chest. "Cyrus, you can hardly stand! No. No way. I'm not going to hide like a scared little girl."

"But you are scared, and you are a little girl. Now go!" His words made her throat ache. "Claire! You must protect the stones. I cannot protect you and them both. Do *not* make me tell you again." His voice had changed—was suddenly powerful and commanding. He towered over her now. A force to be reckoned with.

She pushed her fear down and went to the front door. He did not wait to see her go, striding quickly from the porch, out onto the lawn. She wouldn't have known he was suffering with the way he moved now.

At the front door, she looked out over the field. Her eyes scanned the tops of the corn stalks, sweeping back and forth. Then her blood ran cold. The stalks were moving, bending and parting like a rolling wave. *Oh, God!* Something was advancing through the field towards the house. She stood frozen, watching, barely breathing.

In her hand, she clenched the warm leather pouch of precious stones.

Within moments, her pulse was roaring through her ears. Like a scene playing out in a movie, the stalks of corn parted and she felt a scream rise within her chest. Her hand flew to her mouth to stifle it.

The figures gliding towards Cyrus were assuredly vodar wraiths in every sense of the word. Their bodies were covered in black oily smoke. The illusion created rotting cloaks to cover the true terror beneath. Tendrils of black smoke trailed behind them like slithering snakes. Everything they touched died. The grass itself dried up in their wake, turning scorched and brown.

Smoke oozed like fog through the holes in their shrouds, as if they were smoking and burning beneath them. These wraiths had wings too, transparent wings of smoke that sprouted from their backs. They held them limply at their sides. There were six, and each grasped a sword much shorter and narrower than the one Cyrus held at the ready.

Her body trembled as she watched her beloved Cyrus. How did he expect to fight *six* of these things? How?!

"There's no way," she muttered. "There's no possible way."

She was his only hope.

Without wasting another moment, she slipped quietly inside. Cyrus may have commanded her to bolt the door, but a bolted door wouldn't stop these creatures. She raced to the dining room and pulled her mom's *Starry Night* painting from the wall. Her hands trembled as she entered the safe's combination. At last she ripped the large metal door open and flung the stones inside. Her grandfather's revolver was there—she grabbed it and the little case of bullets. Then she slammed the door shut, turned the dial, and replaced the painting.

Her father's shotgun was upstairs in his closet—two guns were better than one. With speed she never thought she possessed, she took the stairs two at a time. Recovering the shotgun and the box of ammunition, she flew down the stairs. She nearly slammed into the front door as she came to a halt.

Cyrus was out on the lawn, surrounded by predators. She allowed herself a quick glance as reassurance. He was still alive. The vodar were circling him, closing in. He held his sword in position, waiting for their attack.

She dropped to her knees and began loading the shotgun first and then the revolver. Her unsteady fingers dropped bullets everywhere. *Plunk—plunk—plunk.* They fell and rolled away across the hall floor, but she managed. She also stuffed some shotgun shells into her pockets for later. When the guns were loaded, she stood at the window and watched, still shaking.

Should she storm out firing, or wait until the fighting started before bursting through the door? Did she possess the courage for either? Having courage meant acting in the presence of fear. She was afraid, terrified, but could she take action?

Tears of fear clouded her gaze. Damn it all to hell! Why did heroism seem so effortless in movies and books? How come being brave looked easy? It wasn't easy! She wasn't even sure if it was possible for someone like her.

Her heart pounded in her chest, adrenaline racing through her system, but she kept her eyes glued to Cyrus. He was moving, keeping his opponents in sight, waiting for the first move. This wasn't the first time he'd done this.

She gasped.

In a rush they attacked all at once. His body burst into motion.

Air whooshed from her lungs as admiration welled up within her. Cyrus moved with effortless grace. He performed a memorized dance—one he had done many times before. Even though there were six of them and only one of him, he sliced and dodged and kicked and ducked as quickly as they did.

She steeled her spine. If he could do this, so could she. After all, he didn't run scared when he could have. She wanted to be like that.

Quietly, she turned the doorknob, opening it just a crack. Then she hesitated, giving herself a final moment of clarity. She looked at the entry hall in front of her—filled with so many childhood memories—allowing her mind to go to its happy place. Then she tucked her grandfather's single action revolver into the back pocket of her jean shorts. She would use the shotgun first. That meant she would need to be close enough to pack a punch.

Concentrating, she went through each of her dad's drills in her head. Then she placed her non-firing hand on the hand stock of the shotgun, right in the middle just as he'd taught her. Her firing hand went on the grip of the gun, forefinger at the ready. The shotgun was double-barreled, so she would only get two shots before needing to reload. Each one had to count.

The sound of metal striking metal rang in her ears. She tried to ignore it. "Now or never," she whispered. "Now or never!" Taking one final deep breath and closing her eyes, she wedged her foot in the crack and kicked open the door, slipping through.

CHAPTER 12

THE VODAR FIGHT

Battle Ground, Indiana

Claire's appearance went unnoticed. The fight between Cyrus and the vodar was a flurry of intense movements. The logical place to target his enemies was from the top of the porch stairs. Trying not to draw attention, she crept into position.

The vodar moved like smoke pouring around an unmovable object, fluidly, relentlessly, unforgivably. Their advantage, six to one, required Cyrus's complete focus. Both of his hands were occupied wielding his sverak, blocking and parrying every blow they dealt. He kicked and lunged, dancing back and forth. She watched, open mouthed, before collecting her wits. His skill was nothing short of incredible, but how long could he possibly keep up?

She placed the butt of the shotgun against her shoulder. Resting her cheek against it and positioning it along her line of sight, she squinted at the black figure furthest from Cyrus. If she missed, if she hit Cyrus...

No, she couldn't think like that. Planting her feet, she braced herself for the kick back. Three, two, one—

The shot cracked through the air, silencing everything. The

world slowed to a stop, except for the wraith she'd hit. It stumbled backwards. Then everything sped up again. Cyrus moved first, taking advantage of the distraction. He swept his blade around and removed the heads from his two nearest opponents, one then the other. She didn't have time to watch.

The black figure she'd hit square in the chest stood to its full height, wings flexing outward. It turned its hidden face upon her. Chills raced down her skin. It shot forward, streaking across the grass.

"Shit!" She glanced around.

Fear and adrenaline dumped into her system. She fired again, this time aiming for its head. The bullet made contact. The wraith exploded in a puff of smoke, disappearing. Her jaw dropped.

"Claire! No! Get out of here!" Cyrus was fighting with two others. She ignored him. The third remaining vodar began gliding towards her, its short sword raised.

Her breaths came in gasps. She flung away her emptied shotgun and grabbed the revolver from her back pocket. Her hands trembled. She held it out in front of her and took aim, then fired. Several pops rang out, one after another, mixing with the sound of clashing metal. Each bullet struck true.

Like magic, the vodar exploded into a puff of smoke and disappeared. She blinked, then her eyes widened. Their *heads*! That was the trick. She had to hit them in the head.

Cyrus did not have the luxury of a gun. He wrestled with the remaining wraiths, their movements a blur. She tried to get a clear shot, but it was impossible. Not without running the risk of shooting Cyrus.

She edged closer in hopes of distracting them. If she could separate them, she could get a clean shot. As she moved, she kept the revolver aimed in front of her. She was ready to pull the trigger at any moment.

"No—Claire!" Cyrus yelled.

One of the two wraiths spotted her. It backed away from Cyrus, moving quickly towards her. She didn't hesitate. Two shots rang out as she fired at the creature's face. It exploded into thin air.

She stared at the place it had disappeared, still not quite believing.

Cyrus screamed. The sound echoed in her ears. Her breath caught in her chest. "Cyrus!"

The final vodar wraith stood over him, its sword lodged deep in his abdomen. Cyrus fell to his knees, his face stricken, tears leaking from the corners of his eyes. *"No!"* She screamed the word.

Taking aim, she sent a single bullet at the back of the vodar's hooded head. It struck true, but she kept firing even as the revolver clicked. Each shot was an echo ringing in her ears. The demon disappeared in a puff, leaving wisps of smoke behind, and then nothing.

She stood, gasping for air.

"Claire," Cyrus cried out. Her head snapped towards him. She dropped her revolver and rushed over, sinking to her knees. Taking his face in her hands.

"Cyrus. Cyrus. Cyrus." She spoke his name like a plea. Like she was begging him to stay with her. Begging him to be okay.

She ran her fingers through his hair, pushing it back from his face, caressing his head to comfort him. His sverak lay on the ground beside him. Both of his hands were wrapped around the hilt of the vodar's weapon. It was all that remained of the terrifying creature. Her mind didn't have the foresight to realize that the other swords had disappeared with them, except for the one lodged in Cyrus's abdomen. That would come later. For now, her focus was entirely on the man before her.

Cyrus wheezed, his breaths labored. He attempted to remove the blade, gasping with effort as he pulled. It didn't budge.

"The…" He gulped. "The poison. The poison—I can feel it. Get it out. Get it out of me! Get it out! Get it out!" He repeated the same, frenzied words over and over, lost to the pain.

She panicked. He'd never acted like this. So…helpless. Her body trembled and her hands shook. She met his wide eyes and said, "Tell me what to do, Cyrus. Tell me!"

"Help me get it out," he gasped, tugging again. He looked at her like she was the only person left he could count on. That thought strangled her heart. She was all he had left.

"Okay." She nodded. Fortifying her nerves, she placed her hands gently over his and pulled. The blade came free with a squelching sound and dropped to the ground, releasing a hissing black smoke. It laid in the grass like a filthy enemy. With it gone, his blood flowed free.

Cyrus coughed and sputtered before falling forward. She caught him, rolling him over onto his back. Each gasp was a precious gift of extended life—life that was quickly melting away.

Tears began seeping from her eyes because deep down she knew this was the end, even if her mind refused to admit it.

"It's going to be okay," she whispered, stroking his forehead. "Everything is going to be okay." She peeled back his blood-soaked shirt and flinched. The incision, though narrow, was deep and weeping. This wasn't something she could fix.

Her pulse rang in her ears, turning into a roar. She ripped off her own shirt, leaving behind her camisole. Bundling up the fabric, she pressed it over the wound. "It hurts," he cried. "Make it stop! *Please!*" His knees bent and he rocked them back and forth, the movement helping him cope with the pain.

Her tears broke free.

"I know." She stroked his hair. "I know it hurts. But—but only for a little bit. I'm going to make it stop. I promise. I'm going get you fixed up and feeling better. Just—just like last time, remember?" Her voice shook and she choked on half the words. Words that were lies.

Her gut soured, making her sick to her stomach. Cyrus wasn't going to survive this. Not now.

No—she had to try. Something! She had to try or she'd never forgive herself. Every second was precious. Her shirt was already soaked in blood. She needed to get to her dad's medical supplies.

"Cyrus? Can you hold on for just a minute?" she murmured gently. "I'll be right back."

She tried to rush away, but he grabbed hold of her hand.

"Please—please do not leave me." His begging came in between each staggered breath.

"But I've got to! It's the only—it's the only way I can take away the pain." The words ended in a cracked, high-pitched voice. He opened his mouth to speak, but a fit of coughing left him shuddering. "I'll only be a moment. I promise!"

She tried to pull away, but he tightened his grip. "Please—no. Not alone!"

"Cyrus, you'll die!" she squeaked. "You'll die if I don't—"

"Claire! Claire listen...listen to me!" He coughed violently this time. Blood came up.

"Cyrus..." she whimpered. Her stomach lurched into her throat. She could barely see him, her eyes so blurred with tears. He wouldn't let her leave. He wouldn't let her save him. Out of everything, that hurt the most.

"Please, Cyrus. This isn't how it's supposed to be. Please..."

"Listen—listen to me, Claire." He struggled to speak. "I have little time. You must...you *must* deliver the stones. Take them to King Talon."

"I..." She shook her head. "I *can't*!"

"You can!"

"But I don't—"

"You *must* do this—" He coughed again. "Do this for me."

She wanted to scream at him. Anger and sadness battled each other, beating against her insides. Why was he being so unfair? Why was he asking her to do this? It was bad enough she was forced to watch him die. She wanted nothing to do with the horrid dragonstones. They were the cause of all this.

"Please, Claire!"

Overwhelmed, she collapsed and began to sob. Her body heaved and shook. She draped herself over his chest, wrapping her free arm about him, clinging to him as if holding on would keep him from slipping away.

"*Cyrus?! Cyrus!*" Voices screamed in her mind, mirroring her own pitiful cries, as if even her subconscious was chanting his name. "*Cyrus!*" it called again. "*Cyrus!*"

Except, her subconscious didn't sound like three distinct male voices. She sat up and looked down at him, wiping at her tears. "Do you...? Did you hear that?"

Cyrus's eyes went unfocused, beginning to cloud over as he stared up at the sky. He blinked, muttering to himself.

"Cyrus?"

"Claire, there is something—" He let out a long groan, tightening his hold on her hand. "Listen to me now. Do you...the names I gave you...the betrayers...the nasks. Do you remember?"

"I..."

"Their names, Claire...the king...you must tell him. Tell him everything...tell no one else. You must keep your mission secret. Consider everyone a suspect. His nasks...could be everywhere."

"*Cyrus! Cyrus!*" More voices echoed in her mind. She tried to ignore the absurdity of it. The shock of his death was breaking her apart. Making her go crazy.

"Claire, promise me."

"I don't think...I can't," she cried. "I don't have the courage for it!"

"Courage?" He sounded surprised, even in death. A faint smile appeared on his face. "You were so brave today...so brave." His approval made her sob harder. "You are my last hope, Claire." His voice was little more than a whisper. "Please...I must let go...I must."

"Let go? No! Cyrus, you can't!"

"I cannot hold the poison any longer. It is...it is *agony*. Let me go!" All she could do was shake her head. "The names—do you remember the names?"

"No! Cyrus, I don't..."

"Repeat...so I know you will remember. Do you understand?"

She tried to speak but merely croaked. He gave her both of the names, one after another. She obediently repeated them twice to make sure they would be remembered. "Good," he said, then exhaled, shutting his eyes. "Say them...every day. When you wake in the...in the morning...and before...you sleep...Do not forget them!"

"I—I won't."

"Good. Now make...make your promise...the *unbreakable promise*...so I can die in peace."

"The—the *what?*"

Another fit of coughing took him. Blood splattered up during his fit. It leaked from the corners of his mouth. The poison blackness was quickly seeking to consume his face.

"It will be easy," he panted. "You need only...repeat after me..."

Her panic felt visceral, so real she could taste it. "No, Cyrus. Please..."

"You owe me one favor...remember? I call upon that favor now. Will you go back on your word so easily?"

"No." Her chest sank and she caved in on herself. She'd forgotten the wager. "I...I will be true to my word," she said, hating herself for it.

"Cyrus! Hold on brother. Hold on! We are coming for you."

She gasped. "The voices. What...? Didn't you...I swear I heard—"

"You must repeat after me, Claire. Make the unbreakable promise."

"Okay," she breathed, wary of whatever this promise was. Cyrus shifted, but not without releasing an anguished cry through clenched teeth. He squeezed her hand so hard, she thought her bones might break.

Suddenly distracted, Cyrus began muttering and looking at the sky. His eyes were milking over. This was the end. She had seen it happen when her grandfather died. The way Cyrus's breath rattled, like death, she could hardly bear it. The death rattle, when a person was close.

"No," he muttered. "No. Please! I cannot go with you...I have things...things I must do...my time cannot...I must stay."

She stared at him, eyes wide. "What—Cyrus what is it?"

"Daudagher is here. He is here...ready to take me...but I cannot go with him. Not like my...My work is not done. Hurry. We must hurry!" He turned his unseeing eyes upon her. "Claire? Claire, where are you?"

"I'm here. I'm here." She lifted his hand and placed it against her cheek.

He sighed. "Good...good. Repeat after me. Do you understand?"

"I...I understand." She could not refuse him any longer. She owed him a favor.

"Now repeat. I, Claire..."

"I, Claire." She echoed his words.

"Will transport the stones...and...and the information I carry... directly to the king. I will not speak...not speak of it to a single soul...until my burden is safely delivered. I will not discuss anything that might jeopardize my mission. I will do everything... everything in my power to keep the stones safe. This promise I make...the unbreakable promise...with the power vested within my soul. I will not...I will not rest for all the days of my life...up to my last...until it is fulfilled." He said all of this with great effort, gasping and wheezing in between.

She repeated his words, sentence by sentence. The moment she said the last word she felt a tingle—like a thread of energy—leave her body. Was it magic? Was she bound to her new fate?

"Thank the gods..." he gasped at last, laying his head back down, turning his unseeing gaze upwards.

"Cyrus..." She moved her face close to his as she continued to stroke his hair.

"It was not...supposed to be...to be like this," he cried. "I wish...I wish there was another way..." He took a deep shaky breath. "But... it must be done."

"Cyrus—?! He is dying, Reyr! I can feel it. Cyrus? Cyrus! Hold on! We are coming!"

She tried to ignore the shouting in her mind.

"Claire?" Cyrus whispered, unable to see her. "How...how many did you kill? Three? Four?"

"Four, technically," she said. "But you did most of the work on that last one."

"I thought...I was saving you. It is you...who saved me."

"Cyrus!" She swallowed back a sob.

"I must...go now. I must pass from this body. Help me...Claire.

Help me to end it." He lifted his hand, reaching for her face. He groped blindly, so she grabbed it and laid it upon her cheek. "One more favor…I must ask one more favor…"

"Anything." Tears rolled down her cheeks like rivers of pain, trying to carve new paths through her skin.

"One kiss…please…just…one."

She blinked. "All right."

His eyes closed.

"Just a little longer, Cyrus. Please!" She ignored the voice again, battering against her consciousness. Instead she bent her head down, touching her lips against Cyrus's. The world around her began to slow. With heightened senses, she was aware of the soft warmth of his skin and the tingles upon hers. She felt the slow exhale from his nose tickle hers. It was almost magical, the deep feelings that resonated within her, like the humming strings of an instrument.

The invading shouts heightened in her mind. *"Cyrus! Do not leave us!"*

"Nooo!"

"Stay with us!"

They repeated, changing, morphing into sounds of anguish, of disbelief and grief. Of loss.

She opened her eyes and pulled away from Cyrus. Her gaze traced his familiar face. It was completely still, motionless, empty. Cyrus was…he was dead.

CHAPTER 13
IN NEED OF AN HEIR

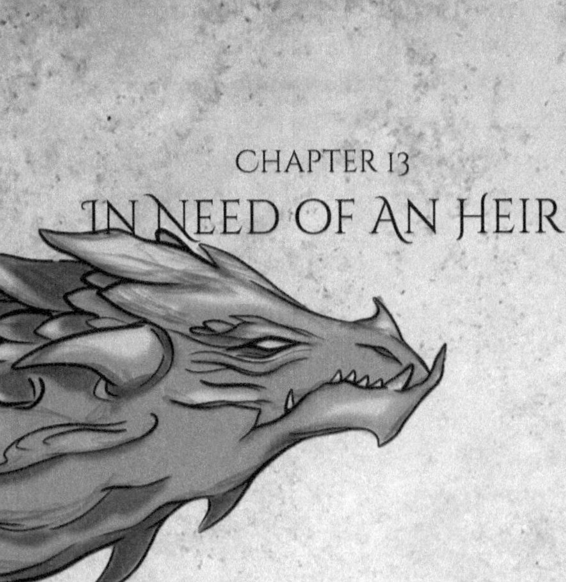

Kastali Dun

Talon knew something was wrong. There was a tightness around his heart, gripping him, squeezing him until each beat felt constrained. He took several deep breaths, trusting the feeling would disappear. It did not. He rubbed his sternum. What in the name of the gods was the matter?

"If we are all in agreement, we may proceed to the next matter of business." The steward's voice presided over the lower council meeting. Oh, how he abhorred these matters of formality—*council meetings*. He would have rolled his eyes, but he refrained. As stale as these procedures were, they were necessary. His people needed to believe there was more than a single decision maker holding the kingdom together.

"Very well. Let us move on," the steward said. The steward stood next to the chronicler, who sat in a separate, portable desk to the king's left. The rest of them sat around a large, polished oak table. It sat twenty-two—ten on one side and ten on the other. No one sat at the foot of the table. That would have been the queen's place.

Upon the chronicler's small desk was a large scroll. On it was written each of the meeting's discussion topics. At the end of each discussion, the chronicler scribbled his notes detailing the verdicts reached, tasks to be completed, and so on.

Aside from himself and the twenty members of his Lower Council, the steward and chronicler were the only others allowed to attend these closed meetings. His six shields did not; there was no need. He met with them nightly, filling them in on matters of importance.

Despite the belief that the decision making was left to the lower council, it was the upper that truly controlled the lower. The decisions they made in this room were driven by whispers planted by his six.

"Ahem," the steward cleared his throat. "The next matter is..."

Talon sighed. "Today, please, Mathis. For the love of the gods." This last he muttered under his breath.

"Forgive me, Your Grace." The steward was sweating profusely. He removed a handkerchief and wiped his forehead. "The next matter of business pertains to you, Your Grace."

Talon waved his hand in annoyance. "Let's hear it then."

"Very well, Your Grace. There has been talk amongst the people."

And so it goes, he thought to himself. Talk amongst the people was a favored way to lead many matters in these meetings. "What talk?" He didn't bother hiding his boredom.

"Well, Your Grace, with all that is happening...well...the people are worried about...about..." Mathis sighed.

"Out with it," he snapped, obvious annoyance seeping into his tone.

Several in the room shifted uncomfortably before Mathis spoke again. "It is the wish of the people that you produce an heir, Your Grace, as you do not yet have one."

He blinked, speechless. Then his annoyance transformed into the familiar anger he knew so well and his teeth clenched. "I would be more than happy to produce an heir, except, in case you have failed to notice, I have nowhere to place my seed."

There were several low, male chuckles around the table. He

watched Mathis turn a deep shade of red. The man was practically trembling. He usually had this effect on people. He turned his gaze to the table—they fell silent.

Mathis worked up the courage to speak. "Forgive...forgive me, Your Grace. I *do* indeed know this. Yet, it is the wish of the people that you take a bride and with her, *create* an heir."

It was so easy for the people in his kingdom to forget important facts about the drengr race. He turned to the rest of the council and said, "Did you know about this?" He met each of their gazes, at last settling on Lord Richard Rosk. He disliked Richard the *least*, with the exception of Lady Saffra, who was the only female council member, and almost never present, except for days like today.

Lord Rosk shrugged. "You know how the people are, Your Grace. Having no heir makes them nervous. It makes all of us nervous." After saying this, Lord Rosk sat up a little straighter, squaring his shoulders.

"What say the rest of you?" Talon looked from one council member to the next. Seeing this as an invitation, they began voicing their opinions, as they generally did. The only member to remain silent was Lady Saffra. Out of everyone, she had the most sense. Ironically, she was the youngest—a child in his eyes. He would always see her as the ten-year-old she was when she first arrived at the keep, despite the fact that she was now a woman grown.

He sighed, loudly. The table fell silent immediately. "You are all aware, I presume, that I am a *drengr*?" He looked from one person to the next. "Good. And I am sure you are further aware of the customs that govern my race? The customs that govern the monarchy?"

Silence.

"Good. I am glad to see that you are not idiots. So then, surely you know that the only life partner a drengr takes, or in my case, the only *queen* a king takes, is his mate? The king's mate is the making of his destiny, which the gods *alone* ordain. Has it not been this way for the last fifty thousand years?"

His words were met with low grumbles, many in agreement

with what he said. He held back the most crucial bit of information, which the council failed to see. Even if he took a bride, one who was not his fated mate, he would fail to produce an heir. That was how Drengr magic worked. Only his fated mate could bear his child.

"So I ask you this, have the people forgotten our customs?"

He waited several moments. Lord Rosk cleared his throat. "They have not forgotten, Your Grace. Your circumstances are special, as we can all agree." Lord Rosk looked around at his fellow council members, each nodding in turn. "We are falling into desperate times. Surely you cannot argue that. Perhaps it is time to reign in a *new* era—*new* customs. Perhaps it is time to abandon the customs of old, in favor of preserving your line. If you do not agree with that, then maybe we council members ought to demand a *Tournament for the Crown*."

He sighed. This entire matter was ridiculous, but deep down he knew there was relevance to their worry. He was the first king in the Drengr monarchy to fail at finding his mate. He had tried—for nearly a hundred years he tried. His mate simply did not exist anywhere in the world. And once he obtained his scars, the hope of finding anyone to love him evaporated. No one, mate or not, could stand to look at him.

"Tell me, when I gave my coronation speech, did I not make it clear that I would be the first of my line to rule *without* a queen? I promised the people that I would do as good a job, if not better, than any king before me. Have I not?"

"You have done excellently, Your Grace." Many nods circled the table. "The only problem is, the people to whom you *gave* that promise died nearly two hundred years ago. It is their offspring you now answer to."

"Yes, yes." He knew that. Humans led such short lives. Perhaps he would play along for now. If hope would make the people happy, then why not? "Very well, my lords. I will consider this request. And *who*—which lady specifically—do the people believe I should take as a wife?"

"That, Your Majesty, is entirely up to you." Lord Stefan Rosen spoke up, leaning forward in his chair. "I believe that it would be wise to take a woman of *noble* birth. She should be young, as you will outlive her by many years. Might I be so bold as to suggest—"

"I know exactly who you might *be so bold as to suggest*, Lord Rosen. Your daughter, Lady Caterina, is the youngest and most eligible when it comes to those families belonging to our beloved council members, is she not? A favorite among the people."

Lord Rosen preened. "Aye. She is, Your Grace. And I am sure many of us cannot deny her beauty, either." Several whispers of agreement resounded.

He held his tongue. There was little about the wretched woman he found beautiful. By traditional standards she was uncommonly pretty, with symmetric features, dark hair, supple breasts, and a tall figure. Her selfish personality that preceded her. It drowned out the rest. Then again, many of his nobles were selfish.

There were murmurs of approval at the idea of wedding Lady Caterina. "It would be a most fitting match, Your Grace." Lord Rosk looked at him, stroking his goatee thoughtfully.

"Aye, Your Grace, a smart match too." Lord Euan Doyle nodded vigorously.

"Is this truly what you wish?" he asked, looking from one to the other. Every single occupant muttered their agreement, except Lady Saffra. She wanted as little to do with the council as possible.

He considered the request. Marrying for the pure sake of producing an heir had never before crossed his mind. Obviously, no heir would be produced. But perhaps it would keep the people off his back for a short while. Then he would be free to tackle the more important matters at hand.

Except, if it was Lady Caterina he was forced to wed, he would be stuck with her longer than a handful of decades. Unlike a human, she was a mage in training and would live much longer—a couple of centuries. He shuddered at the thought of having her around that long. Then again, he took solace in knowing she would have to see his scarred face every day. That almost made him chuckle. How fitting for the vain creature.

"It would make the people happy, Your Grace." The steward

stepped forward, finally inserting himself into the discussion. "The gods only know the kind of unrest we are facing. Perhaps the prospect of a wedding might bring renewed excitement to the kingdom."

Excitement?! He'd enough of *that*. Every day felt like diving head-first towards the ground with his wings closed tightly to his body, only to pull up in the final instant. The last thing he needed was more excitement.

His thoughts turned to Cyrus and again, his heart tightened.

"What say you, Your Grace?"

"Very well, Mathis." At this point, he was ready to do whatever necessary, if only to be done with this stifling room and these stifling people. "Charlan, you may jot down in your chronicles that I will *consider* the matter of taking a noble woman to wed, perhaps even Lady Caterina, if it will please you, Lord Rosen."

Lord Rosen looked like an excited toad. His chubby cheeks were rounded and plump as he smiled widely, nodding fervently up and down, so hard that his head bobbled like he was experiencing a spasm. He half expected the man to begin croaking. The thought made his lips twitch.

"Very well. You will have my answer on the matter in a fortnight. May we move on to our final matter, Mathis?"

"Aye, Your Grace. We may."

"Good." He looked back at the council. "It has come to my attention that Cyrus is in danger." There were whispers around the table. Of course, no one knew what had befallen his beloved shield, but it was time to reveal all, or suffer the criticisms of the people for withholding valuable information.

"Seven months ago, Cyrus departed the capital. I told you he was traveling to the North on business, but I was not wholly forthcoming regarding his mission." The room remained silent. Lady Saffra fidgeted, everyone else sat stock still. "I did not send Cyrus to Northedge. Instead, I sent him on a secret mission to obtain a weapon within the Gable Forest. Unfortunately, it would seem that his mission has ended in failure. He has disappeared from our world and traveled through the Kengr Gate."

Sounds of outrage and disbelief broke out around the table. It took him some time to calm everyone down. At last, he handed the discussion over to Lady Saffra. As he did, a thought occurred to him. No one had suggested *her* as a viable option for a wife. She held higher titles than all of them, despite coming from a low birth. Yet, none mentioned her as a candidate for marriage. It made him curious. Why was the council so supportive of Lady Caterina? Had Lord Rosen bribed the members?

"Yesterday I conducted a scry," Saffra explained. "I searched for Cyrus and found him." She proceeded to describe what she had seen. When she finished, the same shock and surprise circulated the table.

"I believe you have not been fully truthful with us, Your Grace," Lord Rosk said. "Tell us of this weapon you mentioned."

He sighed. There was no point in hiding it now. Given that his council members were sworn to secrecy, nothing they discussed left the room anyway. However, tongues liked to wag, and no one was perfect. He especially knew that Lord Rosen would immediately run to Lady Caterina and inform her of the news. The prospects of marriage would greatly thrill her, even though he had not yet agreed.

"The weapon of which I speak is an ancient one. I find it unlikely that any of you have heard of it. They're called dragon-stones—" His stomach clenched. He placed a hand over it to calm it. "A thief has...has attempted to steal them." Whispers broke out, which rose to loud protests as the council members argued over their speculations

His stomach lurched again. His heart pounded and the pressure in his sternum doubled, as if his heart attempted to jump from his chest. Extreme pain seared him and his vision flashed white. He gritted his teeth. It was like he'd been stabbed. His six shields were bound to him, but it felt as if one bond was being ripped away.

His wide eyes found Saffra. She was slumped in her seat, unconscious. The council was too preoccupied to notice her blackout. Moments later she opened her eyes—they were wide and horrified. What had she seen? Cyrus's death? The same death he was feeling now?

Another spasm of agony took him. He tasted blood in his mouth as he bit into his tongue. And then as suddenly as it began, it ended, leaving him...empty.

"The King is unwell," Saffra cried, jumping to her feet. "This meeting will continue tomorrow. All of you—out!" Following her orders, the council room cleared. He was hardly aware of it.

"He's dead!" he hissed through the pain, trying to stand. "Cyrus is dead!"

Tears began pouring down Saffra's face.

He turned away from her and let forth an agonized cry, then he fled. On the balcony of his tower, he transformed into a great black dragon, releasing himself into the sky. He opened his maw. The sound that came out was pitiful. It was called the *Death Cry of the Drengr* for a reason. The eerie wailing embodied his incomprehensible grief. Others heard the sound and joined him, jumping into the sky to pay their respects. Soon the entire capital was alight with dragons—all keening mournfully. Of the six brotherhood bonds, one was now shattered. He couldn't bear it. There would be no more white dragon amongst his guards. Cyrus was gone.

CHAPTER 14

TOO LATE

Battle Ground, Indiana

Claire was vaguely aware of the unfamiliar voices in her mind, arguing. She wished they would shut the hell up. Her body shook with sobs. She was still draped over Cyrus. It felt like nothing mattered anymore.

Cyrus was dead, and it was all her fault. He'd warned her this would happen. He'd told her that his death was certain. Each warning was brushed aside and discarded. She'd refused to believe it before, and now she had no choice but to accept it.

There were things she could have done differently, and maybe it would have saved him. Maybe they could have gone somewhere safer together, somewhere the vodar wouldn't have found them. Maybe she should have insisted he go to the hospital and done everything in her power to get him there. She shouldn't have waited so long before shooting the vodar. If she'd killed them faster...

Guilt settled into the pit of her stomach, making her sick. She was to blame for this. Cyrus had been her responsibility and she had failed him. All those days sitting around chatting. "I was so stupid!" she sobbed, "I wasted all your time with my stupid fantasies."

She lifted her head to look at his face, disgusted by what the poison had done to him. "I'm so sorry. So, so sorry." She collapsed across his chest again. "Please forgive me..."

You are not to blame, came the voice of reason. It sounded almost like Cyrus, like what he would say to her if he were still alive.

"But I am! This is all my fault!" She cried harder, completely heartbroken.

"There he is, Reyr!"

She jerked upright and looked around, wiping her eyes with the backs of her hands.

"He's not alone. Who is that? His killer?"

The hairs on the back of her neck prickled. Someone could see her, but she could not see them. Her eyes darted around.

"Kill her!"

What?! She jerked her gaze towards the sky and gasped. Three giant dragons dove straight towards her, wings tucked tightly to their bodies. Her mouth fell open—too shocked to react. Then their bodies morphed into men. In an instant, harsh hands gripped her, dragging her up and away from Cyrus.

"No!" she screamed, fighting back, trying to reach for him.

She was forced to her feet. The sharp edge of a blade met her throat in warning. She froze, the fight going out of her.

One of the drengr fell to his knees, hands moving over Cyrus with care, examining his body. "No! It cannot be!" His body shook with suppressed sobs. Another drengr came up beside him, placing a hand on his shoulder. She couldn't see their faces.

These were his friends, she realized, and they were too late.

The one kneeling had golden hair, layers of thick locks that fell to the nape of his neck. The one standing beside him had brown hair with auburn highlights. She wasn't sure about the one behind her.

Tears continued down her cheeks. Cyrus had believed himself

forgotten. He'd thought no one would come for him, but they had. They were here. Not that it mattered anymore.

Her body flushed with heat. "This is all your fault," she hissed, ignoring the blade at her throat. She struggled against the iron grip holding her. "You're too late. Too late to save him. He's dead because you couldn't get here faster."

"She dares to speak?!"

She jumped at the sound of the voice in her mind, certain that it hadn't been spoken aloud.

"So it would seem," another answered.

"We must find out what she knows then kill her."

She blinked, the realization crashing over her. The voices belonged to the drengr standing here before her. She could *hear* them. But...why?

"She reeks of guilt. That much is obvious."

The golden haired drengr stood to his full height and faced her. His eyes turned flinty and he said, "I would be careful with your accusations, if I were you. Your circumstances paint you a murderer, so watch your tongue."

"Reyr, say the words and I'll slit her throat. We can be done with this!" The blade pressed more firmly against her.

"Not yet, Koldis. Let me speak with her."

"She deserves to die for what she has done!" Koldis growled. *"How can you show her leniency?"*

"If she is his killer, the king should be the one to do it. That honor belongs to him. Do you disagree?"

The blade's pressure lessened. *"Yes. You...you are right. Forgive my rashness."*

"It is forgiven. We are all troubled by this."

She opened and closed her mouth, not quite believing. Did they know she could hear them? Was there something...something *wrong* with her?

"Look, I know this looks suspicious," she said, managing to find her voice. "But I didn't kill him. I...I tried to save him." The last bit came out as another sob.

Reyr gave her a stony expression. He was built just like Cyrus.

They all were. With large muscular frames that towered between six foot five and seven feet. But it was their deadly expressions that frightened her the most.

"If you did not kill him, then what of this?" The male standing beside Reyr bent and grabbed the vodar sword out of the grass. "Is this the weapon you used?"

"I—no! It's not mine. I swear."

"Is that so? Jovari, let me see that." Reyr held out his hand to examine the weapon.

If ever there was a time to tell them everything, it was now. They needed to know about the vodar, about the attack, about the dangers Dragonwall faced. They needed to know about Kane and the dragonstones.

"Look—" She prepared an explanation, but nothing else came out. Her jaw snapped closed. She scowled and tried again, this time pushing harder. *Croak.* Her cheeks flamed red with embarrassment and her eyes widened. What was happening? Where was her voice?

"Where did you get this sword?" Reyr asked.

"I didn't. I told you! It's not mine. It came from...from..." Again she lost her voice. What the hell was going on?

Her eyes widened. It was as though she was under a spell, rendered speechless. The words she'd spoken to Cyrus—the promise.

"It's not mine..." she whispered, defeated.

"Then whose is it?" Reyr asked.

"She's lying!" The blade at her throat pressed harder. She couldn't see Koldis behind her, but she recognized his telepathic voice now.

"I'm not lying!" she cried. "I...I promise."

"Be that as it may, there's no one here to claim this sword."

"Reyr, look at his skin," Jovari said. "He's been *poisoned*."

"I know." Reyr lifted the sword to his nose and sniffed. "It's the blade, Jovari. The work of dark magic."

Good lord! This was becoming a nightmare. She couldn't explain herself. They really thought she was guilty, and they had a weapon to prove it.

"I think it's high time you tell us *everything*," Koldis snarled in her ear.

"I didn't kill him!" she cried, trying to struggle free of him. "You must believe me. It was the...the..." Her lips mouthed the word *vodar*, but again, she was forced into silence.

"Speak up, *girl*. I cannot hear you," Koldis hissed, his mouth nearly touching her ear.

"I'm trying!" she insisted. Tears of frustration flowed down her cheeks.

You made a promise, said a logical voice in her mind. *The magic binds you to it.*

"I—I'm not allowed to say." She sniffed. "I promised Cyrus that I would take this matter to the king—to *your* king."

"What do you mean?" Reyr's amber eyes pierced hers. Amber, with flecks of gold around the edges. Beautiful.

"I made an unbreakable promise," she explained, trying to keep her voice steady. "I am bound to it—to Cyrus. I cannot tell you what happened here. I must speak with your king."

She realized how unfair Cyrus had been. It wasn't a mere promise she had made. When he'd said unbreakable promise, he had meant unbreakable in every sense of the word. Magic bound her to it. There would be no backing out, no running away. She was a prisoner.

"An unbreakable promise?" Reyr opened and closed his mouth. "You cannot be serious."

"She lies, again!" Koldis said. *"Can you not see?"*

"You must believe me!" Her eyebrows were tightly drawn. A headache throbbed at her temples. "I promised him. I didn't do this—I didn't kill him. I cared about him. I took care of him. You must believe me! You're all in great—" Her breath whooshed out of her lungs. She was going to say *danger*, but even that word was against the terms of her promise. She went limp in Koldis's arms. Utterly defeated. There was nothing her promise permitted her to say that would erase her appearance of guilt.

"The unbreakable promise is rare magic." Reyr set the vodar's sword on the ground and crossed his arms, still watching her.

Perhaps trying to determine what to do with her. "For more reasons than one, I find it difficult to believe Cyrus would resort to such measures."

"He didn't think you were coming."

"Well that is nonsensical, is it not?" Jovari also crossed his arms, eyeing her. "Of course we would come for him. He should have known that."

"He didn't..." She keenly recalled Cyrus's sadness when he believed himself forgotten.

Reyr ran a hand through his hair. "This matter is out of my hands. I think it is best if we let the king decide her fate."

Both Jovari and Koldis erupted into objections over Reyr's suggestion.

"Silence! Both of you," Reyr hissed. "We have flown a vast distance to get here, only to fail. I think it is time we rest for the evening. The sun is quickly setting. Our journey can wait one night."

"You truly wish to bring her back with us?" Jovari sounded surprised, even outraged.

"This is madness, Reyr. Madness. Kill her. Be done with it."

"What choice do I have, Koldis?" Reyr asked. She followed the telepathic conversation, pretending she heard nothing.

"She hides too much from us, and I do not like it. I am sure the king will understand our decision in time. I need only a single slip of my sword. Her blood will drain before she realizes what I've done. It will be less to carry—less to worry about."

"Come now Koldis, calm your wrath. Look at the poor girl. She's distraught. She's crying. She certainly hasn't fought us with any magic since our arrival. If she were a great mage, she would have already tried. I am beginning to find it hard to believe her capable of besting Cyrus...of besting anything, really."

Her chest caved in. *That* stung. Because if she had been capable, perhaps Cyrus wouldn't be dead. Just another thing she'd failed at. She could add it to her growing list.

"Think about it," Reyr added. *"Look at her."*

Her breathing began to calm. Reyr was defending her. For all the harshness he had shown, he was clearly the most reasonable one in the group.

"*I do not like it,*" Koldis said, reluctant. "*But I trust your judgment.*"

Reyr gave a brief nod. Then he said for all to hear, "We will rest here for the night and begin our journey in the morning." He looked straight at her. "You are coming with us."

She gave him the barest nod, but relief washed over her. This was exactly what she needed. Perhaps their distrust was a blessing in disguise. Had they believed her innocent, they would have simply departed with Cyrus. Now they would take her with them.

Her promise required her to travel into Dragonwall and for that, she needed a guide. She had no idea where the gate was, but these drengr would show her the way. They would take her exactly where she needed to go. If that required feigning guilt, then so be it.

CHAPTER 15

DRAGON FLIGHT

Battle Ground, Indiana

Claire was less than thrilled about her new house guests. They were not patient like Cyrus. Koldis looked at her as if she were a monster, Jovari avoided her gaze altogether, and Reyr simply wore an expression of defeat. They hardly conversed, and when they did, they did so telepathically to exclude her.

They were grieving, she got that, but she was too. She wasn't their enemy, but they acted like she was. It hurt.

Cyrus was no longer in the yard beside the cornfield. He'd been shrouded in sheets and moved to the porch. Koldis had insisted on standing watch beside him, probably because he couldn't stomach being around her. She was happier for it, eager to be rid of his ominous gaze.

Long after dark, she'd cooked dinner for everyone, hoping it might win them over. She'd been wrong. The only one who had thanked her was Reyr. Of the three, he appeared to have the kindest heart.

All in all, it had been a miserable night!

When she finally retired to her bedroom, she cried herself to

112

sleep. Her dreams that night were filled with strange scenes, strange people, and strange events. As if her brain no longer belonged to her. As though her mind was shared with another's.

She woke to find dark circles under her bloodshot eyes. It took several moments to recall the harrowing events from the day before, to remember that Cyrus was dead, and not simply waiting downstairs. Inside, *she* felt dead. How long would it take to heal from something like this?

Your sadness will not last an eternity, her mind argued, even though it certainly felt like it would.

She was just coming downstairs, heading towards the kitchen, when voices reached her—

"She's nothing but a burden, Ryer." It was Koldis. "Why should we trouble ourselves to bring her? She's hiding something and you know it."

She hesitated, her stomach clenching painfully, then crept closer, stopping just outside the kitchen.

"We already talked about this yesterday," Reyr grumbled. She heard the scrape of a chair. When she glanced around the corner, it was to see them gathered at the breakfast bar, snacking on fruit.

"We are talking about it again," Jovari insisted. "You know the laws regarding the gates. Are you truly willing to take such a risk?"

"Laws can be suspended in extreme circumstances."

Koldis gave a derisive snort and said, "Are you not ashamed to carry this human upon your back? I mean, truly. Carrying her is dishonorable! What would your Gemma think? What will other people think? Other drengr?"

Her face burned hot. She swallowed down the lump building in her throat. What was so shameful about carrying her? The only thing she'd been looking forward to out of this—this disastrous *mess*—was the possibility of getting to fly with a dragon. Now, they'd ruined that too.

"What choice have I, Koldis? You expect me to carry her in my claws? We have a long way to go before reaching Kastali Dun, and she'll slip through my grasp long before that."

"I'm not that heavy," she scoffed, coming around the corner. It was hard to hide her anger, her hurt.

"It's not your weight, human." Koldis glared at her. She glared back. "It's Reyr's dignity that is at stake."

Be patient with them, said the same voice of reason she'd been trying so hard to ignore. *Grief has clouded their judgment.* How was she supposed to be patient when they were being so mean? And why was she arguing with the voice in her head, anyway?

"To undirfold with my dignity!" Reyr said. "Have I not already failed? My dignity is lost. Claire comes with us, end of discussion."

"Fine, then let us depart and be rid of this place. Claire, go and gather your belongings, whatever you wish to carry. It will be a long journey." This, from Jovari, which surprised her. All she could do was perk up and nod. "Make it quick," he added, his tone snappish, ruining whatever hope she'd just had at winning him over.

She grabbed an apple from the fruit basket and bit into it, eating it as she rushed upstairs. In her bedroom, she frantically began gathering whatever she'd need. When she had a pile of stuff, she took inventory of it. Protein bars, candy she'd found lying around her room (because she loved sugar), bottles of water, at least ten pairs of undies, a couple of bras, two changes of clothes that included her sturdiest pairs of denim, a travel pack of toiletries and other feminine products, the bedroll she used for hunting trips with her dad, the loaded revolver, and finally, the leather pouch containing the dragonstones.

Yes, she hadn't forgotten about them.

The drengr had searched for them the night before. She'd witnessed their panic when they couldn't be located. They'd expected Cyrus to have them, and when he didn't, they'd accused *her* of stealing them. God, she'd never even wanted them in the first place!

She'd denied it, of course. Even still, Koldis had insisted on searching her, patting her down with his harsh hands. Only after they'd failed to find them were they satisfied with dropping the matter.

With everything gathered, she stuffed the pile into her Osprey hiking backpack, which was now bursting at the seams. Finally, she scribbled a note to her parents reassuring them that she was okay, and that she might be gone for a while. She left it sitting on her bed. At least they would know she was alive.

The final preparations she made were outdoors for the farm animals. She ensured their food stores were full. The farm hands would be returning the day after tomorrow, so the animals would be okay.

With everything in order, they assembled on the farmhouse lawn. The morning's glaring sunlight beat down on them. "Do you have everything you wish to bring?" Reyr asked.

"Yes, I think so." She shouldered her pack, nearly buckling under its weight.

"Good. It is time to go." He led her away. "You will be flying with me."

She knew why. None of the others could stomach the idea of flying with her. She held her tongue, even though she had plenty to say.

"Once I transform, you will climb upon my back. I have no harness, so you will have to hold on tight." She nodded as he spoke. "And I should warn you, in our dragon form we cannot speak to you. We drengr do not possess the ability for human speech when we are dragons. However, you may call to us if needed. We can hear and understand you."

"Right." She already knew this but pretended otherwise. Happy with her understanding, Reyr moved away from her. Koldis was already in his dragon form near the barn. Cyrus's shrouded body was strapped to his back. It was hard not to stare at his giant, hulking body taking up so much space.

Without further warning, Jovari and Reyr also shifted, their clothes melting away as their bodies grew. In an instant, they transformed into dragons. Her jaw dropped as she watched the process.

In the brightness of day, the sunlight glittered off their scaly hides. Their beauty swept everything from her mind. She almost forgot how poorly they'd treated her. Almost.

Up close, they were much larger than the one she'd seen falling from the sky. This presented her with a significant challenge. It took multiple tries to hoist herself from Reyr's foreleg to his back. With each failed attempt, she heard Koldis snort impatiently. He was laughing at her. She did her best to ignore it. Why did he have to be so *mean*?

She finally succeeded, swinging her right leg up and over. Then she did her best to get comfortable with the hard scales beneath her rear. Her backpack was strapped to her back, but she double checked to make sure it was secure.

In spite of everything, it was difficult to believe this was happening. She looked from one dragon to the next. They sparkled with color, their bodies both beautiful and fierce. Each hulking shape was covered in dazzling scales from head to tail. The spikes on those tail-tips were different styles. The underside of their bodies turned from scales to smooth, snake-like skin. It was impossible to decide which one was the most impressive.

Koldis was a stunning shade of emerald green. He stood a bit taller in the shoulder than Jovari. Jovari's scales were the color of blue sapphire. Each glassy scale shimmered in the sunlight. However, it was Reyr's form that dominated the scene. His hulking body was larger than both of his companions. He was a brilliant golden color. It gave him a statuesque appearance, like something malted in gold standing guard in front of an important building.

"I am ready to leave this forsaken place." Koldis broke the mental silence, intruding into her thoughts. She continued to pretend she couldn't hear them. She had bigger fish to fry, much bigger fish. Her best bet was keeping her mouth shut, complying with their orders, and getting to the king as soon as possible—those were the inklings of urgency her promise created. Already she was eager to get this whole ordeal over with.

Several moments passed before she heard Reyr's orders to launch. A giant roar escaped his jaws, vibrating up through his throat. His rumbling gave the death place of Cyrus a final goodbye, and then they were in motion.

With a great leap, Reyr propelled her upward. Her body jolted as the downward force of gravity took effect. She felt heavy, like she was being squished. The ground fell away. Huge golden wings at least twenty feet in length stretched out from both sides of Reyr's body, catching the wind.

She was speechless.

As they ascended, her body was full of sensations. Her heart hammered violently in her chest. The wind whistled as it rushed past her ears. Her head began adapting to the pressure change. And once they gained some altitude, her ears plugged up and popped.

Beneath her, she felt the smooth hard scales of Reyr's neck. They were almost too hot to touch. She took a deep, calming breath, and allowed herself to look around. This was *unbelievable*. There were white cotton ball clouds not far above them, and beneath them, the ground stretched out in little green and brown patches. She loved it! It was all she'd hoped for and more.

The world was better this way—detached—as if she wasn't part of the heavens or the earth. She was somewhere in between. It was exactly how her heart felt, losing Cyrus—disconnected from everything, lost in her own grief.

Jovari's voice sounded in her mind. *"Reyr,"* he said. *"Let's get out of here. Lead us to the gate."*

And that was that—she was off to find Dragonwall.

CHAPTER 16
LEAVE NONE ALIVE

Shadowkeep

Kane considered the map before him, moving his eyes from marking to marking. This was not a common map. No, it was very different from any other map in existence. Not because of its tar-black ink, which never faded over the years, though that was certainly abnormal. Nor was it because of the map's size, for it was monstrously large, spilling over the sides of the great table. It wasn't because of the map's age. Such a document should have been tattered, its color faded with time, its surface wrinkled and creased. This one was embossed with a powerful anti-aging incant. Still, that was not the reason.

No, this map was unique because it did not simply end at the borders of Dragonwall. Dragonwall's maps, every one of them, only went as far as the boundaries around the kingdom—the Northern and Eastern Barrier Ranges, the Dragonfire Sea to the west, and the South Seas to the south. This map continued northward and eastward, well into uncharted territory, except the territory *was* charted, it was laid out upon the parchment in fine detail. There was no other map like it.

Kane enjoyed knowing things no one else did.

Studying the parchment, he made annotations, notes for later. Every so often he muttered to himself like, "That won't do." Or, "Surely not there." He analyzed each option available, taking great care as he spanned the whole of Dragonwall.

His task was an important one. He needed hiding places for his three Dragon Stones. These locations needed to be unreachable for anyone except him, and easily accessible should he need to recover them on short notice, like when he obtained the remaining two.

He leaned over the map and made several transcriptions near a set of caves not too far east. "Yes," he decided. "This will make an excellent hiding place." High on the cliffs, the caves were unreachable, except for perhaps mountain goats, or maybe a dragon, for that was how he intended to arrive. He scanned several more places along the parchment. Two locations remained unselected, but which would he choose?

There was a knock on his door.

"Enter." He laid down his quill, careful not to smear any of the wet ink. Gerard shuffled in, overly bent at the waist such that his nose and eyes faced the floor. His posture looked rather ridiculous. Behind him marched an armored goblin, helm tucked under its elbow.

"My Lord," Gerard croaked. "A visitor." Even standing, the servant's posture was stooped, evidence of the many hours spent bowing and simpering...and cleaning. Yet Shadowkeep was still in ruins, full of dust and cobwebs.

Gerard stayed extra still.

He looked them both over. "You may go, Gerard, that will be all. And do take extra care when scrubbing the hall today. I saw spiders the size of my fist lurking in the shadows." The servant shuddered before backing from the room.

The goblin stepped forward. Goblins were short; this one did not quite reach his chest. Its sinewy muscles made up for its lack of height. "Greetings, Your Malevolence. I bring word from Supreme Leader Tazak." The goblin's accent was harsh and guttural.

"Good. I will hear it."

"Supreme Leader Tazak wish Unka tell Your Malevolence,

troops assembled as request. March from Pavv into Eastern Barrier Range, begin immediately. In mean time, Unka and Unka's men sent as gift good will. May alliance be strong, last long." Unka brought his fist to his chest in a powerful gesture of respect.

Kane sifted through his broken language, piecing it together. "Yours is welcome news, Unka." The gods only knew he'd had little of that as of late.

Unka was one of few goblins who spoke the common language. This pleased him. Better still, Tazak's troops were assembled in the Eastern Range, ready to march. The goblin king had hundreds of thousands under his command. "How many follow you, Unka of Pavv?"

"One hundred strong males," Unka answered, pulling his shoulders back proudly. "More from Supreme Leader come if Your Malevolence desire."

"Very well. One hundred will suffice for now. Since you are a gift to do with as I please, I have a task for you. I must ensure that the lands surrounding my fortress remain free of wandering trespassers. See to it that your troops patrol. Kill any who come within ten leagues unless they look suspicious, in which case, bring them to me."

"Yes, Your Malevolence." Unka bowed deeply. "Unka go patrol."

Upon Unka's exit, he returned to his task. Perhaps it was his focus upon the map, or the safety provided by the fortress that made him careless, for he did not immediately notice the smoke in the corner. It materialized like hissing steam oozing from lava rock, seeping through the cracks of the walls. He turned to face the vodar wraiths just as they arose like shadows come to life.

A brief assessment of their appearance told him everything he needed to know. They had failed. Again.

"You have returned empty handed." He scowled. A muscle in his jaw twitched. "Once more I find myself disappointed."

"My lord." One of the six stepped forward. "We were met with opposition—a powerful girl."

"A...a *girl*?" he sputtered, not quite sure he'd heard correctly. "You failed at the hands of a *girl*?"

"She used strange magic. A weapon. Next time, we will be ready."

He knew very well that the world beyond theirs was void of magic; it was created that way. His ancestors had made it to exile the *magicless* of this world, human scum they deemed unfit to serve. With the laws implemented after the creation of these portals—laws prohibiting the use of any gate punishable by death—none dared pass.

"Of what girl do you speak?"

"She was young, my lord. She needed no sword to vanquish us, no fire to drive us away. Her magical weapon was—*unusual*."

There was a moment of silence before another stepped forward. "We underestimated our task, my lord."

"Obviously. You failed to obtain my prize. I am beginning to think you are pointless sacks of smoke, useful for nothing at all."

"I killed the white one, my lord." A third stepped forward. Unlike the others, this one's short sword was missing.

"Well, there is something—one small success dwarfed by your colossal failure. And the girl? Tell me you killed her too."

"She lives."

His mood darkened. "Find her. Kill her. And *bring me my stones!*" The last part he hissed through his clenched jaw.

They were off at once, and good riddance too. Anything drawn from the depths of undirfold was unsettling, even for him.

He returned to his map, muttering. "You still have three," he reminded himself. He enjoyed the power they provided, the confidence, the strength, should he need it. He would accomplish his goals, and the stones would aid him on his road to domination. Hiding them away was unfortunate but necessary until their safety was guaranteed.

Gerard knocked at his door; he knew it was Gerard because the servant's smell permeated the air. He gritted his teeth in displeasure. A day full of disturbances was an unpleasant day indeed!

"What is it?" he snapped. He was all but ready to kill the next intruder.

Gerard entered again, this time pale and fidgety. He stood there silently with bulging eyes until Kane said, "Have you no floor to mop? No hole to hide yourself in?" The servant muttered something inaudible and continued his twitching, eyes still wide enough to burst. "Well? Have you something to say? Or did you simply come to gawk?"

Gerard whispered, once more mumbling incoherently. Of all the servants he employed, this one was certainly the most annoying—and meddlesome too. Were it not so difficult to recruit common scum, he would have done away with Gerard long ago. "Well? Spit it out!"

"D—dragons...my...my lord," he managed to say. He pointed to one of the loopholes in the room. "Dragons," he repeated. "Dragons, over Ice Lake. Look, my lord. See them? There."

Ice Lake was the large, partially frozen lake at the basin of Shadowkeep. He knew very well about the dragons. He also knew why his servant was so surprised. Dragons were extinct, or so everyone believed. They were nothing more than fairy tales used to scare little children.

"Look," Gerard repeated.

"I need not look. What of them?"

"They are...they are *wild.*"

"Good observation." What a simpering idiot. "Is this all you wish to tell me?"

"But...but how is it possible? How can...how can it be? Why are there wild dragons over Ice Lake?"

"Why?" he all but roared. "Because I commanded it of them! Do you see this sword here?" He pointed at the weapon lying propped against the wall.

"Y—yes, my lord."

"If you bother me one more time today, I will use it to slice off your idiotic head from your idiotic shoulders. How I would love to see it roll. Would you like that?" Gerard cowered in fear, whimpering. "Now, leave me."

He almost regretted not taking Gerard's head. Death always made him feel better. But one death would be nothing compared to the numerous lives he was about to take. He felt the muscles on his face pull at his lips, until his teeth were exposed. Yes, why not have some fun, there was no more need to wait.

He went to the loophole and looked out upon Ice Lake, taking in the sight that Gerard was so terrified of. He took pleasure in Gerard's fear. The people of Dragonwall would have similar reactions of disbelief. Nearly one hundred, swooping and diving as they caught fish and game from the lake. Every color imaginable on display, but he looked for one in particular. A blood-red flash caught his eye. There he was. Wrath. The leader of the Ice Clan. The Ice Clan was the oldest and most infamous of the ancient dragon clans. It was also the only clan still in existence, unbeknownst to Dragonwall and its king. How overjoyed he was upon discovering them hiding away in the North. Kalderland had been full of surprises. Now he offered them the one thing taken from them some fifty thousand years ago. Their home. But only a portion of it. The northmost parts of Dragonwall would be theirs if they cooperated, and the south would be his.

"Wrath, it is time." He sent the telepathic thought to the wild dragon. Watching the creature from a distance, he noticed that the red beast changed its flight pattern.

"Time to fly? Time to kill? Wrath yearns to deal death—yearns to kill." Dragons often spoke of themselves like this.

"Yes, Wrath. It is time to deal death."

"Wrath shall begin at once."

"Good. Fly south, to the base of the mountains. To Belnesse. Burn the city to the ground. Leave no one alive."

CHAPTER 17
SMOKE ON THE HORIZON

The Kengr Gate

Claire's next two days were mostly uneventful. The drengr scarcely spoke to each other as they flew. She'd only her mind for company. It gave her too much time to think about what had happened to Cyrus, to beat herself up over his death. Too much time to worry about the future.

They had avoided human settlements, doing their best to fly around them, all except for one. A small town nearly a day's flight north. And only because she had begged them to stop during one of their infrequent breaks.

Stupidly, she'd forgotten to bring sunscreen. Though the sky was cold, the sun's rays were harsh. It had only taken a few hours before her fair skin had reddened and she'd realized her terrible mistake.

The town was small—a pass through, really—and had a long highway snaking through it, heading north. To hide their forms, the drengr landed a ways away, in a deserted field. *"I don't see why she can't simply deal with it,"* Koldis grumbled. Of course, he had no idea what it felt like to be sunburned. He had scales to protect himself, and in his human form, the ability to heal his skin. She

125

didn't bother explaining it to someone who didn't care to understand.

"I shouldn't be too long," she said instead, placating. Already the sun was setting, and it was almost nightfall. A quick check of her phone—because yes, she'd brought it with her—said they were just north of the Canadian border.

"You are not going there alone," Reyr insisted, having shifted back into human form along with the others.

"I'll be fine."

"I will go with her," Jovari said, surprising her, surprising all of them. "What," he added with a shrug. "I'm curious to see how humans live on this side of the gate."

"Fine," Reyr said. "But do not be gone longer than two hours, or we will come searching. And keep us updated."

They set off, walking alongside the road leading into town. She didn't mind Jovari's silence or his suspicious glances, not that he ever paid her much attention. While he wasn't as hostile as Koldis, he also wasn't as polite as Reyr.

"I have to warn you," she found herself saying. "Most humans aren't accustomed to seeing a man fully decked out in—"

"In what?" he snapped, making her bristle.

"—medieval clothing," she finished. He merely lifted an eyebrow, clearly uninterested in having any sort of conversation. She sighed, then, throwing out the idea that maybe she'd win him over as an ally. "I'm just saying, people in my world dress differently than people in your world."

"And how would you know that? You have never *been* to my world."

"I haven't. But the clothes you are wearing are extremely outdated." Only by about three hundred years. She kept *that* part to herself.

"I beg your pardon! They are not." He sounded offended; his entire face had morphed into a scowl.

She sighed. "Fine. But you're going to stick out like a sore thumb."

He merely huffed and dismissed her in that way they were

skilled at, by turning his attention away and ignoring her for the remainder of the walk.

The town materialized around them. She spotted a drug store and breathed a sigh of relief. If ever there was a time to congratulate herself on keeping spare cash in her backpack, it was at this moment, even if the place she ultimately ended up, in Dragonwall, wouldn't accept her currency.

Jovari looked enamored the moment buildings appeared. His head was in constant motion, turning this way and that, taking everything in with a furrowed brow and wide eyes. When they stopped at a crosswalk, he gasped. "What...what are those things?"

Cars. He was talking about cars. She felt a pang of sadness, remembering Cyrus's similar reaction. "They're vehicles," she explained. "It's how we get around. Cars, trucks, vans, that sort of thing."

"But, you do not use horses as your main mode of transportation?"

"No. Now, come on." She took his arm, pulling him across the street. It was a testament to his wonder and awe that he didn't complain about her touching him. Koldis surely would have.

When they arrived, the doors to the drugstore whooshed open, which made Jovari jump backwards with another gasp. Again, she had to pull on his arm, walking him inside.

"Welcome to McKesson," a female clerk said from behind the nearest register in a bored monotone.

"Why, thank you," Jovari answered with enthusiasm, as if he'd just been welcomed to a party. The clerk looked up at that, eyes widening, and gaped. It was only by dragging him down a nearby aisle that they avoided whatever questions lurked in the clerk's eyes.

Jovari continued to gape. He'd gone from a grown man—a grown *drengr*—to a childlike version of himself, caught in wonder at all the brightly packaged items on display. Makeup, candy, incidentals, even tools.

"I have never seen a place like this."

She ignored his excited explanation to the others, searching for the correct aisle.

"What kind of place is it?" Koldis asked.

"The strangest kind. Everything is wrapped in odd, brightly colored packaging. Even their food!"

Suddenly Jovari dragged her to a stop. "What is this?" he asked, facing an endcap.

"Those are tools—for working on your car." He tilted his head to the side, contemplating. "For if you get a flat tire," she added, since he clearly didn't understand.

"Then...they are not weapons?"

A customer walking by came to a full stop, staring at them, at *Jovari*, before continuing on.

"No! Not weapons," she hissed, trying to keep her voice down. "Now come on. The sun care is down that aisle."

She stuck to the necessities. Sunscreen and aloe gel. They'd just reached the checkout counter when the clerk from earlier, a woman with dark brown hair and large rimmed glasses in her late teens or early twenties, greeted them again with far more excitement than when she'd welcomed them into the store. She had a magazine in front of her, but had long since abandoned it to watch them.

Claire set her things on the counter, ignoring Jovari as he began picking up various items on a nearby display meant to tempt shoppers last minute. She reached into her back pocket when she heard a *pop* and a *whoosh*.

"Oops!" Jovari said.

She whirled towards him just as he unloaded a plastic tube of marbles all over the floor. They plinked, one after another, rolling in every direction. She felt the blood drain from her face as she hissed, then whirled back towards the clerk, afraid of how the woman would react.

"Pardon me, miss," Jovari said at the same time. "I did not intend to make a mess of your wares or your fine establishment."

"Oh." The woman behind the register simply gawked. "It's... that's...no worries. I'll clean it up later." Never mind that they were marbles and a tripping hazard. The woman couldn't seem to take her eyes off Jovari. Or think clearly, for that matter.

"That's why I told you not to touch anything," Claire snipped at him, irritated.

"It's really no trouble," the woman repeated, this time to Claire, before turning another bright smile on Jovari, who grinned back at her as if she were the prettiest thing in the world. The woman's cheeks turned bright red.

"Do you accept American money?" Claire asked, trying to recapture the woman's attention and get the hell out before Jovari did something else stupid.

"Sure do."

She'd hoped so. They were so close to the border, as it was. As quickly as possible, she grabbed the cash from her back pocket and began counting it out as the woman rang up her items.

Jovari chose that moment to materialize beside her. "I'd like to buy this," he proudly declared to the clerk, placing a child's toy on the counter. He reached for his coin pouch but Claire clamped her hand over his wrist, stopping him. The last thing she needed was him spilling gold coins out onto the counter.

"I'll get it for you," she whispered to him, covering for his near slip. "Just...wait for me outside, okay?" It was easier than trying to argue with him, or refuse.

He nodded, leaving the toy. She picked it up to examine it, pushing the button on the baton before snorting. It was a spinning light up toy that had little illuminated balls in the shapes of planets that whirled around. The label on the handle said, *Galaxy-Drive Inc.*

"He's a handsome one, your friend." The clerk scanned the toy and added it to her bag. "He always dress like that?"

"No, only sometimes. Today he thinks he is a knight from the Middle Ages."

The woman's expression fell, which gave Claire immense plea-sure. "So...he's not right in the head, then?"

"Sure," she said, a wicked smile morphing on her features. It felt like payback for how Jovari and the others had treated her. "You could say that."

"Damn. The cute ones are always crazy, aren't they?" the clerk added on a sigh, taking Claire's money and handing her the bag.

"Yep, thanks, keep the change," she blurted before dashing out of the store where she found Jovari walking around a parked truck, examining it. The truck, thankfully, was empty.

"Come on," she said, tugging him back towards the crosswalk. "If you're a good boy, I'll even give you your toy."

"Toy?"

"The thing you wanted me to—oh, never mind."

Who was she to rain on his parade? He probably believed it was a fancy weapon or something, but she was wrong. He really *had* known it was a toy, and took great pleasure in showing it off to the others when they returned. She hoped Koldis might snort and turn his nose up, but even *he'd* been fascinated, snatching the thing from Jovari and watching the planets whirl and flash.

They arrived at the gate the following afternoon.

She'd expected it to be a spectacular structure, some kind of extraordinary thing to behold, or at least a door. It wasn't any of that. Its mundane appearance was hardly distinguishable amidst the wooded grove where it lived.

Jovari was the first to walk through. When he vanished, all she could do was blink, gazing open-mouthed at where he'd just been. Watching something disappear into thin air was unsettling, even after what she had been through.

"What...what will happen to us?" She turned to Koldis and Reyr.

"Your insides will explode and you will cease to exist. It's pretty painful if you ask me, especially for a *human*." Koldis sneered, then hoisted up Cyrus's body and followed Jovari, vanishing through the gate.

She watched the spot where he'd vanished and swallowed down her rising fear. "He was only joking, right?" Of course her insides wouldn't explode, that would be silly. Yet, she still felt the need to ask.

"He was only joking," Reyr confirmed.

"So...so we will just walk through and come out in your world?"

"That is the gist of it."

She adjusted the straps of her backpack, overly nervous, stalling for the inevitable. Even now, she could feel the bonds of her promise like invisible hands, pushing her where she needed to go. "What will it be like on the inside?"

"You mean between worlds?"

She nodded.

"When you travel through, it will be cold as ice and darker than a moonless night, but only for a few moments." He waited patiently beside her. A welcome relief. After nearly three days of flying, he seemed a bit more relaxed towards her. He was especially nicer now compared to before.

She hesitated, turning to face him. "Reyr, you know I didn't kill Cyrus, right? I don't know any magic. I especially don't know how to fight. I could never overpower a drengr. I could never kill a king's shield." She wouldn't dream of saying this with the others around.

Reyr's eyebrows knitted together. "King's shield," he repeated, surprised to hear the term coming from her. "How much did Cyrus tell you?"

She worried at her lower lip. "Everything."

The promise allowed her to reveal that much.

Reyr sighed. "I hardly know what to make of you, Claire. Either way, you must go to the king."

"I know."

"Shall we depart?"

She looked over at the gate and her heart began to race. Of a different mind, her feet took several steps backwards. It wasn't the gate that frightened her, but rather, the thought of leaving her home world behind. She was about to make a monumental decision, one she had little say in. There was so much uncertainty. What would be waiting on the other side? Would she ever come back? Would she ever see her parents again? Her friends?

You can do this. You are braver than you know.

She shut her eyes for a moment and took a deep breath,

ignoring the reassurance coming from the back of her mind. Inside, she was so conflicted. Part of her felt stretched, pulled towards the gate, as if she were being tugged and manipulated like a marionette. The other part held firm to the ground beneath her, terrified and full of doubt, reluctant to move so much as a muscle.

"You have nothing to be frightened of," Reyr said, his voice softening. "Passing through is not a thing to fear."

She opened her eyes to look at him. His amber gaze met hers. She traced the planes of his face. In truth, he was hopelessly attractive. A strong jaw bone and straight nose. He carried himself with poise, with overwhelming confidence.

But...he wasn't Cyrus.

"Here, take my hand." He reached for her. She stared at his hand. This was the first nice gesture he showed her. Taking a deep breath, she gladly accepted.

His skin was warm and rough, but not overly so, not like her father's hands after working for years on the farm. She was happy to latch on to him, squeezing his hand as if her life depended upon it. They walked forward together.

She did not know where the veil to Dragonwall lurked, somewhere in between the boulders they passed through. The moment she stepped through the barrier, she knew. Everything around her vanished, just as Reyr said it would. She saw only blackness, and her body felt a freezing chill. She gasped. Reyr's hand wasn't there anymore. He was...gone! Her heart began to race. She cried out, but she could not hear her own voice.

It lasted seconds. Darkness was quickly replaced by bright sunlight and warmth. Her eyes sharpened into focus. A new world came into view. The air here was warm. It also lacked the humidity she was used to. A light breeze, gentle and refreshing, rustled her hair and tickled her cheeks. She squinted against the sunshine, trying to get her bearings.

Reyr dropped her hand and moved away, but she hardly noticed. She was too busy taking in her surroundings. Shielding her face with her arm, she looked around, releasing a huge sigh of relief. She'd made it. This was Cyrus's world. *Dragonwall.* She was one step closer to fulfilling her promise. All that stood between her now was a vast stretch of land.

She stood on a giant hill covered in long, dry grass. It crunched under her feet. Beside this hill there were many others, stretching out in rolling waves that quickly fell flat. Beyond that, the prairie extended endlessly onward.

The air was cleaner here, she realized. No man-made pollutants smudged the horizon. Even the sky looked bluer, with puffy clouds scattered across it.

She turned in a circle, a laugh bubbling up from her chest. Behind her, she was greeted by jagged peaks of a mountain range. It towered up over the land like a wall, stretching to the left and the right as far as her eyes could see. Her gaze fell on Reyr, Jovari, and Koldis. They stood in a circle talking about logistics. She ignored them and looked past, continuing to gaze along the range.

"Do those mountains have a name?" she asked.

"The Northern Barrier Range," Reyr answered absentmindedly, returning to his conversation with Jovari and Koldis. Cyrus's body was on the ground beside them, still bundled up.

She blinked and looked away, back towards the mountains. Nothing came close to their magnificence. Even Mount Everest would have paled in comparison. The peeks were lost amongst the clouds. Then they fell straight down into the hills. She slid her gaze along them, then stopped short. There was smoke on the horizon. A lot of smoke.

"Something's burning," she said loudly, pointing. "Over there."

Reyr, Jovari, and Koldis turned in the direction she gazed.

"Is that—"

"Smoke. Yes." Reyr cut off Jovari's question.

"That's a lot of smoke," Koldis said. "Too much to be good."

"Your sight is better than ours, Jovari. What do you see?"

He was quiet a moment. "The aftermath of a blaze. But it is some distance away. What cities lie northwest of here? Any?"

"There's only one large enough to create that kind blaze," Reyr said. "But...surely it can't be."

"Belnesse?" Koldis ventured.

"Aye."

"I don't understand," Jovari ventured. "Why would it be burning? Why would an entire city be burning?"

"That, Jovari, is a very good question." Reyr had his hand over his face to shield his gaze from the sun.

"I see no signs of life," said Koldis, searching the skies above them.

"Drengr of the north! Are there any sweep teams in the area? Can anyone hear my call?" Reyr's voice sounded very loudly in Claire's mind. She flinched. It was as if he'd shouted at the top of his lungs. He was calling to other drengr, she realized, to see if any others in the kingdom were nearby. There was no answer.

Again he called out, *"My name is Reyr. I am a shield to the king. If any are near, I would have you answer."*

Cyrus had explained to her that telepathy depended on distance. If no one was around, Reyr's calls would go unanswered.

"All is silent," Jovari concluded after several long minutes.

"Then I must fly to their aid. Immediately." Reyr's declaration left both Jovari and Koldis protesting.

"Have you forgotten Cyrus? Have you forgotten this *girl?*" Koldis demanded, now angry. "We must stick to the plan."

"Koldis is correct," Jovari said. "It is too far out of our way."

"Then what would you have me do?" Reyr sounded helpless. "Am I to leave Belnesse to its fate?"

They were all silent for a time. "What of Davi?" Koldis asked at long last. Reyr shook his head. "Doubtful that he would be aware of it. Not with the lack of sweep teams in the area."

"We cannot afford to linger, Reyr. Flying nonstop, it will take a full day to reach the city. With added weight—" Koldis paused to glance at Claire. "Several."

"Then I must go alone. The two of you must continue on with Claire and Cyrus."

"I do not think this is a good idea." Jovari wiped his brow, looking uncertain.

"I cannot turn my back on them. I cannot do nothing. It does not sit well with me. They aided us greatly in our war with the

Kalds. Koldis, you can carry Cyrus. Jovari, take Claire upon your back." Jovari looked as though he wanted to protest, but Reyr silenced him with a single stern look. "Get over it. There are more important things in this life than *your* dignity. You need not worry about what is proper out here." He spread his arms wide. "Not a soul will know that you did something considered...distasteful."

Her face burned. There they went again.

"I will fly fast. If all goes well, I can discover what happened and return to you in three days, maybe four. We can meet at the marble dragon. Wait for me there."

Before Jovari and Koldis could further protest, Reyr transformed into his behemoth golden form and leapt from the ground. Each flap of his great wings took him further away. As he receded into the distance, flying towards the smoke, she heard his voice in her mind. *"Do not mistreat Claire. She is innocent in my eyes until the king decides otherwise."*

"You cannot possibly be serious, Reyr." She sensed Koldis's mental sneer as he said this.

"I am entirely serious, Koldis. I gave you an order. I expect you to follow it."

Jovari said nothing in response. Instead, he shrugged and knelt beside Cyrus, fussing over the ties holding the shroud in place.

Eager to look anywhere but Cyrus, Claire finally noticed the gate standing behind them. The name was fitting. Two square columns rose from the earth. They were made of black onyx. She went to them and brushed her fingers along the glossy surface of the left pillar. Both were covered in symbols and runes. Nothing she could read.

She flattened her palm against the onyx and felt the rigidity of it beneath her skin. Under the intense sunshine, the surface was hot. She gasped. The world around her went dark, as if taken by a powerful storm. Rumbling with anger, clouds quickly moved in. Unable to pull her hand away from the shock of it, she blinked.

There were people, lots of people. They stood in an orderly line, a procession that stretched far down the hill. Something was wrong though. These people weren't solid. They were slightly translucent, almost like ghosts. Still unable to pull away, torn between horror and fascination, she allowed her gaze to shift over them.

The longer she looked, the more disgusted she became. They were dressed in rags. Many in the line wore manacles, others clutched children, crooning to their frightened babies. There were people of all ages, but they each bore the same expression, of devastation.

Then she saw powerful shrouded figures on horseback, patrolling the procession. Sometimes they used whips to keep their prisoners in line. One by one, these poor individuals were forced through the gate where she now stood, disappearing forever into the world she called home. Not a single being saw her as they passed *beyond*—she was invisible to them.

The masters on the horses were evil. She knew this immediately when she saw one of them whip a mother who was moving too slow. The woman stumbled, earning another lash. "Stop it!" Claire cried. "You're hurting her!"

Just as the words fell from her mouth, her blood chilled. Looking up from the horse, the hooded man's gaze found hers. Red eyes stared back at her—eyes like Kane's—eyes that she'd seen recently in her dreams. The people couldn't see her, but the evil being could. Like a rippling effect, the other hooded riders looked up. They too found her. They too had red, glowing eyes and pale faces.

Yelping, she quickly pulled her palm away from the pillar. Everything disappeared. There were no more clouds, no more wailing people, no more evil masters. Everything around her was exactly as it had been moments before.

Blood rushed past her ears, drumming in her head. Had she seen a distant memory of the past? She couldn't help but wonder if the gate contained a history darker than its own surface.

Despite the sweltering sun, she shuddered and turned in search of her companions. Had they witnessed the same thing she had? From the looks of it, they had not. Koldis was already in dragon form. Jovari was busy strapping Cyrus to his back. Neither of them noticed her activity. When Jovari was finished, he moved over to her. "Let us depart," was all he said before changing into a stunning blue dragon.

She had an easier time climbing onto his back. He wasn't nearly as large as Reyr. Plus, she'd had practice over the past few days. On his back, she got herself situated, adjusting the backpack she carried so that it sat in front of her. "I'm ready," she said at last, loud enough for him to hear.

They immediately launched into the sky. She held on for dear life, clutching tightly to the ridges along his neck. Her constant fear was that she would slip off and fall. After a few days of flying with Reyr, the sensation hadn't departed.

At least Reyr would try to catch her if she fell. Would Jovari? Koldis certainly wouldn't.

Beneath her, the black pillars fell away. So too did the large hill that had held the many prisoners and their masters. Try as she might, she couldn't leave the scene behind, though she wished it would disappear as quickly as the ground did.

Minutes later they were airborne, steadily flying towards the flat prairie. It stretched out in front of them all the way to the horizon. She glanced over her shoulder in the direction that Reyr had gone. Squinting hard, she could no longer see him. But at the last moment, just before she turned forward, she thought she noticed a bright glimmer of light reflecting off his golden scales.

"With our added weight," said Jovari, *"how many days do you think it will take to reach the marble dragon?"*

"Two, likely."

The marble dragon....

She mulled it over. It was a strange name, but she liked it. Not only did it have a nice ring to it, but it sounded like the name of a tavern or pub. She really hoped that it would be. After days spent flying and nights spent sleeping on the hard ground, she was eager to be done with this whole escapade. More than that, she was desperate to wash away her stink with a hot bath. All she could do now was hope. Hope, and wait.

CHAPTER 18

UNCERTAINTY

Kastali Dun

Saffra cursed the gods more times than she could count in the days following the death of Cyrus. The austerity of her sorrow was suffocating. More stifling still were the walls and people surrounding her. There was no way to escape any of it.

"Lady Saffra," Jocelyn spoke softly. Her handmaiden had busied herself, tucking away their morning breakfast remnants whilst paying her worried glances. "Might we take a turn about the keep's gardens this day? It is such a lovely sunrise. The fresh air would do you great good, my lady."

The moments following her vision, those moments when she knew Cyrus was truly dead, she had confined herself within her chambers, refusing to leave. She hadn't the courage to face the keep's occupants. Suffering their questions, their mournful gazes, their looks of sympathy, it was too much for her broken heart.

Unlike most, she had truly known Cyrus; he had been like a brother to her.

Saffra heaved a sigh. She was indeed in need of fresh air. Perhaps it would help her mood. "I suppose, Jocelyn. I cannot avoid it forever."

"Wonderful. I will see to your attire then, my lady."

"Thank you. My gray gown will do for today, and for every day following until I say otherwise." She planned to wear the color for some time. Nothing demonstrated mourning more accurately than the ashen shades of drab melancholy.

Nodding, Jocelyn retreated.

As she prepared for the day, Saffra's mind continuously reverted to the very sights she tried so hard to avoid. Every time she closed her eyes, she saw Cyrus lying motionless, his body cold and lifeless, a stab wound to his abdomen, and skin blackened. It was horrific. Even now, she felt bile rising in her throat.

She pushed it down.

There had been another. A golden haired woman with unnerving green eyes. She'd cried over his dead body. Saffra had seen her since her earliest visions, this woman, but had never understood why.

Glancing in the mirror, she chewed on the inside of her cheek. Should she tell the king? Almost as quickly as she thought it, she shook her head. No, better to leave him alone, as he wished to be. He'd locked himself away and was refusing to take visitors. He'd even dismissed his personal servants. She'd heard rumors, likely started by the guards who stood watch outside his doors. Rumors that in his grief, he'd gone into a rage, destroying the inner chambers of his tower.

Even his own shields kept their distance.

Should she trouble an already troubled man? Was it really necessary to tell him of this…this woman? Knowing Cyrus was dead had to be enough. The rest was simply…extraneous details. Unnecessary.

Yet…what if this woman had more to do with Cyrus's death than she realized? What if she *knew* something? Or, what if…what if she was guilty? She considered the possibility, but dismissed it almost as quickly . Her gut told her it was impossible, even if her logic told her she shouldn't ignore what she'd seen.

"Here, my lady. Let me lace your ties." Jocelyn prompted her to turn. She acquiesced, only half-aware of Jocelyn as she went through the mechanical motions of dressing. "There now. You are ready."

She gazed at her figure in the mirror. Every aspect of her appearance spoke of death. The blandness of her attire, the pale shade of her brown skin, the redness of her eyes. Even her expression spoke volumes about her sorrow.

She gazed blankly at herself, just staring—

"My lady? Shall we depart?"

She shut her eyes, giving her head a subtle shake. "Yes, yes. Let us go."

Together they walked through the flowerbeds and trees contained within the vast gardens of the great keep's lower levels. The beautiful greenery was a small island of paradise within a sea of wretchedness. How horrid cities were, with their awful stench, their filthy streets, their loud obnoxious noises. Not a day went by that she didn't long for her country home, poor as it was. She would have traded a hundred lavish lifestyles for the single possibility of returning to her family, especially in such times of sadness. But duty and honor—these were the things that bound her. This was her position now, to which she was condemned. She was Lady Saffra, Royal Prophetess to King Talon. Hers would be a long life. A cursed life. Where she went, only grief and bad tidings seemed to follow.

"My lady?"

She turned. "I apologize, Jocelyn. What did you say?"

"Oh, no need for apologies. I was merely admiring the orange peonies there. Are they not beautiful at this time of year?"

She nodded. "Aye. They are. Cyrus's favorite flower, I do believe. He used to keep vases of them in his study." A silly, random thought. How long would it take her to stop thinking of those little details?

She inhaled, caressing a bloom. They were so beautiful. A calm sense of familiarity rushed over her. And then...

And then blackness took her.

She was in the wilderness, set before the tall backdrop of monstrous mountains. The Northern Barrier Range. She saw the gate, its black pillars gleaming in the bright sunshine, akin to ominous sentinels of the landscape guarding the realm of Dragonwall.

A familiar face emerged. A relieved laugh bubbled up in her chest. It was Jovari! He was a welcome sight. Almost immediately, Koldis appeared. He too stepped from between the black columns, but what he carried with him made her stomach drop. Cyrus lay shrouded within his arms. The air fled her chest.

She looked at the two of them as they silently regarded the landscape. Their eyes fell in her direction, as if they looked directly at her. It was almost...eerie.

But she knew it was really towards Kastali Dun that their gazes rested.

She patiently waited for the third and final member of their party. She sighed when she saw movement between the pillars. Reyr came forth, but he was not alone. She gasped. He emerged hand in hand, guiding someone.

"Oh, gods!" she whispered, unheard by no one but herself.

It was the very same golden haired woman she'd seen before.

"My lady?" Jocelyn caressed Saffra's face. "My lady? Is everything all right?" Jocelyn was used to her frequent fainting spells. They always left her handmaiden pale and scared.

"I'm fine, Jocelyn," she said, offering her handmaiden a weak and unconvincing half smile. Several whispers sounded from behind them. She could only guess that she had collected an audience. It was no wonder the keep's residents thought her strange. Many of them avoided her when they could. It was easy to see why. Dropping unconsciously in public must have appeared wholly unnatural to them. And it happened often, especially as of late.

"Help me to my feet, if you will," she asked. With Jocelyn's assistance, she was able to stand, although her limbs remained shaky and unstable.

The aftermath of the vision left her stomach churning. "I must see the king. Immediately."

Although Jocelyn did not reply, Saffra did not miss her handmaiden's intake of breath. It was a clear sign of her reluctance. It was not as if Saffra *wanted* to visit him under such circumstances.

On the contrary, she desired to run as far as possible from him. Even the thought of him frightened her, knowing what a state he was in.

"My lady, surely you are too unwell to visit the king. Let me take you back to your chambers to regain your strength."

"Thank you, but I must go to his tower directly."

None feared the king more than the common people, but he was only frightening on the outside, to those who did not know him. Even if that encompassed nearly the entire population of Dragonwall. Their reasons for fearing him were obvious: the awful scars upon his face, his hulking build, and his temper. *Especially* his temper.

He had a beastly reputation. And yet...he was a good ruler. She knew that the king would never harm her, despite Jocelyn's worry. Jocelyn listened to too many rumors.

When they entered the corridor leading to the king's tower, she dismissed her handmaiden. "I will be fine from here, Jocelyn. Thank you." Her handmaiden bowed her head and departed.

Saffra stood alone, hidden in shadow while composing her thoughts. The castle's keep was quiet this morning. It was a blessing. She needed time to think.

Her mind was fraught with uncertainty. The king was entitled to know that Reyr was well, that the search party had indeed located Cyrus, and that they were now returning with him to the capital. He also deserved to know that an outsider accompanied them. To give the king adequate forewarning, such a surprise was best relayed in advance, and in private.

Her stomach clenched uneasily. She understood the tight spot this woman would be in. Outsiders were not permitted through any gate. Stories *did* tell of such cases where strangers found themselves within the kingdom. These otherworlders always touted the same explanation, that they had traveled through a mysterious portal to find themselves in a strange land filled with dragons and magic. Such a retelling was ever their downfall. The penalty associated with using any gate was death, especially if the traveler came from the other side. Too many dangers came with that unknown world.

The king would surely insist upon such a verdict when he learned of her. But furthermore, what would he do upon discovering that she was also present at the side of Cyrus's dead body? Would he pronounce her doubly guilty?

It felt as though she held the power of this person's fate in her hands.

Perhaps she could omit the truth, offering only a small portion of it. She could leave the second part out. She could pretend that she had never seen the woman before. She could avoid mention of her, claiming to have only witnessed Cyrus lying dead upon the grass, and Koldis, Jovari, and Reyr returning. But that would require lying to the king.

She...she couldn't do that, could she? Pursing her lips, she wiped her sweaty palms upon her gown and straightened her skirts. Then, she proceeded forward to the king's tower.

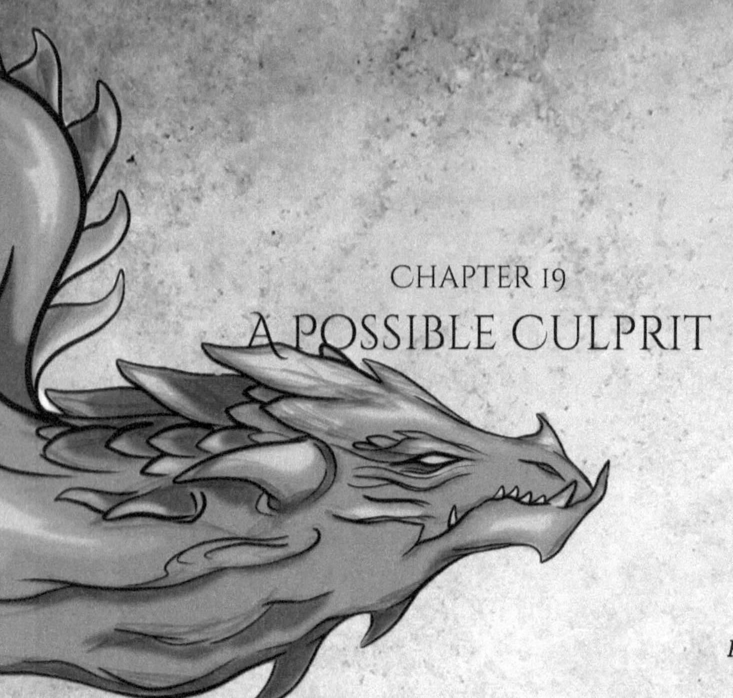

CHAPTER 19

A POSSIBLE CULPRIT

Kastali Dun

King Talon recognized his torment. He knew it well, for it found him as it often did. In so doing, it greeted him the way an old friend might after a long winter or distant journey. And this friend? He hated it. Cursed it.

Loss was not something he did well. For a king, loss meant guilt. Loss meant failure. Cyrus had been his to protect. The bond they shared went deeper than blood. It was a profound connection that perhaps only mated drengr could understand, but even then, it was different. Incomparable.

To accompany it, the rage and anger he so often wrestled with burned brightly, engulfing him within a blaze of uncontrollable emotion. He hated himself when he became like this. Yet this was how he coped. He had always been more dragon than human, and it showed. In times like these, by the gods, it showed.

Fury was easier than grief, it was easier than sorrow, though both were cowardly roads to take. Still, he took them. He took whatever he could. Life was hard enough as it was. And yet, though it was easier to be angry, it was not easier than the torment accompanying his loss. It was not easier than the guilt he felt from his failure.

The dragon side of him dominated. Such powerful emotions—not necessarily coherent and certainly not controllable—had wreaked havoc on his surroundings. Most of the belongings in his private quarters had been smashed and broken. Even though wrecking them brought no comfort. He had done it anyway. Even afterward, he hadn't the heart to say the words that might make such objects whole again. *He* was no longer whole. Why not allow the state of his living quarters to be an accurate reflection of himself?

If only the gods would grant him one small mercy. He wanted nothing more than to remain locked away for eternity, never to face his duties, never to admit publicly of his errors, and most certainly, never to show how broken he felt.

A knock at his door sent fire through his veins. Angry fire. The guards knew better than to enter. He kept them terrified. Ignoring the rapping, he gave no response. Instead, he sat on the torn armchair, swirling the contents of his brandy in a glass. It was the only thing that calmed him, to some small measure.

His tower looked as though he had taken up his dragon form to rampage through the rooms. Maybe he had. He could not remember. Regardless, such an unflattering sight should remain private and unseen. He had no desire for anyone to behold it.

More pounding followed. He let out a low growl in warning. "Leave me be!" he roared at last. And for a moment the knocking stopped. Only then, the door slowly opened.

He shot to his feet. Just as he was about to lose control and perhaps condemn a guard (or two) to the dungeons, Lady Saffra stepped through. Her eyes were wide as she took in the state of things. Silently, she shut the door behind her.

Her brow was furrowed, worried. Yes...he frightened all, except those who mattered most to him. Saffra was young, just under twenty if his memory served. Why should she *not* be afraid? Still, her obvious feelings brought only annoyance.

"I do not wish for your horrid tidings this day, Lady Saffra. You would do well to leave me before I act in a way that is not kingly." Somehow, his voice came out more controlled than he expected.

She curtsied, clenching her skirts with fists. "Your Grace, I—"

"Talon will do, Lady Saffra. I am no king today." He hated the respectful title. He did not deserve it.

Lady Saffra blinked, taken aback. She opened and closed her mouth several times. All the better to leave her speechless. He wanted naught to do with her. At last, she gave a small nod. "I apologize for coming to you at such a time."

"Bah!" he waved a hand. "As always, you display the utmost politeness. I have not the patience for it." At that, he threw himself back into the only seat in the room, the only piece of furniture that was not otherwise destroyed. There he took up his glass once more. Saffra watched him silently, judging him harshly, no doubt. But rather than run away, she remained. He gave a sigh that was more snarl than anything. "Very well, *Lady Saffra*, tell me what you have seen. And I swear to the gods, if it is more bad news, I will have you locked away, never to trouble me again. You bring only vexing matters that are better left for another time."

It felt good to make threats, even if they were empty. The truth was, he *needed* Saffra. If he was to succeed, even to a small extent, he needed her greatly. She flinched slightly, but she did not cower away from his threat. A thing to be admired, surely. Though she was still very clearly apprehensive, hesitant.

"Your Grace, I have seen them! Just earlier," she said. He straightened, knowing exactly who she spoke of. "I saw them enter the kingdom through the gate in Kengr. But..." She picked at a stray thread on her sleeve, nervous. "They didn't come alone." He edged forward, the glass in his hand forgotten. "They brought Cyrus, dead and wrapped in a shroud. And...and a woman."

"What did you say?" He blinked.

"A woman, Your Grace, from beyond the gate."

"A woman..." he mused. Then his mood darkened, all sorts of theories coming to mind. "Tell me of her. Who is she?"

Saffra hesitated, as if considering something. "She was young,

Your Grace, perhaps my age, maybe a little older. Beautiful, to be sure. With golden hair and green eyes."

He frowned. "That's it? Nothing more? You do not know who she is?" he asked.

Again, Saffra hesitated, then gave her head a little shake.

He huffed. This was the *last* thing he needed, especially now. "Again. Tell me again, everything you saw. Every detail. Leave nothing out," he demanded, standing to pace back and forth. She did as commanded. As she spoke, a single dominant theory developed. "And you're sure this woman was *with* Reyr? That he was holding her hand when they came through the gate?"

Saffra nodded with a whispered, "Yes, Your Grace."

"Hmm." Reyr had to have a good reason for breaking the law. He knew his shield better than most. Reyr was honorable. For him to resort to such drastic measures—bringing an outsider into the kingdom—it could mean only one thing. It meant that this person had done something terrible enough to warrant the king's justice.

Yes, that must have been it. This woman was responsible for Cyrus's death, to be sure. Searing rage and hate roared through him, but this time, instead of directing it towards himself, he had somewhere else to send it. "I'll kill her for this," he snarled.

"Your...Your Grace," Saffra stuttered. "I do not believe her guilty. It would seem impossible. I beg that you reconsider your allegations."

"I did not ask for your *beliefs*, Lady Saffra, nor your begging." His voice was closer to a hiss. "You are a prophetess, a young one at that. Here you stand before me, arguing against my judgment. Titles of king aside, I have walked in this world far longer than you. You would do well to hold your tongue from such decided opinions, and refrain from giving them so freely."

It wasn't that he didn't trust opinion, even if he made it sound that way. It was because he didn't *want* to. For the first time in days, he felt better. Felt like he could breathe. If she took this away from him, destroyed this new theory that was pulling him back from the brink of madness, he'd be right back where he was this morning.

Saffra fell quiet after that. He could see the clench of her jaw and tightness of her balled fists. In the silence, a new thought occurred to him. "Tell me, Lady Saffra, I have only just remembered. In the council chambers a few days ago..." He could not remember how many; time had spun itself together in a never ceasing array. "What did you see when you slumped unconscious in your chair? It happened in the same moment I felt Cyrus's death. Did you witness it? Did you see him die?"

Saffra's eyes widened briefly. She did not answer immediately.

"Answer me!" His rage was close to bursting.

"I...I saw his body, Your Grace. I saw his dead body. His skin was the color of soot—blackened with poison."

He waited for her to say more. He knew there was more. She was too easy to read. A frown furrowed his brown and pulled at his lips. Saffra was usually forthcoming, so this...this reluctance was unlike her. He narrowed his gaze. A threat.

She flinched. "The woman was there. She was there beside him."

"I thought as much. I needn't remind you Lady Saffra that it is a terrible crime to lie to a king."

"You are no king today," she replied at length. Her voice shook as she said it, betraying her. Only now did he see her look of disdain, directed towards him. It was well warranted. That she had the nerve to stand up to him kept his temper from spilling over.

"You are correct, Lady Saffra. Today I am nothing like a king. Now leave me."

"But..."

"But, *what*?!"

Saffra started. "The woman did not do anything, Your Grace! I am sure of it. She merely cried over his body. You must believe me. She is not his killer."

"Have you proof?" he demanded. Saffra shook her head and remained silent. "I thought not. As such, *I* will make the decision regarding her guilt. Not you. Now go."

Saffra fled without another word.

Several days later, when the time came to call an assembly of his lower council and inform them of the recent developments, thanks to Lady Saffra, they reached the same conclusions as he. Lady Saffra stayed away from this meeting. She often did unless he required her attendance. He would have stayed away too, if such a thing were possible.

In the end, the verdict was unanimous. This woman, whoever she might be, was surely guilty of a great crime. "You must condemn her to death, Your Grace, and kill her immediately," Sir Rosen said after hearing the information. "Such a woman is surely a great sorceress and must be eliminated before she can do more harm."

"She is an immense danger to our kingdom," the others argued. "But surely a trial will be more fitting with our customs."

"And allow her to speak? Allow her to curse us all?" came the rebuttal from someone else.

In truth, he wished very badly to hear what she had to say. Though, he doubted her words would be of any importance. At the least, he wanted to hear her admit to her crime. Such a declaration might bring him a measure of satisfaction. Of closure.

"I will not kill her immediately," he decided. Upon hearing his verdict, the chronicler recorded his words, scratching away with his quill upon parchment. "I must think the matter over for now. As such matters go, a vote will be taken before I give you my final decision. But know this, if she is his killer, a painful death will await her. There will be no mercy."

A great deal of mumbling followed his words. Not everyone agreed. Their objections taxed him, and he was eager to be alone.

Once everyone was gone, he poured himself a goblet brimming with a strong dark mead from north of Squall's End. There he sat, drinking his fill beside the firelight, surveying his surroundings. The room was orderly once more. He had finally righted it as a first step towards regaining his composure, but healing was a long way off. He could not begin to traverse such a path until all loose ends were tied.

It started with this mysterious outsider...this *woman*. Who was she? What had she done to Cyrus?

Saffra said she was beautiful, but even beauty could be deceiving where magic was concerned. Yet he wondered about her, what she was about, what she might look like. He pictured golden hair and green eyes. Then he shook his head and rid himself of the distraction. He had done away with women long ago, and even the most beautiful would not tempt him.

Especially not Cyrus's killer.

Instead, he considered the matter at hand. By morning—which was adequate time for someone on the council to leak the information—the entire city would be in an upheaval. His citizens would demand justice for Cyrus's death, and rightly so. She was the only culprit—she would stand no chance against the people's demands. When the time came, justice would be served. He would be the one responsible for dealing it, and deal it he would.

CHAPTER 20
A FOOL'S ERRAND

Landow

Mikkin took his wife, Mardra, into his arms, burying his face in her red hair. With his eyes closed, he could outline her features in his mind. He saw every freckle upon her skin. He saw the way her cheeks dimpled when she smiled, and the way her gaze danced with mischief. She smelled of lavender and charred wood, evidence of many hours spent before their hearth. That simple thought—knowing how hard she worked—drove him to tighten his grip. He couldn't let her go.

"But you must," she whispered, gently stroking his hair. "My time has come."

No! Curse the gods! He would deny their wishes. She was not theirs. "Take me instead," he begged. "Let her live." The void beyond their entangled bodies gave no answer.

"Mikkin, my love, you must let me go."

"I can't. Please, Mardra. I cannot lose you. I cannot lose Devden and Thomas." Hearing their names, their sons materialized, running to him, clinging to his legs.

"Don't go, Da-da," Thomas said before Devden burst into tears. Two sets of brown eyes gazed up at him in earnest, glistening.

"Please don't cry, children." Mardra patted their heads. "We go to a better place now. We go to the gods."

"But...I want to stay with Paaaa." Devden tightened his grip. Mikkin's heart constricted, strangled by ropes of despair. How could the gods be so cruel?

Mist crept towards them, tendrils outstretched like eager arms, lapping about his ankles like lake water. His heart quickened. "Don't leave me..." His words—his prayer—died on his lips. The world around him was nothing more than blackness. His arms flailed, grasping at the emptiness where Mardra disappeared, where the boys ceased to exist. There was nothing but the void, and tears left behind upon his cheeks. He fell to his knees. The emptiness engulfed his mind until he remembered— he remembered everything.

The sting of physical pain returned to Mikkin's body. He felt it like an afterthought, dwarfed by his torment. He refused to open his eyes. If he did, his torture would be real. Tears leaked from beneath closed lids. A sob escaped his chest as reality manifested. "Mardra..." he whispered her name, clenching his fists. "Mardra..." It was all gone, everything he ever knew, everything he ever loved, taken from him.

Taken by *beasts*.

In a sudden jolt, his eyelids flew open. Gone...everything was gone. The fragments of his memory reoriented, until consciousness returned in full. His mind roved over the killers stalking his memory, billowing flames of death. He gasped. His body felt like a hollow shell.

His gaze darted about, unseeing, until settling upon the ceiling above, wooden and aged. His raw fingers twitched, grasping, clawing at the bedding beneath him. The linen was soft against his burns. Where *was* he?

He thought he'd died, but this was not the wilderness he tried to die in. This was not his grave.

"Mary!" A woman's voice cried out. "Mary, he's waken' up. Go and get Tynen. Hurry, quick-like!" He struggled to turn his head, his movements slow and stiff, his eyes still wide. He found a dark-haired lass sitting at his bedside.

She smiled kindly. "All will be well, mister. You're in Tynen's house—good hands to be sure." Her words swept through him faster than a river, in and then out, with no meaning. "Gods above though," she cried, "If I might be sayin', sur, you gave us a fright, you did! We wasn't sure you'd wake."

I never intended to, he said to himself. Damn these people for trying to save him, from trying to take him from his family.

"Here, drink this." The woman held a cup to his lips, reaching her hand under his head. He turned away just as the water rushed out, spilling all around him. The woman swore, "Gods above!" Once more she tried to set the cup at his lips. Again he turned. "Come now, sur. Cooperate."

"Let me die," he hissed. The croak was hardly audible.

"No one be lettin' you die today. Drink." This time, she held fast to the back of his head and forced his lips to the cup. Cold water rushed into his mouth, gushing down his parched throat.

Several people burst into the room all at once. He coughed and cleared his throat as his sights settled upon two men, one old and grizzled, the other a strapping young lad, and a woman, similar in appearance to the lass beside him. The older man stepped forward and crouched beside his bed.

Their eyes met for several moments before he spoke. "Ho there, mister. I'm Tynen, and this is my home. We aren't accustom' to findin' unconscious strangers on the outskirts of our little village. There's been terrible rumors circulating..." The man shook his head. "We seen the smoke on the horizon."

Mikkin flinched. Blazing orange flames leapt into his mind, followed by the strong scent of smoke. His stomach lurched. He threw himself over the side of the bed and began retching. Only water came up, and then nothing. Tynen let him finish before hoisting him back into bed.

"You look as though you seen death." Tynen spoke again. "What happened?"

His throat was raw, his tongue more so. He tried to speak, but only one word pierced the silence, rolling from his tongue like a curse. "*Dragons...*"

"Dragons, you say?"

He gave a jerk of his head. Tynen's eyebrows pulled together before he glanced back at the others. The lass beside him covered her mouth, stifling a surprised hiss.

His gaze returned to the ceiling. He cared little for their shock. Swallowing, he tried to regain his voice. Countless screams and days without water left talking nearly impossible. "More water," he croaked at last. The dark-haired lass lifted the cup to his lips. This time he drank deeply. Again, he tried to speak. "They came from the mountains." His voice cracked from disuse. "They burned everything. Belnesse is gone. It's all gone." Those last words came as a sob, cutting him like a knife. More tears leaked from the corners of his eyes. His gaze remained fixed upon the ceiling.

Panicked whispers met his ears. Then Tynen spoke, "We saw the smoke on the horizon and wondered..." A slight pause followed. "Jamie, how quickly can you get to Belnesse?"

"If I take Lizzy—a day. I might make it by nightfall if I leave now."

"Off you go then, lad. Make haste." The door closed with a thud. Still, Mikkin gazed up at the ceiling. "Jamie is a right good lad. He will return to us on the 'morrow with confirmation of your claim."

"Little good it'll do you," Mikkin muttered. "He won't be findin' anything but ash."

The room fell silent. In the wake of that silence, new sounds arose. An argument took place somewhere outside. It was a man's voice, and a woman's. "Please, sur!" she said. "If you wait here, I shall be gettin' him for ya."

"No waiting, miss. I must speak with him now." The man's voice was rich and proper, each word spoken with perfect enunciation. "My time here is limited."

A door slammed and moments later, two more people filed into the little room. He turned his gaze upon them. The female was dressed in drab clothes. The man however, was of a princely appearance, with a large frame wrought of thick muscle, fine traveling clothes, and a mane of golden hair.

Mikkin looked the man up and down before his gaze settled on the long sword strapped to his waist. The likes of this weapon were something he had never seen before. It was finely crafted, and covered with gems and jewels.

"Beggin' your apologies, Tynen," said the new woman with wide eyes. "This man refused to wait when I be askin' him to."

"No matter, Kera, you may leave us." Tynen rose from his crouched position and presented himself before the stranger. "I ain't seen your kind in Landow since I was a boy. How can I help you?"

A drengr! Mikkin's eyes widened.

"I was informed that a man was rescued—a man who knows something of the smoke rising from Belnesse. Is this that man?" The golden-haired stranger peered around Tynen until his eyes fell directly upon Mikkin.

"Aye. This be him. What is your name, Drengr? I am Tynen, the elected village leader here."

"Pleased to meet you, Tynen. I am Reyr the Gold, king's shield to King Talon the Black." Tynen sputtered at the title—they all did. A prince, indeed! The drengr held forth his hand to clasp Tynen's forearm in greeting. "My time here is short. I must speak with this man immediately."

Tynen nodded. "Very well. He sings a strange tune, this one. Mayhap you be makin' more sense of it than me."

The others retreated as Reyr moved forward. Mikkin watched Reyr, eyes narrowed. For a moment, his mind was rebellious and his body in need of revenge. What was the difference, truly, between a drengr and a dragon? Both breathed fire. King's man or not, he could inflict the same destruction those wild beasts had.

The drengr pulled up the vacated bedside chair and took a seat. He straddled it, resting his arms atop the high back. Then he leaned forward, his strong body towering over Mikkin's weakened form. "Tell me of Belnesse," he commanded. "The city was burned to the ground. I have seen it with my own eyes."

"Then you know of the devastation wrought. So what need have you of me, Drengr?"

"More need than you can imagine. Tell me what happened."

It was no small request. This drengr required him to relive every harrowing moment as the words of explanation tumbled from his lips. He told the king's guard of the dragons, of the way they swept in with their fiery breath, igniting everything in their path. As he spoke, he saw his sons in the flames, screaming, writhing in agony while their skin melted from their bodies. He tried to save them, but he was too late. He was forced to watch as a red dragon, scales darker than the flames themselves, snatched his beloved Mardra into its maw. The sound of Mardra's wails echoed in his ears. "I cannot go on," he cried at last, a fresh wave of tears pouring from his eyes. "Forgive me, Lord Reyr, but I cannot."

Reyr placed a hand upon his shoulder giving a nod of understanding. Then the drengr's eyes closed tightly. "I, too, lost someone I loved to evil. Long ago. The pain has never departed. My condolences for all that you have endured."

Mikkin said nothing and his gaze returned to the ceiling. The drengr spoke once more, "You have confirmed my worst fears. I must get this information to the king immediately." With that, Lord Reyr gave his shoulder a gentle pat.

When Mikkin next looked over, it was to see Lord Reyr exit the room. Tynen returned shortly thereafter with a pitcher of water to refill his cup. "Mary," he gently called, "make our guest some food." Then he turned back to him. "What's your name?"

"Mikkin. My name's Mikkin." Already he felt his consciousness slipping away. He hadn't the energy to tell Tynen of his conversation with Reyr, or that Reyr had already seen Belnesse with his own eyes. By this time, Jamie was well on his way to Belnesse—now a wasted effort—but he could not say the words that would call the lad back. He hadn't the energy for anything but the slumber that forced him to drift away until there was nothing left but blackness.

When he next woke to the fragrant smell of food, even the conversations he'd had with Reyr seemed like a dream. The light seeping into his small room from the tiny window was dim. Nightfall was upon the little cottage. He was alone, but he could hear sounds of movement outside his door. Pulling back his covers, he sat up. Even such simple movements took a great deal of effort. Evidence of his weakness and the hardships he'd endured. Several days had passed since his last meal. Despite his desire to die, food was the only thing he could think about. It was the smell of sustenance that had woken him.

He swung his legs over the cot, ignoring his bandages, and his bare feet touched the dirt floor. Using what little strength he had, he managed to stand and steady his shaking limbs. He made his way to the door. It opened into a large main room. Mary was hovering near the hearth stirring the contents of a large pot. In the center of the room, there was a wooden table with benches, and off to the side were several ancient looking armchairs. It was a homey place, both warm and inviting.

Mary turned to see him. She wore a weak smile. "Just in time for supper," she said. In her voice he heard her failed attempt to sound cheery. "How are you feeling?"

"Like hell," he croaked. He shuffled to the table and sat down on the bench, letting out an exhausted sigh. Mary dished up contents from the pot and brought them to him in a bowl. He thanked her with an emotionless voice.

Hungry as he was, he observed proper manners and used the spoon to eat, though he was tempted to lift the bowl to his lips and drink the soup down quickly.

"Tynen will be back shortly," Mary said as she studied him. "He has called a village meeting to explain who you are. Everyone's been wanting to know..." She trailed off, returning to the hearth, muttering.

Tynen returned just as he finished his soup. The man's face was grim. He nodded at Mikkin as he entered, then went straight to Mary, wrapping her in his arms. Mikkin could not hear what was whispered. He did not care to. Their show of affection made him uneasy. It reminded him of what he'd lost. A fresh wave of grief resurfaced.

Standing quickly, he fled the cottage. The sky's stars were

beginning to show. The small cottage was set much farther back than the others. He walked to its rear, locating a grassy place to sit. There, he doubled over and wept.

He remained there a long while—just a shell of a man. By the time he went back inside, it was long into the wee hours of the morning. A still and silent cottage greeted him. All that was left of the evening's fire was now embers. He made his way back to his room and went to sleep, praying that it would be dreamless, but his prayers were in vain. Flames consumed his nightmares until he could no longer subject himself to them, at which point he rose.

Dawn light was only just spilling in through the windows. He sat at the wooden table in quiet reverie, watching the sky grow brighter. Mary and Tynen emerged not long after, greeting him. Mary quickly cooked and served breakfast—porridge and bacon— and they sat around the table eating.

Now that he had the energy for it, he told Tynen and Mary of the conversation he had with Lord Reyr. When he finished he added, "It is a shame the lad wasted his journey. Reyr saw all that I spoke of, and more."

"And you are sure of it?"

"Aye, he said he saw it with his own eyes. Did he not tell you?"

"Reyr spoke no more than a few words once he finished with you. Nothing was said of Belnesse. He appeared in a great hurry to be away."

"Then I hope you will take my word for it—Belnesse is gone."

"Aye. If the drengr saw it with his own eyes, then I suppose we must believe it. Do not fret about Jamie. The trip will do him good, wasted effort or no."

Mikkin nodded before saying, "I thank you both for showing a stranger like myself kindness." Despite thanking them, he silently hated them for helping him stay alive.

"It is the least we can do. If you have your strength about you," Tynen added, "the south fields need work. I wouldn't mind a helpin' hand."

For a moment he said nothing, then he nodded, glad to be given something to do.

They spent the day in the fields, uprooting large weeds, plowing the dirt, and preparing it for mid-summer crop. It all seemed so dream-like. He felt out of place, like a ghost in the world, all...*wrong*. For all he had hoped, there was no hiding from faces that refused to leave his mind, no matter how much he busied himself. Red hair, smiling lips, brown eyes—these were the images that followed him everywhere.

Jamie returned late that afternoon. From the fields, they heard Mary calling to them, so they rushed to the cottage. They arrived just as Jamie dismounted from his horse. The look on the lad's face said more than words could. Mikkin did not want to hear it. Whatever the lad might have to say. It was unnecessary.

"It is gone." Jamie's voice was choked. He shook his head as if trying to rid himself of what he had witnessed in Belnesse. "We rode as fast as we could, Lizzy and I."

Mary reached for Lizzy, escorting her to their barn. Tynen clapped Jamie on the shoulder in an effort to comfort the boy. "Let's get you some food, son." They escorted Jamie inside.

"What did you see? Were there any survivors?" Tynen asked once they were indoors.

Jamie shook his head. "It was all ash. There is nothing left. Belnesse is gone."

News of Jamie's trip spread through Landow, leaving in its wake a slew of frightened villagers. They all speculated that Landow would be next, should the dragons return from the mountains. It was unsettling for everyone, so the next several days were spent preparing for such an outcome. Watchers were set to keep the village on full alert. Weapons were collected and inventoried, even though the villagers knew such protections would do little good against fire.

Three days after his arrival, after his initial shock and loss began morphing into furious anger, Mikkin felt that his stay was at an end. He was of no use to anyone here, merely a burden for Mary and Tynen. They did not see it that way. They assured him that his help was appreciated. Still, he had no desire to work the fields when vengeance was to be had. A restlessness settled over him. He held fast to the hope that he might seek retribution for the ones he loved.

When his morning duties in the fields were complete, he left Tynen and went to the house to make preparations for his departure. Mary worked outside in her garden, so she did not notice his actions in the cottage. He collected the things he needed, hoping he could be ready to depart before the midday meal.

Tynen returned much faster than he anticipated. "What do you hope to accomplish by this, Mikkin?" Tynen questioned him. Instead of answering, he continued to place provisions into the rucksack he commandeered. "It's a fool's errand, Mikkin. A fool's errand! Surely you can see it. You'll be getting yourself killed, you will."

"I know the range better than most, Tynen. There is nothing for me here. Nothing for me anywhere, matter fact, because I have nothing left. Who better to go than me?" There was no changing his mind. He knew what he needed to do. With proper provisions and a weapon, he could make it to the range. But he did not plan to stop there.

The wild dragons had come from the range and returned to the range. That meant there was a lair of them somewhere. He intended to find it. He would kill every last beast he could get his hands on. How? He did not know yet. But sitting in Landow day after day accomplished nothing. He couldn't ask anyone to accompany him. Others might have something to lose, but he didn't. He was the perfect candidate.

"And what do you expect to do once you find them?" Tynen asked, pointing out the flaw in his plan. It was a shortcoming, yes. Mikkin shrugged his shoulders. At least if he found the lair, Dragonwall would be one step closer to destroying them.

Someone banged on the locked door and got their attention. Tynen moved to open it and Jamie entered. He looked from Tynen to Mikkin. "You are leaving?" Jamie asked.

He nodded.

"Mikkin thinks he can single-handedly track down the wild dragon lair and seek retribution for his losses. If I raised you right, boy, then you will tell him it's a fool's errand, as I have. Though I can't say he'll listen to reason, yours or mine," Tynen growled.

Jamie was silent for a moment, thinking. "I'm going with you."

"In the gods' hell you are, boy! Absolutely not."

"Yes, Father, I am. Don't forget that I am of age now. This is important. I agree with Mikkin. No one in Landow will be safe until these dragons are killed. It'll be ages before our messengers reach Fort Squall. Even then, what can they do for us?" Jamie asked. Tynen shook his head. "Father, he should not be doing this alone. At least with me, he has a better chance of survival."

Mikkin stayed silent, letting the two of them argue. He had no intention of allowing Jamie to accompany him. This was his task—his alone.

He finished packing everything and turned to them. "I will travel through the range faster alone." He moved towards the door to leave.

Jamie snorted. "Alone? Faster? Begging your pardon, sur, it will take you days to reach the mountains on foot. My horses are the fastest." Jamie squared his shoulders proudly. "Without them, you will surely be exhausted before getting into the range."

He could not argue with that.

"Let me accompany you. We can be at the range in a day. My father is right, if you do this alone, it'll be a fool's errand."

He stayed silent as he considered the idea. "And what do you suppose we do with the horses once it is time to climb through the range?" he asked Jamie, who did not answer immediately. The Northern Barrier Range was no place for horses.

"Father, escort us to the range. I beg it of you. Then you can see us off."

Mikkin shook his head. This was not part of his plan. There were dangers ahead. It was not fair to risk the lives of others for his own personal vendetta.

Tynen was silent for a moment. "Your mother won't like the idea, you know. Not one bit. But if it is your wish, then I will escort you."

Jamie breathed a loud sigh.

It was settled, then. They were going to the range. And as soon as he found the dragons, even the gods would not stifle his wrath. He'd kill as many as possible, or die trying.

CHAPTER 21

THE MARBLE DRAGON

Kengr Planes

Claire adjusted her position in the dip of Jovari's neck where it met his wing joints for the zillionth time. She scooted around on the bedroll folded beneath her, wishing it offered more padding. Dragon scales were as hard as glass, and although the scales themselves were smooth, the places where they joined together were anything but.

Her body ached with soreness. Each movement sent her muscles screaming. It was impossible to get comfortable. She ground her teeth and gave up, turning her attention to the land beneath them, wondering how Reyr's trip north was going.

The grassy landscape was completely flat. Monotonous, even. Every so often, they passed over a small grove of trees. These clusters of irregular growth were the only distinct features in the otherwise lifeless world below, which appeared to stretch indefinitely.

They'd been flying for nearly two days. The excitement had long worn off, replaced by her increasing worry. There was nothing to do but speculate about everything that might happen, everything that might go wrong.

She couldn't tell what made her uneasy, exactly, but she had a hunch as to why the pit of her stomach wouldn't relax. Her nights were filled with dreams of dark, cloaked demons. They hunted her, even in sleep, looking for the dragonstones. Unease prickled the back of her neck. She glanced over her shoulder. A dark smudge on the horizon caught her gaze, but when she blinked and squinted, there was nothing there, just wide open sky.

They will not stop hunting you until they have the stones.

Her conscience had grown increasingly annoying, offering opinions. It especially showed when she had misgivings, but she didn't question it anymore. She was too overwhelmed.

Their second day in the sky was just as tedious as the first. Jovari and Koldis were courteous enough to stop twice so she could stretch her legs and relieve herself, but they never transformed to talk to her.

It was...lonely.

Her thoughts often drifted to Cyrus. If he were still alive, how might things have gone differently? Would he be in her place, weak and delirious on the back of Jovari, getting rushed to the capital by his companions for magical healing? Would she be sitting at home in her farm house, condemned to live out the rest of her life wondering if everything had simply been a dream?

"Dusk is approaching." Koldis sounded in her mind, drawing her from her thoughts. *"We should be upon the marble dragon soon."*

"Not soon enough if you ask me. I am eager to be rid of my...added weight."

She clenched her jaw, desperate to say something cutting in return. There were few things she hated more than being considered a burden. But when she opened her mouth, her voice died. She didn't have the gut to do it, to reveal that she could hear them.

Only one positive thought improved her otherwise dismal mood. The hope that the marble dragon would afford her rest. Their journey south from the gate had taken them out of the hills and deep into the flatlands. The ground was hard and uncomfortable, littered with pebbles and rocks. She desperately craved a soft bed and a hot meal.

She felt her eagerness rising as the day progressed.

The sun was sinking when Jovari descended toward what looked like a giant white boulder starkly distinguished against the dull landscape. The marble dragon was aptly named—a giant chunk of white marble carved into the shape of a sleeping dragon. It wasn't a pub *or* an inn. There was no settlement to speak of. The landscape was as empty as it had been since entering Dragonwall. Her shoulders fell. Hot frustration coated her skin. She was so, so tired. She should have known better than to get her hopes up.

What was she doing, anyway?

She wasn't cut out for this, for what she'd agreed to do. Yet, here she was, forced to live up to a promise she'd had no business making. Now, she had no other choice. Would she even survive what she was setting out to do?

She snorted, and didn't care if Jovari heard it. Cyrus hadn't given her a task, he'd *condemned* her. How could he be so unfair?! Why'd he have to fall into *her* cornfield when he could have picked a hundred others? Her teeth clenched and she felt the first needle pricks of anger—anger for what he had asked of her.

He'd had no right.

The drengr descended towards the ground. Jovari landed, back legs touching down before his forearms settled. She dismounted as quickly as possible, eager to be away from him—from all of them. She just wanted to be alone.

Her legs took her towards the hulking white shape on the landscape.

Despite her inclination to hate the marble statue—mostly because it wasn't what she'd wished for—the sight of it stole her breath. It was slightly larger than her companions, and reminded her of what Cyrus looked like. She pushed all thoughts of *him* from her mind.

Jovari and Koldis had already shifted into their human forms. They were searching out a good spot to make camp, ignoring her as usual. So she ignored them, too.

The dragon was incredible, so lifelike. So real. She frowned. In a world filled with dragons, what was the point of carving one out of marble and plopping it here at random?

"Where did it come from?" she asked, before realizing that she'd voiced the question aloud.

Jovari and Koldis prodded the ground with their feet.

"No one knows, exactly," Jovari answered. He didn't look up from his task. "Its existence is heavily shrouded in myth. One legend says that it was made by those who spoke the old language, the great Asarlaí sorcerers. They speculate that it was forgotten when the time came to wake the dragons."

Koldis snorted. "That's nonsense. It is one of Rage's generals cursed into stone. Everyone knows that."

Jovari shrugged. "How about here?" He didn't wait for an answer as he began smoothing out the area, muttering.

Koldis nodded. "It'll do. I will locate some dry wood. Claire, you remain here." Koldis's expression hardened. "Do not consider wandering off, or the wolves will eat you. And if that happens, we won't bother saving your skin."

Jovari gave a pleased grunt, as if the thought of her getting eaten alive amused him. The two of them stalked off, leaving her alone. She glared after them until they disappeared, then turned her attention to the giant, marble creature. At first, she did follow their orders, keeping her feet firmly glued in place. But one small step led to another. Curiosity drew her closer and closer, until she was close enough to reach out and touch it. Even with dusk approaching, she could see that there were dark blue lines etched in the marble, giving it an authentic appearance, like blood veins.

"Incredible," she whispered. How could someone from a primitive world carve marble this way? Every curve was perfect. Unless... they'd used magic?

It was evil once, until it suffered the wrath of Queen Isabella.

She frowned. This wasn't a fact she should have known. She certainly had no idea who Queen Isabella was.

She wandered around the statue, getting a good look at every inch of it. Truth be told, at any moment she expected it to wake and lift its head, or to yawn and spread its wings. It was merely resting until it was ready to rise and take flight.

The longer she stared, the more it drew her in, stealing her attention. She forgot all about Jovari and Koldis, all about her mission. Would its scales be warm like the Drengr? Would they be smooth as glass? Was it strong enough to whisk her away upon its back?

Arm outstretched, she laid her palm atop the marble body. Instantly, the ground began to spin beneath her. Pain stabbed through her mind. She gasped. A strong force grabbed hold of her, stealing her thoughts, slicing through her. She pushed back. For a moment, the force faltered, as if deterred. That was all she needed. She cut into its mind, instantly, breaking in.

Her eyes widened, unseeing. There was awareness—an eternity of consciousness. Scenes flashed through her thoughts, but none of them made any sense. She was flying over cold mountains, wings strongly beating against the thin air. She was hunting in a wildflower meadow that glowed in the afternoon sunshine. She was surrounded by enemy dragons. Fighting. Betrayed.

Golden hair and bright blue eyes swam into her mind. She saw a face not so different from her own—or maybe it *was* hers, in some other life. The woman's body was covered in strange markings. It was unnerving, seeing herself like this.

The beast living within the stone fought her, trying to eject her from its mind.

Waves of anger flowed from it, washing over her. It wanted very badly to hurt her. And it was. She felt the flash of pain, searing through her. Her pulse raced, blood roaring past her ears. She tried to breathe. Her lungs constricted, but nothing happened. She opened and closed her mouth, trying to scream, but nothing came out. Something was siphoning her life away, stealing her energy, feeding on it to attack her, to weaken her, to *kill* her.

Fight it, Claire. You must fight it.

At last, a scream tore from her lips. She tried to call for help, but she couldn't form words. She wasn't even sure if she was connected to the real world. Darkness pressed in around her. A single foreign thought invaded hers.

"*Your life is mine,*" it said. "*Mine.*" The word echoed, bouncing around in her head. "*Mine...mine...mine...*"

Everything stopped. Her hand broke contact with the marble surface. She was dragged away from the dragon gasping.

"Claire? Claire!" Jovari held her by the shoulders at arm's length, shaking her. Her head bobbled. "What in the gods' hell is wrong with you?"

She blinked. Slowly, the world came into focus. "I...I'm sorry. I'm sorry!" The words were mumbled, weak. Where *was* she? What *was* this place? She traced Jovari's face, as memories of her life began flooding back in.

Her body shook violently. She tried to suppress the lingering feelings that had overpowered her. She felt as though she had been brought back from the dead.

The word *mine* still echoed in her mind.

"What...what happened?" She looked back at the dragon, breathless. It was unchanged, sitting curled up, exactly as it had been before. As if nothing had happened.

"You tell me," Jovari hissed. "You're the one acting strangely." He let go of her, still scowling. She recognized the scowl, the one that told her she was ever an inconvenience. "You...well...you sort of went rigid. You looked like you were suffocating—grabbing at your throat with your hand." His eyes hardened. "Are you well?"

She ignored his question, pointing instead at the marble dragon. "That *thing* isn't marble at all," she said. "Maybe it feels like it, but it *spoke* to me. There is something...something *living* inside it." Jovari barked a laugh, looking at her like she was crazy. "I felt something," she argued. "An intelligence? I don't know. I can't explain it. But it was trying to kill me." The words hadn't sounded crazy to her until spoken. No wonder he looked at her strangely. "Touch it," she said. "Touch it and see for yourself."

"Claire. This is—"

"I know it sounds insane."

"I was going to say *impossible*."

"I'm not making this up." She crossed her arms.

"Look, I have touched the statue before. It's nothing but marble. See?" He laid his hand down on the statue's surface. Nothing happened.

"I'm not lying!" Her fists clenched and unclenched at her sides. "When I touched it, I saw things in its mind. It was angry with me. It tried to kill me, like it was claiming…claiming *me*." She'd almost said, *my powers*, but thought better of it. She didn't have any powers—

"*Have you arrived?*" She twitched at the sound of Reyr's voice in her mind. "*What is your status? You never checked in with me.*"

"*My apologies,*" came Jovari's immediate answer. "*We had a minor…incident.*"

"*What do you mean, minor?*"

"*Nothing—nothing serious. There was an incident with the marble dragon. I am not sure how to explain it properly. Claire was behaving… strangely. We can discuss it when you arrive.*"

Their correspondence took seconds. Jovari's eyes came back into focus. "Listen, Claire. I never said you were lying. We can discuss it with Reyr when he arrives."

"*Very well,*" Reyr said to Jovari. "*We will discuss it upon my arrival. I, too, have news to share.*" Something was wrong with how he said this. Whatever it was wouldn't be good.

"*What sort of news?*" Jovari ventured.

"*Later.*"

Tired of his accusatory glares, Claire left Jovari to go sit at the campfire Koldis was preparing. Somehow, he'd managed to go hunting while she'd nearly been killed. She put her bedroll under her as a cushion and watched Koldis, eager for Reyr's return. He would believe her.

Koldis ignored her presence as he piled firewood in preparation for their fire. She watched the way his muscles bunched beneath his tunic. Why did they all have to be so handsome? Ugh!

When he was done, he stepped back, held his hand up, and muttered something. His lips hardly moved. Flames burst into life and the wood blazed brightly. She sucked in a sharp breath. "How did you…?" She never got to see Cyrus perform magic, though she had wanted to.

Koldis turned to her with a flat stare but said nothing.

"The fire," she added. "You started it without a match." Since their journey's start, the only fire they had were the fires she prepared, which had been nothing compared to what Koldis had conjured up.

"I am supposed to believe you've never seen magic?"

"I haven't."

"Right…"

To kill Cyrus, she would have needed a good deal of it. Naturally, Koldis thought she was lying. "I swear. I'm…I'm impressed, that's all."

"Eldár is the word I used. It means *fire* in the old language, but surely you already know this."

"I-I don't." She tried to be civil with him, but what did it matter? She watched him walk over to a spot on the other side of the fire, farthest away from her. He sat down with a scowl. She was about to say something more when her conscience advised otherwise.

Let him be. He has suffered a terrible loss.

So had the others, but they didn't treat her nearly as poorly. Still, she decided to let it go. Instead she watched the flames, allowing her mind to drift back to the giant white beast behind her.

She'd experienced so much mindfulness within its body, as if it had once been alive. Its strength had nearly killed her. That was another bizarre aspect of magic she could hardly wrap her head around—the idea that her energy could be yanked from her body. But why? Why her? The marble dragon seemed to have no effect on Jovari. Was that because he was a drengr while she was merely a human?

You are not merely *human.*

The idea made her itch, but it had to be true. After all, she could hear the drengr speak to each other telepathically. She could touch seemingly inanimate objects and read beyond their surfaces. She had done it at the gate, and now she had done it with the marble dragon. She had dreams filled with things she couldn't quite explain. Her mind seemed to know answers to questions when it shouldn't.

Holy hell! What was happening to her?!

Just two weeks ago, she seemed as normal as normal could be. If anything, she was *too* normal. College education, no job, terrible ex-boyfriend issues, living with Mom and Dad, student loans...The list went on. Now she was anything but.

Maybe her companions did have a good reason to be wary of her. It seemed that she hardly knew herself anymore. What she was capable of, the strange things that happened to her, the strange things that happened *around* her, the inexplicable pathway her life now traversed. All of it was shrouded in mystery.

Reyr returned the following morning. When he landed, Koldis untied the neatly-wrapped packages on his back, then Reyr transformed into his human form. He seemed agitated as he opened the parcels and began distributing the supplies. He said nothing while he did this. There were blankets, water skins, pots for cooking, bowls for eating, and a burlap sack full of buns, dried meat, carrots, and potatoes. The sight of the food left her stomach growling, but that wasn't what caught her attention now.

Folded in cloth, Reyr removed a sword, which he handed to her.

"You cannot be serious, Reyr. Giving her a weapon?" Koldis was disgusted. Reyr gave him a look that immediately silenced him.

"What is this for?" She realized afterward that it was a stupid question. It came mostly from shock that Reyr trusted her enough to hand it over.

"You are supposed to stab an enemy with it. What do you think?" Koldis muttered, going back to sit by their breakfast fire. She shot him a nasty look.

"Rumor is that these lands are being roamed by demons. It is best that we be prepared." The sun was rising high into the sky as he spoke. The brightness of day made the idea of dark demons seem absurd. But she knew that come nightfall, the terror of his words would set in. If vodar wraiths were truly roaming the wilderness, then what would happen when they found her?

"By demons, do you mean the vodar?" she couldn't help but ask.

Reyr jerked. "You have knowledge of them?" She nodded. "Let me guess, you cannot speak of it?" She chewed on her bottom lip but again, nodded. "I see…" His face went hard, but he hid it by turning to Jovari instead.

"What news?" Jovari asked as he came up to stand beside them. He had been out hunting and had only just returned.

"There is no time to speak of it now. We will discuss it tonight. Let me catch my breath and then we must depart." It was obvious that he was in a hurry to return to the capital, now more than ever. She couldn't help but wonder what it was, what he'd discovered. The two of them left her to go sit with Koldis, but only for a short while. True to his word, Reyr gave the order, and they departed south shortly thereafter.

CHAPTER 22
AN UNEXPECTED ATTACK

Claire sat with her knees pulled up to her chin, deep in thought. In the darkness, the flames of the campfire danced before her eyes. Hypnotized, she watched them flicker and wave and crackle and pop.

This close, it was almost too warm, but she enjoyed the fire's comfort nonetheless. Especially after Reyr's news. The fragrant smell of cooking stew even had her inching closer. The thought of a warm meal left her stomach growling with impatience. She had eaten little else besides dried meat and bread all day, and even less in the days before.

Jovari broke their pensive silence. "Tell me again, Reyr, what happened? What did you see when you flew over Belnesse?"

Reyr sighed. He had already gone through the details more than once. "The ruin of an entire city. I saw it from a distance at first, even before my wings carried me directly overhead. Dark ash in piles where buildings once stood. Not even the tower was left. By the time I arrived, the smoke had long since vanished." He paused, shaking his head. "Seeing it...so many people must have died. So many lives. I can't imagine what they went through."

"It's barbaric!" Koldis let his disgust be known. "They deserved better."

"Aye." Reyr shook his head. "Seeing it was like a nightmare. All I could hope for were survivors. But even then, there was nothing. *Nothing.* The whole city...burned. All but a single survivor." He threw a handful of dried grass into the flames. It crackled.

"Only dragon fire can exact such terrible damage," Jovari said.

Reyr inhaled then let out a loud exhale. "I can still smell it," he scoffed. "Charred flesh and misery. Ick. It's like my nostrils are tainted." He fell silent.

"This is troubling." Koldis rubbed the back of his neck, his eyes far away. He had become thoughtful and level-headed in light of the news. "I think we would be wise to believe this Mikkin fellow. He is the sole survivor, after all."

"I see no other option. His word is all we have." Reyr hesitated. "I was told he walked for days before falling into exhaustion. His caretakers found him unconscious in the fields, his clothing singed and torn, his feet bloody, and his lips parched from days in the sun without water. I don't think someone like that would lie."

"It is a wonder he escaped at all." Jovari voiced the same thought bouncing around in her mind.

"Escaped...do you think?" Reyr tilted his head. "I'm not so sure. Perhaps he was set free."

"If he was set free," Koldis said, "then it was done to send a message."

"Fear mongering." Reyr pressed his lips into a thin line.

"Yes." Koldis sighed. "How can it be that dragons, after thousands of years, could possibly exist?"

Reyr shook his head. "I will tell you this, when we bring this news to the lower council, they will laugh at us. The very idea—the existence of dragons—is something no one would dare believe."

"It does seem absurd." Koldis stood and threw another branch on the fire, glancing quickly at her before looking away. "Strange things are happening in Dragonwall," he muttered, almost too quietly to be heard.

She breathed a sigh of relief when dinner was ready, eager to change the subject. The stew was the best thing she had tasted in days, which was sad, because it consisted of watery broth, carrots, potatoes and meat. Consequences of her ever-present hunger, she supposed. Going back for a second and a third helping, she ate greedily and in silence.

"Mikkin said there were nearly one hundred dragons," Reyr blurted during the meal.

"Far too many for my liking," Koldis answered.

She pushed down a grumble. It wasn't easy, knowing the answers to their questions. In fact, it was incredibly frustrating. The longer they spoke of it, the worse their speculations became. At one point, Jovari insisted that the dragons intended to take over the kingdom. She alone knew the truth, that Kane was the one behind everything.

She wanted to join in their discussion, but couldn't. Besides, she had different things to think about. Cyrus had known something big was coming for Dragonwall—something devastating. He'd known it was only a matter of time, that the people needed to be warned. Reyr's news confirmed Cyrus's worst fears. Kane had made his first move. How many more would die before she could relay Kane's existence to the king?

The conversation about Belnesse carried on late into the night. Her incident with the marble dragon was completely forgotten by everyone but her. She had hoped to tell Reyr about it, hoping that he would have some answers, but in the end, she never got the chance to ask. She finally gave up and curled up in her bedroll.

Sleep was difficult, at first. She tossed and turned for what felt like hours, drifting in and out of odd memories that were certainly not hers. On occasion, voices filtered through her consciousness. Whether they belonged to the strange memories or came from outside her head, she couldn't have said.

Just as she was drifting into another strange dream, a hand gripped her shoulder. She sucked in a breath. She was urgently shaken awake. Her eyes flew open. Reyr crouched over her, a finger pressed to his lips. A deep sense of unease settled over her, prickling her neck. This was a familiar feeling. Her pulse accelerated.

"It is as I feared. Spread out," came Reyr's telepathic command.

Something heavy was thrust into her hand—the sword Reyr had gotten her. Her eyes went wide. She tried to catch a glimpse of her surroundings, but there was no moon out, and the stars were hardly bright enough. All she could see were black shapes moving around the perimeter of their little camp. She knew without needing to see that the vodar had found her. They had come for the stones.

Instinct took over. She reached for her backpack and put her hand over the pocket where her revolver was hidden. She had killed them once before, she would do it again.

"They are closing in, Reyr. We are outnumbered. Keep them in your sights," Koldis said.

Her drengr companions used telepathy to keep quiet.

Reyr stood. His hand was on the hilt of his Sverak, ready to remove it from its sheath. She swallowed, her mouth suddenly dry.

"Beware of their magic. On my count—" Reyr was slowly moving away from her, his back now turned. Through the loud rush of blood pounding in her ears, she heard the scrape of swords being drawn.

Using this as her cue, she quickly unzipped her backpack and removed the revolver. She kept it loaded for this very purpose. Hands shaking, she got on her knees, trying to digest what was about to happen.

This was real. They were here for *her.* They would not stop hunting her until they had the stones. In a few moments, that very same notion might become obvious to her companions, jeopardizing her entire mission. If they found out she'd hidden this from them...

Reyr's voice was in her mind again. *"Ready? Three, two, one—"*

There was a bright flash of white light. She cursed, momentarily blinded. The sound of clashing metal reverberated loudly. It seemed to hum through her body. But these were not the only noises to greet her ears. Pops and crackles like sparks of electricity echoed around her, paired with more bursts of blue and white brilliance as her surroundings flashed from light to dark.

"They are going for Claire!" The sudden shout exploded into her mind. *"Stop them!"*

Freeing herself from the chains of shock, she jumped to her feet. Two of the six black shapes were gliding towards her. The other four were trying to free themselves from their fight with Jovari, Koldis, and Reyr.

Without further hesitation, she held the revolver out, both hands gripping it tightly to keep from shaking. She fired. The shot split through the air. The head of the nearest Vodar exploded into smoke, quickly followed by its body. There was a momentary silence that came after, but she did not act stunned like the others. Once more she took aim, both hands on the gun as she pointed it at the head of the next wraith. She pulled the trigger. This time something entirely different happened. The air around the vodar grew opaque, flickering as the bullet encountered an invisible shield. When it passed through, it turned to dust and disappeared.

"Not this time," a voice hissed. Chills raced across her skin. For a moment, she could not move as fear sank its claws into her.

The wraith moved towards her, gaining speed, arm outstretched. A glittering sword slashed through the air beside her, followed by an aggressive cry as the weapon made contact with the vodar's neck. Reyr's appearance saved her. He took off the wraith's head in a single sweep. It vanished.

She did not have time to thank him. A burst like fireworks illuminated the air around her, followed up by another. The strange orbs she had seen were exploding. Reyr must have erected a shield of protection around them.

A renewed sense of duty took hold of her. Kane would not win. Not today. Fiery courage blazed up within her. She grabbed her sword from the ground.

Relax your mind. I will guide you...

The thoughts in her brain were absurd, especially now in the heat of battle. She ignored the commentary, thinking only of what she wanted in that exact moment—the death of the wraith standing before her. Crying out with a passion she didn't know she had, she took several strides forward and lifted the sword to meet the Vodar. It raised its own weapon in response. She did not stop to think about what its blade could do to her. Instead, she focused on what happened next.

Their swords met. The reverberation crashed around her.

"Claire, no!" She heard Reyr's shout of surprise. She ignored it, swiping at the vodar and then jumping backwards. If she'd had time to think about it, she would have been dumbfounded. She had never used a sword. Not once. How the hell was she fighting with one?!

Lifting the blade again, she swung it around, spinning on her heel as she ducked from an oncoming blow. She let her blade follow her movements. She struck the vodar's legs, hidden beneath its smoking robes. It hissed and tried to lash out at her, but she jumped back. Back and forth they fought, evenly matched, it seemed. As they continued, she began to get the impression that the vodar was toying with her, going easy on her. As soon as she let her mind lose focus, she erred, moving in the wrong direction. The Vodar's blade sliced along her leg and she felt white-hot searing pain.

She screamed, the raw sound scraping up the insides of her throat. A second later, she managed to jump aside. She lifted her sword to block another attempt, but a different sword beat her to it. This one glittered with dark green emeralds. Koldis was beside her, taking over. It lasted only the length of a breath before the vodar's head was removed.

The world around them fell silent, almost as if the universe had come to a halt. She was vaguely aware of the searing agony in her leg. Her mind was spinning. *Everything* was spinning.

Fight it. Fight the poison. You must.

A surge of something that could only be described as energy burst through her. Squaring her shoulders, she turned. Koldis stood beside her, arms limp at his sides. He was breathing hard, staring blankly in front of him where the vodar had just vanished. Then, as if coming out of a trance, he turned to her. "How are you going to explain your way out of this one, Claire?" Even in the darkness, she could see his angry glare, but that wasn't what surprised her. He had just saved her life. Her mind whirled with confusion. A moment later, the world dimmed. She felt her legs buckle beneath her as she dropped to the ground. The last thing she noticed were arms reaching out to catch her.

CHAPTER 23
CONTENDING WITH POISON

Kengr Plains

Claire woke to a blur of shapes moving around her. The world faded in and out of focus for several long minutes—minutes that seemed to last an eternity. From light to dark, her vision moved as she pulled her drowsy mind from its dreams, *strange* dreams. Foggy images of vodar wraiths, sword fighting, bright flashes of light, and worse. It all swam in and out of her consciousness.

She forced her eyes to focus on the sky above, swallowing against her dry throat. The moment her mind came into focus, a sharp pain traveled up her leg. She groaned, clenching her teeth. In the same instant, a switch flipped in her brain. She hadn't been dreaming. All of it had been very real. Her heart took off in a gallop as a wave of panic raced through her.

The burning in her leg hummed, making her gut clench. There was nothing in the world more real than what she felt. She was careful not to move for fear of making the pain worse. She lay motionless, utterly traumatized by what had happened. Was she going to die?

Another cry rose up from deep in her chest.

She closed her eyes and swallowed a few more times. She was too young to die, and how would she fulfill Cyrus's promise if she did? The pain wasn't nearly as bad as the fear that came with it, but that told her something. Surely her wound wasn't as bad as it felt, because if it was, she would have been *begging* for death.

She opened her eyes and pushed herself up. Everything began to spin before settling into a steady state. She felt a hand on her shoulder. Reyr crouched beside her. "Not too fast," he warned. His voice was warm, soothing. She looked from his worried face to her wound, her eyes widening. The lower part of her pant leg had been rolled all the way up to her knee. There was an angry gash, but no blood, which had to be a good sign. In the middle of the gash was a black line sending out little black veins like a collection of small tributaries leading into a river. The poison was there—she'd recognize the signs anywhere.

Reyr followed her gaze. "You can thank Koldis for his quick actions. It is he who saved you. He is the only one of us skilled at reversing the effects of poison in its early stages. He was able to keep it from spreading—at his own expense." Reyr motioned with his head to where Koldis was sleeping, an arm thrown over his face. He looked more handsome when he wasn't scowling. "He must regain his strength before we can continue."

It was dawn and the sky was a flat gray. The air was humid and sticky, making her more uncomfortable than she already was—if that was possible. "How...how long have I been out?" Her tongue felt thick, her throat like sandpaper, her voice rough and unused. Which meant she'd probably done a lot of screaming while Koldis was healing her.

"Only a few hours. The rest of us, except Koldis, haven't slept."

"And...and my wound?" she squeaked. She did her best to hold still. When she wasn't moving, she could almost block out the pain. Almost.

"It will not kill you. The poison will not spread, Koldis has seen to that. But it will hurt until it is properly healed. None of us here possesses the ability to fix it. Not even Koldis."

A new panic set in. "You mean, I've...I've got to carry on like this until...until I get to the capital?" By the end of the sentence, her voice was barely a whisper.

"No, fortunately not. We will reach the forest in less than two days. There, you will find the healing you need."

"The...the *forest*?" She swallowed down her fear, because there was only one forest he could possibly be referring to.

"Aye. We will be there by nightfall tomorrow."

She stared at him with wide eyes. "But..."

They couldn't go to the Gable Forest, nor Esterpine. That was where the sprite queen lived. Cyrus had told her about the queen and how angry she'd been with the drengr monarchy for removing the stones from their protection. Moreover, he hadn't trusted her.

Apparently, he'd marched right into Esterpine, right up to their queen, and demanded they return the dragonstones to their rightful owners. Despite the warnings given, and their need for spriten protection, he'd taken them anyway. There was no way the sprites would forget the offense.

Reyr's forehead furrowed. She swallowed. "What...what makes you so sure that I will get help in the forest?"

"I cannot be sure. Perhaps if you ask nicely, the sprites might take pity upon you."

She snorted. He really had no idea, did he? No idea what had happened when Cyrus took the dragonstones. How could he? He'd hunted Cyrus for weeks, following the bond they shared, which took him straight to the gate and through it. It was likely that Reyr had never entered the forest in search of Cyrus—never visited the sprite queen to find out what had happened.

Reyr stood and walked away to speak with Jovari. Their voices were low, so she heard nothing of their conversation. But not long after, they woke Koldis in preparation to leave.

"How is she?" Koldis yawned as he looked over at her. Upon finding her eyes on him, he quickly looked away and didn't bother waiting for an answer. He merely rose and stalked off. She had no idea what to make of it.

Several minutes later, he returned. After having a quick look at her leg, he went to the fire and removed a pot, pouring some of its liquid contents into a bowl. "Drink this," was all he said before leaving her alone.

She smelled it apprehensively. Tea, perhaps? It was odorless. She drained it. The effect was almost instant as her pain numbed.

Breathing a sigh of relief, she did her best to stand and quickly pack up her belongings, limping pathetically around their little camp. The others did not pity her, and she was happy for it. The last thing she wanted was consolation from any of them, especially after the way they had treated her in the past.

She was even more relieved that they said nothing about the attack. She expected to be bombarded with questions, but their demands never came. They must have been in a hurry to resume their journey.

They were soon airborne. She sat nestled in the dip of Reyr's neck, right where it met his wing joints. It hadn't been easy climbing up to her perch. All the technique she'd developed was no longer useful with a wounded leg.

Despite their lack of conversation on the ground, in flight, their words flowed freely. They wasted no time in erupting into an open discussion regarding what had happened.

"*They were after her,*" Koldis started by saying. "*Surely none of us can argue with that.*" There was both confusion *and* surprise in his telepathic voice.

"*No. I cannot argue against it, Koldis.*" Reyr gave a mental sigh. "*It was obvious to me as well.*"

"*I grow tired of her silence,*" Koldis continued. "*She knows the exact reason for the attack. Yet we are left in the dark. It angers me. She may have known they were coming for us. She could have warned us!*"

"*I understand your frustration. But what would you have me do? Torture the poor girl into disclosure?*"

Jovari spoke up then. "*She has been tortured enough. The blade of a vodar wraith is lethal. I cannot begin to imagine her pain.*" The others, in turn, agreed. "*It is a lucky thing, Koldis, that you were there to save her.*" A short silence followed before he spoke again. "*Her wound, the black poison. It reminds me of what we saw on Cyrus. No?*"

"So you think it was a vodar who killed him?" Koldis wondered with obvious skepticism.

"Aye, I am beginning to wonder," Jovari answered.

"It seems entirely possible," Reyr agreed. *"I have no solid explanation as to why, Koldis. But perhaps if she observed Cyrus's death, perhaps if she saw those who were responsible, then I could argue that their attack was an attempt to tie up loose ends."*

"And create three more by assaulting her before our very eyes?" Koldis scoffed.

"Yes, it is indeed odd."

"Clearly they want her dead," Jovari said. *"That tells me she knows something. I would like to know what it is?"*

They continued on like this for some time, speculating over her involvement. What bothered them more was that she hadn't immediately died from the poison. It was something she hadn't yet considered. Cyrus had told her much the same thing when he'd suffered. He'd said that a human would die instantly. She hadn't.

Why?

Because she was no ordinary human.

"And what about her fighting?" Koldis asked. *"That was entirely unexpected. You got her that blade, Reyr. She looked at it like it was a snake, like she'd never seen anything like it. But then she wielded it like it was an extension of her arm."*

"Hmm. Yes. I am aware."

His observation made her stomach squirm. Koldis was right. She'd never used a sword before, and yet...

"Her style was unique," Koldis went on. *"Did you notice? It reminded me of..."* He trailed off.

"It reminded you of Cyrus," Reyr finished. *"Indeed, I noticed it too."*

"Cyrus was incredible with a sword. I will always remember him for it."

Her cheeks flushed. She didn't know what to feel. It was an uncomfortable conversation to overhear. She wished, more than ever, that she could tune them out. It felt wrong to listen in, but what choice did she have? Only one positive thing seemed to come from it. They no longer harbored hostilities towards her. Curiosity had replaced their doubt and mistrust.

Hours passed until her exhaustion overtook her. She sank into a fitful sleep as her body tried to forget its pain. If she thought riding a dragon was uncomfortable before, it was nothing compared to flying with an injured leg. The longer she nursed it, the more aware of it she became.

Think of other things. Keep it from your mind.

She almost laughed at the absurd advice. Think of other things? She was sitting in the sky on the back of a dragon with nothing else to occupy herself. What the hell else was she supposed to think about?!

"If we make good time, we will be in Esterpine by tomorrow night." She was hardly cheered by Reyr's announcement later that afternoon. The muscles in her right leg were clenched tightly, as if that would help with the pain. Even her teeth had become sore from unconsciously clenching her jaw.

Eventually, the flat gray sky gave way to rain. It began to fall in great sheets, cooling the world around them. She was glad to have a bath, even though it left her clothes and everything else sopping wet. She was also happy when the clouds passed overhead, moving off to the north. It did not take long for everything to dry.

As the afternoon waned, a great smudge of green appeared on the horizon. It stretched to the left and right, before her. She knew that she was seeing the Gable Forest. An odd feeling of familiarity accompanied her recognition as it settled over her. Her heart thudded wildly in her chest. Whether it was because she hoped the sprites would offer healing, or for some other reason entirely, she could not be sure, but seeing the forest on the horizon put her mind at ease.

The land here was not as barren as it was further north. They passed over several small settlements. As they continued south, she began hearing foreign voices in her mind. They were whispers at first, growing louder and softer as they moved along. It took several of them for her to realize these belonged to other drengr.

A particular set of voices grew increasingly louder over time.

There were drengr in the vicinity and they were getting closer. Her eyes scanned the distance, eventually spotting a smudge of color far away, to her right. Jovari, Koldis, and Reyr were no longer the only ones in this patch of the sky.

She listened as the first voice said, *"Look ahead! If I am not mistaken, those are king's shields, three of the drengr fairtheoir."*

"Let's fly to greet them," said another.

Her companions failed to notice. It was strange. Couldn't they hear the conversation the way she did? The thought left her frowning in thought.

What if drengr telepathy was as simple as any sort of conversation? What if a drengr could pick and choose who they wished to speak to, but exclude the rest. If that was true...

Her frown transformed to a smile. If that was true, she could overhear conversations that weren't meant to be overheard. She could hear *all* of them and they had no idea.

The approaching drengr were curious. She picked up the snippets of their conversation as they speculated what a trio of shields were doing this far north. *"Look!"* one surprised voice said, catching her attention. *"One of them carries a human! It's Lord Reyr —Davi's brother! I thought his mate had died."*

"Have you ever seen a drengr fairtheoir carrying a human?" one of them asked.

"Nay. Never," came the reply.

Her cheeks flushed. She was beginning to feel uncomfortable. Their shocked reactions reminded her of how Jovari and Koldis had complained at the thought of Reyr carrying her. Why was it such a big deal?

"Reyr!" She heard Koldis speak up. *"Look there. A group of drengr. From Fort Squall, if I'm not mistaken."*

"It is, indeed!" Excitement rang in Reyr's voice.

Just then, the new party hailed them. *"Greetings drengr fairtheoir! Well met!"*

The two parties came together and continued flying south towards the forest. She counted five sets of colorful scales, each with a rider. And every rider's eyes were on her. She immediately feigned interest in her backpack, fussing with it to avoid their gazes.

"We are surprised to see you so far north, Lord Reyr. What brings you to this part of the king—?"

"Did someone die?" another voice cut in. *"Whose shrouded body is that upon your back, Lord Koldis?"*

"Let us discuss this on land," Reyr said. The invitation was accepted. They landed and greeted each other cordially. When the drengr shifted, she noticed that they were all male. Were there no female drengr?

There has never been a female Drengr. Not since the beginning of our history.

She didn't mistake the bitterness in the thought. But...why? Why no females?

"You carry a human with you," one of them stated, looking straight at her. "And the body? Who is it? Anyone we know?"

"That is grave news," Reyr said. "Grave news indeed. Cyrus is dead."

"No! Surely not!" There were gasps all around.

"How could this be?" A tall female stepped forward. She was dressed in what Claire assumed to be flying gear. A lighter form of armor.

"We do not have the answers you seek," Koldis said. "But we plan to determine them in due time. We are going straight to the king with this matter."

"The king does not know yet?"

Reyr shook his head. "Alas, he does not. We will tell him as soon as we are free of the forest."

"Understood." The drengr who led their charge nodded. "And who is this—this female?"

"This is Claire." Surprisingly, Jovari stepped forward to her defense. She blinked at him, taken aback. "She's with us."

To her relief, the drengr and their riders didn't question them.

"Greetings, Claire," many of them said, bowing their heads briefly. She didn't miss their quizzical expressions.

"Tell me, what news of my brother?" Reyr asked.

The male in charge nodded, cracking a happy smile. "Lord Davi is well. He and Lady Emmy would surely be delighted to see you."

"And my nephew?"

"Also well! Perhaps after you are free of the forest, you might pay them a short visit?"

Reyr bowed his head in agreement. "I intend to."

"Wonderful. We do not wish to delay your journey. Please give the king our sincerest condolences," said the male drengr in charge. Jovari, Koldis, and Reyr nodded. The newcomers backed away and transformed, quickly leaving them as they took to the sky. She watched their ascent in awe. It was the first time she had witnessed drengr-rider pairs, since hearing about them from Cyrus.

"May as well break here for a few minutes before we continue on," Reyr told her. She gathered his meaning and made her way to a private spot to relieve herself, returning several minutes later.

"Are all riders female and all drengr male?" she asked Reyr. It seemed a little too *confined* for her liking.

"There has never been a female drengr." He hesitated, not quite answering her question. "You seem...surprised."

"Why aren't there female drengr?"

"I cannot say for certain. It's one of the mysteries of our race. It is believed that none were able to fledge after the dragons took on Queen Isabella's blessing."

She started at the mention of the queen, a name she'd only recently heard before. "I...I see. That doesn't seem entirely fair, does it?"

Reyr shrugged. "You'll have to take it up with the dead queen. You can give her an earful from me when you do." He winked at her.

She let out a nervous laugh. "And your riders?"

"They are our mates. The bond we develop is lifelong and inti-mate. That is why the others were surprised to see you upon my back. It is considered quite...unethical to carry another who is not a mate."

"But...why?"

He sighed. "The act of flying with another is considered nearly as intimate as making love."

Her mouth dropped open and she had to stifle a choking sound from the back of her throat. She had no idea that flying with Reyr was seen that way. It seemed incredibly absurd, and far too old-fashioned for her tastes. But...this was a different world. Clearly people did things abnormally here.

"It appears that I have answered your questions. Are you ready to take flight?"

She nodded, eager to reach the forest and get that part of their journey over with. As she climbed upon Reyr's back, she had to bite her tongue to keep from crying out. Searing pain shot through her leg. They were back in the sky almost immediately. She was glad, thankful that they needn't walk the distance to the forest.

They did not stop again until it was time to make camp. Already the trees were much closer on the horizon. Koldis took the first watch. She was relieved to rest her aching muscles, relieved to sleep in hopes that she might escape her pain, relieved that by tomorrow night she would hopefully gain a reprieve from it.

That night, she kept her sword beside her. She intended to do so for the remainder of the journey. There was no telling when the vodar might return. And if they did, she wanted to be ready.

CHAPTER 24
INSIDE THE KEEP

Kastali Dun

Desaree inhaled and her stomach gave a rumble. In the mornings, the great keep's cookery always smelled of freshly baked spiced bread. She crept over to the countertop beside one of the massive brick ovens. Several loaves were already out and sliced. They sat steaming, taunting her with the heavenly scent of apples and cinnamon. She snuck a few slices, buttering them before anyone noticed. She bit into one and groaned—

"Desaree!" She jumped. It was Tess. "*There* you are."

Tess was head lady, which meant she managed all the servants and could most often be found within the cookery. Most importantly though, Tess was like a mother to her.

"Come now, m'dear! Do not keep me waiting." She waved her famous wooden spoon, the one she always carried around to smack no-gooders with when they were making trouble. Desaree rushed to her side. Although Tess was a kindly woman, her wrath was unpleasant. She'd slept in once—just once!—and Tess had assigned her to clean pit toilets for a month She'd never been late again.

The cookery was bustling, especially this morning. Trays were being assembled and loaded with the contents of the morning's breakfast. Porridge, spiced bread, butter, cheese, apples, and pots of honey. The keep's more prominent nobles often took their morning meal within the privacy of their chambers. Those nobles of lower birth generally could not afford such lavish indulgences, so they took their meals in the dining hall. As of recently, however, given the state of things, many were willing to pay the price for the privacy of their accommodations.

News spread through the capital like dragon fire—Lord Cyrus was dead. Rumors had taken form in a ridiculous manner, as they often did. Many speculated about Cyrus, his death, and about the mystery girl who had come to Dragonwall with the king's own shields. No one fueled these fires more than the servants. Her kind overheard plenty of gossip while they attended to their duties.

Preparations for the impending funeral were in full swing. Food stores were under intense scrutiny as every apple, potato, and carrot was inventoried. Candle sticks were taken from storage, dusted of their cobwebs, and polished to their full brilliance. Guest rooms were to be readied today and tomorrow in anticipation of visitors who traveled from afar. Many wished to pay their respects. The servants would be busy for days to come.

Desaree's morning duties included breakfast deliveries to the grand apartments throughout the keep. She had a long list of other duties too, but she liked this one the best. It was easy, a lot of walking to be sure, but she enjoyed that.

As she nibbled on her bread, Tess yammered off the names of those she would serve this morning, which were written upon a list. "...The Boyce's, Sir Roly Daven, Lady Tania, Commander Daxton, and Lady Caterina—"

She bit her tongue, giving a little squeal of pain.

"Is there a problem?"

"Not Lady Caterina," she said. "Please, Tess."

"You're still on about that woman?"

Lady Caterina was Desaree's least favorite person in the entire keep. In fact, Caterina was her least favorite person in the entire capital, better yet, make that the whole of Dragonwall. She *despised* her, and for good reason, too. To the rest of the world, Caterina was an angel, but Desaree saw right through it.

"*Yes*, I'm still on about her," she said. "You know how she treats me."

"Desaree, have we not been over this already, child? You cannot get out of your duty each and every time." Tess paused to sigh. "Were it any other day, I would send someone else in your stead. As it is, everyone is busy." Then she leaned closer and added in more of a whisper, "None of the other servants like her either. Just do your best."

She groaned and gathered up the first tray for the morning—the tray going to the Boyce family—and left the kitchens. The first few deliveries were painless enough. It was always the same routine for each delivery. Knock gently on the door and announce your purpose. Place the tray on the occupant's bedroom table. Set out the contents. Curtsy. Smile as much as possible. Then bid them a good day and leave.

Some of the nobles were friendlier than others, especially Lady Tania, who also happened to be the biggest gossip in Kastali Dun. Lady Tania always knew the latest happenings. Nothing slipped past *her* perceptive ears.

She knocked at the lady's door. "Breakfast delivery," she called. A few moments later, Lady Tania was ushering her inside. Desaree noticed that she still wore a robe and nightclothes. The woman disliked handmaidens and favored her privacy. Her lack of assistance showed. Desaree followed her over to the table.

"I was hoping it would be you," Lady Tania said, "and not that dratted Nessle boy, or whatever they call him. He is so dull!"

"Nestley," Desaree said, smothering her laugh.

"Right. Dumb name. Would you mind helping me tidy up a few things? I would be more than happy to share my breakfast." As she spoke, she winked at Desaree.

The lower level servants rarely got enough to eat for breakfast and midday meal, even though dinner was always plenty. Lady Tania often shared with her in exchange for a little tidying service.

She was never one to turn down food. She began by opening the curtains and making the bed, moving quickly throughout, collecting the woman's dirty clothes into a pile.

"So what do you think about the woman everyone is speaking of?" Lady Tania asked through a mouthful.

"The golden haired outsider they are calling her. I do not yet know her name."

"No one knows her name yet, dear, but I mean, what do you think about it all? About *her*?" Lady Tania was so persistent. "I'm told she is strikingly beautiful."

Desaree considered. "Beautiful or not, many say she is guilty of a great crime." By many, she meant the servants. She had yet to agree with them on this matter. A mere human capable of killing a drengr?

"Aye, they are all crying for justice."

"What do you think about it, Lady Tania?"

"I think it is ridiculous if you ask me! A human woman—killing Lord Cyrus. But what do I know about these matters..." She stuffed more food between her chubby cheeks. "I am of no consequence, after all. We poor females...no one takes us seriously."

Desaree watched her, happy that Lady Tania was of the same opinion.

"Come dear girl. Eat," she said.

They spent a short while eating and speculating about what had happened to Lord Cyrus, as well as what would happen to the strange woman when she arrived in Kastali Dun. Desaree was certain that as an outsider, she would be killed. "They will want retribution," she argued. "People always want a scapegoat—someone to blame."

"Nonsense, lass. The king is smart. He will deal fairly with the situation, especially if she is innocent."

Desaree did not know much about King Talon, but what she *did* know, scared her. Despite never having interacted with Dragonwall's ruler, she had heard enough from the other servants.

"How do we know that this woman is innocent, my lady? She is from beyond the gate; no one knows what she is capable of."

"You make a good point. Perhaps she has powers unknown to us." Lady Tania set her napkin down on the platter then continued. "I'm simply happy to have something new and exciting to talk about. Surely you are too? Life has been rather boring." The woman gave a big yawn and stretched.

"Thank you for the breakfast, Lady Tania, but I must be going. I have two deliveries left." She was dreading Caterina's. It was her last for the morning, and she was anxious to get it over with.

After delivering Commander Daxton's breakfast, she rushed down to the cookery to grab the final tray—the dreaded final tray. Tess cornered her as she was leaving, waving her spoon. "Wait a moment, dearie!" Desaree stopped in her tracks and turned to face her. "There has been a late order. I need you to deliver one more when you are finished with Lady Caterina's." She motioned to the tray Desaree carried. "To Lord Verath. He will be taking breakfast in his chambers this morning."

"Lord...Lord Verath?!" she sputtered. The contents on her tray teetered and her cheeks flushed with embarrassment. She gave much the same reaction every time Lord Verath's name was mentioned. He was one of the king's six shields. Not only did she fancy him—secretly and from afar—he was the *last* person she wanted to see after her impending visit with Caterina.

Tess reached forward to ensure the tray wasn't dropped. "You will be fine, child. Now, hurry up!"

Desaree made her way to the upper levels of the keep then tapped at Lady Caterina's door. "My lady, your breakfast is here," she called with a shaky voice. The door opened to Lady Caterina's handmaiden, who was quickly pushed aside as Lady Caterina herself came into view.

There she stood, scowling at Desaree. "*You!*" she spat. "*No wonder* I have been waiting an eternity."

"I am sorry, my lady, they put you at the end of my delivery list this morning."

"Excuse me? How dare you!" Red patches appeared on Lady Caterina's otherwise flawless skin. "Would you speak to a *queen* in such a manner? I bet you haven't any idea, have you?"

"Idea of what, my lady?"

"That I will soon be your queen."

For a moment she stared blankly back at Caterina, struck dumb by the notion. Then her head began spinning. What was Caterina implying? Had the king asked for her hand? Never in a millennia would she have believed anyone could possibly desire this woman as a wife.

"Well, it hasn't yet been finalized." Caterina plucked a piece of lint from the arm of her gown. "My father still awaits the king's answer, but it is only a matter of time. I bet you never would have guessed it—how far I would rise. Well soon, I shall be all the way at the top. You *always* believed yourself superior to me when we were children. Well look at us now. You will be scrubbing floors for the rest of your life. Me? I shall be queen."

Caterina fell silent for the span of several heartbeats, then as if coming out of a dream, she looked down at the tray Desaree held. "Gods! Look at the state of my food. Did you *throw* it on there?"

She had forgotten to rearrange the tray's contents after almost dropping it. "I apologize my lady." Her voice quivered, more from fear than anything. She was the only person in the world who knew what Caterina was capable of.

"Hurry up then!" Caterina grabbed her arm and dragged her into the room. Her fingers dug into Desaree's flesh. Desaree had to bite her tongue to stifle a cry of pain. She refused to let Caterina know how it hurt.

She began setting out the woman's breakfast. Caterina's handmaiden, Seraphina, rushed forward to help. Caterina hissed and grabbed the back of her handmaiden's gown, stopping her. "Desaree can do it herself. There's no need to help her."

Desaree's hands shook so badly that she accidentally knocked over the small pot of honey.

"You clumsy idiot!" She felt the sting of Lady Caterina's hand against the side of her face. Stars swam in her vision. The force of the blow was surprising. Then again, Caterina wasn't merely a woman. She was training to be a mage. She never understood why the gods had blessed her with magic.

"I—I am sorry my lady," she stammered, and quickly cleaned up the spilled honey. Backing away from the table, she separated herself as far as possible from her.

"Get out of my sight," Caterina barked. "And tell them to send someone else next time. I never want to see you in my chambers again."

Desaree escaped from the room. By the time she reached the kitchens, tears were streaming down her cheeks. She had to give herself a few minutes in the empty corridor to wipe her eyes before presenting herself to Tess for the last tray.

"Child! What happened?" Tess grabbed her face with both hands. She could feel the bruise that was beginning to form around her cheekbone. "Has she ever hit you before?" Tess asked.

Desaree shook her head, though that was a lie. Caterina had hit her many times when they were children.

"Very well. I will send someone else next time."

She was given the last tray to deliver to Lord Verath. She reached his door, shaking and upset. This was not how she envisioned their first meeting, and it was true that she had imagined their first meeting many times. Usually it took place in the royal gardens, where he plucked her a flower and offered to place it in her hair. Or in passing down one of the many corridors, where he stopped and told her that her hair looked lovely, or that he wanted to know her name.

Certainly not this.

She clutched the tray with her right arm, took a deep breath, and knocked. "My lord, I've brought your breakfast."

"Enter," he called from the other side. The sound of his deep voice, the anticipation of entering his room, the thought of seeing him in private—it was nearly too much. She squared her shoulders, remembering that life had not always been this way, and turned the knob on the door.

Lord Verath stood near the fire with his back to her. He had one arm propped upon the mantle, gazing into the flames. He looked like the perfect picture of elegance and poise! Like something from a painting. Her cheeks flushed and she turned away.

Remaining silent, she prayed that he would not look upon her. As she made her way across the room, no matter how hard she tried, it was impossible to keep her beating heart calm. Thank the gods he faced the other way.

She began positioning his meal on the table, removing each of the contents from the tray. As much as she wanted to rush through it, she refused to be careless. So she placed everything perfectly. Just so—

"Stop." She froze, eyes downcast. "Just a moment." He strode over. She kept her face turned downwards, felt the blood rushing past her ears. Had she done something wrong?

"What in the name of the gods happened to your face, Desaree?"

She jumped at the sound of her name, nearly dropping the utensils in her hand. Her gaze darted upwards. She found Lord Verath standing across from her, as handsome as ever, with his dark hair and dark eyes and bronzed skin. His eyes were fixed on her face—on the place Caterina had slapped her. She flushed. The bruise forming on her face throbbed.

"My...my lord, it...it's nothing," she managed, turning her eyes down again. In a blink, he rounded the table and took her chin in his fingers, turning her head this way and that to better see the bruise.

"It does not look that way to me. Who did this to you?"

"I..." She thought about it, she really did. She couldn't lie to him, but she also couldn't tell him who it was, for fear of retaliation.

He frowned. "Well?"

She shook her head. It was difficult, considering he still held her chin in his fingers. His touch alone left her heart fluttering. She pressed her lips into a thin line, in obvious refusal.

"I see..." He scowled, but released her. He could have pushed the subject, demanded an answer. He was a lord, and that's what most lords did, wasn't it?

Instead, he simply dismissed her with a quiet, "You may go."

She left him as quickly as possible, breathing a deep sigh of relief the moment she was alone again. When she returned to the kitchens, she was engulfed in shock. In her entire time at the keep, she had never spoken to him. There were a few times when he had caught her eye, likely by accident. And each time it had happened, her face had burned like a thousand fires.

Gods! She was such a silly girl. But who could blame her? This was *Lord Verath*!

She had been thirteen when she first arrived at the castle, becoming a servant within the keep's walls. As a young girl, she had admired him from afar. Everyone knew the names of the king's six. They were famous, even idolized. She knew plenty of stories about Lord Verath in particular, about his bravery, and his loyalty to the king. It came as no surprise when she grew older and began developing feelings for him. Half the women in the keep, and even some of the men, looked at him with stars in their eyes.

She'd never told anyone, of course, and she'd certainly never expected him to notice her. But he'd said her *name*! Spoken it like he'd known it for a long while. He'd even shown concern for her. It made her almost giddy with delight. Lord Verath—concerned about *her*, Desaree, a mere servant.

Once she checked in with Tess, she made her way to the second-floor chambers where she was scheduled to perform the day's chores. Her mind was on Lord Verath. For the rest of the day and many days to come, she thought of nothing else but him.

CHAPTER 25

INTO THE MOUNTAINS

Northern Barrier Range

Mikkin adjusted his position in the saddle. Little good it did to ease the ache in his rump. Gods, how he hated this form of traveling. It wasn't so much the horse as it was the riding. He would have preferred walking, but Jamie was right. On horseback, it would take them a little over a day to reach the mountains. Already, the uninviting peaks loomed up before them, casting dark shadows on the hills at their base. But that part of the journey would wait for tomorrow. They had traveled far enough and it was time to make camp. In the morning, Tynen would take the horses and return home to Landow, leaving Mikkin and Jamie to continue on foot. The range was no place for horses, and he was glad of it.

Mikkin was comfortably familiar with this environment. He'd grown up beneath the gloom of the mountains, hunting in them, exploring them, and camping in them with his children. But he'd never journeyed deep into their midst. His knowledge and memory would only take him so far. The rest would be a real test.

Together, the three of them located a small grove of trees through which a small, shallow stream ran, its lyrical trickle was inviting. "I'll tend to the horses," Tynen said. "If you two wouldn't mind lookin' for wood, we can get a fire going." They agreed and set off to search. Having brought only dried meat and bread, there was no need for a fire, especially in the summer heat, but it would be a nice comfort once the sun went down.

Jamie insisted on starting the fire so he humored the lad, understanding full well that Jamie was eager to prove himself. As soon as a crackling blaze was struck, they sat around to eat. Traveling food was never satisfying. They needed to keep their packs light. Once they began their ascent into the range, they would be happier for it.

Before leaving Landow, Tynen lent him a fine bow with a set of arrows. Hunting was second nature for him, and there would be game aplenty, but wild game was not what the bow would be most handy for. None could say what kind of danger they would find lurking in the depths of the great pines.

"Do you have a plan yet?" Jamie asked after dinner. He shrugged. He had a rough idea, but only just. Locating the beasts was first and foremost on his mind.

"Once we are in the range, I am sure we will spot the dragons flying overhead. After that, we can follow their flight patterns and track them back to their lair. I'm still working out the rest." Jamie looked skeptical. "You got anything better, lad?" It was a rhetorical question, and Jamie shook his head, so he continued, "I am familiar with the lower parts of the range. I used to hunt there for my family. I can take us in far as I remember, but the paths run out before long. After that, we'll be forgin' new ones."

"I am sorry about your family, Mikkin," Tynen said. "It's a terrible thing to lose the ones we love. I still have my wife and son at least." Tynen made eye contact with him and the hint was not overlooked.

"I will watch out for him, Tynen. You have my word."

Tynen gave him a curt nod.

It was past dark now, and the stars twinkled brightly above them. Jamie began humming. It was a tune he recognized. One that wasn't often sung, since it was more of a soldier's song. Even still, he invited the lad to sing aloud. After the first stanza, he and Tynen both joined in. Their voices melded together in unison:

O'er the mountains do we march—
O'er the mountains high.
O'er the mountains to battle gods,
To battle kings, to battle warriors.
O'er the rivers do we march—
O'er the rivers deep.
O'er the rivers to battle gods,
To battle kings, to battle warriors.
Bring your sword and shield and knife.
Bring your courage, honor, life.
To battle gods,
To battle kings, to battle warriors.
O'er the realm do we march—
O'er the realm so vast.
O'er the realm to battle gods,
To battle kings, to battle warriors...

He thought the lyrics were appropriate, given the journey they had ahead, except it would not be kings or warriors they battled, but dragons. "It is getting late. We should rest," he told the other two, so they spread their blankets around the fire and slept.

For Mikkin, it was a restless sleep. He could not escape the confines of his nightmares. He always saw Mardra's face, followed by Devden and Thomas. They burned in flames hot enough to melt stone. He often awoke drenched in sweat, burning up as if he had just come from the fire. That night, the scent was so strong in his nostrils, he retched into the grass before drifting off once more.

The sun rose early and so did they. The dead embers of the fire were left to smolder; they would soon be extinguished. Breakfast, which consisted of more bread and dried meat, was eaten quickly and in silence. Tynen's anxiety for his son's departure was evident, but he bore his worry quietly.

When they finished, they packed what little they had. It was important that they make haste and take advantage of the coolest part of the day. So, Tynen rounded up the horses and bid them farewell, heading south.

Mikkin and Jamie began their journey north on foot. It felt unbearably slow compared to the fast pace of horseback. Still, he was glad to be on his own two feet again.

Onward they trekked into the Northern Barrier Range. The farther they walked the steeper the terrain became. They were soon in the foothills, but they had some way ahead before gaining significant elevation. As they walked, Jamie hummed the same tune from the night previous. This time he did not join in. He saved his breath. They would tire soon enough.

By midday, the sun was scorching. There was no shelter on the knolls. Even these were becoming too steep to climb, so they stuck to the gorges between. He was eager for the shade of mountain trees, and they were close. At their rate, they would reach the great pine forests by nightfall.

When the sound of running water met his ears, he declared it high time for an afternoon respite. To his pleasure, they located a nearby creek, possibly the same that they'd camped upon the night before. Filling their water skins, they drank deeply. To ease his skin of the blistering heat, he splashed water upon his face and neck, but it was no use. At last, he resorted to plunging his entire head into the icy depths.

"It's too damned hot to travel under this blazing sun," he told Jamie. "We can continue on in a short while." They sat and snacked on some of the dried meat.

As they rested, the sound of a breaking twig captured his attention. He swiftly held a finger to his lips, signaling silence, then he tiptoed over to the side of the creek where the noise had emanated. A large cottontail was on the banks near the water, foraging through the grass. Reaching for the bow on his back and nocking an arrow, he calmly pulled the bowstring taught. There was no hesitation before he released. The arrow struck true. The creature was dead instantly. He turned to smile at Jamie. They would eat fresh meat tonight and save the dried meat for later.

By nightfall they were at last under the shelter of the great pine forest. The evergreens were fragrant, reminding him of the many nights spent hunting. Despite these memories of happier times, sadness came, too. No matter what he did, he was constantly plagued by his loss. Gods, was it torture! It was Mardra he missed the most. Her red hair. Her freckles. Her soft touch. He pushed the recollections out of his mind.

The spit they constructed was crude. He turned it carefully so that both sides of the meat cooked evenly. A wonderful scent permeated the air as the cottontail cooked. His gnawing appetite was overwhelming. He knew Jamie was hungry too. The lad hadn't taken his eyes off the prize.

When it finished, he divided up the portions equally. They both scarfed down the majority of the meat, leaving only a little for breakfast. The leftovers were wrapped up in cloth for the next day. As they watched the fire, they sat silently. Neither had the energy to talk.

The next morning, Mikkin woke early. Jamie was still asleep next to him. His quiet snores were just enough to breach the silence. Something about the noiseless forest did not sit well with him. He sat up, straining his ears for sounds of anything abnormal. He heard nothing, and that disturbed him. There ought to be birds chirping and bugs buzzing.

He remained motionless, listening, and sat that way for several long minutes before he heard them—faint voices somewhere not far off in the distance. They sounded low and harsh, but familiar. He'd heard voices like these once before. The back of his neck prickled and a cold sweat broke out over him.

There was only one explanation. Goblins. He laid frozen a moment longer, too surprised to move.

Goblins were nasty little creatures, and he had no idea how many there might be. He reached over and shook Jamie awake, putting a finger to his lips. Jamie understood, his eyes wide with alarm. He picked up the bow and quiver, motioning for Jamie to follow him. Together, the two of them crept through the trees towards the harsh, guttural sounds.

They dodged behind the large pine trunks as they went, both in sync with each other's movements. When they were close enough, he signaled Jamie to stay put. Peering around the tree that hid him, he looked towards the source. It was goblins—three of them. The little creatures sat around a campfire, cooking breakfast. They were excited about something. Their ugly, stunted green bodies were alight with movement. They talked, wildly moving their hands and waving their arms. Mikkin exhaled quietly. What luck! The goblins had been right under their very noses. Had the creatures made their camp just a little closer, they would have discovered Mikkin and Jamie fast asleep.

They had a choice. Either they could creep away silently, or they could fight the goblins to the death. In the case of the latter, they were outnumbered, and the feat would be a tricky one. He liked the first option better. Making eye contact with Jamie, he motioned for them to return back the way they had come. He was just about to take a step forward when the voices stopped. The forest fell silent. Both Jamie and Mikkin froze.

Goblins were known for their keen sense of smell. This morning the wind was not in their favor. It blew their scent towards the creatures. He silently cursed. There was only one thing he could do now. Quietly, he reached over his shoulder for an arrow. With deft movements, he loaded it, keeping his body still, holding his breath tightly in his chest.

One goblin grunted something in its harsh tongue. Another responded. He dared not peek around the tree now, but he did not need to. Already, he could hear them coming to their feet. The moment they stood, leaves and twigs crackled.

Taking advantage of the distance and the element of surprise, he jumped around the tree, letting loose an arrow straight towards them. It hit the nearest goblin square between the eyes. Behind him, Jamie gasped. The other two goblins stood blinking, processing what had just happened. Then they charged.

"Run!" he shouted. He was already reaching for another arrow. He released it right as the two goblins closed in on him. They were no more than a few arm spans away. His second arrow struck true, right in the goblin's neck. It went in the front and out the back and remained stuck there. He did not have time to watch the creature fall.

Jamie had already fled. He did the same. The third goblin gave chase. Outrunning it would have been stupid. They were wicked fast. So as he ran, he grabbed another arrow from the quiver on his back.

It was imperative that his motions be quick. The goblin was too close and there was no time to use the bow. He positioned the arrow pointing outward then immediately stopped dead in his tracks, spinning around to face it. The goblin did not expect this. It crashed right into him, its head colliding with his chest. The arrow plunged directly onto it.

The blow was not lethal, but it was enough to severely wound it. The creature howled in pain, shouting what he assumed were profanities. It tried to grab hold of him. He attempted to move away from it, but the goblin latched on to his clothing and pulled him backwards. Spinning around, he felt his tunic stretch and twist.

Its grasp was strong. He gave it a hard kick in the groin. This momentary distraction allowed him to reach for another arrow. Once again, the creature hollered and yowled. He took the arrow and plunged it into its eye. The action elicited another scream of pain.

The little wretch tried to grope for him, wildly moving its arms about, but missed by several yards. He reached for one final arrow, nocked it, and let it fly. The point struck the goblin in the forehead, sending the creature to the ground. It was dead, though its feet twitched several times before falling still.

Putting his hands on his knees, he took several large gulps of air. It took a moment for his astonishment to set in. Never once had he killed a goblin, and certainly not three. It felt good. *Too* good.

"Mikkin!" Jamie's call rang through the forest. He silently

swore. Blasted boy! The last thing they needed was to draw more attention. Then again, the goblins had already done that for him.

"I'm here," he called back in a much quieter voice. He was still breathless.

Jamie appeared a few minutes later. He looked from Mikkin to the dead goblin at his feet. His eyes were wide. "You...you killed them? All of them?"

He nodded, standing up straight, stretching his arms and shoulders.

"Are you all right?" the lad asked.

"I'm fine. A little winded, to be sure." With his foot, he kicked the goblin over so that it was face up. Gods! What an unpleasant little thing. It looked as though it had never seen a bath, or water, for that matter. He examined its clothing. There was a pouch tied about its waist, and a small knife latched to its belt.

Though goblins had an excellent sense of smell and could not be outrun, they were dull as rocks and had terrible eyesight. They were also smelly. This one reeked of rotten fish. He held his breath as he unlatched the knife and the pouch, moving quickly so he could breathe again.

He opened the pouch to find several gold coins and a red ruby. He held it up to the light just to be sure. Goblins were greedy urchins. He handed the contents of the pouch over to Jamie. He had no need for such things. However, his curiosity got the better of him, and he wondered what the other two might possess. Eyeing the arrows that stuck out of the wretch's body, he decided it would be better to keep them. So, once more, he held his breath and moved to retrieve them. They made a squelching sound as they were removed.

"What are you doing?" Jamie sputtered. He finished his task before answering. The sight of the blood and gore covering the arrows made his stomach heave. He did his best to wipe it off on the goblin's clothing.

"These arrows are our only protection right now. We cannot afford to waste them. Unless you want to make more?" Jamie shook his head. "Good, let's find the other two. We also need to search their camp. They may have weapons. Then we need to be on our way."

Together, they reclaimed the other two arrows and discovered more gold coins, along with several gems in the goblins' personal pouches. Then they located the campfire where it all began. They found three traveling packs possessing nothing of interest to either of them—some nasty looking food, or what Mikkin assumed was food, and stinking clothing. The only things of value were their short swords, wide and curved outward at the waist, which the goblins had been too stupid to grab. Mikkin tossed one to Jamie.

The lad looked at it in disgust. "What do I want with a goblin sword?"

Mikkin rolled his eyes. "You are supposed to use it, lad. I doubt these will be the last goblins we happen upon. Besides, goblin steel is hearty. They will serve us well."

They made their way back to their campfire and packed up their belongings. He tied one of the knives to his ankle and tossed another to Jamie, then he wrapped one of the short sword sheaths around his belt and tied the extra one to his pack. He immediately felt safer. He did not know what else they would find lurking in the forest, but he was sure that they would be better prepared for it the next time around.

CHAPTER 26
THE GABLE FOREST

The Gable Forest

Claire sagged with relief the moment they reached the Gable Forest. The trees towered above them like sentinels, their branches stretching up to the sky as if giants themselves praised the heavens. Her heart fluttered as she gazed up with wide eyes. Within just a few seconds, a strong desire to plunge herself into the forest's depths consumed her. Was it her eagerness to be cured of the vodar's poison? To rid herself of the pain? Or was it something else entirely?

Just yesterday, the thought of venturing into the forest, traveling to Esterpine, sounded like the worst possible idea. Absolutely absurd. Cyrus—on behalf of his entire kingdom—had insulted the sprite queen and her people by demanding the stones be returned. It felt almost humiliating to present themselves, on the run with their tails tucked.

But now? Now she wanted nothing more than to venture beneath the green cover that beckoned her. What had changed?

She looked at her companions. Reyr stood to the left of her, carrying Cyrus's shrouded body cradled in his arms. His forehead was furrowed. The same could be said of Koldis and Jovari, who also eyed the forest with an uneasy disquiet. They stood silently, waiting on the brink of the unknown. She shifted her weight, impatient.

"Well, best get it over with," Reyr said, stepping forward.

They followed after him. She did her best to keep up, limping along as spasms of pain shot up her leg. With every step, she felt herself beginning to slow. Her breath began coming in ragged gasps. The pain deepened, especially when her companions increased their pace, all but leaving her behind.

She gritted her teeth. "You three just go on ahead then," she called. "I'll catch up later."

Reyr gathered her meaning and slowed. The others followed suit. "We should keep our voices down," he warned, looking over his shoulder as they stepped into the shadows. Shadows that would stay with them for the entirety of their journey through the trees. "Best we not draw attention to ourselves whilst we are here."

"Who knows what we will find lurking within," Jovari muttered, giving the forest a dark look. Koldis said nothing and merely clenched his jaw.

This was the first time she'd seen them like this. Even when the vodar attacked their camp, they appeared far more sure of themselves. What was so worrisome about a bunch of trees?

There are many things to fear within the forest. It is a hostile place for outsiders.

She snorted, earning a stern look from Reyr. Perhaps her conscience was correct, but her heart disagreed. The forest was nothing more than a forest, after all. Part of her rejoiced to be here.

They soon passed beyond the trunks of the first trees, which were not nearly as thick as those that followed. Each grew larger than its predecessor. At first, the growth around them was sparse, but the density of greenery increased. Within minutes they could no longer see the light from where they had entered, but neither were they in complete darkness. An otherworldly glow permeated their surroundings. It was as if the air itself provided the illumination they needed.

The forest was *very* much alive.

A smile crept across her face. Happy tingles started in her fingertips and toes, before traveling up her arms and legs, until finally, joy reached her heart. What she felt...it was hard to explain. Like she wanted to dance. The nagging pain in her leg was hardly noticeable.

The others didn't share her sentiment. All three displayed tension as it rolled off them in waves. "I don't like this place at all," Jovari muttered not long after entering,

"Only a mad man would," Koldis replied.

She held her tongue.

They walked for what seemed like hours. She was enamored by everything, finding each sight more enchanting than the last. The forest floor was no longer grassy, but covered in a blanket of foliage and moss. Creeping vines ejected from the bushes and shrubbery growing up around their tree hosts. The flora was home to firefly-like bugs, which blinked and flickered, making the undergrowth look possessed.

She gazed up at the vines in wonder, winding around the enormous tree trunks. They were twisted so tightly about their hosts they could be climbed like ladders. But to where? When she craned her neck back, their tendrils vanished, reaching up into the sky.

A little laugh escaped her lips, earning a glare from the others. She felt like Alice in Wonderland after drinking a shrinking potion. It was a different world.

So many sounds met her ears. Although she could not see the source of them, birds chirped, bugs buzzed, and even a faint trickling of water echoed. The cacophony created a lovely backdrop to the fairy-like world she now found herself in. A world she wanted to stay in forever.

"How much longer?" she asked, once her excitement began to wear off. It wasn't that she was impatient, she was merely eager to see Esterpine.

"I do not know," Reyr said. "I thought perhaps we might have arrived by now."

"You don't know?" she asked, eyebrows drawing together. "But don't you know where you're going?" They had been following Reyr the whole time.

"Hardly."

She faltered, turning to Jovari and Koldis. They looked just as lost.

"If you ask me," Koldis said, pointing at a knobby trunk gnarled with age. "I would say we have seen that tree four times already and are simply traveling in circles."

"The rumors of travelers losing themselves in the Gable are well founded." Jovari stopped in his tracks as he spoke. "We should never have come, Reyr."

"What does he mean?" she asked, turning to Reyr.

"The sprites guard their secrets jealously," Reyr said, his voice hushed. "It is said that the Gable Forest is bewitched. The trees themselves have minds of their own." She glanced around at the giants, wondering if it was true. Somehow, the concept wasn't impossible to believe. "The forest moves and reforms to ensnare its victims. *They* made it so outsiders cannot hope to navigate it. Few make it out alive. Those who do are babbling with madness by the time they emerge."

Babbling with madness? The hairs on her arms stood on end and she frowned. "Why did we come here then? Just because of my leg?"

Reyr sighed, his shoulders slumping. "We had to come regardless," he said. "Traveling around the forest would have left us exposed to the vodar. They will not venture into the midst of the forest."

"Well, now we may be lost in here forever," Jovari muttered.

"Cyrus found his way through, didn't—"

"Cyrus sent word to the sprite queen before arriving." Koldis cut her off and she scowled back at him for it. "He was given emissaries to guide him, else he would have been just as lost as we are now."

"Oh...I—" She jumped as a monstrous crash echoed all round them.

"Quick, hide!" Reyr whispered. The others rushed away while she stood frozen, glancing about for the source of the sound. A hand closed around her forearm. Reyr pulled her away. The four of them rushed to a nearby tree, pushing themselves into the vines of its undergrowth. They retreated just in the nick of time.

Thundering through the forest, came something that strangled the air from her lungs. The creature did not notice them as it passed by. She watched it with an open mouth.

The body of this *thing* was tall and tree-like, but it was no tree. It was made entirely of wriggling worm-like tree roots, which snaked down its waist creating the appearance of a skirt clothing its lower half. These roots connected themselves to the ground and seemed to crawl and slither along as it moved. That was why it rumbled. The earth had to break away from the roots as they reattached themselves to new dirt. There were also roots flowing out behind its back and head like streamers on a kite. These fluttered around too, looking for somewhere to attach.

Within its hands, it held glowing green orbs that threw off illumination identical to what filled the world around them. This glow sparked and flickered like fire. The being carried the substance with care, like a gardener carries its little plant-lings, devoting its focus to the task at hand.

"What is it?" she whispered with awe. The others were silent for a time. At last Reyr answered. "I have heard stories of the root men. I never imagined them to exist."

"*Root* men?"

"Aye. They tend to the forest. Very little is known about them. And that is not their true name either, but I do not know the spriten name for them."

"Simeik..." she whispered and then frowned.

"What did you say?" Reyr turned to her, his brows drawn.

"I...I don't know." And in truth, she didn't. She could not have repeated the word had she tried. It fled her memory as quickly as it had come, leaving her increasingly afraid of herself.

Their focus returned to the strange spectacle before them. At last, the root man's clamor retreated into the distance, and all the normal sounds of the forest returned. Only then did they climb from their hiding place.

"We should turn back," Koldis said.

"No. We must go forward." Reyr maintained his stance. Going through the forest was the only way for them to proceed. The three of them began arguing.

She stepped forward, clearing her throat. "We should go this way," she said, pointing. They stared at her. "What? I think I know the way. It's through those trees there." A pair of large trunks to her left looked particularly inviting.

Her companions frowned.

"She will get us more lost than you have, Reyr," Koldis grumbled.

"Just...trust me, okay?" She was feeling more confident by the moment. "I know you have little trust to give someone like me, but I'll get us there, I promise. The forest doesn't scare me like it does you. That clouds your ability to find the way. I know the way. It's just through there." She pointed again in the same direction, this time, more certain that she was right.

"You are not simply saying this?" Reyr asked.

"No. This is the way."

"Very well. We will follow you."

She quickly hid her surprise. Jovari and Koldis looked furious, but they knew better than to continue the argument. She was determined to prove them wrong. Taking a deep breath and trusting her instincts, she began limping her way to where she believed Esterpine was. The other three followed.

She let the sounds of the forest guide her, doing her best to connect with her surroundings. Sometimes she allowed her fingertips to graze the bark of a nearby tree or caress the dangling vines that hung about them like veils. Reyr had been correct. There was a sentient awareness in everything she touched, as if every growing thing in the forest had a mind of its own. When she quieted her own mind just enough, she almost heard them whispering to her.

The idea was insane, and most times her eyes flew open so that she could laugh at the absurdity of it. These plants didn't possess intelligence, did they? It was silly.

But...why, then, was she finding her way?

Not long after they set out, she noticed that her feet had discovered a well-worn foot path. Just to make a point, she turned back to her companions and lifted her eyebrows. Reyr merely shrugged. The other two ignored her completely.

She continued upon this path, following it as it twisted and wound its way through the forest. Soon after, chills raced across her skin. She felt the creeping sensation of being watched. Although she tried, she could not find the source of this scrutiny. She pressed on, and the further they went, the more she saw signs of civilization.

Perhaps the others had not noticed, but she had. There were well-disguised statues covered in ivy placed throughout the eucalyptus, oak, and sycamore trees that grew in this part of the forest. Each was posing, but they all pointed in the direction she was heading, as if leading her where she needed to go. She took this as a good sign.

Then, she saw something that stole her breath and filled her heart with wonder. A massive gate structure jutted out of the earth, rising above her. She stopped dead in her tracks. Jovari, Koldis, and Reyr collided with her back.

It was unlike anything she had ever seen. Aside from its sheer size towering over them like a giant sequoia tree, it was made entirely of roots, branches, and leaves. The posts were the trees, each manicured and grown to the same cylindrical diameter, stretching up into the ceiling of the forest. And in between these posts, elaborate roots grew, grafted in spiraled patterns. Some were shaped into strange, geometric symbols.

In the middle was a vast doorway. Two trees were bent together at their tops to form a perfectly symmetrical arched curve. Above this, the posts mimicked the same arched pattern jutting straight up, allowing their tops to bow and take form. In between, roots filled in the empty spaces with more elaborate configurations.

Everywhere around them the scent of pine filled the air, reminding her of Christmas. This was it. This was Esterpine. They had finally made it.

It felt like coming home.

CHAPTER 27

QUEEN JADE

Esterpine

Claire trailed behind an envoy sent to escort them into the city. He had appeared shortly after their arrival at the large entry, startling them all as they gazed upwards.

"The queen bids you welcome," he'd announced, making them jump backwards. It was unclear how long he'd stood there watching them, waiting to be noticed.

He was not at all what she had expected. His midnight blue hair was pulled back into a ponytail at the base of his neck. He wore nothing but a loin cloth and a sword, displaying luminescent markings that swirled and twisted across his pale skin. These elegant tattoos arranged themselves in all sorts of patterns, some similar to what she had seen across the walls of the gated doorway. A few crept up to his face, which was angularly shaped, framing two almond-shaped eyes, one blue and one green. The same shade of green as her own.

"My queen is most eager to meet you," he'd said, looking directly at Claire. "Come, I am to bring you to her." She had quickly closed her mouth and quit her gawking. "This way," he added.

Jovari, Koldis, and Reyr said nothing as they followed behind her. She merely gave them a quick backward glance to ensure that they were keeping up, before returning her focus to the curiosities of the forest sprite.

As he led them, she continued to watch him. It was a trial keeping her eyes where they belonged. He was far taller than was normal for a human, and he moved with effortless grace as his feet found all the correct places to step. Not a single sound came from his motions. Her companions, on the other hand, were louder. The dead foliage beneath their feet crunched noisily.

The forest whispered around her, sending comforting thoughts. Her eyes briefly closed and reopened, expecting to see nothing more than cornfields, but the sprite was still there, leading the way. This was all real.

It was difficult to fathom. Things like this simply didn't happen. It was like she'd fallen asleep reading one of her fantasy books and woken up inside the pages.

When she'd seen Cyrus fall from the sky, she'd hardly believed it. Dragons? Impossible! But this? This forest was beyond comprehension. The sprites who lived here were merely an extension of the vast ecosystem. Nothing was clearer as she watched her guide's markings pulse and glow brighter with each tree he recognized and every flower that greeted him.

She increased the pace of her limp, ignoring the fresh wave of pain, and caught up with him. More sprites were beginning to appear. Each was similar to the one leading them, but subtle differences were obvious. Few of them had blue hair, for instance. Yet they all had markings.

"Are your tattoos real?" The words tumbled out of her mouth before she could stop herself. What she really meant was, did he put them on his body, or were they something he was born with.

"My tattoos?" His voice was rich and musical. There was a hint of playful amusement.

"I mean...your markings," she said. More and more sprites could be seen wondering the forest paths now. They all stopped to stare at the strangers moving through their midst.

"My markings are as real as the eyes I see with, or the feet I walk on." She frowned. He noticed and added, "They are my identity. Evidence of what I am. I am a sprite of the forest. All sprites bear their identities proudly."

"How do you get them to glow like that?"

"They glow of their own accord."

He seemed fond of short answers, and reluctant to give even that. So she slowed her pace and fell behind, gazing once more upon her surroundings. Only then did she notice the little houses that had materialized. These weren't normal, nor were they like the earthen cottages one might expect in a forest. They were adaptations to the world in which the sprites lived.

The trees in this part of the woodland had grown monstrous, their ominous branches cascading up towards the roof of the forest, covered with thick layers of moss. The root systems beneath were so huge, they lifted the trunks high off the ground like stilts. Glass dwellings had been built beneath them, the sheets of which were shaped to fill in the empty spaces between the roots, almost like soap bubbles. Each tree looked as though it had a glittering tree skirt.

Within, there were many common household items like tables, chairs, and book shelves. Uncommon were the hanging decorations from the root ceilings. Gemstones and crystals the size of baseballs dangled on vines in various shapes and colors, glowing and glittering like ornaments.

Distracted, she didn't immediately notice the spiraling staircases carved into the sides of the trees. These twisted around and around until they were lost in the floating mist above. Where did they go? What lay at the end of each one?

More and more glass houses sprang into existence until the whole of Esterpine materialized before them. She could hear her companions whispering loudly behind her. Perhaps they were as beguiled as she was. Although, from the tone of their lowered voices, it sounded as if they weren't eager to be here. She, on the other hand, *loved* this place.

The city was full of sparkle. Glowing orbs decorated the world around them. Some were recessed into the knots of grizzled trees, others hung from poles along the walkways like lanterns. Some even floated without assistance, defying the laws of gravity. Most were yellow, but a few took on other colors like pink, blue, purple, and green.

Utterly magical.

Sprites emerged from their glittering homes to point and whisper. How often did strangers find themselves here? Given their reactions, it was rare.

Nearly every sprite had the same kind of markings but in different patterns. However, she was shocked when she saw their children. There weren't many, but these youngsters had no markings at all! They looked...*nearly* human, with the exception of their angular features and otherworldly beauty.

She tried not to gawk. Something stepped out in front of her path. She sputtered and stopped dead in her tracks. "A unicorn?!" she breathed, delighted.

The majestic animal wandered freely across the narrow dirt pathway. Its silky white coat shimmered like a pearl as it caught the light. Flowing behind it, its pure white mane fluttered in the gentle breeze.

"Amazing," she whispered. Perhaps it heard her, or maybe it sensed her amazement, because it stopped and turned its head to look at her. For a brief instant, their gazes locked. She felt as though she were floating on air.

Without thinking better of it, she reached a hand out to invite the unicorn over, silently begging it to come, hoping that it would. It did. It trotted right over and placed its nose against her open palm, nuzzling her gently. The velvety fuzz on its skin was softer than any horse.

The exchange was brief, merely meant as a welcome. Before she knew it, the creature was trotting off into the forest mist. She watched it go, sad to see it leave. A moment later, she felt a gentle nudge from behind as Reyr reminded her that they were supposed to be following their guide.

"Just this way," the sprite said.

They rounded a bend in the path and she gasped. A giant glass castle came into view, dominating city's center. Until now, she had been too preoccupied to give the queen of Esterpine any thought. Anxious butterflies took flight in her stomach.

What would she be like? Would she know that Claire had the dragonstones? She regretted not asking Cyrus more about her.

They made their way up a large set of crystalline stairs. As she gained height, she looked beneath and saw all the way to the bottom. Her stomach jolted. The entire hall was that way, completely transparent. Were it not for the rainbows glistening upon the surface, she would have appeared to float in midair. The idea was unsettling.

They were taken into the queen's great hall without ceremony. Before she could absorb her surroundings, her eyes fell upon a woman with the blackest hair she had ever seen, braided elegantly as it fell down her front. It was as though her plait had swallowed up all the light to obtain such a shade. For all that it was lacking, the rest of her radiated light in waves. Her clothing was made of a shimmery translucent cloth that did very little beyond hiding her feminine parts. Like the others, shimmering markings flowed across her skin. She possessed far more than most of her people. Perhaps they were a symbol of one's magical ability, and the queen held the most.

"Welcome to the crystal palace." Her voice was pure like the sound of a singing wine glass. She stood from her throne and descended the stairs of her dais. Her gaze remained fixed on Claire's. The throne room was silent. Not even the queen's feet made a sound as her bare soles struck the floor. "You are the first outsiders to stumble successfully upon our hidden kingdom. I am both shocked and impressed. Tell me, how did you manage it?" It was clear that her question was directed at Claire.

"I..." She swallowed. "I followed my heart, Your Majesty." Her words felt clumsy and unconfident.

The woman smiled, pleased. "It is no small accomplishment. The magic of the forest ensures that no outsider will find his or her way through. To this day, no outsider ever has, nor will they ever, until the end of time. Welcome, Claire," she said, opening her arms wide, "to the city of Esterpine. I am Queen Jade."

Claire closed her mouth. The queen knew her name! There was no time to question it.

"Now, we have pressing matters to discuss." The queen lifted her gaze and descended the remaining steps, stopping before Cyrus's shrouded body, now laying at the foot of the dais. "I am saddened by the circumstances that bring you to my kingdom. Tell me, Lord Reyr of golden scale, what dangers have befallen your brother shield? He left us months ago, very much alive. I warned him, but he did not listen, to his own demise."

Claire frowned. Months? He'd only been with her a week. Did time move differently in this world?

Reyr may have been surprised, but he hid it well, taking a step forward. "We know little of the events leading to his downfall, Your Majesty. Poison was involved. The vodar dealt Claire a similar wound, but Koldis was able to address it quickly. His timeliness saved her life."

From the corner of her eye, she saw Koldis stand a bit taller.

"And the stones?" the queen asked.

"I believe that his killer stole the them before we arrived." Reyr hung his head in shame.

Reyr felt responsible for this failure. Guilt bubbled up inside of her. She wished that she could tell him the truth, that it wasn't his fault.

"So it is true? The stones are gone?" The queen lifted her dark eyebrows. The others shifted on their feet but said nothing. She sighed and said, "Then it is as I feared."

Claire frowned. The queen's words did not accurately fit her tone. She should have sounded worried, disappointed.

"And what role did *you* play in this, Claire Evans?"

"Uhm." Her face heated. "I didn't kill him—"

Reyr stepped forward. "An important role, Your Majesty. Unfortunately for us, she has made an unbreakable promise. We will not know her true involvement until she speaks to King Talon."

"An unbreakable promise, you say? It is not *sprite* magic."

"Aye. Asarlaí magic."

"Deceitful magic, you mean?" Reyr swallowed, then nodded. "Very well." Her regard fell once more on Claire. Without looking away, she ordered the others out. "I wish to speak with her alone. Oh, and while you are here, we will see to your needs. You may stay and rest as long as you wish. Consider it a reward for discovering our city."

Her companions left, and she found herself alone with the mysterious queen, whose dark blue eyes bored into hers as if the woman were discerning the very secrets of her soul. "Humans are terribly easy to read," she said at last. "But you are no human, are you?"

Claire gave a brief shake of her head. It would be pointless to lie.

"If you were, the poison of a vodar blade would have killed you instantly. However, I can read you for other reasons." She hesitated, studying Claire's face. A deep, uneasy frown settled upon the queen's features. "Yes, I know you now. I have sensed your depths and come to a startling conclusion. Yours is a difficult path ahead, full of twists and turns. Someday you will learn the truth of who you are and what you are capable of."

The queen's words frightened her. "Who..." She tried to speak, but her voice was a weak whisper. "Who am I?"

"That road of self-discovery lies within your *own* heart. I cannot take it from you, nor can I make it for you."

"But, I can't figure it out. I've already tried. What's happening to me?" Surely the sprite queen would have answers.

"Many things, Claire. Many things are happening to you. You must remember, it is only through great struggle and strife that we become who we are truly meant to be. All great destinies are born that way. I believe your role in the days to come will be more important than any of ours." The queen smiled, as if making some secret realization.

Claire merely frowned, noting that the queen's advice wasn't the least bit helpful.

"I admit, finding one's self is no easy task. The difficult roads you must face will leave you stumbling and perhaps, at times, hopeless." Her voice grew soft and comforting. "In that darkness, you will face your worst enemies, but you will also learn to recognize your true friends. If you choose correctly and do what is right, you will come to learn your strengths."

"Do what is right?" Claire repeated. "How am I supposed to know what is right?"

"When you face difficult decisions, just know this, the easy choice is rarely the correct one. You will know—if it hurts—you will know."

Claire opened her mouth but didn't know what to say, so she closed it again.

Trust her words. She is wise.

"You must promise me one thing here and now," the queen said as their conversation came to a close. "Promise me that you will protect the dragonstones to the end of your very being."

Her eyes grew wide. She knew! The queen knew! Was this one of the many secrets she had seen within her?

"I will protect them. I have no choice. I must."

The queen nodded, satisfied. "Come now, that wound needs tending to. My singers will heal it, but it will never be fully sound. The discomfort will depart, but you will never forget that the remnants are there. Can you accept that?"

She nodded, eager to be rid of the nagging pain shooting up her calf.

Queen Jade led her from the glass palace, summoning her healers as they went. They walked for some time in silence. As they went, she tried to process all that the queen had told her, but her sleepy brain made little sense of any of it.

At last, she was brought to one of the beautiful glass houses they had passed coming into the City. "You will reside here while in Esterpine. Your drengr companions have been given similar accommodations, and you may find them when you are well again." As if on cue, others arrived to tend to her needs and prepare her for the healing process, laying her gently upon the dwelling's feathered bed.

Already, her attendants were humming a comforting tune, allowing their soft voices to meld together in song. It was beautiful, and she thought that if she listened closely, she could just discern the meanings of the foreign words upon their tongues. Her eyes grew heavy and her body, desperate for sleep.

"Here is where I leave you now, Claire. Just know," Queen Jade added, hesitating, "you are always welcome here in Esterpine. So long as you can find it, the city will welcome you with open arms."

It was the last thing she remembered before her induced slumber took her.

Esterpine

Reyr kept watch over Claire's sleeping figure from his chair in the corner, careful not to disturb her. Her chest gently rose and fell, but her sleep was fitful. Her eyes twitched beneath their lids and her body fidgeted.

She had surprised him at every turn. When he'd first beheld her, she'd brought emotions to his surface that had long since been buried—feelings that were better left unacknowledged. She reminded him so much of Gemma. Beloved Gemma. Nearly two hundred years had passed since her death.

Claire would complicate his life. Somehow he knew this within an instant of meeting her. In those first few minutes, standing over Cyrus's corpse, he'd wanted so badly for her to be guilty. In truth, he'd needed her to be. Having a culprit—someone to blame for Cyrus's death and the torment it brought—would have made things *much* easier.

Deep in his heart he understood that she was no killer, though he did not trust her, not at all. She showed no obvious signs of magic, but that meant little. A good pretender could do the same.

Claire stirred, bringing him from his thoughts. Her body

regained consciousness as her eyelids fluttered. Her eyes opened. He gave her time to lay there, staring blankly at the ceiling ornaments, while he silently informed Jovari and Koldis of her condition.

As if on cue, her head snapped in his direction. "Reyr?" she croaked.

He stood and moved over to her bedside. "How are you feeling?"

"Better than I can remember in...in a long time." She smiled, looking at the ornaments above her. A strange look passed over her expression. "This journey has been harder than I imagined. How stupid of me to think it would be easy," she scoffed, lowering her voice. "Perhaps we can stay here a while and rest?"

The gods knew he could use some rest, but Claire's healing had already slowed their progress. The forest was safer, to be sure. The vodar would not *dare* venture into the kingdom of the sprites, but they needed to be on their way.

When he did not answer, Claire's face fell. "Well, it was worth a try. How long have I been asleep?"

"Since the night before last." It was late afternoon. She had slept two full days. "We must depart at first light in the morning. Come, get yourself dressed. Supper will be soon, and we have been invited to dine with the sprites in their city center."

"Good!" she said, jumping to her feet with renewed excitement. "I'm starving!"

He was, too, but not for anything that the sprites might serve them. Allowing her privacy, he left the room.

When she emerged, he could not help his lingering eyes. She looked stunning—a stark contrast to the weeping girl he'd found in the other world. Far more like a woman.

The sprites had given her a shimmery silver gown. It was less revealing than what Queen Jade wore, but beautiful all the same. It left her arms bare and fell to her ankles. A silvery cape of a slightly different shade and cloth clasped around her neck. The ensemble brought out the golden color of her hair and green of her eyes.

She caught him staring and her cheeks flushed.

"Forgive me," he said. "I did not expect to see you clad in their garb."

Her smile was shy. "Neither did I, but someone must have left it for me. It's lovely, isn't it?" She gazed down at the fabric to study it.

"Aye. It is." Her stomach growled loudly and he smiled. Stepping aside, he held out his arm, motioning her forward. Part of him felt inclined to offer his elbow, like he would for any lady, but he refrained. They walked side by side down the city's main path.

Having dined alone in his accommodations since their arrival, he learned earlier that day that many of the sprites gathered for the evening meal in a vast, outdoor dining area. The ceiling of the city center consisted of vine arches laden with flowers. The heady floral scents mixed with the ever-present pine. Though he was reluctant to admit how much he enjoyed it, he found the smell relaxing.

When they arrived, he did not miss Claire's sharp gasp. Most of the seats were filled with hungry sprites. He found Jovari and Koldis sitting at a long table nearby. They, too, spent more time than was necessary gazing at Claire's clothing. Strangely enough, he disliked the attention she received and a rush of protectiveness stole over him.

They sat down to eat.

Claire said very little. None of them were in any mood to converse, though the sprites sitting with them did trade bits of news. Except for Claire, who did not mind the table's presentation, they ate very little. Sprite food was just as poor as the reputation that preceded it. He was a drengr and meat was his sustenance—preferably raw and freshly killed.

At the end of their meal, their guide with the blue hair stopped by their table. "If it would please the Lady Claire," he announced, his gaze settling on her. "My mother has suggested that I take you up into the treetops. Your companions are welcome to join us, if they desire."

Claire appeared confused. "Your...your mother?"

"Ah. Yes. My mother. Forgive me for not introducing myself before. I am Prince Feowen." The prince bowed deeply, keeping his gaze upon hers. Claire's eyes grew wide with understanding and her mouth shaped into an *oh*.

His stomach tumbled, watching the interaction. Watching the way another male made her face light up. What was *wrong* with him?

Claire glanced from the prince to Reyr. He nodded. "You may go, if you wish." Then, turning to the prince, he said, "We would also like to join you. I've always longed to see the forest in its entirety." He understood that the honor was not often given to outsiders. It surprised him that Queen Jade had extended it to Claire. Then again, her obvious fondness for Claire completely bewildered him. That woman had thousands of years on him. She was wise beyond accounting. If she trusted Claire, surely he should too, but he simply could not bring himself to it.

Prince Feowen led them to a great tree, larger than any surrounding it. Many of them had stairs carved into their sides, spiraling up into the tops of the trees. On and on they climbed, but it was well worth the effort.

The world looked different in the branches of the trees, whimsical and dream-like. Little light bugs fluttered about them like glitter in a sea of blue and green. The breeze sang as it whistled melodies through the leaves. The mist shimmered and shifted around them.

At last, they exited the stairs onto a platform. The prince chose this tree because it stood much taller than those around it. It made for an excellent vantage point.

"This is the highest place in the forest," he explained as they filed out onto the landing. Claire was breathing hard beside him. The climb had left her winded. That didn't stop the awe upon her face.

There were green plumes—treetops—as far as the eye could see, and in every direction. Almost like a lumpy blanket. He saw nothing of the mists below. It was a warm, clear night. If he strained his sight far enough, he could just make out the southern border where the trees ended. They would make their way there tomorrow.

He hadn't realized how much he'd missed the stars. Letting his head fall back, he looked upon the sky. The moon was a small sliver, and the constellations sparkled around it.

"How come we didn't just fly here?" Claire asked, drawing his attention. "Couldn't we have just flown to this landing and taken the stairs instead of getting lost in the trees?"

He opened his mouth—

"Dragons cannot fly over our forests, Lady Claire," Prince Feowen explained. "We have made it so."

"What do you mean?" she asked, frowning.

"The magic placed upon the trees extends up into the sky. You may not see it, but the barrier exists. Any creature of magic or not, be it dragon, drengr, bird, or otherwise, would merely slam into an invisible wall. Consider it one of our best safety precautions, aside from the maze we have created within."

"Oh…" She fell silent. "So you really *did* make it impossible for people to find Esterpine?"

"No, not impossible for *everyone*. Those of spriten blood have no problem finding home."

Reyr did not miss the peculiar look Feowen gave her, as if he was hinting at something. It left his mind spinning. Queen Jade had said much the same two nights before. Claire's ability to locate the city was unexpected. Even the queen was surprised by it.

The unlikely theory that Claire might have sprite blood crossed his mind, but he discarded it almost as quickly. It was impossible, completely absurd to presume that a human from beyond the gate —a world that was supposed to have nothing *but* humans—could have anything other than human blood. The sprites were not human. They had markings to prove it.

Claire was human. She had to be. Still, a little voice in the back of his mind nagged at him. Why then did she live through the vodar's poison?

He slept little that night, unable to get his mind off the same repetitive question. Who was she, really? Part of him believed that if he spent a few more minutes pondering it, the answer might come. The other part of him grew frustrated.

Queries like these forced him to unnecessarily dwell on her. It was dangerous, because it compelled him to admit how different she was—how much she stood out. Spirited, strong of heart, and stubborn to the core, she was unlike most of the women he knew, except perhaps Saffra.

Not only that, but she was bold, cheeky. The King's Shields were elite. She cared little for their titles and spoke to them however she pleased. He admired that about her. It's what set her apart. Most would be cowering in her shoes, which led him to wonder, where did she derive her strength? And just like that, he found himself back at the same question about her identity. Groaning, he flopped over to his other side and forced his mind to go blank. At last, sleep took him.

The following morning he was eager to rise. Apprehension settled upon his shoulders. Once they were free of the trees, he would be able to stretch his mind with the help of Jovari and Koldis, and contact the king. He dreaded this part of the journey. The king's wrath would be absolute. He had failed, and King Talon would not be happy.

Their breakfast was more of the same—fruits, bread, roots, leafy greens, and nuts. The stewed bark broth was the worst. No amount of spices could possibly make it drinkable. And he could not help but glare at Claire as she willingly devoured everything placed in front of her.

"It's almost like tea, isn't it?" she said as she sipped from her steaming cup. "I love it already."

"It is almost like garbage, if that is what you mean," Koldis muttered from across the table, glaring at her. Claire blatantly ignored him.

He shuffled around on his cushion and tossed a handful of nuts into his mouth. The sooner they departed, the sooner he could rid himself of these trees and go hunting. Perhaps they might find some grazers outside the forest—

"Please tell me we can leave Claire and go hunting once we make it out of here," Jovari begged, all but reading his mind. *"If I do not get meat soon, you will find me to be a real grouch."*

"As if you aren't already?" he teased.

They departed Esterpine shortly thereafter. Claire was the only one reluctant to go. The expression on her face made it look as if this *pained* her. Once more, his absurd thoughts nagged at him.

After hours of endless walking, their guide bid them farewell. Reyr could not help the sigh of relief that tumbled from his lips. They came out on the south-western part of the forest, ideally located for his quick trip to the western coast. He owed his brother Davi a visit. Mikkin's outlandish tale of wild dragons required the fort leader's attention.

"We will rest here for a few minutes," he announced, setting his rucksack on the ground and taking a seat. They would hunt before departing. Jovari and Koldis already knew of his plans to go west and rejoin them two days thereafter. They had discussed this in some detail while Claire was with the sprite's healers. Fort Squall would be little over a day's flight from where they emerged, and he could easily make up time on the flight back if the wind ruled in his favor. But first things first—the king.

Claire wandered a short distance away, but he paid her little mind. His focus was on his two companions. *"Are you ready?"* he asked. Judging by their silence, their hard expressions, they were as eager as he. Which was to say, not at all. *"Very well then."*

Together, the three of them allowed their minds to meet and meld, becoming a force of strength as they pushed their thoughts forward. Like searching tendrils, they stretched their consciousness out over the plains of Eigaden, southward, going farther and farther, until at last, they reached Kastali Dun.

"Explain yourselves!" The king's voice boomed in their minds the second they reached him. His paired emotions were like a thundering avalanche. *"Better yet, explain why you have brought a murderous witch into our kingdom."*

"Your Grace, my apolo—"

"You should have killed her! Have you any idea what problems this has created? Gods above!"

"Please, Your Grace. I do not think Claire killed Cyrus. She—"

"You dare exonerate her? I am disappointed in you, Reyr."

"*Your Grace...*" He felt the king's emotion disappear. "*Your Grace?*" He reached out with his consciousness, using Jovari and Koldis to amplify the connection. Except, there was no sign of the king.

"He blocked us," Koldis said out loud, shaking his head. "He *actually* blocked us out."

As if it was surprising.

"Indeed, it seems so." In his anger, King Talon did not so much as allow them to explain. It was rather unfair, after everything. "This is going to be much harder than I anticipated," he said. The others agreed. Confronting the king was going to be an uphill battle. He dreaded it, but what he dreaded more was what might happen to Claire in the process.

CHAPTER 29
THE FLYING PIG

Weldon

Claire held back her tears until they were airborne. She couldn't bear for Jovari and Koldis to see her cry, and she *dearly* needed to cry. Once again, she found herself on Jovari's back with Reyr nothing more than a golden speck on the horizon.

She pawed at her cheeks, wiping away her silent tears as they fell.

How was it possible to hate someone *so much*, when she'd never met them? The king that Cyrus had served, the king he had pledged his life to, should have been honorable and just. Level headed. After all, Dragonwall's shields wouldn't serve a tyrant. And yet...

King Talon's words, his anger, replayed over and over in her mind. He'd called her a *murderous witch*. Was that what he really thought?

She hated how naive she'd been.

After everything Cyrus had told her—all the little snippets about King Talon—she'd failed to learn what he might be like. Now she knew. Never had she been so disillusioned.

If he mistrusted her this much, he'd never agree to speak with her. So much for fulfilling her promise. She'd be lucky if he wasn't waiting in the capital with his sword drawn, ready to lop off her head.

She wiped away more tears.

She'd mistakenly believed that her biggest challenge would be her journey. Flying across a vast stretch of land with little to no creature comforts. She'd been *so* wrong.

Her biggest challenge would be the king, and if he didn't thaw towards her, if he killed her before she could fulfill her promise, his kingdom would fall. She snorted at the thought. Maybe he deserved it. Perhaps a great man like him should be taken down a notch or two. But...what would that accomplish?

Kane had to be stopped. Dragonwall wasn't the only kingdom threatened. Nothing more than a thin veil straddled her world and his. With the gates unprotected, Kane could easily spread his devastation to everyone she loved.

King Talon was her only hope. She *needed* him. She needed his cooperation.

Bring him to the light and he will see reason...

She ground her teeth together. Why did it have to be *her* job to make him see reason? She wasn't anyone special.

Because you made a promise.

She snorted. It wasn't fair that this kind of responsibility had fallen into her lap. She couldn't turn her back even if she tried. The pull from the unbreakable promise was too strong. It wouldn't allow her to walk away.

Promise or not, this is your world too, even if you refuse to admit it.

Of course she refused! It was the most absurd thought—how could she? Still, a part of her ruminated over what Queen Jade and Prince Feowen had said. Their *not so subtle* hints about how only a sprite could find Esterpine, and only a sprite could have made it through the forest without getting lost.

~

Jovari and Koldis flew for hours until the sun was in the middle of the sky. She never knew what time it was anymore. Supposing there was no need, she still disliked the disorientation it caused.

At long last, Koldis broke the silence with something to distract her. *"Weldon is there,"* he said.

"Aye. I see it now," came Jovari's answer.

She squinted south, but her eyes saw nothing more than gently rolling hills scorched from the summer's heat. And then, nestled amongst the knolls, she spotted the first road she had ever seen in Dragonwall. It was hardly discernible at this height, but it was there, twisting and winding its way in the same direction as the *Flat River*, which they had followed south since leaving the forest.

She nearly gasped with excitement when she spotted a horse pulling a cart. It was miniature, barely the size of her fingertip, and moving much slower than Jovari and Koldis. Soon they overtook it. She could have sworn that the little man sitting at the reins looked up and waved hello with his cap.

"I would suggest we give the town a wide berth," Koldis advised. *"But I cannot deny my longing for a drink and a feathered bed."*

"You cannot possibly be serious," Jovari all but snorted. *"Have you seen the way Claire is dressed? You want to parade her through Weldon?"*

She gave an audible *tut* in response. Her companions loved talking about her, especially when they believed she couldn't hear them. And it wasn't like her clothes were *bad,* per se. Sure, she had changed out of her sprite garb and tucked it away, but there wasn't anything wrong with a sturdy pair of jeans, paired with a T-shirt and jacket.

"I am sure she will bring many curious glances, but so too will we. She is not the only one who will stick out. I imagine the people will want to know what brings two of the king's own, and a dead body, into their midst."

"Exactly. Best to avoid such questions," Jovari said.

"Since when have we feared questions? We are the king's drengr. They dare not question us."

She hoped very much that Jovari would agree with Koldis, and almost laughed at herself when she realized it was Koldis she was rooting for.

"*I fear the rumors more than I do the questions,*" Jovari said. "*Besides, since when am I the voice of reason when you are not?*"

"*I suppose there is a first for everything.*"

"*Very well. I take it that you are resolved in this matter?*"

"*Aye. I am resolved. Besides, Reyr is the true voice of reason, and I do not see him here to stop us.*"

"*Well, you are my superior. I dare not argue.*" She didn't mistake the lack of reluctance Jovari showed, as if he too welcomed the idea of food, drink, and a soft bed. Nor did she miss the snort Koldis gave in response.

It was in that moment that Weldon finally rose up before them. Little wisps of smoke twisted up from tiny chimney stacks, and as they grew closer, slowly descending, she began to make out the cottages dotting the landscape below. More horse carts now traversed the road they followed.

Within minutes, they were on the ground. Jovari quickly transformed, explaining their plan while he untied Cyrus's body from Koldis.

"Are you sure that it's wise to show ourselves in the village?" she argued, mimicking Jovari's original sentiments. She too was eager for the same comforts as they were, but...what fun was it hearing their conversation if she couldn't act on it?

"That is for *us* to worry about. Not you." Koldis gave her a stern glance.

"Aren't you concerned about all the questions and rumors our visit will create?"

It was difficult, but she did her best to hold back a wicked grin as Jovari and Koldis shared a knowing look.

"*See?*" Jovari said telepathically, lips pursed. "*I am not the only one thinking reasonably.*"

Koldis glared back in response. "*Quit pointing fingers. Had you thought reasonably, you would have given your complaints a greater effort.*"

Oh, she liked this very much. Pretending she couldn't hear the silent tirade, she shrugged and stirred the pot a little more. "I only brought it up because any *reasonably* thinking person would use caution. I thought perhaps the two of you could benefit from the voice of reason." She felt her nostrils twitch as she said this.

Koldis scowled. "Our actions are not for you to decide or question," he snapped, picking up Cyrus and stalking away towards the dirt road. Her nose was now flaring something terrible, so she quickly turned away from Jovari and followed Koldis. It was all she could do to keep from bursting into laughter. Better that, than the tears that had fallen earlier.

Little farm houses lined the dirt road leading into the village. She took everything in, trying to absorb and memorize each detail. The dwellings were of a similar style, with thatched roofs and multi-paned windows. As they got closer, the cottages grew nicer. Some were two and three stories tall, with stone roofs. They were not quite perfect. She found it comical that some leaned drunkenly to one side or the other as age got the better of them. What she liked most was that many had small fences and pens holding chickens, pigs, grazers, and horses.

All sorts of sounds met her ears, from the children running about making mischief, to the mothers screeching their warnings as they scolded them. There were shouts of advertisement from the merchants in front of them, clip-clops from horse's hooves pulling their carts, and many hushed whispers from those who noticed the passing of two large drengr males carrying a shrouded body, accompanied by a strange girl.

A sentry holding nothing more than a spear stood watch at the wall's stone entry. He said nothing as they approached, merely gazed at them with wide eyes. They passed under the archway and entered Weldon.

The quaint little village was entirely adorable. She smiled wide, trailing behind Jovari and Koldis. The cottages within the walls were nicer. Most of them were touching, with shared walls. Only a difference of paint color and height made each one discernible from the next. Like Tudor style town houses, though not nearly as fancy as the ones she had seen in pictures.

Her foot landed in something soft, accompanied by a squelching sound. She froze, looking down at her hiking boot. It sank into a puddle of muck. "You've got to be kidding me!" she groaned. A gooey mess of mud and…excrement, no doubt. The entire thoroughfare was much the same. She crinkled her nose and continued on, doing her best to dodge the muck.

Jovari and Koldis had failed to see her misfortune, so she set off at a jog to catch them just before they rounded a corner into a nicer part of Weldon. When Jovari did finally notice her, he laughed. "Perhaps watch where you step next time," he said.

She glared at him.

Ignoring them both, Koldis hailed a man passing by. "Tell me, friend, is the mead at the *Drunken Maiden* still as good as it used to be?"

Recognition passed over the man's face and his eyes widened. He bowed deeply. "Begging your pardon, Lord Koldis—"

It surprised her that the man knew Koldis by name. Almost like he was some kind of…celebrity. Maybe that's how the king's shields were viewed.

"—I hate to say it but the *Drunken Maiden* fell under new management. I'd be tryin' the *Flying Pig*, were I you. Up two streets and make a left, if it please ya."

"I see. You are certain?"

"Aye, milord. Best honey mead for a hundred leagues o' here if you must know."

"I highly doubt that," Jovari muttered as Koldis nodded, tossed the man a coin, and sent him on his way.

They continued further down the streets of Weldon. "Did you know that man?" she asked Koldis.

He grunted. "Of course not. Why would you ask?"

"Because he knew your name."

Jovari clucked. "Everyone knows our names, Claire. Best grow accustomed to it."

"Right." She turned her attention back to Weldon. This time, instead of gazing at the buildings, which had grown even taller, she looked at the people passing by. She finally understood why she stood out. She may as well have been at the renaissance fair. All the women were dressed completely old fashioned, just like her companions. Just like Cyrus had been when she found him. She should have guessed it, especially because of what the sprites wore. But seeing this made it real—these people and the way they lived.

She was an outsider in every sense of the word. It didn't help that all the people looking at her whispered and pointed as she passed. Her skin heated and she avoided their eyes.

"They're all talking about me," she muttered so that only Jovari and Koldis would hear her.

"Aye. They are not used to a beautiful maiden such as yourself, gracing their midst," Jovari said.

She snorted, happy to be teased. "You and I both know it's because of how I'm dressed."

"Very well. Believe what you must." Jovari gave her a smirk that looked more like a reluctant smile before turning his gaze forward. It was a rare nice gesture, and somehow, it improved her mood just a little. Moments later, the *Flying Pig* came into view, just in time for her growling stomach to greet it.

Sounds from happy patrons floated towards them through its open door. Her mouth watered instantly when she smelled roasting meat wafting into the street. Jovari and Koldis came to a halt, surveying the entrance.

Koldis shrugged. "Looks reputable enough to me."

"Aye. Shall I buy the first round?"

"Only if I might buy the second," Koldis agreed.

"Together we will drown our sorrows and woes properly."

"Indeed!"

She watched their exchange, hiding a grin. The hope of a hot meal, mead, and a comfortable bed seemed to lighten all their moods.

Turning to her, Koldis motioned with his arm. "Shall we?"

She stepped across the threshold. Her nose was immediately struck by the dank scent of pipe smoke and stale alcohol. This, mixed with the lingering stench of dirty men, quickly stifled her appetite. She'd been in plenty of bars, but this was...altogether different.

The torch-lit room was much darker than outside, and after her eyes adjusted, she noticed that many tables were scattered around. Most were full. The room went quiet as they entered.

"Welcome sirs," came a friendly voice. They turned toward the source. "Beggin' your pardon, miss," the barman added as he spotted her with them. Then his gaze studied her companions a little more closely. "Gods above! I ain't never *ever* be havin' *lords* in my tavern before. Welcome, milords. Welcome! What can I be helpin' ya with?" As he spoke, his eyes finally noticed Koldis's burden. They widened briefly at the sight of the well-disguised body. However, he pretended to ignore what he'd seen. The sprites had done an admirable job with Cyrus, binding him in better cloth than Claire had provided, and masking the stench of his now decaying body using magic. She quickly looked back at the barman, eager to look anywhere other than Cyrus.

Jovari took a step forward. "We require three beds, if you have them, and mead. I hear you have the finest honey mead in the village." It was an admirable subject change, and the man quickly forgot what his gaze had fixated on. Instead, his face lit up from the praise.

"That I do, milords! That I do!" he said. "Come!" He didn't wait for them to follow as he led them up the stairs to his vacant accommodations. Mediocre at best. Certainly not a Hilton. But welcome in lieu of a night spent in the wilderness. "You'll be finding all your needs accounted for here," he assured them. "The chamber pots are under the beds. My maid will see to those in the mornin'. Once you've washed up, come on down for a spot o' supper."

"Many thanks," Jovari said. He removed his coin pouch. The bar man looked greedily at the gold that tumbled onto Jovari's palm, but his honor must have gotten the better of him. "No need for payment, milords. I'll not have it said that I charged the king's own." His expression was genuine as he battled between propriety and his clear desire for payment.

"Nonsense," Jovari insisted. "We will pay for what you provide, and we will pay well."

The man smiled wide. She noticed he was missing several teeth. The rest were blackened and rotting. Aside from perhaps the drengr, who probably had nice teeth simply because of magic, it was clear that some people in Dragonwall hadn't heard of toothpaste, or a toothbrush for that matter. From the stench below, she doubted they even bathed.

Hopefully that was merely a common theme among country folk.

"Very well then, milords," the barman decided. "Very well, indeed. I shan't be refusin' payment if you insist. Bless you. Verek will surely favor thee well for such generosity."

She supposed that Verek was another of their many gods, but she didn't bother asking. Taking Jovari's money, the man shuffled away. She watched his retreat before Koldis spoke, "Well. You both heard the man. Let us stow our burdens, clean ourselves up, and have some supper." With that, he entered his room and shut the door. Jovari did the same, leaving her alone on the landing. She sighed and followed suit.

Supper that evening was unexpectedly eventful. A fiddler heard about their arrival and graced them all with his presence. A number of drunken men performed their own versions of a dance on the tables, having lost all dignity. She couldn't help but laugh as they tripped over their own toes.

Things got especially exciting when a fight broke out on the other side of the room. Many gathered around the spectacle, eagerly making bets. She'd witnessed her fair share of bar fights, but for once she was happy to watch without the responsibility of putting a stop to anything. Funnily enough, it seemed that the barman hadn't a care in the world. Maybe the thrill brought him better business; he didn't bother interfering. It was only when the shorter of the two men was knocked unconscious that the crowd roared and applauded, and the fighting stopped. Satisfied, the larger man moved away and continued his evening as if nothing had happened.

The barmaid was an excellent cook. Claire eagerly scarfed down two bowls of stewed, meaty broth. When the woman emerged from her kitchen and spotted her, she made it a point to come by the table and introduce herself. Friendly as she was, Claire didn't miss the maid's curious eyes as they roved over her appearance, taking in her clothing.

She was almost relieved when the woman finally went back to the kitchen. "You had better get used to it," Koldis whispered, butting her shoulder with his. He was clearly in a good mood. She did her best to keep up with his drinking and Jovari's too, but these were drengr, and after her second tankard, she could already feel a drunken buzz kicking in.

Many people stopped by their table to pay their respects, trading stories and gossip. Much to her surprise, she found her two companions very amicable drunks. They avoided any mention of their true business. It was evident that they were smooth talkers. In fact, much to her relief, it seemed that they held her in higher regard the drunker they got, perhaps forgetting to blame her for what had happened to their beloved friend.

Yet, for all the fun they appeared to be having, she could see in their eyes that they were hurting. In those moments, it hit her hard. She wasn't the only one who'd lost Cyrus. He had been their brother in all but blood. She couldn't begin to imagine how much it must have pained them to lose him.

"How will we go on without him?" Koldis quietly asked, falling into melancholy. It was clear that behind the exterior he often displayed, he was heartbroken. That made things harder for her, especially because she wanted so badly to continue hating him for the way he had treated her.

That night she lay in her lumpy feather bed, tossing and turning, trying to fall asleep despite the loud sounds coming from the bar below. And there in the darkness, she finally admitted to a truth felt deep in her chest. She *did* want to help Dragonwall. Not simply because of her promise, but because she was growing fond of her companions, even if they didn't feel the same way. Jovari and Koldis weren't her enemy, despite the way they regarded her. The king wasn't her enemy either, even if he did think her a murderous witch. The real enemy was Kane. No matter how much her companions distrusted her, mistreated her, and frustrated her, at the end of the day, they were all on the same team. That had to count for something, didn't it? She only hoped that the king would see it that way, too.

CHAPTER 30
KANE'S NASKS

Kane descended the lower stairs of Shadowkeep in a flourish, circling around and around, deeper and farther underground. Down he went into the bowels of the fortress, into the darkness of the mountain. Along the way, he heard anguished cries, wails of despair from the cells within the rocky depths of his stronghold. Tools were useful until they weren't, and his magic required vast resources.

Somewhere beyond, a bat cried out. Its screech echoed down the tunnel, warning other beasties of his approach. The creatures beneath Shadowkeep dwelt in darkness their whole lives, but they did not mind. They were drawn to the magic of the place, to the evil that oozed from the walls, just as he was.

Before him, torchlight sent a mischief of rats scurrying and squeaking as they hurried to flee from his quick step. Behind him, failure nipped at his heels. There were too many to count. Five hundred years of meticulous planning, and for what?!

Gone were the days of old when the Asarlaí ruled. Ruined were their plans to remove all those of non-magic descent. *The Five* had seen to that by creating dragons. Dragonwall belonged to *his* people, not the humans, not the drengr, and certainly not the drag-ons, beasts forged from rock and stone out of pure *stupidity*.

He alone could restore the great destiny intended for his world. Everything rested upon a fragile point, as if battling for balance at the pentacle of Shadowkeep's tallest turret. It seemed that now his plans tilted in the wrong direction. It simply would not do!

The face of the golden-haired woman swam into his mind's eye —*again*. He cursed under his breath. Who was she? How much did she know? What might her knowledge cost him? These questions gobbled him up the way the creatures beneath Shadowkeep devoured a dead carcass.

He had seen her, oh yes, he knew her face. He scried her in his Dragon's Eye. Mind you, the basin wasn't truly the eye from a dragon. It was the bowl-portion of a dragon's skull, the place where its brain once rested, hollowed out and upturned. Dragon skulls were rare in these times, difficult to find, harder still to trans-port. They were immensely important, as they were useful for a number of magical spells and potions.

His Dragon's Eye was filled with the magical water that allowed him to view anyone, provided he had some of that person to call upon. Fortunately for him, he had obtained what he needed from the woman named Claire. His vodar wraiths wounded her during their fight. Initially he was furious that his assassins had failed again—he was still quite angry—but he soon realized how to turn the situation to good use.

After Claire and her companions had made their way south, he'd visited the place of the fight. Once there, he'd found bits of dried blood—Claire's blood. He'd scooped it up, dirt and all, every bit that he could find. What a prize! Claire's blood was his only consolation now that she had slipped through his fingers. He could no longer count on his wraiths. With three of the king's own protecting her, and the Gable Forest at her back, it was too risky. Fortunately he had other contingency plans, one of which he was about to implement.

Coming to a halt deep within the lowest cavern of the moun-tain, he stood before a waterfall. This was not merely *any* waterfall.

It was special—he had made it so. Now it would serve him well, as did the many slaves it cost him to build it.

Icy water cascaded down from a rock ledge far above, disappearing into a narrow slit in the floor and the caverns below. He watched the water for several moments before sending his consciousness outward. He felt his mind stretch across the mountains, forcing it to push past the planes in the north and well around the Gable Forest as it moved southward. Only when his awareness reached its target in the capital did he allow it to settle. Two minds he penetrated, and two minds he led, until they were alone and positioned where he desired them to be. Then he withdrew.

They were ready. Concentrating on what he needed to see, he waved a hand before the sheet of falling water. Its surface rippled, beginning from the middle and moving outward, like a stone tossed upon the flat surface of a pond. Lights emerged. The scene before him materialized. Two men stood within a dimly lit room inside the great keep of Kastali Dun. They faced the transparent portal he had created.

Upon seeing him through the rippling surface, they bowed. "Greetings, my lord." His nasks had answered his summons. "What is your command?"

"Tell me, have you succeeded in your venture? Have you convinced the king to kill this woman—this outsider?"

The one on the left spoke first, "We have planted deep mistrust, my lord."

The other added, "The king has not yet agreed to kill her. A vote will be taken. It is likely there will be a trial."

He considered their words. A trial would not guarantee the outcome he desired. "My orders to you were simple—the woman must be eliminated."

"Of course, my lord, of course. We have, *and will*, continue to poison the king's mind against her. The remainder of the Council is already in agreement, she is a threat to our kingdom and guilty of a great crime."

"Very well. There is still time to convince the king of this. He must believe that she killed his guard." He did not wish to send his vodar into the capital just yet, so for now, he relied on his nasks. "I hope you understand what must be done, should the king spare her life." His narrowed eyes made them nervously twitch.

"We do, my lord. The woman will be eliminated if the king should fail."

"I certainly hope so. Now, I have another task for you." This one was nearly just as important.

"Anything, my lord."

A new threat had emerged. This one was long on his mind, growing more meddlesome as the years passed. "The king's seer— eliminate her," he ordered. He could no longer risk his plans to this young mage. He knew of her visions, and with each report, he grew angrier. She was beginning to anticipate his every move.

"The Lady Saffra, my lord?"

"Yes, you *imbecile*, the Lady Saffra, unless you know of another seer who requires death?"

"No, my lord, but she is a powerful mage. We—"

"I know what you are. Do you expect me to come down there and perform the task myself?"

"Of—of course not, my lord."

"If you fail me in this, I will walk through this sheet of water and kill you myself, do you understand?" It was an empty threat. He could not risk placing himself in Kastali Dun. Not yet, anyway.

"Yes. Yes, my lord. We will not fail."

He did not care how they did it, so long as the job was done. His nasks were incompetent. That was partly why he had chosen them. Smarter minds were harder to control. "The poison maker in the city. William Collier. He remains a servant to my cause. Find him." He looked at the man on the left, giving him a knowing stare. One that said much without words.

"We will do as you bid, my lord."

"Good. Then go, both of you." They looked relieved to be dismissed, and he was happy to be rid of them. Waving his hand once more, the scene before him disappeared, and the portal became nothing more than a sheet of water.

CHAPTER 31
FORT SQUALL

Fort Squall

Reyr flew hard against the eastern wind. It sang in his ears, whistling past him. He battled it with each downward sweep of his golden wings. His breath came in short gasps, searing his chest as if his own fire burned through him. His shoulder muscles screamed in pain, begging him to slow his pace, but he did not listen. He disciplined himself unfairly, pushing harder than ever before, because he could feel nothing but the wrenching cries of his own heart—the sadness he felt from losing Cyrus, the failure he felt from disappointing his king, the fear he felt for what was to come.

Beneath him the ground sailed past. He hardly noticed. His mind was too consumed with King Talon's disapproval. He blamed himself for everything. Before departing Kastali Dun, it was *he* who had tried to dissuade Cyrus from going north. No one else had bothered, not the king, not any of his fellow shields, only he, because he knew then that something was wrong, even if the others failed to sense it.

In the days following Cyrus's death, he often wondered, what if things had gone differently? Many alternatives crossed his mind, and each scenario resulted in a better outcome than the one he now faced. If he'd been more insistent, perhaps Cyrus would still be alive.

This pattern of thinking was familiar to him. He'd done the same thing when Gemma had died. He'd asked similar questions. What if they never flew north to fight in the battle? What if he ignored the summons for the war? What if they left Dragonwall together, abandoned their honor, left duty behind, and lived only for themselves? She would still be with him. They would still be together. He would still be happy.

It was dangerous to dwell, and though he tried to free his mind of its burdens, it was impossible during the long flight to Fort Squall. What worried him most were his thoughts about Claire. His mind eagerly strayed to her as a reprieve. Even in his dragon form, he could not control himself. Although he was reluctant to admit it —he hated himself for it—he missed her presence upon his back. It reminded him of better times, happier times, when he would fly with Gemma. He should have loathed her for it, for renewing the pain he'd locked away after his mate's death, but he found it impossible.

A fiery glow appeared on the horizon. He exhaled a plume of smoke, one that tasted a lot like relief. The sun was dropping into the Dragonfire Sea, lighting her waters with hues of orange and red. And there, sitting at the edge of Stormy Bay, was Fort Squall. Still miniature, perhaps as large as his tiniest claw, its battlements stood tall like a proud warrior.

Warmth blazed in his heart, melting all his icy worry away.

Slowing his pace, he inhaled. Salty air filled his lungs, laced with so much familiarity. It felt like coming home—it always did. He knew every silhouette before him, every distinct feature, every tall tower rising up beside the city. Kastali Dun was his home now, yes, but Squall's End and Fort Squall would always be his *true* home. The fort was in his blood. His fathers and forefathers had held it for thousands of years, passing it from father to son. It could have been his, and would have been, had Gemma lived.

Instead, it had gone to Davi.

Dusk was upon him when his wings brought him close to the glittering city. And to his delight, joyous bugles rent the silent sky. The welcoming heralds of dragons surrounded him as the fort's drengr swooped in to greet him.

"Welcome, Lord Reyr! Welcome home!" many cried.

Some were too young to recognize, while others he knew by name. Many had been companions and friends during his time growing up in the fort. All were glad to see him.

"Reyr!" Davi's voice sounded in his mind. *"You did not tell me you were coming! Welcome home, brother! I have missed you."*

When was the last time he'd been here? A pang of guilt squeezed his chest. He should have visited sooner. Far too often, he found himself caught up in the king's business.

Descending towards the torch-lit courtyard, his drengr escorts followed close on his wing tips. Their Riders were all smiles, anticipating the happy evening to come. Every time he returned home, Davi insisted upon throwing a most lavish feast. He hadn't the heart to tell them—this time there would be no feast.

As he closed in on his destination, he shifted into his human form, landing perfectly on two feet. His sverak jingled at his side, metal scabbard clanking against his belt. Davi was already strolling happily towards him from an adjacent corridor. Davi wasn't *merely* his brother, they were twins. Rare, but it happened.

They locked into an embrace while others watched, grinning to behold the happy moment. When they pulled apart, Davi clapped him on the back. "Next time, do not wait so long to visit! We will feast well tonight!" he added for those near enough to hear. In a quieter voice he said, "I heard about Cyrus. Are the rumors true? Is he really gone?"

Unable to voice such a devastating confirmation just yet, he merely gave Davi a brief nod. Word traveled fast when the drengr lent themselves to it. It was likely that the sweep team they'd encountered days' past had backtracked closely enough to relay the news.

"And a human girl from beyond?" Davi whispered. "Is it true then?"

"Let us talk in private," he said. Davi agreed, escorting him to the fort leader chambers. They entered the study. He still freshly recalled when it had been used by their father. The sight of it, even now, brought memories flooding back—the day he burst in to tell his father that Gemma had become his mate. Rorck's proud expression was etched permanently in his mind.

Davi took a seat behind the desk. The position suited him—though he would not have thought so in years past. He admired his brother for stepping up to the responsibility. Davi never anticipated this outcome. When they were younger, Davi often boasted that he and Emmy would fly off into the sunset. They were eager to explore distant lands and discover new peoples. How it must have killed them to settle down.

He took a seat opposite Davi. "I must be on my way shortly," he explained, hating his business-like tone.

Davi looked both surprised and disappointed. "You have only just arrived," he said. "Surely you can spare a little time. We are all tense. Many could use a bit of merrymaking." It was true. Even Davi looked worn and tired—much like how he felt.

"We certainly could," he said, sighing reluctantly. "But I must return to Jovari and Koldis. We must make haste to reach the capital." He paused to recall King Talon's words. The king mistrusted Claire. He seemed certain that she was guilty. This left him in a very tight position. At last he said, "The news is true. Cyrus is dead, and a young woman from beyond flies with us to Kastali Dun."

Davi's expression softened. "I had hoped to find the news false," he admitted. "Tell me, how did it happen?"

Reyr shook his head. He did not know. He hated not knowing. The sooner they got answers, the better. But would King Talon choose answers over his own selfish need for justice? "I wish I knew the cause with certainty. Poison seems likely. Alas, this woman is the key. She possesses the answers we seek." He proceeded to tell Davi of all that had happened since Cyrus's departure north. The fort leader listened quietly.

When his recounting reached Belnesse, Davi swore. "It cannot be true! The entire city is gone?" he cried, face going bloodless.

"It's...gone."

Davi fell silent. Together, they sat in the dim light of his study. They said nothing in their mutual need for quiet consideration.

At last, Davi spoke. "So much death and destruction. Tell me of this Mikkin fellow. You trust his word?"

"I trust it completely." He relayed everything Mikkin had told him. "I have no reason to believe ill of the man. I saw the burned city myself."

"Surely it was a mere cooking fire run astray."

"Cooking fire," he grunted. "If only. There were no survivors aside from Mikkin. This was no mere accident. It was intentional. Dragons live among us once more."

Davi dropped his head in his hands and groaned. "So rarely do our sweep teams venture that far north. There has never been much need to with the mountains protecting us like a barrier. It is the coast we focus on." Davi sighed deeply. "If what you say is true, then I have failed them. I have no one to blame but myself." It was difficult news to bear, especially for Fort Squall's leader. Everyone living in this territory was Davi's responsibility. "How was I supposed to anticipate a wild dragon attack? Dragons are legend now, nothing more."

"So we thought..." He shook his head. He too struggled to accept the idea. "None of us could have anticipated this, brother. Blame yourself if you will, but it is a mistake any one of us could have made."

Davi flashed him a look of helplessness. "More than forty thousand years have passed without a single sighting," he said. "Do you know what this means?"

"It means that the days of old are coming back to haunt us. It means that if we do not do what is necessary, many will die."

Davi picked up a quill from his desk, twirling it between his fingers. When he next spoke, he continued to gaze absentmindedly at it. "The wild dragons banded together to burn Belnesse. Wild dragons never organize for a common cause—not since the days of Rage. What do they want?"

"I can only assume their desires are the same as before."

Davi looked up at him. "They have come back to claim owner-ship and dominion over Dragonwall?"

"So it would seem, unless we can think of a more likely purpose driving them."

"What does King Talon say?"

As far as Reyr knew, King Talon did not know. Wild Dragons were not discussed during their abrupt conversation. The news would likely come as a shock, especially considering everything else taking place within Dragonwall.

Davi read his mind. "With goblin raids to the east, vodar sightings across our northern territories, and pirate attacks along the coast, dragons can mean only one thing. Our kingdom is close to war. You must tell him, Reyr. We must prepare our defenses."

He agreed. "You will do what needs to be done here, I presume?"

"Aye. Would you expect anything else?"

He shook his head. He trusted Davi's leadership to its fullest. He was about to say so when the door behind them burst open. They both turned to find Lady Emmy. She stood stock still, her face pale. The two of them rose, and for a moment they all fell silent, gazing upon each other.

Emmy was Davi's mate. She knew all that Davi knew. The minds of mates were melded, and it became clear that Emmy's features mirrored everything Davi kept hidden. They were afraid for Fort Squall, afraid for their people, afraid for their lives.

"Wild dragons brought nothing but death and destruction upon our people," she whispered from the doorway. "Our sole exis-tence was to rid the world of them. You cannot *possibly* believe they are back." She looked at Davi, as if begging him for comfort where there was none.

Davi and Emmy had every right to be scared. They all did. Wild dragons had far less to lose compared with their drengr cousins. It left his people at a disadvantage. The dragons had no riders to protect. They lacked the humanity that afforded better judgment. Everyone knew that dragons were bloodthirsty warmongers who thrived on death and destruction, though the bards would have people believe otherwise.

"They will feast on our undoing," Emmy said, walking forward as Davi took her into his arms. She was resilient—a perfect mate for his twin.

It did not take long for Davi to comfort her before they found themselves sitting and talking like they used to do, discussing strategy and trading news. Aside from everything else, the fort was doing well for itself. Even now, searches were underway to accommodate its need for support.

When they discovered his hunger, Emmy had serving staff bring meals up for them. He ate in a rush. "It is a shame you must go," she said. "Your nephew will be sore over it. He talks often of you."

"His search goes well, I take it?"

"Aye. Quite well." Davi was beaming as he discussed his beloved son. "Still no mate yet, but he is young. I am confident."

Reyr nodded. "He will find one. As you say, he is still very young."

At last, he took his leave, much to the disappointment of all, but he was too eager to return to his companions. The idea of them alone and exposed, should the wraiths return, left him uneasy. He especially disliked being away from Claire. He felt that it was his responsibility to look after her now. With her being many leagues away, he could hardly do so.

He flew all night, and well into the following day, trekking south. As it was before, the wind was not in his favor. At the end of the day, as the sun crept towards the horizon, Jovari reached out to him.

"We have made camp along the Flat River. There is a grove of trees south of Weldon. We will wait for you here."

Weldon. He knew of the small settlement. *"I should be there by nightfall. What of Claire? No problems while I was away?"*

"Of course not. Claire is in good hands. After some time with her, we have decided that she isn't all that bad." Something in Jovari's tone was different. Had he finally warmed towards her?

With an extra burst of speed, he pushed himself onward. At last, after darkness had fallen, he spotted a small glowing campfire nestled amongst a grove of trees. Breathing a sigh of relief, he descended.

"Welcome," Jovari and Koldis said. He transformed before landing, surveying their camp. In truth, his gaze searched for one thing. It was only when he saw Claire sitting beside the fire looking serenely up at him, did he allow himself to relax. She was safe. They were all well.

"We've got stew," Claire said as she stirred a pot over the fire. Eagerly he went and took up a seat. He was just about to spoon some of the broth into his mouth when a familiar voice blasted into his mind. The king was finally ready to speak.

CHAPTER 32

HISTORY

Eigaden

Claire sloshed stew everywhere the moment King Talon's voice bombarded her mind. Reyr had only just returned from his trip, and the king's contact was not something she'd been expecting. "Careful with that!" Jovari held out his hands and took the bowl from her, eyes narrowing. Except...she hardly paid him any mind.

"The people cry for justice, Reyr," King Talon snarled.

"We all cry for justice, Your Grace."

The king scoffed at Reyr's patient tone. *"Gods above! You could have saved us from this added burden."*

"Added burden?"

"Yes, added burden. The instant you found that girl standing over Cyrus, you should have slit her throat."

"Your Grace—"

"Saffra tells me she was found covered in his blood. His blood, Reyr. What more proof is needed?" Claire's heart lurched.

"Your Grace, with all due respect, there ought to be a fair trial."

"Yes, yes. I have agreed to a trial," King Talon said, begrudgingly.

"Still, many of the council members have argued against it. They are calling for her immediate death." A shiver raced down her spine.

"Is it unanimous then? There has been a vote?"

"No, not unanimous. One vote remains in opposition."

"Whose?"

"Lady Saffra maintains her stance."

Reyr frowned down at his bowl of stew. *"When you say stance...?"*

"Saffra maintains that Claire is innocent."

Claire exhaled—

"Is everything all right, Claire?" Jovari forced her attention away from the private discussion. "You look...unsettled. I certainly hope you plan to eat."

She offered him a weak smile and nodded, noticing that he and Koldis had nearly finished. She dished up a bowl for herself and sat back down.

"Your Grace, I believe Saffra has good reason to claim Claire's inno-cence. I too must side with her." She dared a glance towards Reyr, warmth seeping into her chest. He *believed* her. After all this time, she'd finally won him over.

"You are being careless, Reyr," King Talon growled. *"I know you. You have always been quick to forgive and forget. You have spent too much time traveling with this girl. Perhaps you have forgotten that she is an outsider."*

And...just like that, her smile faded.

"Perhaps you are correct, Your Grace. Yet, Claire has shown no signs of dan—"

"You do not know what she is capable of!" She flinched at the roaring voice. *"Have you considered that she claims an unbreakable promise as a foolproof way of manipulating you?"*

A long pause. *"I considered it, and I believe it unlikely."*

"Cyrus would never do such a thing. Withdraw your trust from her. Until there has been a full trial, she is guilty."

"As you wish, Your Grace."

Pretending she heard nothing, she turned her attention to her stew. If Reyr discovered her ability, it would only make matters worse. He would be furious if he found out she had secretly listened to everything. Right now, she needed all the trust she could get.

Try as she might, she couldn't stomach her dinner. She pushed the chunks of meat around in her bowl. When the others began chatting about Reyr's trip, she poured the contents back into the pot hoping they might not notice.

Her companions talked long into the night about Reyr's twin brother and preparations to come. Under different circumstances, she would have been interested in the discussion. She was eager to learn everything she could about Dragonwall. But in her current state, she curled into a ball beneath her blanket and tried her hardest not to cry.

THE NEXT MORNING they departed at dawn, flying south. She noticed no difference in Reyr's behavior towards her, though she expected him to turn cold after the king's command. It was an uneventful day. She thought perhaps the king would contact them again. Truthfully, she dreaded it. But he did not, nor did he reach out to any of them the following day.

As the days passed, her mind often drifted to him. Each time it happened, her skin flushed with anger. He considered her guilty without any evidence. How could he be so stubborn? So obtuse? His narrow-mindedness *infuriated* her.

The night before they were set to arrive, her nerves took a turn for the worse. All sorts of scenarios flashed through her mind. If everyone on the council wanted her dead, then she would not be safe in the capital when she arrived. If the king planned to try her as a criminal, how would she relay Cyrus's message? How would she fulfill her promise? Would she ever get the chance to speak to him alone?

She tossed and turned, getting no sleep whatsoever. Long before the sun had risen, she got up to find Reyr. It was his turn to keep watch over their little camp.

He saw her coming and patted the ground beside him, inviting her to sit. It was rare that she ever got time alone with him. They were silent for a while before she worked up the nerve to say anything. "We never got a chance to talk about what happened with the marble dragon statue."

"Ah yes," he said, glancing at her. "Truthfully, I forgot all about it. Why don't you explain what happened."

She did, relaying every detail. However, she held back her suspicions because she worried that the experience had something to do with her ability to hear the drengr.

"Huh," he said at last. "It's rather strange, I'll admit."

"But...you believe me?"

"Aye, I do not think you would make this up." A small laugh burst from his chest and he shook his head. "It is too far-fetched. Besides, some of the things you mention are written in history."

Her shoulders relaxed. Perhaps she wasn't crazy after all. With all that had happened, she was starting to believe it.

"When you say written in history...?"

"Well, for instance, the woman you described seeing in your mind is very likely Queen Isabella."

"She's a sprite queen?"

At the time of the incident, she'd known little about the sprites. But she remembered seeing the woman's appearance and the markings upon her skin.

"At the time, yes. In fact, Queen Isabella was Queen Jade's aunt."

She sucked in a breath. Aunt? There was so much to unpack there. Instead, she said, "Why was she inside of the marble dragon's memories?"

"Some legends claim that it was *Isabella* who turned the infamous dragon to stone."

"Didn't all the dragons come from stone?"

Reyr chuckled. "Did Cyrus tell you that?" She hesitated, then nodded. He smiled. "You know, when this is all over, I would like to hear all that he told you."

"When this is all over, I would be happy to grant your request."

They fell silent for several moments. "So, tell me about the dragons, if they were created from stone, who made them?"

"Hmm...that's a bit of a story. Though, I suppose we have time." The sun wasn't due to rise yet. "Make yourself comfortable."

She was as comfortable as she was going to get.

"It is said that the world did not always have dragons. Ages ago they were created—carved from stone by powerful sorcerers known as the asarlaí."

She knew about the asarlai from Cyrus—Kane was one of them.

"Dissatisfied with their already impressive powers, a group of asarlaí known as *The Five*, sought to rule the world. It was they who worked tirelessly, chiseling from color enchanted lava rock the beastly forms that would later be called dragons. Before breathing magic into them, none of them knew what to expect. As a fail-safe, they each removed a small palm-sized chunk from their lifeless bodies." A thrill shot through her. She knew exactly where this tale was going.

"These stones were polished and rounded, later becoming known as the dragonstones. The Dragonstones offered a way of rendering inert the giant dragons should they become too power-ful. The asarlaí could not stand the idea of losing control; after all, the world was theirs to rule.

"The dragons cooperated with The Five for a time, using tele-pathic powers bestowed upon them to communicate amongst themselves and with their makers. Together they claimed the terri-tory and named it Dragonwall, in honor of the mighty beasts who conquered it. Thus dawned the Second Age."

She almost shivered with excitement.

"The dragons were too much like their masters—greedy, power hungry, and proud. They truly believed that they were never meant to be controlled, so they plotted in secret against The Five, stealing the stones and killing their creators."

She hummed with interest. Even from the start, the stones had a terrible past—a past built on deceit and treachery.

Reyr stared out over the landscape, now smudged with a faint hint of pink and orange. "After killing their masters, the five dragons did not stop there. They swept through Dragonwall in search of any remaining Asarlaí, sending the last of the great sorcerers into hiding. Some say they traveled to distant lands, sailing across the sea. To Oshea."

"So...they all left? The Asarlaí?"

"Aye. We have not seen or heard from them since."

A roaring filled her head, lifting to a fever pitch. She wanted *so badly* to tell him about Kane. Even though she knew it was impossible, she opened her mouth and tried. The words were formed and everything, but just like before, no sound came out.

"Are you all right?" he asked, eying her. She must have looked like a fish out of water, or a croaking frog who'd lost its voice.

Clearing her throat and coughing a couple of times, she nodded. "Sorry. Just a tickle."

"Very well. Shall I continue?"

"Please."

"When the dragons were happy with their work they settled down, proliferating throughout Dragonwall. Thirteen clans were formed. These clans divided up Dragonwall into territories over which they presided. For the most part, they left Dragonwall's inhabitants alone to work the land as they saw fit. Great houses were established with long ranging dynasties. Humanity thrived. Aside from the occasional goblin raid, humans and beings of magic worked and lived in harmony. Over time, the dragonstones were lost and even forgotten."

"Oh..." It was the only thing she could think to say. Suddenly nervous, she rubbed her chest and felt the bulge hidden in her bra. All she needed was for Reyr to discover the little leather pouch hiding there. If that happened, her entire mission would be over.

"So..." She cleared her throat. "What happened to the thirteen clans?"

"Rage. Rage happened."

"Who's Rage?"

"He was the leader of the Ice Clan. He commanded that general you saw, the marble dragon, if history is written correctly."

"Wow."

"The words I recall go something like this," he said, his eyes taking on a far away gleam.

> *Thirteen clans there were—*
> *Thirteen clans when Rage did rise—*
> *Thirteen clans to conquer.*
> *And so he fought with tooth and claw,*
> *Then pronounced himself their ruler.*

SHE CHEWED on her lower lip. "Rage tried to conquer the clans and take control of the dragons?"

"Very good. Yes."

"That's...greedy."

"The dragons were always greedy. Rage went to each of the clans petitioning his cause. The Fire Clan was first to swear allegiance to him, followed shortly thereafter by the Storm Clan and the Desert Clan. Soon, even the Cave Clan came out of hiding to profess their loyalty. However, there were many who did not. One clan in particular, the Iron Clan, rallied the remaining clans to fight against Rage, but it was not enough. Rage's evil acts washed across the land instilling fear into the inhabitants of Dragonwall, giving all the dragons a bad name, even those who wished to continue living in peace.

"As a result, they were hunted. Quite brutally slaughtered—the good ones and the bad. After all, how could humans distinguish between an evil dragon like those of the Ice Clan, and a good dragon, like those of the Iron Clan, who simply wanted peace and to be left alone."

"I thought all dragons were bad," she said, frowning. Reyr shook his head, a strange expression crossing his face. "No. Not all were bad."

He hesitated. A golden light peeped up along the eastern horizon.

"It was a brutal time," Reyr said. "Very bad for dragon kind. Then came a young dragon from the Iron Clan by the name of Vigilance. Seeking to unite the population of Dragonwall against this evildoer, he wanted the humans and magical peoples to band together and fight alongside the rallying clans, but Vigilance had a dilemma."

"I can already guess," she said.

"Can you?" He grinned.

"Vigilance didn't have a way of communicating with people, did he? Since he was a dragon, and dragons can't actually talk, how could he tell them he was good?"

"That's correct. Dragons cannot talk out loud, and humans cannot hear their telepathic voices."

"None of them?" she hedged. Her heart began to race. She hadn't anticipated this opportunity, but it was too perfect to pass on.

"No. Humans do not possess the ability for telepathy. Some sprites do, but humans have never been able to communicate with us."

"What about your mates?"

"Ah. That is different. When a drengr develops a bond with a mate, the telepathic ability is established to allow for telepathic communication."

"I see." Another question popped into her mind. "How is a bond developed?"

"You have *many* questions." He chuckled in good humor, flashing her a charming and utterly disarming smile. "Already, we have digressed."

"Sorry," she mumbled.

"Shall I continue? Good. Where was I?" He paused for a moment. "Ah, yes. Vigilance needed a way to bridge the communication gap between dragon and humankind. He needed a way to explain that not all dragons were evil. He went in search of a solution, one that would change Dragonwall forever."

"He became a drengr," she whispered, guessing the end of the story.

Reyr nodded. "In the forest, Vigilance came across a powerful sprite—Queen Isabella."

Her eyes widened. "The same queen I saw? *She* created the drengr?"

"Aye. Queen Isabella was so beautiful and so enchanting, that at first sight of her, Vigilance bowed his great spiked head and surrendered himself to her, pleading with her to help him defeat Rage." Goosebumps prickled down her arms. She could almost picture Vigilance in the Gable Forest, bowing before the beautiful sprite queen.

"Fortunately, Queen Isabella heard the pleas of Vigilance. She was one of the rare few blessed with telepathic abilities to hear *all* of dragonkind. She took pity upon him, offering a trade. This trade would ensure his success, but granting his wish would come at a cost. It would change him, and that change would be irreversible. He willingly agreed, desperate to do anything and everything to save Dragonwall. So, she blessed him with humanity, bestowing upon him the ability to shift into human form.

"In so doing, the sprite queen gave him a way to speak to the people so that he might rally Dragonwall's inhabitants. Several of his comrades followed suit, taking on Queen Isabella's blessing and becoming drengr—which means *dragon warrior* in the old language."

Her jaw hung loose and she quickly shut it.

Reyr grinned, clearly pleased by her surprise. "Vigilance and his newly formed force of drengr rallied the humans to their side, but they did not stop there. Sprites and dwargs joined their cause. Never had Dragonwall witnessed such a uniting of peoples. Together, they battled the clans that supported Rage, driving them from the lands until all that remained was the Ice Clan, but they too eventually fell in some of the greatest battles Dragonwall has ever witnessed. When Vigilance defeated Rage in a show of aerial combat, the world rejoiced. Since then, our inhabitants have flourished under the rule of the drengr monarchy."

"So…where does the marble dragon come in?"

He chuckled. "I believe the Ice Clan sold him out."

"They betrayed him?"

"I think so. Perhaps it was done to save their own scaly hides. Isabella found him and battled him, at last turning him into stone. I suppose she intended to punish him for all eternity, forcing him to dwell forever upon the land as a monument."

"That's…"

"An impressive story. I know. We take great pride in our history."

She nodded. "Thank you—for telling me."

"I am always glad to share history with those who are willing to listen."

"I admit, I find your world so fascinating. We don't have magic where I come from. There are no goblins or dwargs, and especially no sprites, or drengr or unicorns or dragons."

"That seems rather boring to me."

She laughed, feeling immediately lighter. "Well, yes. I suppose it is."

She didn't bother telling him all the things they *did* have— things that Cyrus was amazed by. It would be too difficult to explain technology.

"Reyr?"

"Hmm?"

"What's going to happen when we arrive? I know…I know I broke the law. According to Dragonwall law, my people are forbidden from entering into your kingdom. Then there's the whole Cyrus thing. Everyone thinks I killed him."

Reyr stiffened, his demeanor changing in an instant. "How do you know the law about the gate? Did Cyrus tell you?"

"Yes," she whispered. "He said the crime was punishable by death."

"That is correct."

"Are they going to—are they going to kill me? Is the king going to kill me?"

There was a long silence, heavy and uncomfortable. When she

looked at him, he was gazing east, watching the sun peep up from the horizon. "The king is suffering from a great deal of grief."

"So are you!" she cried. "But at least you're being reasonable."

"Aye. I try to be. The king..."

"The king, *what*?"

"He has been through far more in his lifetime than many have had to suffer. He will come around."

She chewed her tongue to keep from speaking. Life experiences were hardly a good excuse to kill her. "Can't you do something? I need to speak with him about Cyrus, about Dragonwall. About..."

"Aye. You mentioned that when we found you."

"Well, I wasn't lying. Cyrus told me everything."

"I see, and did he tell you about the dragonstones?"

She cleared her throat, her cheeks heating. When she couldn't meet his gaze, he said, "I shall take that as a yes. Look, Claire, I cannot make any promises. You made your choice. You chose your path. I will speak to the king *when* and *if* he will hear me. I will do my best to facilitate a meeting between the two of you."

"Thank you," she whispered. It was the best she could hope for.

The sun came free of the horizon, warming everything it touched.

"Come, let's get some breakfast and depart."

She nodded, following him back to their camp.

CHAPTER 33
KASTALI DUN

Claire savored her last day in the sky. She loved flying, even though it made her sore and achy. She adored the freedom, the cool wind that whistled past her ears, the sense of separation between her and the ground. The closer she got to the capital, the more she wished she could remain aloft forever.

A deep foreboding settled over her, which intensified around midday, when the king's voice sounded in her mind. He addressed all three drengr. *"How long until you are upon the city?"*

"Several hours still, my king," came Jovari's response. *"We will arrive before night falls."*

"Good. I need not remind you that we are to pay proper respect to Cyrus when you arrive. All the traditions will be upheld."

A procession through the city was scheduled for that evening. Cyrus would then be taken to the pyre and burned by the fiery breath of King Talon himself. Following this, three days of funeral games would commence, as was custom for their people.

"We will observe the proper grieving time before we divert our attention to this girl you've brought."

"Of course, Your Grace," Reyr said. *"What then is to be done in the meantime, until Claire can speak with you?"*

"Speak with me? She will not be speaking with me. I will face her at her trial, as is customary for criminals. If she is found guilty, she will beg for mercy before the end."

Claire gasped, unable to conceal her emotions. She was not generally weak stomached, but the king's words made her insides twist with nausea.

"I do not think that is wise, Your Grace," Reyr answered.

"My verdict is not up for negotiation. When she arrives, the guards will be there to take her."

"Take her where?" Reyr's words were measured. His golden scales heated up beneath her legs, as if the fires within him were stoked. She shifted uncomfortably.

"To the dungeons."

"The dungeons?"

Her heart stopped beating for a second, then sped up until it raced. Angry tears clouded her vision.

"Your Grace, if I may—" Jovari cut in.

"You may not!"

She glanced over at the sapphire blue dragon beside her. He'd been about to defend her.

"These are my commands," the king said. *"They are not up for negotiation. This girl has poisoned your minds. Do not assume her inno-cence."* Silence fell heavy between them before the king's voice sounded once more, this time softer. *"The three of you have spent far too much time with her. When you arrive, you are to sever all contact and leave her to the guards. That is final."*

"Yes, Your Grace," came their responses. And then the contact was broken.

Reyr gave a frustrated growl. It reverberated through her legs. The others said nothing.

She wanted to scream. Emotions flooded through her—anger, frustration, fear. Especially fear. It turned her blood to ice. She shouldn't have come. Shouldn't have agreed to Cyrus's request. Shouldn't have made an unbreakable promise.

She was about to find herself in a huge city, very much alone. The king wanted her locked up like a common criminal. He failed to see what she was doing for him. He was so blind!

A groan left her chest. This was hopeless. Absolutely hopeless.

She furiously wiped at the tears sliding down her cheeks, sniffing. She had cried too many times since losing Cyrus. Enough was *enough*.

She inhaled, squaring her shoulders and lifting her chin. There was nothing else for it. She'd just have to beat the king at his own game. If he wanted to behave like a selfish, nearsighted *brat*, she was going to fight back.

THE DAY PASSED IN A BLINK, with her mood taking on shades between dismal and fearful. Long before Kastali Dun materialized on the horizon, she heard the city's drengr. The cacophony of voices began as intermittent whispers, growing in strength with each beat of Reyr's golden wings. Closer and closer the king's shields brought her. Louder still the voices became. Soon she could make out full conversations.

The things she heard were of little importance, but still, she listened, if only to keep her mind off her impending doom. This ability was the *one* thing that she could use to her advantage. Despite the growing headache it gave her, she was determined to listen, just in case some snippet of information proved useful—

She gasped.

The vast expanse of Kastali Dun materialized, stretched out before her. Behind it, the dark blue sea went on and on until it met the horizon. Located on a rocky outcropping was the biggest castle she had ever seen—the great keep of Kastali Dun. It was the largest keep in Dragonwall. Like a scene from a fairytale.

Its tall ramparts were topped with spires and turrets that starkly dominated the skyline. The sight of it left her heart pounding. She was both impressed and afraid.

Trumpets sounded in the distance. An announcement of their

impending arrival. The proclamation was dreadfully beautiful. It spoke in so many ways to her heart.

Reyr increased his pace, as if eager to be home. She leaned into him for comfort, placing her cheek against his warm, scaled neck. As they arrived, her eyes swept over the city, taking it in. It was so many times larger than Weldon—unfathomably large.

There were wisps of smoke rising from chimneys, and below the smoky tendrils, a sea of rooftops. Everything was tightly packed together. In between the buildings, narrow streets gave way to wider ones. These snaked their way uphill to the keep.

She sucked in a deep breath. Out of nowhere, drengr swooped in around them. The sight left her wide eyed. It was a rainbow of colors. Dragon scales sparkled brilliantly in the late afternoon sun. She had never seen so many at once. Nearly all of them had riders.

It took a matter of moments before they were surrounded. At least one hundred strong, the pairs assembled into V-formations as they escorted them over the city. Some of the riders looked at Cyrus's body strapped to Jovari, as if confirming that he was truly dead. Most just looked at *her* instead. She saw their searching gazes—their suspicion. It left a tight ball in her stomach.

Ignoring all the telepathic speculation shooting from drengr to drengr, she kept her face forward, determined to stay strong. Even if on the inside, she was crumbling like broken rock.

You are strong. Do not let their misguided words steer you off course.

The voice that spoke jarred her from her emotions. She'd been hearing it a lot.

What if I am too weak? she dared to ask.

Be brave. It was you who saved me, remember? You are strong.

It felt like a punch to the gut. Those words—they were the same ones Cyrus said just before dying.

"Cyrus?" she gasped, far louder than she intended. The voice in her mind did not answer. She needed to pull herself together. If she was going to get through this, she needed to be strong. Shaking her head, trying to clear it, she turned her attention back to the city.

The keep loomed up before them. Reyr began to descend. With

each bit of altitude lost, her heart beat faster and faster. She tried to ignore it, focusing on the sight before her. The giant castle.

The rocky edifice looked almost green. Thin sheets of velvety moss from centuries of accumulation blanketed it, giving the walls their eerie sheen. This place was old, very old. She could feel its magic too, ancient and powerful, as it radiated towards her and tingled across her skin. What an odd sensation! Almost like charged air before a thunderstorm. Goosebumps erupted across her skin.

Reyr landed in a vast courtyard on the keep's lowest level. He was followed shortly thereafter by Jovari and Koldis. Everywhere she looked, hordes of people had gathered. She hated all of them for their desire to gloat.

She dismounted gracefully. Her limbs were trembling, but she didn't let that show. The moment her feet touched solid ground, guards latched on to her arms. The metal of their armored gloves chafed against her sunburnt skin.

"Reyr!" she cried, pulling against them. "Reyr!"

They dragged her away. Her voice was drowned out by the boo-ing of the crowd. The guards forced her away. She wasn't given a chance to say goodbye.

All around her, the crowd screamed.

"Murderer!"

"Traitor!"

Slap. She jerked. Her eyes watered as something wet hit her cheek. The guards held her too tightly to wipe it away. When she looked down at her shirt, she saw what looked like fruit juice. It smelled rotten. *Smack.* Something else hit her chest and splattered against her face. A sob escaped her lips but she clamped them closed, refusing to react.

She had just enough time to look over her shoulder before a shadowy corridor swallowed her up. Reyr was transforming into his human form. Above them, the capital's drengr circled like vultures. Koldis took flight to join them.

Her chest tightened until it hurt. It's like they'd forgotten her. Abandoned her.

She'd never felt more alone in all her life.

"You can do this," she whispered under her breath. "You can do this." It was nearly impossible to find her courage, harder still to maintain her fortitude as the guards pulled her away from the *only* familiar thing she had left in this world. Silently, they escorted her into the bowels of the keep. "Where are you taking me?" she demanded, even though she already knew.

The keep's dark walls were foreboding and unfamiliar. She was taken down a series of stairways and corridors. She tried to note their path, in case she could somehow escape, but failed. It was like a maze. She would never find her way out. The lower they went, the shallower her breaths became.

She was tossed into a cell. She scrambled to her feet and turned as the door slammed in her face. "Manners would be nice!" she cried at the guard's retreating footsteps.

She stood motionless, blinking at the closed door. Minutes passed, and still she did nothing. The entire experience left her too shocked to respond.

Eventually, she came out of her daze. The guards hadn't bothered to remove her backpack or confiscate any of her belongings. The dragonstones were still safely tucked in her bra. A small, surprised laugh burst from her lips.

Perhaps she was luckier than she'd realized.

Coming to her senses, she wiped some of the muck off her face and arms, getting it all over her hands. It stank. So did she. At that very moment, she would have given *anything* for a proper bath.

She looked around her cell the way a caged animal might. She removed a flashlight from her pack and tapped it against her palm several times before light blazed around her. The cell was small, maybe half the size of her bedroom at home. It had stone walls, no windows, and a dirt floor. It was completely empty, except for a small pot—a chamber pot. She groaned in disgust.

Venturing into the corner, she sank to the floor and burst into tears. So much for strength, for courage, for all her determination to avoid crying. Her body shook with great sobs, her eyes blurred and her nose ran.

What had she ever done to deserve this?

It was impossible to gauge the passing of time. Eventually her tears stopped and she removed the dragonstone pouch from her bra, where it was becoming uncomfortable, and tucked it safely into the pocket of her jeans. From her backpack, she pulled out her bedroll and spread it on the floor beneath her. She removed a cloth and used it to blow her nose and wipe herself off. Even still, she was exceedingly filthy. Even a change of clothes didn't mask her smell.

There was nothing to do but sit and wait. She wondered what was taking place outside. What special respects the kingdom paid to honor Cyrus? None of them would understand what he had been through—not like she did. *She* was the one beside him in those final moments.

She hated that she would not get to honor him the way Dragonwall's citizens would. That she was stuck here, instead. So, she said a little prayer for him, closing her eyes. Then she shifted her body, trying to get comfortable.

She might as well settle in for a long wait.

She'd be here for three days. Three long days until the grief period was over. Three long days of confinement in the darkness before the monster who called himself a king sentenced her to death.

CHAPTER 34

A DARING PLAN

Kastali Dun

Saffra pulled an arrow from her quiver. Although her movements were practiced, today they betrayed her true feelings. Her fingers shook with every use. Even her aim was imperfect.

While everyone had gathered in the lower courtyard to witness the highly anticipated arrival of the king's shields, and more importantly, Claire, she was here. Alone. The city's trumpets had set her off, turning her stomach into a tight knot. They'd gone on and on, forcing her to think over her plans, which had only made it worse. Rule breaking was unlike her. She wasn't one for deceit, especially towards the king of Dragonwall. But...what choice did she have?

Whoosh.

She let another arrow fly, squinting against the setting sun as she followed its path to the target. *Thud.* It was a full handspan off center. *Whoosh.* She repeated the motion. *Thud.* Over and over she drew and fired. *Whoosh. Thud. Whoosh. Thud.* The sound was soothing.

Minutes ticked by. She ignored the sight of drengr in the sky.

275

She ignored the cries that drifted across the castle's grounds, almost frenzied. She ignored what might be happening at this very moment. Instead, she focused only on her movements.

Eventually, the noise in the lower courtyard quieted and she felt calmer. Archery was her tonic, after all. The more her muscles ached, the better she felt.

She inhaled, letting her breath out in a slow exhale. It was refreshing to feel the sun's dying heat upon her face. To enjoy the fresh air outside the castle walls.

She hadn't done it nearly enough lately. Mostly, to avoid questions about Cyrus—about his death. Just because she was a seer, didn't mean she had *all* the answers. Everyone seemed to think she did.

Darkness began to fall. She thought over her plan again. She'd hatched it only this morning, after the disaster that was the king's announcement. She'd been at court, hidden beneath a cloak. Claire was to be thrown in the dungeons after she arrived. "Put her where she belongs!" his courtiers had cried, a crazed delight taking them. Others had even called for her death.

She let another arrow loose as her cheeks heated with shame. These were the same people she served. The same people she shared space with.

How could they be so cruel towards someone they knew nothing about? So hasty in their judgment? Grief and anger were fickle, yes, but a poor excuse. Then again, it wasn't exactly the courtiers she blamed. It was King Talon. He was supposed to be an example to the kingdom. Instead, he chose to make decisions with his emotions and not his head.

Hence, her plan.

Walking over to the target, she removed her arrows and returned to her chambers.

"My lady, welcome back," Jocelyn greeted her. "Desaree will be along shortly with our evening tea. Shall I ready your gown for the procession?"

Her gown. The one Madame Rosanne had made for the occasion. It was a light gray number, to symbolize mourning. It matched the tunics to be worn by the king's shields. Like their attire, her dress had a silver dragon's head embroidered on the left breast—the king's sigil.

"Thank you, yes. And the matching cloak, too."

"But my lady, it will be too hot."

"Never mind that," she said. "Oh, and Jocelyn?"

"Yes, my lady?"

"Tonight I would like for you to attend the procession with Desaree."

Jocelyn hesitated then said, "As you wish," before returning her attention to Saffra's gown.

Many ladies of the court required accompaniment no matter where they went. Handmaidens were accustomed to following their mistresses around, but Jocelyn understood that Saffra was different. Saffra often chose to do things on her own. She wouldn't question the request...would she?

Jocelyn helped her into her gown. The fabric was soft and soothing. Regardless of how soft, she could not breathe. "Must they be so tight?" she cried. "Can you not loosen the laces?"

"You complain every time, my lady. And every time my response is the same. No. The gown is meant to be this way."

She huffed in response.

Sitting down, she took up the large tome lent to her by the grand mage. For days she had thumbed through it, reading the stories one at a time, hoping to arrive at the tale Marcel spoke of— the one about the marble dragon. Her scrying lessons with Marcel left her exhausted, so there was little time to research her dream. It was slow going.

As she waited for her evening tea, she flipped through the pages, skipping all the narratives she had not yet read. Much to her frustration, none of the titles contained the key words for which she searched. When she reached the final page, she sighed loudly and began again, this time digging deeper until she gasped. "I found it, Jocelyn!" she said, calling her handmaiden over.

"*How Fright the White Met His Downfall*," Jocelyn read, albeit shakily. She was still learning. Most handmaidens did not read.

Saffra had been teaching her. She smiled. *Fright the White* was a fitting name.

"Shall I read it aloud?" she asked. Jocelyn nodded, taking a seat opposite her. There was an epigraph and an authors' note. She started with those first.

Pale as snow his scales do gleam,
It seems they will forever,
For cursed he was by one supreme,
A most challenging endeavor.
Now he rests in grassy plains,
Entombed by solid stone,
For only blood can break these chains,
To free him from his own.

"What do you suppose that means?" Jocelyn asked.

"Well, it is obvious is it not?"

Jocelyn shook her head. "I do not understand the 'Only blood can break these chains,' part."

"I think it means that someone of the blood, I am not sure which blood, could possibly break the spell to free Fright from his stone form."

Jocelyn's jaw dropped. "But my lady, is he not a dragon?"

"Aye. A dangerous dragon at that." She was too eager for the story to ponder the poem further. She began reading the author's note.

"The following is an interpretation of a tale disclosed by the sprites of the Gable Forest, as told by their bards. To understand this legend, we recommend the reader first familiarize themselves with the stories of Rage—"

"Who is Rage?" Jocelyn asked.

"A dragon you never want to meet." She barked a laugh. "But we may never get through this story if you continue to ask questions." She gave Jocelyn a knowing smile before continuing, "The legend goes as follows. There was once a powerful dragon by the name of Fright, for he was truly frightful as his name suggests. Most commonly he became known as Fright the White, for his scales were that of moonstone. It is said that many onlookers mistook him for a full moon during dark skies. Thus the saying, 'Beware of the traveling moon' became common in stories told to scare children."

"I've heard of that!" Jocelyn cried. "My mother used to read me stories about the ancient dragons."

Saffra chuckled. Hers had, too. "Fright the White was the leader of the Storm Clan, one of the many clans to pledge allegiance to Rage. He was desperate to prove himself and eventually, he secured a most prestigious position in Rage's hierarchy. As his right hand and trusted general, he carried out many heinous crimes against the people of Dragonwall. Next to Rage, he was the most feared.

"For a time, they coexisted, sharing their love of blood thirst. But there came a day when Rage's hold upon Dragonwall began to weaken. Near the end of his campaign, many of Rage's sworn clans were defeated by the newly formed drengr. For Rage, the need to protect his claim to kingship grew dire, so much so, that he betrayed Fright.

"The mighty sprite queen, Queen Isabella, had been working hard to track down the last of Rage's supporters. To save his own hide, Rage and his Ice Clan betrayed the Storm Clan, resulting in the brutal deaths of all their clan members, except for Fright. Isabella had no intention of killing Rage's evil general. Her intentions were far worse."

"She turned him to stone!" Jocelyn clapped her hands together. She knew all about Saffra's dream and was eager to discover the truth of it.

"It would seem so," Saffra said, turning back to the story. "At long last, Queen Isabella came upon Fright in the lands north of the Gable Forest. She faced him alone, but she did not fear. Her magic was from the oldest bloodline in the kingdom. Her ancestors, the *Spirit Singers*, settled the lands of Dragonwall long before it was named thus, even longer still before the dragons existed. She was confident in her ability to curse this beast.

"And curse him she did, albeit not without great effort. They battled for many hours, testing the might of their powers—the magic of the sprites against the magic of the great asarlaí who birthed the beasts into the world. When at last the dust settled, all that remained of Fright was the form in which she cursed him to bear, the form from whence he originated. That of stone.

"From that day forward, the people of the land would rest easier knowing that a great evil had been destroyed—"

There came a knock at the door.

"That would be Desaree." Jocelyn jumped up and rushed to the door.

She set down the large tome, pushing aside her curiosities for now. They both greeted Desaree. She entered carrying their evening tea and honey cakes. As always, Saffra was delighted to see the young woman. "Tell us, how have you been?"

"I am faring quite well, my lady. Thank you." Desaree busied herself with the tea and cakes. Something was different about her this evening.

"What has you in such a good mood? Come, tell us. We would love something positive."

Desaree's face turned deep red and her eyes darted towards the floor. "Nothing at all my lady. It is simply a good day."

Saffra opened and closed her mouth. *A good day?* With an impending funeral and the keep in an uproar? She decided to let it go, because yes, Desaree was hiding something. "Were you given time to attend the procession tonight?" she asked, instead. "I had hoped that Jocelyn might attend with you."

"Oh. Yes, my lady. I am. All the servants are."

"Good. She may join you, then?"

"Of course. I'd be delighted." The two women exchanged happy smiles. "Sarah will be joining us, too."

"How wonderful!" Saffra looked from Jocelyn to Desaree. "Have you a few minutes to join us for tea, then?"

"I'd like that."

Together, they snacked and chatted until it was time for the two women to depart. As soon as Saffra found herself alone, she jumped into action, taking up the remainder of the honey cakes and stuffing them into a basket. Already there were cheeses, bread, salted pork, and other delectable items stowed within. She'd spent the day filling it, careful to keep it tucked away from Jocelyn.

She trusted her handmaiden, but this task could be dangerous and required secrecy. Claire was considered a threat to the kingdom. Most believed her guilty of murder. Cyrus was beloved by all. No one could know of this meeting.

With everything in order, she had only to wait. She wanted to ensure that no stragglers spotted her, so snatching up a half-finished wine bottle, she slipped it into the basket. Then she pulled one of the new bottles she had just received earlier that day and filled a goblet of her own. As the ruby liquid flowed into the cup, she hesitated. There was a strange and abnormal smell. She lifted it and inhaled. It reminded her of something...off-putting . Unease crept into the pit of her stomach.

Picking up the bottle, she studied it and smelled its contents. Her nose crinkled. Poison. It was ever so subtle, but she recognized it, thanks to some of Cyrus's efforts.

Disgusted, she set the bottle down and poured the contents of her goblet back inside. Unease prickled the back of her neck. The bottle was new. It had arrived with a set she recently ordered. Was someone trying to...to *poison* her? Her heart sped up. She glanced around the room. Nothing looked amiss. There was no one hiding in the shadows.

A dangerous game was brewing, and she had a feeling it had to do with her dissension from the lower council.

With a frenzy, she began uncorking the other bottles. She smelled each one before breathing a sigh of relief. They were fine, it was only the one. She returned the cork to the poisoned bottle and set it aside, determined to take it to the king when she had the chance. Until then, she took a deep breath and refocused her mind. She needed to mentally prepare herself for the task ahead.

This time, she poured herself a new goblet of wine from a new bottle, free of poison, and began sipping it. The wine was a deep red from the vineyards of Dalry. She drank deeply until none remained. Setting the goblet down, she rose and gathered up her basket, then waited.

Drums. The beat started low and slow. It grew louder. The procession had begun.

At the door, she paused, pulling her velvet hood over her head to shadow her face. Taking a deep breath, she turned the handle and stepped out into the corridor. There she breathed a sigh of relief. Aside from the drums, the keep was silent. Not a soul was in sight. Squaring her shoulders, she set off into the night for the dungeons.

CHAPTER 35

THE DUNGEONS

Kastali Dun

Saffra peered around the corner and into the guard room. A wall of keys stretched up to the ceiling. Numerous prisoners were housed within the dungeons. Some would never again see the light of day.

Four guards sat around a table of crates playing cards. They taunted each other, tossing coins onto a growing stack. With the activity taking place in the streets, their watch was relaxed. She smiled, already basking in her imminent success.

She pulled away and rested her back against the cold stones of the wall, breathing quietly. Her ears pricked at the sound of coins clinking.

"Loser of this hand does the next rounds," one of them said.

She tensed, stepping away from the doorway.

"I already know it's goin' ta be Eddy, eh lad?"

"You don't know what I got in my hand, Derrell. So, shut your hole." Eddy had a higher voice. He looked much younger than the others.

She continued to lurk, listening.

"Well, let's see 'em cards then." There was a pause, followed by a roar of laughter. "Ha! Told ya so, Eddy! Told ya so! To the rounds, boy!"

Eddy growled in annoyance. "Curse you, Derrell. Everyone knows you's a cheat!"

The scrape of a stool made her flinch. She concealed herself within the shadows. Moments later, Eddy emerged with a glowing lantern. He made his way down the hallway away from her. She watched his yellow glow until he was swallowed up by the darkness.

Long minutes ticked by.

Eddy returned and the guards went back to their cards, swearing and laughing, having a grand time. She crept past the open doorway and began down the hallway. When she was far enough from the guard room, she created her own light.

"*Eflae dagar*," she muttered, using the words of the old language. A small white orb, bluish on the edges, materialized, floating above her open palm. She thrust her hand forward, releasing her hold upon it. Floating along, it followed her.

The torches were extinguished in these corridors for good reason. Intruders would have a difficult time navigating the darkness of the hallways. Escapees would find themselves lost. The dungeons were made to be confusing. Their tunnels were purposefully built like a maze, but she knew which way to go, thanks to a large scroll she'd purloined from the keep's royal library. Had the king known it was there, it would have been removed from the shelves. Now it was safely hidden within her chambers.

Taking the first left turn, she made her way down a narrow tunnel. Prisoners awaiting trial were placed in the cells nearest to the guard room and farthest from the torture chambers. Perhaps it was to save them from the screams of those poor souls residing within the depths of the vast dungeon. She sniffed. The air was rancid.

Heavy doors lined both walls with small, barred windows. She looked through them one at a time. Her heart quickened, fearing what she might see within. Most of the occupants were male. Plenty were deranged and aggressive. At one door, just as she peered in, a toothless face loomed before her, laughing. A hand shot out between the bars. She yelped and jumped back, heart pounding.

She reached the wall at the end, but no Claire. A frown pulled her eyebrows together. Claire should have been here. Chewing on the inside of her cheek, she went to the second tunnel, and then the third. Unease crept into her stomach the deeper she went.

Soon, she found herself in the very back of the dungeons. It heated her blood and set her teeth on edge. The guards had locked Claire in the same tunnel as convicts serving life sentences. Her shoulders shook with anger. Taking a deep, calming breath, she placed her palms flat against Claire's door. She had no keys. If the wood was impervious to magic, her mission would fail.

Truthfully, that was one aspect of this mission she'd failed to find information about.

Clearing her mind, she focused on her words. "*Hinga laesa,*" she commanded. Her voice was no more than a whisper, but magic always knew. A click split the silence, and then another. The light pressure from her palms pushed the door open. There was a yawning darkness beyond.

Her light orb shot in and bathed the room in brightness. She blinked. Claire stood backed against the wall, eyes wide. Their gazes locked.

Saffra breathed a sigh. Claire looked exactly as she'd expected —exactly the way she had appeared in visions and dreams. She entered the cell and closed the door.

"Have...have you come to kill me?" Claire's voice rasped.

She shook her head. "I always wondered what meeting you would be like. And no, I have not come to kill you. Quite the contrary. I have come to help you." She held her basket forward. Claire eyed it but made no move to take it. So instead, she moved across the cell. "May I?" she asked, pointing at the blanket spread over the dirt floor. Claire nodded, but still watched her.

"I didn't think anyone would want to help me." Claire hesitated. "Is that...is that for me?"

Saffra was already removing contents from the basket. She

placed them upon the blanket, spread out as if they were merely having a picnic.

"Aye." She smiled. "I thought you might be hungry."

Claire's face crumbled. She could not have been much older than herself. A few years perhaps. A moment later, Claire plopped down beside her.

"I've seen that before." Claire pointed at the small orb of light, still looming about her. "You can do magic. Reyr used one when the vodar attacked us."

Saffra froze, chills racing down her arms. "The vodar attacked you?" Claire nodded. "Does the king know?"

"I don't think it matters," Claire scoffed. "I don't think he cares."

"Surely he does," Saffra said.

Claire snorted. "Not likely. All he cares about is ruining my life. Sorry, but who are you?"

"Oh. I'm Saffra."

"Saffra..." Claire's eyes grew wide, then a small smile formed on her lips. "*You're* Saffra? You're the reason I wasn't killed!"

"Killed?"

"A vote was taken. You were the only one who disagreed with my immediate death."

"I...yes." Saffra's eyes narrowed, suspicious. "I highly doubt the king would have killed you had I ruled with the majority."

"He absolutely would have. I know he would have."

"Here. Try these. They're my favorite," she said, lifting the honey cakes from the parchment. To prove her point, she popped one into her mouth, enjoying the sweet corn and honey flavor as it exploded on her tongue.

Claire hesitated, then did the same. Her eyes closed in delight and she made a humming sound of appreciation. After she swallowed, she said, "Thank you for coming. I thought I was going to starve in here."

"Please, it is the least I could do."

"Does this mean that you don't think I'm guilty? Everyone else thinks I am."

"Because they have not seen what I have."

"You saw me standing over Cyrus, covered in his blood."

"I...How do you know that?"

Claire shrugged. "The king told Reyr about it."

"And Reyr told you?" Saffra studied her.

Claire froze, mid-bite. "I...I overheard Reyr tell Koldis and Jovari."

"I see..."

"Wait." Claire's brows drew together. "If you saw me, does that mean you can see—"

"I can see things that others cannot," she explained. "I am a seer. The king's prophetess. Furthermore, I am the reason Cyrus is dead."

Claire's mouth fell open. "You don't...you don't honestly believe that, do you?"

"Of course I do. It was my vision that sent him away." A heaviness settled in the pit of Saffra's stomach, turning the honey cake into a rock. Cyrus's death *was* her fault. Had she stayed quiet about her vision, Cyrus would have remained within the keep.

"Is that why you aren't at his funeral?" Claire asked. "You blame yourself so you don't feel deserving?"

Heat flooded Saffra's face; thank the gods it was shadowed. "I came here for another reason," she said. "But...I do admit that avoiding his funeral was easier because I played a role in his death."

"No! Just... just *stop*. You can't..." Claire exhaled. "Look, I saw what killed Cyrus. I know what he was up against. You had nothing to do with *any* of it. If anything, blame the king, but don't be unfair to yourself."

The back of Saffra's neck prickled. "You saw what killed him?"

"Of course I did. I was there."

"And...does the king know—that you saw the killer, I mean?"

Claire shook her head and snorted. "I'd tell him if the asshat would let me." Saffra's jaw dropped. "Anyways, I can't tell him now, can I? The stubborn asshole won't speak with me. He insists upon a trial. *What*?!"

"I...it's just that...I do not think I have ever heard such colorful insults, especially not aimed towards the king."

Claire huffed. "Well, he deserves them."

Saffra sighed. Claire did make an excellent point. "So...if you saw his killer—"

"You don't think I would have said something to Reyr, if I could have? Trust me, I want to. I would have saved myself a trip."

"So...?"

"I cannot tell anyone before I tell the king. Cyrus forced me to make a promise."

"Oh." Saffra frowned. "But surely you are not so honorable that you would rather remain true to your word and risk your life over it. Why suffer the king's wrath? Why go through any of this?"

"Because I can't break my promise! I swore to Cyrus. I made an *unbreakable* promise."

She blinked. "An unbreakable...but...I never would have imagined—"

"Neither would the king. Which is why he thinks I'm bluffing about everything."

"So whatever you must tell him—it is important?"

"Extremely."

Saffra picked at her bottom lip with her teeth. What could be so important? Whatever it was, she trusted Cyrus. If he'd felt this need, then there was good reason.

Claire cleared her throat. "You said there was another reason you came here tonight. Why?"

"Oh. I..." Saffra glanced down at her basket before taking in Claire's face, her features. "I came here to figure out who you are."

"That's it?" Claire looked disappointed. She picked up a bread roll and pulled a chunk off, shoving it into her mouth.

"This is going to sound a little impossible, but I've seen you before."

"I know," Claire said through a mouthful. "You saw me standing over Cyrus, covered in his blood. You said that like two minutes ago."

"No, I mean..." Saffra sighed. "Claire, your face was the first face I ever saw in a vision. I was eight."

"You..." Claire's throat bobbed as she swallowed the remainder of her roll. "You're joking right?"

"I wish I was."

"But, what did you see? Like...like private stuff? You didn't see..." she trailed off.

"No. No private stuff. You need not worry about your personal business. I only saw bits and pieces."

"Why?"

"I wish I could say. I was hoping you would know." Even as she spoke the words, her stomach sank.

Claire slumped back against the cell wall. "You didn't happen to see the king releasing me in any of these visions, did you?"

"Unfortunately, no."

"Well, it was worth a shot I suppose."

"You need to speak with him alone to break the promise?"

"Yes—that was what Cyrus insisted upon. Not in a court full of people. If he knows what's good for his kingdom, then he will allow it. I need to tell him...I need to tell him everything."

"Well, that's cheery, isn't it?" Saffra tried to muster a smile.

"You don't even know the half of it," Claire muttered.

"Perhaps I no longer wish to. Is the kingdom truly in danger?"

"Pretty much. And danger might be an understatement."

"I see. Then I suppose your coming here is as important as I predicted. I admit, I thought perhaps I would discover more about you from this visit, and I have. But not as much as I hoped to."

"What do you mean?"

"Well, to start, I thought you might know why I have visions of you," she said.

Claire shrugged. "You're guess is as good as mine. It's creepy though, don't you think?"

"Creepy...yes, that is perhaps an adequate word for it."

Footsteps sounded down the tunnel. Saffra's blood turned cold. "Quick, put everything in here. The guards cannot know that I am here."

Together they piled everything back into the basket. She extinguished her orb and went to the opposite side of the room so that Eddy would fail to see her if he happened to look in. Holding her breath, she waited until his footsteps passed and then retreated. Then she waited a few moments longer just to be sure.

Silence returned.

"I'm afraid I must leave you now," she whispered, lighting the room once more. "Is there anything else I can do before I depart?"

"I doubt you can convince the king to set me free?" She gave a quick shake of her head. "Right. I didn't think so. Well then, a bath might be nice. I smell like shit."

A smile tugged at Saffra's lips. "Now *that*, I can do."

"Wait...really?"

Saffra grinned, moving to the other side of the cell. Speaking words that summoned up the dirt from the floor, she formed a clay-like bowl. Claire gasped as it took shape. As soon as it hardened, she finished her incant. Then, taking a water skin from the basket, she poured it into the bowl. Alone, it was hardly enough. But she knew the words for multiplying water.

"*Aukae vaten.*" The water rose to fill the bowl.

Claire gasped. "I...I don't believe it. I was only...I didn't think..."

"Your wish is my command, Claire. But, now I must leave you. Do *not* let the guards see the bowl or the basket." She cleared her throat then added, "I suppose the next time I shall see you is in the throne room."

"Great. I can hardly wait." Claire did not hide her lack of excitement.

"You are braver than I could ever be," Saffra admitted before departing. If anyone could stand up to the king, it would be this outsider, and wouldn't that be something!

CHAPTER 36

AN UNEXPECTED REQUEST

Kastali Dun

Desaree and Jocelyn found Sarah just after sunset. Together they made their way to a vantage point right outside the keep's gatehouse. It was an ideal place to watch the start of the procession. Ranks had already formed as everyone assembled to watch Cyrus travel through the city.

The warm summer air had not yet let up, and those carrying torches added to the heat. As if afraid to disrupt the mood, mourners cried soundlessly. Only hushed whispers could be heard as they floated through the orange glow. The speculation of a thousand onlookers created a sea of undertones that carried itself down the lines of progression where Cyrus would soon be carried.

Packed tightly in the crowd, Desaree, Jocelyn, and Sarah stood on their tiptoes to see over the heads of the other watchers.

"I have never seen this many gathered," Jocelyn whispered, eyes wide.

None of them had.

Desaree turned her gaze toward the main assembly. From the portcullis, the parade would snake its way through the city until it reached the defensive walls. Outside Kastali Dun, there was a huge pyre constructed by the cryptons. In keeping with tradition, Cyrus's body would be burned by the fiery breath of the king himself. It was tradition.

Musicians formed ranks to take the lead. They stood motionless, holding their instruments at the ready. Then, they began. A hauntingly sad tune echoed from the towering walls of the buildings that lined the street.

The musicians took up the march, pulling everyone else along with them. The people in the crowd cast flowers onto the ground, covering the way for the procession. The great sorrow permeating the air burst like an inflated pig's bladder, and the cries of many joined the heart wrenching tunes of the sad music. Grasping Sarah and Jocelyn's hands, she gave each a reassuring squeeze.

"Here comes the king!" Sarah gasped. Indeed, he had just come into sight. His proud form, heightened by the gold crown upon his brow, was difficult to miss. "Do not look directly at his face," Jocelyn warned, her voice hushed. "He will know."

She didn't *dare*!

The common rumor was that the king despised any attention brought about by his scarred face. In truth, his reputation was more frightening than the deep lines upon his skin. But she wasn't willing to take any risks.

They were unable to see much over the heads of everyone else, but Desaree saw the bier lifted by the cryptons who carried it. Cyrus rested atop. An ornate beaded cloth had been draped over him, hiding what lay beneath. Her eyes were drawn to the beauty of the rich beads that shimmered and sparkled. There must have been thousands sewn into place.

Flanking the bier were the king's five remaining shields. The king walked in front, his head bowed in defeat. Like the crowd, the drengr also wore gray—the color of a sad sky—with dragon's head sigils embroidered just above their hearts.

She tried to get a better look at Lord Verath, pushing herself as high as her toes allowed. When she caught sight of him, her heart skipped. His expression was hard, grim. All of the shield's faces were that way, etched with grief.

Just as quickly as they came, they passed. The music died down, and the procession continued further into the city. She heaved a sigh. Most of the crowd trailed after, making its way down the street. With them the sad cries. Her longing gaze followed.

"We'd better run along," Sarah murmured, breaking the spell. "Tess will have a fit if we're late. Jocelyn? Will you be returning with us?"

"I think I'll continue with the procession," Jocelyn decided, bidding them farewell.

Desaree and Sarah made their way back into the keep.

The feast that followed brought many guests. They ate and drank away their sorrows, telling stories of Cyrus. Desaree stayed busier than ever, assembling and delivering platters of food to the dining hall. Steaming rolls, caramelized carrots, potatoes, leafy greens. As soon as one dish was placed before a table of hungry mouths, she was fetching another. By the end of it, her body ached.

Only once that night did she glance up to the head table. She noticed that there was little conversation taking place between the king and his shields. She allowed her gaze to wander along the table until it fell upon Lord Verath. Their eyes met, forcing a small gasp from her lips. She looked away, pretending not to have noticed him, then avoided him entirely for the remainder of the night.

At long last, the feasting came to an end. Nearly everyone had retreated from the dining hall. She found herself delivering the final empty platters to the cookery. Relief drove her, and eagerness. All she could think about was sleep, her bed, tucking herself in beneath the sheets.

"Ah, Desaree! There you are!" Tess rounded on her with another tray. Its contents were hidden by plate covers.

She groaned, eying it. "Another? Can I not rest for the night?"

"Not yet, dearie. Take this to Lord Verath." Tess thrust the tray into Desaree's hands as she sputtered.

"Lord...Lord Verath?" Her stomach fluttered. "But...he was already at the feast. Did he not get his fill?"

"Gods, child! It is not for you to question a lord's command!"

"But...why me? There are others here—"

"Because he *requested* you!" Tess whacked Desaree with her wooden spoon. "Now get. Go on."

Her shoulders fell. Blowing loose strands of hair from her face, she forced one foot in front of the other, trying to hold back another groan as she left the cookery. She hadn't even realized what a mess she was until now. Holding the tray away from her, she looked down at herself. "Gods above," she swore. Food splatters dotted her apron. She looked like she'd taken a tumble in the pigpens. No doubt her hair was in a fit state of disarray, too, as strands freed themselves from her braided plait.

A strangled laugh exploded from her chest. Of all days—of all times. Lord Verath had summoned *her*. She had avoided him ever since their first encounter. The last few mornings when he'd requested breakfast, she'd traded the duty with the other servants. There would be no escaping him now.

A dead silence had fallen over the keep. In their exhaustion, guests and patrons had finally retired to their beds. She wished she could be curled up in her own, hiding under warm blankets. Nonetheless, her tired feet made their way to the *Hall of Kings*, albeit not without minor protests in the form of aches and pains.

She stopped outside Lord Verath's chambers, knocking more loudly than she ought to have. The door opened immediately, as if he'd been waiting beside it.

"Good evening, Desaree." Her skin flushed hot. "Come in."

"Good evening, my lord," she said, entering. A click sounded as the door closed behind her. She kept her eyes on the tray and made her way across the room. Gods! Why did the table have to be so far from the door?

"I apologize for keeping you late," he said. "I am well aware of the hour." She made no reply. "If you will forgive me for it, I believe the need is dire."

A snort bubbled up from her chest; she disguised it as a polite cough. *Dire?* Gods above! He had *just* eaten. How dire could it possibly be?! She set the tray upon the table.

"Have you eaten?" he asked, coming to stand across from her.

"No, my lord." Her face flushed anew. There'd been no time for dinner, and she would have eaten afterward, had Tess not sent her to his room with another gods' damned tray.

"Good. I had hoped not. Stay and eat with me." She faltered, her hand hovering over one of the platters. "Well?"

"Thank you, my lord, for your invitation, but I am not hungry. I must respectfully decline."

"Nonsense. You have not eaten. You must be hungry."

She opened her mouth—

"Sit! I command it of you."

She scurried to sit, afraid to disobey a direct command. He moved around to push her chair in before taking the one across from her. Her hands began to tremble. She clasped them together in her lap, fidgeting with her fingers. The food before her *did* look spectacular. An entire leg of roast goose and gravy, mashed potatoes, fresh baked rolls, and leafy greens. She inhaled, hiding the sigh that threatened to escape her chest. There was even pie! She adored pie.

Her eyes devoured everything as Lord Verath studied her, letting silence stretch out before them. "Have some of everything," he said at last, handing her the only empty plate. "I insist."

As if in a daze, she began dishing a bit of everything. The fragrant scent of herbs left her stomach growling. Mortified, her hand flew over her abdomen. Lord Verath's booming laugh broke the silence. Her skin burst into flame. She stole another glance, only to find that he was laughing at her!

"See?" His eyes danced with mirth. "And you told me you weren't hungry. What say you now?"

She couldn't quite form words, so she gave him a shy smile and returned to the food. It came as no surprise that everything was delicious, the roast goose especially. She ate it slowly to savor it. Once she began eating, it was difficult to remember how weary she was.

"Is it to your liking?" he asked.

"Yes, my lord. It's...excellent."

"Please, no need for such titles. My name is fine."

"Of course, Lord Verath." She didn't dare look at him.

"No, I meant—" He paused to sigh. "Verath will do."

"As you wish, my—Verath." Oh, *gods*! She withered with embarrassment.

He chuckled.

She ignored him, trying not to fall apart. Instead, she turned her attention to the pie, scooting away her emptied plate, greedily setting the slice in front of her. Verath showed no interest in the pie, and why should he? Surely he'd had plenty at the feast.

She stole a glance and caught him grinning. Fine. Let him laugh all he wanted. She had every intention of savoring this.

Maybe that's why he'd invited her here. To entertain him. Well, at least he made it worth her while, bribing her with food. Good food—at that. She was never one to turn down the cook's food, and her curves showed it.

With the first bite, her eyes closed in enjoyment. Instead of fretting over Lord Verath's attention, she focused on the savory taste of berries doused in sugary glaze. And the crust, so flaky and buttery. It was heaven. Absolute heaven.

"I see your bruise has improved."

She froze her chewing and opened her eyes.

"I did not appreciate your refusal when I last asked for the perpetrator's name. You ought to have told me." Her muscles tensed. "Come now. You need not fear me. It merely makes me angry to see such mistreatment, especially towards you."

"Thank you for your concern, my lord. It's healing well enough." She cleared her throat. "Forgive me, but I truly have no desire to discuss it."

"I could make you tell me, Desaree," his voice was low. "I could command it of you."

Her stomach dropped. "I would prefer that you do not. I cannot...I cannot risk her finding out."

"Her?" Lord Verath's brows knitted. "It was a woman and not your lover?"

She sputtered. "My—my *what*?"

"Your lover."

"I...I don't have one," she stammered, absolutely mortified.

His eyebrows rose. "I see. And you are afraid that if you tell me, this woman will find out?" She nodded. "What if I can promise you otherwise? Would you tell me?"

She opened her mouth, then shut it tightly, considering his words. Her heart sped up in her chest. "You promise she will not find out?"

"I promise. You have my word." He laid a hand over his heart. The king's Shields were honorable. They did not lie or cheat. If Lord Verath promised, then she could trust him.

"Very well. I will tell you. It was Lady Caterina."

"Lady Caterina?" His brow furrowed for a heartbeat before he quickly hid any evidence of surprise. She fidgeted in her chair. "I should have known. She is certainly an awful woman, is she not?"

Her eyes widened. A weight lifted from her shoulders and she relaxed. "What did she do to you to make you dislike her?"

He chuckled. "She has done nothing to me, thank the gods! It is what she does to the king that drives me mad."

A tiny gasp escaped her lips.

"Can you keep a secret?" he asked, his eyes twinkling. She nodded. "Lady Caterina has been after King Talon for years. He very much dislikes her, but that does not hinder her. She makes it painfully obvious that she wishes to be queen. Being the petty woman that she is, she is not interested in his...handsome face."

She burst into a fit of uncontrolled laughter. It couldn't be helped. For the first time since entering Lord Verath's presence, she felt all her nerves melt away. "This does not surprise me," she said through her gasping. "I do recall her speaking of her desire to be queen the day she struck me."

"Did she?"

"Oh yes. She claimed to hold the title very soon."

"Gods above!" Lord Verath shook his head. "Sadly, Caterina is delusional. The king has given no answer, nor will he."

"That is a blessing." Her smile faded and she turned serious.

"The king understands her motives, I hope? She is beautiful to be sure, but her charm is false."

"Aye, he sees through her."

"Few have the ability. Caterina has a way with...acting."

"Does she?" Lord Verath lifted his eyebrows, feigning surprise. "I hadn't noticed."

"You're teasing me, aren't you?"

"Indeed."

"Well then, if you had not yet noticed, then perhaps she is not trying hard enough."

He chuckled. "Believe me, she does try. But it is achingly obvious to the king. He knows what her motives are. He has no interest in them or her. He has no interest in women at all, really. He gave them up long ago."

"Truly? He prefers men then?"

"No, no. Not that it would matter." Verath waved his hand in dismissal. "The king is simply not interested in either."

"But he is so young! Surely he still seeks love, despite the common knowledge that..." She trailed off, afraid to mention his failure of finding a mate.

"Some claim that his scars are to blame," Verath said. "We have assured him that they are not so bad, but he will not hear it. Bah! He is entirely too self-conscious."

"I see." She almost pitied the king.

They fell silent and she went back to eating, picking out a few berries and plopping them into her mouth. The juice exploded on her tongue, its tangy flavor overpowering her senses. She glanced up at Lord Verath. He sat watching her.

"Why did you invite me here tonight?" she asked, unable to bear her own theories any longer.

He hesitated, as if considering his next words. "From my observations, you worked hard tonight, as you always do." His gaze darted to the front of her apron. Oh, gods! She glanced down and blushed. "What impresses me the most about you, Desaree, is that I have never seen you in poor spirits. There is always a smile upon your face and a warm greeting to be had. You are kinder than you ought to be to many who do not deserve your gentleness." Her mind tripped over his words. "As to why I requested *you* specifically, I assumed you would be hungry, so I called you here because I wanted you to have a nice meal."

Warmth filled her chest. She opened and closed her mouth, stunned. Stunned that he had noticed all those things about her.

His lips parted slightly, as if he wanted to say more. He drummed his fingertips on the arm of his chair. "We drengr are often selfish."

She barked a laugh. "Forgive me, but I find that hard to believe. I've heard many stories regarding your kind."

"Oh?" The corner of his mouth twisted into a smile.

"Selfish is not the word I would have chosen. Honorable perhaps? Self*less*?"

He chuckled. "Perhaps, but behind all that we are greedy. A drengr is only half human. The other half..."

She knew what he meant, but it was not for her to argue. Dragons in the tales of old were known to be greedy, bloodthirsty beasts. Verath was neither.

"I am selfish, Desaree, because even though I hide behind the pretense of inviting you here to feed you, I felt lonely tonight. I thought perhaps your company would lift my spirits, because you are always in good spirits."

Her heart should have rejoiced. His were the words she both wanted and dreaded. Wanted because they made her so warm. Dreaded because loving a king's shield was dangerous.

"You look...disappointed."

"Disappointed?" she squeaked. She shook her head, doing her best to appear the opposite. "No. I'm...I'm honored, my lord, to be considered fit company for a shield."

"Verath, remember?" He smiled. "I insist that you refrain from titles, especially when we are alone together."

Gods above! Her heart could have failed in that moment. She could have died happy.

"Now then, it is getting late. Off to bed with you. You can take the pie along. I will have my own servants take the rest to the cookery in the morning."

She blinked back at him, dumbstruck. "I...thank you."

"It is my pleasure."

She smiled wide and picked up the pie, leaving his room. That same smile plastered to her face refused to depart even in sleep as she dreamt of him that night, and many nights to come.

CHAPTER 37
THE COLOR BLACK

Talon sat with his remaining shields, eyeing them in silence. Firelight danced across the sitting room, casting long shadows around his tower. There came another loud rumble as a thunderstorm threw itself upon the keep's walls, breaking the day's humidity. Inside, a cozy fire crackled within the grate.

Three days of funeral games had come and gone. What he'd believed would be an adequate postponement of the inevitable was no longer so. Tomorrow, the trial would take place, and he would be forced to confront the outsider who'd caused them so much pain. He had half a mind to delay it further, knowing he was in such a poor state, but this was his duty.

He heaved a heavy sigh and turned his gaze back to the fire. Duty. Always the driving force. He had every reason to despise it. Duty urged him to face each day anew, and duty kept him hard at work late into the night. This was the price of a crown—a lesson that took him many years to learn.

He had never wanted to be king. When he'd been younger, he'd denied such a day would come, but it had, painfully so.

"No good will come from tomorrow," Reyr murmured into the silence. Talon turned and met Reyr's eyes, noticing their intensity. It often felt like Reyr could read straight into his soul, and sometimes, like now, it was too much. He looked away and found the others watching him just as intently.

He rubbed the back of his neck. "What would you have me do, Reyr? Cancel the trial? Policy demands it."

Koldis snorted. "Policy? The lower council, you mean? They demanded Claire's head too, yet you did not acquiesce."

"I have already heard your argument, Koldis. You have given your reasons often and without restraint. All of you have." He glared at them. "You would have me speak to her in private. You would have me look the fool. Without a trial, the people will believe I am weak. The council will feel slighted. They will claim this outsider has me eating from the palm of her hand. Am I to abandon the law?"

"Yes, yes." Reyr waved a hand in dismissal. "The people cry for justice. What's new? Since when have the people come before your duty to do what is right?"

"All right, then, what *is* right? Hmm?" His voice was low, like the warning growl from a berated cat, or the stifled snarl from an irritated dragon. It's was more of a rhetorical answer.

Politics. It always boiled down to that. It was impossible to please everyone. If he leaned one way, his people would cry out in dismay. If he leaned the other, the response would be the same.

"You already know the answer to that," Reyr said. "Speak with Claire. Discover the truth behind what happened. You are not merely depriving yourself of answers. Cyrus was *our* brother, too."

His shields nodded in agreement.

He huffed at the lack of support. Not one of them was on his side. For once, he didn't care.

He turned back to the fire, falling into silence.

"Your Grace, if I may—" Reyr began, again.

"No!" he growled, done with this conversation. "The trial will go as planned, Reyr. Tomorrow, she will face the kingdom. If she chooses to withhold information before the council, then she will go back to the cells."

Reyr opened his mouth—

"*Enough!*"

Silence fell. He suddenly found their company overbearing. His heart felt too much, angered and hurting in equal measure. "Leave me, all of you," he said. "I will see you in the morning."

They complied, rising from their chairs and exiting the room. Reyr was the last to depart. Just before shutting the door, he hesitated on the threshold for several breaths. Finally, he shook his head and disappeared.

Talon found himself alone at last. It was late and the storm had finally moved on. But there would be no sleeping—not tonight. Sleep had become a rare commodity. It often felt as if every bit of him belonged to his people, as if he were the true servant. Most days he offered himself unyieldingly, but there was still one thing that was entirely his own.

Leaving the interior of his tower for the large balcony just outside, he greeted the damp night air. The smell of rain lay thick around him, cleansing some of the smells that often seeped towards the keep from the city. The clouds had cleared enough to show a few stars. He found himself gazing upward. He belonged there within the heavens, lost within the sky and its clouds. No one could ever take that from him.

Resting his forearms upon the parapet separating him from the sea far below, he leaned forward. Only a few golden pinpricks could be seen—ships making their way to and from the Port of Kastali. Gazing out into the night, out into its darkness, he considered the life he had been given.

So much bad luck. So much misfortune. He often wondered if he'd been cursed.

Black dragons were rare. He was the first ruler to bear such a color. Throughout history, there were many reasons the royal family had birthed reds, golds, and blues.

It was said that black was an impossible color to conquer. The epitome of unruliness. Those rare few to be cursed as he was were easily prone to anger, fear, and grief. What was worse, most lost themselves to it. He had very few fears, but losing himself to madness was one.

"The beast within you is untamed," his father used to say. His parents had worried over his color, and had frequently used it to explain away his rebellious nature. Uncontrollable or not, that part of him would always be his.

Besides losing his parents too early, he'd failed to find a mate. Perhaps it was because he was untamable. No one had ever done it, and no one would. He'd never been meant for love. Such a thing was written in other colors, but not his.

Mateless.

He shook his head. Enough of such thoughts. Instead, he listened to the wind as it taunted him, coaxing him, begging him to come and fly. He answered its call.

Leaping into the air, he shed his skin, transforming into the hulking black iridescent scales that fit him better than humanity ever would. It was liberating. With outstretched wings he caught the nearest updraft, letting it carry him far from his responsibilities and further still from his fears. Flying was the only thing that brought him joy, and how lucky he was to never share it. Let the people take everything else, they could never take his wings.

For a long time that night he was one with the wind, letting his body drift and soar, allowing his mind to forget the problems he was doomed to face. He went hunting and allowed the beast in him to take over. On the plains of Eigaden, he located a herd of wild grazers. They snacked under the stars, oblivious to much of their surroundings. If they anticipated his approach, they gave no sign of it, except a bit of shifting from hoof to hoof.

Pleased, he glided silently over them, absolute in his stealth. When he found one suitable for his picky tastes, he overtook it, snatching it up in his claws and breaking its neck. It was a heavy creature, fattened from a season of gorging. All the better for him. He carried it to a perch overlooking the prairie. There he feasted. Nothing felt more powerful than being a dragon. *Nothing*.

By morning, his appetite was satisfied and his mind calmer, or so he thought. When he landed upon his balcony and took up his human form, all his woes came flooding back. The relentless waves of duty always found the one who waited upon the shores of responsibility. With nowhere to escape, it was inevitable.

"Good morning, Your Grace." Reyr stepped out of the shadows and greeted him.

Much to his surprise, he was relieved. "I had not expected to find you here. I certainly do not deserve such devotion." Then without stopping himself, he covered the distance between them and clapped the gold drengr upon the back in greeting.

"I am here, Talon. I will always be here, devoted as ever." Reyr bowed his head. The golden drengr was unyielding in his honor and even more so in his steadfast friendship. His color was a true testament to his heart.

Talon nodded in acceptance. "It was wrong of me to dismiss you so abruptly last night," he said. He wasn't good at admitting to his faults, but after so many years of Reyr's company, it got easier.

"Your burdens are great and many. As my king, you owe me no apologies."

"Yes, but as your friend, I do."

Reyr smiled, squeezing his shoulder. Always quick to forgive. "Come now, we have other matters at hand. Today, we are going to court. Today, you will finally meet Claire."

His heart beat a little faster. From fear, perhaps? Or was it nervousness? Whatever it was, he was suspicious of the feeling. Something about this woman grated on him, threatened him.

"Claire..." he repeated her name, as if saying it for the first time. The sound was nice. He mulled it over in his mind. Keeping her nameless made it easier to place blame, blame that ultimately rested with him. But admitting to it was the added brick that would send him buckling under too much weight. "What is she like?" he found himself asking.

"Well..." Reyr shrugged. "Beautiful, to be sure."

"Since when have I cared about a woman's beauty?" His scars ensured that beauty would never come to him. The only second glances he received were from those brave enough to gawk at the ruination of his face.

Reyr grinned. "You used to care, you know, when you were younger."

"Yes, yes. Thank you for reminding me. As if I could have forgotten."

Before Gemma, he and Reyr had had plenty of tumbles and romps with both the noble and common born alike. It was all good fun, until it wasn't.

"Fine." Reyr sighed. "If you really wish to know, Claire is unlike any woman I have ever met. She is…"

"She's what?"

"Different." Talon's scowl deepened. "She is headstrong, stubborn, determined…" Reyr began ticking off her characteristics as his grin grew, as if he knew something Talon did not. "She is also a little strange. She does not behave like the women we are used to."

"I'll have my work cut out for me, then," he muttered, his annoyance resurfacing. Perhaps Reyr found merit in these traits, but he did not. They were not qualities he looked forward to wrestling with in court—or ever. The dragon within was too quick to anger, and if that happened, he would be helpless against the darkness inside.

"Oh, yes, Your Grace, your work is cut out for you." For a moment, their eyes exchanged silent understanding. Reyr spoke once more, "It is nearly time. Shall I wait for you to prepare?" He was already dressed in his court attire, his large sverak belted at his side. "I thought you might like accompaniment this morning, and I assume you have already eaten."

"Yes, a fat grazer from the herds north of here."

"Good. Then hurry up."

The male servants in his tower jumped into action. Like Reyr, he too donned his best, strapping his black-jeweled sverak to his side. The sword was a drengr's symbol of maturity—a gift from father to son at the coming of age. He wore his proudly.

Atop his head was placed his most regal crown. The weight of it prompted him of what lay ahead. "A crown should always be heavy, to remind you of the burden you must carry," his father had once told him. He'd been a young boy then, and had not yet succeeded in his drengr transformation. As a child, he could not understand why his father bothered with such a burdensome formality.

"Just leave it behind, if the weight is too much," he'd said, watching his father fuss with it as he prepared for the tedious duties of court. "You're the king. That means you can do what you want."

"It is because I am the king that I wear it." His father's stern look was something he'd never forgotten. "Someday you will understand."

King Tallek had been right. He did understand, only too well. It was now his turn to wear the crown whenever propriety deemed it necessary. And today was one of those days.

CHAPTER 38

THE TRIAL

Kastali Dun

Claire caught the sound of footsteps outside her cell. The clink of keys. A moment later, the door swung open, letting the light of a torch into her space. She shrank back into the corner. All this time she had waited, impatiently furious. Suddenly, she no longer wanted to leave the darkness of her familiar cage.

"King ain't got all day, girl. Let's go." Two guards stood framed in the doorway.

She had no other choice but to obey. They moved up through the keep at a quick pace. She was too numb to notice the rich sculptures lining the corridors, or the decadent hangings on the walls. She did not admire the ornate architecture with its arched windows and vine-carved doors. They passed by servants who stopped to gawk and whisper.

A rough hand found her arm, forcing her to stop. Giant double doors towered above her, barring her entry. They led into the king's court, his throne room. She exhaled, relieved that they were closed.

"Can I...can I have a moment?" she croaked, her voice little more than a whisper.

"Fine. Make it quick." They stepped away several paces.

She looked down at herself, readjusting her silver gown, the one the sprites had given her. It was the nicest thing she owned. A good impression couldn't hurt, could it?

She looked back up at the doors and a fresh wave of nausea clenched her gut. She put a hand over her stomach. "I don't think I can do this," she whispered, too low for the guards.

She glanced down the corridor. What would happen if she ran? Would they chase after her? How far could she make it through the castle before they captured her?

Cyrus?

It was ridiculous. She wasn't sure why she called for him. He was dead. But some impractical notion hinted at a connection between them. Her suspicion had been growing.

All she knew was she needed him now more than ever. *Cyrus, what do I do?*

Silence. Was it so absurd to expect an estranged voice to answer?

Cyrus, Please! I need you—

I am here.

She gasped. Emotion slammed into her, powerful waves against a rocky shoreline, sending mist and foam high into the air in a tumultuous crash of water. She exhaled, trying to breathe. Her eyes stung. Was it really him?

I am here. I will always be here.

It had been his voice...all this time? How had she missed that?

Even the best of us can neglect the most obvious signs. Be brave, Claire. You saved me, remember? You are stronger than you know.

She gulped down air. *I want to be brave,* she said, *but I don't feel brave at all.*

You are too hard on yourself.

Was she? Perhaps he was right, but at the moment, she felt like a coward. If she could, she would have run away and left this all behind.

I highly doubt that. A mental snort accompanied his words. He knew she wouldn't flee, even if the guards stepped aside. Deep down, she knew it too.

Tell me what to do?

You truly wish to know? he asked.

She nodded at the doorway, very aware that this silent conversation was certifiably insane.

You hold your head high and proceed. You have no other choice. You were meant to come here—to do this. Think of it as your destiny.

My...my destiny? Her frown deepened. *Don't you think that's a little extreme?*

Cyrus did not answer but from somewhere within, an unyielding confidence radiated through her like flames to paper. Her body burned hot as every fearful thought, every second guess, every misgiving was swallowed up, leaving her with courage and strength.

Was it Cyrus giving her what she needed? No, somehow she knew otherwise. This was the same courage she felt when a dragon had fallen from the sky. It was the same courage that had urged her to save the human she found in its place. The same courage she felt when she faced the vodar wraiths on her front lawn.

Cyrus was just exposing qualities she already possessed.

Never forget, Claire, fear is a snare. Sometimes, a reminder of our strength is the best remedy to our struggles.

He was right. Taking a deep breath, she squared her shoulders and lifted her chin. Cyrus was with her. He would see her through this.

I will always be with you.

The guards resumed their position beside her. One of them rapped three times against the wooden doors with the butt of his spear. The echoing booms resounded. The doors swung forward. She gasped. Colors greeted her. Rainbows of colors, dancing like ballerinas upon every surface, casting beautiful patterns of light throughout a vast space. Multi-story stained-glass windows lined the walls. Her mouth fell open, taking it all in.

They are depictions of the famous battles of Rage, put in place by

King Eymar, first of his name. The same King Eymar who built this great keep.

The hall was immense, with dark slate floors and thickly carved columns, gazing down upon her like proud giants. She took a deep breath, and then another. The heavy scent of wood greeted her like an old friend. The smell was familiar and comforting. For a moment she was back in Esterpine. Whatever goodness, whatever encouragement the hall was willing to give, she would take.

Harsh hands brought her back to reality. The guards were ready to lead her. She had no choice but to move forward. Radiating pride, she took one step, and then another. Dragonwall may not have known, but she did. Cyrus had saved them, and *she* was the one he'd chosen.

"Stand back!" ordered the guards, pushing at the crowd. Their loud voices penetrated the throng of onlookers who pressed together to witness her entrance. In a single sweep they parted, leaving a wide space for her procession, but she could no longer move. Her feet were glued to the floor. There, at the end of the pathway, was Dragonwall's king.

His appearance matched what she already knew of him—he was powerful...and frightening. It showed in his posture. He sat comfortably on his throne, his elbows resting atop the armrests. His fingers were steepled in front of his mouth. This was a man who did not doubt his supremacy. He knew full well of the dominion he possessed.

She hated him even more for it.

"Move." A shove came from behind. She took a deep breath and proceeded forward, keeping her eyes fixed on the source of her unease. The first few steps were difficult, but with Cyrus's encouragement, each step became easier, until her confident strides had the guards huffing to keep up.

"Reyr, it seems you warned me of her beauty, even stubbornness, but you forgot to warn me of her pride." She missed a step when the king's voice sounded in her mind. *"She walks as though I am at her mercy, as if it is I who must answer to her, as if three days in a cell did nothing to wear her down."*

"Yes, well...perhaps I forgot to mention that." It was wonderful to hear Reyr so clearly over the buzz of other Drengr constantly plaguing her. She gave no notice of the exchange and continued.

Reyr was there in front. So was Jovari, Koldis, and two others she didn't recognize. They sat in elegantly carved chairs arranged at the base of the throne's dais, three to one side and three to the other. One was empty.

That was my place.

Reyr sat opposite the empty chair, closest to the throne on the other side. Sitting beside him were the two she did not know. Next to the empty chair on the other side sat Koldis and then Jovari.

When she briefly met his gaze, Koldis winked. She blinked, not quite sure she'd seen it. But yes, he had. Her heart lifted. The simple gesture meant a lot. Reyr, on the other hand, she refused to look at. Of the three, she blamed him the most. He'd promised to speak sense into King Talon. A whole lot of good that had done.

The king's heavy gaze followed her procession. His stare was intense, as if he could read her secrets. But he couldn't read everything, could he? There was one she hoped he'd never discover.

She drew close to the dais and he moved his hands. She faltered. An inaudible gasp fell from her lips. His face was covered in scars. She quickly schooled her features. A thimble of pity welled up inside of her. What kind of horrors had done such a thing? For a brief moment, compassion replaced intense hatred.

She stopped at the base of the stairs and beheld him more closely. He was completely different than she had imagined. She'd expected him to be old, perhaps a white beard, stooped with age. He was nothing of the sort.

Hiding behind his marred skin was a young face. She could see that he'd once been handsome, with a prominent forehead and heavy-set silver eyes. They glittered with flecks of gold. Beautiful as they were, his eyes did not overshadow the rest of him.

Was it difficult for his subjects to see past the mutilations that covered his face? The most noticeable ran diagonally from his right eyebrow to his lower jaw. She forced her gaze away to look at the rest of him.

His jet-black hair was thick and unruly, hardly tamed by the crown of gold atop his head. These two wrestled for power. Order versus chaos. The winner was clear. Yet the untidiness suited him, lending itself to his beast-like appearance.

The guards moved away, shattering the spell that held her captive by the king's appearance. She was instantly reminded of why she was here. She glanced around the hall, acutely aware of thousands of eyes upon her. Only one pair mattered, and these hadn't so much as blinked.

The king regarded her with a stony expression.

What had she expected? Kindness? A warm welcome? Perhaps some shred of compassion for all she had been through? No, it went deeper than that. She despised his judgement. Despised that he'd marked her as a traitor before ever meeting her.

Heat flooded her skin. Anger. She forced her body into motion and gave him the sloppiest bow she could muster, keeping her face upturned rather than lowering her gaze. Challenging him.

His expression briefly flashed, from surprise to disdain. Soon enough it turned back to stone. Only his eyes betrayed him, glittering with anger. Good. She wanted him to know her behavior was intentional. The beast within was stirring and she'd just invited it out to play.

Be careful when crossing a black dragon. Hate him or not, he is still the king.

Without being invited to rise, she stood from her bow. Whispers swept through the hall. Let them be appalled. Let them hate the way she acted, the way she carried herself, the way she dressed like a sprite, an outsider, someone they did not understand. She no longer cared *what* they thought. This kingdom was not *her* kingdom. This king was not *her* king.

"Silence!" a voice called. A man moved forward from behind the dais. He held a quarterstaff, which he rapped several times on the slate floor. His old age gave him a slight stoop. "Silence in the court," he cried again.

"And who are you?" She boldly lifted her brows.

His eyes bulged at her question. "The king's steward." Then he unrolled a scroll and began reading. "To the woman heretofore known as Claire: You come before the king and court this day to answer for your crimes against Dragonwall. Crimes against both the kingdom, and a beloved shield. How do you plead?"

She cleared her throat and lifted her voice. "I plead not guilty."

The crowd erupted into speculative whispers.

"*Siiilence*," the steward cried, drawing out the word until it snuffed out all else. When his gaze returned to her, he continued. "Not guilty, you say? The council disagrees with you on all charg—"

"What, exactly are the charges?" she demanded, intentionally interrupting.

This charade was *so* beneath her, so she humored him as if he were a child. The steward's face turned red. He glanced up at the king, waiting for some form of punishment. The king merely nodded, inviting him to continue.

"Firstly, you stand accused of entering Dragonwall through one of its gates. For this, the council has already found you guilty. The punishment for such a crime is death." He offered her a sly smile. Cyrus began speaking in her mind, a rush of instructions about the laws of Dragonwall. He spoke so quickly that it left her mind buzzing. "Well? How do you counter?" asked the steward.

Remember, you cannot lie, Cyrus added.

She met the steward's eyes and said, "The common law dictates that the use of any gate is illegal. However, the original charters written by King Eymar state that under extreme circumstances—such as mine—a person may venture through any gate from either side."

The king shifted upon his throne.

"And how is it that you, an outsider, could possibly know that?" the steward demanded.

"You are welcome to have a look, if you do not believe me. The sub clause can be found in article six, residing within *Laws of the Land*, one of three charters written and signed by representatives of the drengr monarchy, the sprites, and the dwargs."

The steward gaped at her, speechless.

Tell him where they are, Cyrus said.

"The original documents can be found hanging in their frames within the royal library. If you would like to go and have a look, I can wait." She crossed her arms, shifting her weight to one leg. This drove the court crazy with excitement. "And by all means, take your time. I have nowhere *else* to be."

"I know where they reside," the steward sputtered. "And I am well aware of the sub clause to which you refer." With all the side conversations, he was forced to yell over the courtiers. He began slamming his staff against the slate floor, calling for silence. Again.

"Well...good. You then understand, then, that based on my stance, the council must deliberate for at least twenty-four hours to reconsider the circumstances that have brought me here. Shall we reconvene tomorrow?" she asked, knowing full well he would refuse.

"We—we shall *not!*" he cried. "We have other crimes to discuss."

"Oh, very well then, let's get on with it." The only sign of her nerves were her trembling hands, which she kept clenched in tight fists beneath her crossed arms.

"The second charge stands as follows. You stand accused of withholding information from Lord Reyr, a king's shield. This is another act punishable by death."

She sighed. How unsurprising. A quick glance at the king showed his face cold and impassive. He wasn't even looking at her. He stared straight ahead at the opposite end of the hall.

"What say you, regarding *this* claim?" the steward asked.

"Well, *Steward*, you can ask Lord Reyr if you like." She glanced at Reyr. He shifted uncomfortably in his seat. "He knew of my reasons. It was *he* who approved my request, granting me permission to withhold my information and pass through the gate."

"Because you gave him no choice." A commanding voice swept through the hall, rich and powerful in its address. Silence fell.

"I believe, *Your Majesty*, that you also know the reason for Lord Reyr's approval. You know exactly why he granted my...request."

The king smoothed his expression and said nothing. He'd never believed her promise was legitimate. According to him, she was merely using it as an excuse to gain entry into his kingdom. As if his kingdom was such a great place to be.

"How do you plead?" the steward asked, regaining control. She gave the king her best expression of disgust before turning away.

Plead guilty…

She sucked in a breath. *What?! But….*

Kane's nasks cannot know about the promise.

She glanced towards the left and right sides of the dais. There she found the lower council. She swallowed the lump forming in her throat. Which of them were his nasks?

A row of seats, ten in length, were arranged on each side of the throne room's dais. All twenty were filled. These mediators sat just below the king's throne in height, giving them a good vantage point of all that transpired. Her eyes flicked from one side to the other. Saffra was there, but she did not make eye contact.

If Kane's nasks knew she had the power to sell them out, what would they do? Sneak down to the dungeons and kill her in her sleep? Perhaps they would call for her immediate death here and now, to which the gathered crowd would respond with glee. Or worse still, they might flee, never to be held accountable for their treason.

Give no indication that you know. Kane has no idea how much I saw within his mind.

Her heart hammered, sending blood roaring past her ears. Guilty or not, the king wouldn't dare kill her, not yet, not before she could tell him what she knew. She gulped down air and said, "For these charges, Steward, I plead guilty."

The hall erupted into chaos. The steward failed to withhold his malicious grin. He was delighted. How much had Kane's nasks paid him to tip the scales?

"Are those my only charges?" she asked, voice raised. She was tired of entertaining the courtiers. She wasn't some…some *spectacle* to be gawked at.

"Of course not!" he claimed eagerly. "There is one more."

"I'll have it then." The poor man was trying so hard. It irked him to see her stand tall against him.

"You are charged with the murder of Lord Cyrus, a beloved king's shield and advisor to the king. How do you plead?"

She sighed. "I plead not guilty." As she said it, she met the king's eyes. They were cold and accusing. Her stomach knotted. After everything, he still didn't believe her. What was worse, he looked as though he might kill her himself.

From this distance, she noticed a muscle ticking in his jaw. He hid it well enough, but he was furious. Why? Had he *wanted* her to admit to killing Cyrus?

The steward stepped off the last step of the dais. "Not guilty, you say?" He made a show of his skepticism. "We shall see, won't we?" Snapping his fingers, he called forth a man who emerged from the crowd. This man carried a long object wrapped in cloth. Her blood ran cold. She'd forgotten about the vodar sword, the one that had been buried in Cyrus's abdomen. The man unwrapped his bundle for all to see and handed it to the steward, who was careful not to touch the blade.

"What do you make of this?" he asked. A fresh wave of panic struck her, threatening to shatter her composure. "Well?"

Cyrus stayed silent.

"It isn't mine."

"Isn't it, though? It was in your possession when you were discovered. Reyr has confirmed it. Hmm..." The steward feigned thoughtfulness as he looked over the blade, studying it. "Well, if it is not yours, if there is another to whom it belongs, let it be known. An accomplice perhaps?"

She opened her mouth to speak, but nothing came out. The promise would never allow her to say the truth with such an audience. The steward gave her a toothy grin. Letting him win riled her. It wasn't fair.

Better to appear ignorant. The nasks cannot know.

"If you cannot explain this sword's existence," the steward said, "you may as well claim it as your own. Own up to your crime." He looked over his shoulder towards the lower council. In his mind, her silence was evidence enough to convict her. He was met with many nods of agreement.

"It isn't mine!" she cried for a second time. Her composure began to slip. The council members whispered amongst themselves, appearing smug. Saffra alone remained silent.

A councilor abruptly came to his feet. The king looked over, acknowledging his desire to speak. "The council has already come to a majority agreement. If this woman cannot explain the sword, then we are forced to accept it as hers. We are forced to believe she killed Lord Cyrus."

The king gave a brief nod and the man sat down.

She clenched and unclenched her fists.

Hold yourself together. You must remain composed.

She looked up at the king. "I didn't do it, Your Majesty. You must believe me. I didn't kill him."

The king finally stood. Like dominos, the entire hall fell to one knee. She looked around. She was the only one still standing. Even the stooped little man with his staff was kneeling. Let them pay their respects—she had none left to give.

Perceiving her rebellion, the king's towering figure descended upon her. She took several surprised steps back, afraid that he might strike her down.

Do not fear him. He will think less of you if you fail to stand your ground.

Swallowing against her dry throat, she bravely lifted her chin to meet the king. When he stopped before her, she discovered just how mighty he was. It took everything to keep from cowering.

She was tall by female standards. Despite this, the king stood a whole head taller, towering over her. His body was powerfully built. He could have easily flung her across the hall in a single sweep of his fist, if anger drove him to it.

"If you did not kill Cyrus, then who did?" he hissed, keeping his voice low. Only those closest could hear them now. They remained kneeling upon one knee. The king had not yet bid them to rise.

It was an answer she could not give—not in front of a sea of onlookers. Her eyes nervously flicked towards his shields. Their faces were composed, but their shifting betrayed their uneasiness.

"Well?"

"I—I cannot say, Your Majesty." She faltered under his towering stance. The strength and fortitude she initially possessed was quickly evaporating.

The muscle in his jaw began ticking again, faster this time. His features finally cracked and she saw his fury. This time, he didn't hide it. "You cannot say?" he snarled. "Or you *choose* not to?" He scoffed. "*I* think it is the latter. You *will* tell me. I command it of you."

"Oh, you command it? Well then." Before she could stop herself, she rolled her eyes.

He flinched. "You—you dare?!" To his credit, he looked utterly shocked. Had anyone ever defied him? "You—"

"I made a *promise*, Your Majesty, and my word means everything to me."

"You expect me to believe that? I know what it is to wear a crown. My obligation, my *life*, is pledged to my people. You owe them an explanation. Until then, you are guilty in the eyes of all."

But what of *his* eyes? She searched their depths and what she saw surprised her. Sorrow. Deep wells of sorrow. He'd disguised it well, hidden it to protect his vulnerability.

Seeing this human emotion from someone so monstrous made her snap. "If that is my only option, then I shall be guilty!" she cried. "I owe your people nothing! Yet, I have done more for them than they will ever deserve. If only you knew," she scoffed. "You, who locked me in a cell for three days! Fine. I'll be your villain. I'll enjoy watching your kingdom crumble."

His mouth dropped open. The look on his stunned face was worth the cost she would surely pay for it. He quickly mastered his expression. "Did you expect something better?" he demanded. "A hero's welcome. A soft bed and a warm meal? Did you think we would welcome you with pomp and circumstance?*You?* The woman who would deny an entire kingdom the truth they so justly deserve."

"Truth?! That isn't what you're after. No, you're enjoying this. I am here for the amusement of all." She spread her arms wide. "I am not blind, Your Majesty. Behind your monstrous facade, there is only desolation. You hide it in hopes of disguising your true faults. Oh, yes. How painful it must be to know the role *you* played in all of this. The role *you* played in *his* death."

Words tumbled out of her mouth—dangerous words. She couldn't seem to stop them. Even knowing she was sealing her death sentence.

"Tell me, Your Majesty, does it keep you up at night? Does it cripple you knowing that he died because of *you*? Because of *your* rash decisions? I see you clearly enough. Hurt has driven you to a dark place and now you must live with regret." She huffed. "Do us both a favor. Don't dig yourself into a deeper hole. Pain is understandable given the mistakes you've made. That doesn't make your behavior towards *me* acceptable. You know—?" she barked a laugh. "I find myself disappointed. I thought I was coming here to meet with a king. Instead, all I have found is a rogue beast!"

Her breaths came fast and sharp as adrenaline coursed through her. She'd just dug her own grave. But at least it was a good one.

The silence in the hall was profound. She expected the king to strike her down. She'd just humiliated him in front of everyone. His eyes flashed with emotion. She thought she saw a hint of something crawling across his skin. Black and iridescent. There, and gone again. Dragon scales?

"Are you finished?" His lips hardly moved. She stood frozen in place, wishing he would prove her right, wishing he would show his subjects what a monster he truly was. But he didn't lift so much as a finger.

"I—I'm finished." She squared her shoulders, defying him with a lift of her chin.

"Good." His low voice sent chills racing down her arms. "You will find no mercy from me. You have weaseled your way into my kingdom like a worm, blood on your hands and evil in your heart. You have bewitched shields into proclaiming your innocence. You have stomped through my lands with little regard for its rules. You make silly demands upon my time, while failing to deliver what is rightfully owed to myself and to my people."

She gaped at him.

"And now—" He paused to catch his breath. "And now you *dare* stand before me to lecture me? To tell me what a monster I am?"

"Even the wisest man can learn from the lowest. Only a fool knows everything."

King Talon's reaction was immediate. His eyes widened a measure and his expression froze as if she'd struck him with her palm. Then, every bit of color drained from his scarred face.

They were Cyrus's words. She wasn't sure what had prompted her to say them. Probably Cyrus, acting in the back of her mind.

She stood motionless, waiting for his wrath, but it did not come. Instead he gave his head a little shake and took control of his emotions. "These...these words of *wisdom* are your final defense? You will give no explanation for his death? Be aware that your refusal will result in a final verdict of guilty. You will be returned to the dungeons to await your death."

Taking a deep, steadying breath, she said, "I am aware of what awaits, Your Majesty. My words are final, as you well know."

"Fine. You must return to your cell." King Talon put his back to her and ascended the dais. At the top, he turned to face her once more. She caught a glimpse of something strange upon his face. He had an odd way of regarding her, like a lion watching its prey. It left the hairs of her arms on end.

He looked over his throne room. "I pronounce this woman guilty of a most terrible crime. Her final days will not be easy, and her death will be the only release she finds." His verdict should have been terrifying. She was too numb to understand the implications of his words. That would come later.

"Guards!" he ordered. "Return her to the dungeons." Her two escorts materialized, each with an iron grip to turn her away.

In that final moment, as she looked over her shoulder, she caught a brief glimpse of Saffra. The seer was sitting erect, looking down upon her with dark, chocolate eyes. Her gaze was soft and encouraging, and within it she found strength, strength she would greatly need in what was to come.

CHAPTER 39

RESPONSIBILITIES

Redport

Tamara turned her head this way and that, studying her reflection in the looking glass. Gemstones glittered in her hair as they caught the glow of orange light from the setting sun. Her hair was fetching, but not nearly as lovely as her ice-blue eyes.

"Hold still!" She received a warning tug upon her unfinished black tresses. A pile of hair was already gathered upon the crown of her head as a braided bun took form. Jeweled pins were placed throughout the twisted plaits. The ornaments cost a fortune that only the richest girls could afford. Ordinarily, riches were of little interest to her, but tonight was different—tonight was special.

She smiled at herself, the gesture hesitant. There in the reflection was a hint of emerging beauty where before there had been none. Gone were the days of her childhood. Her womanhood would soon be upon her.

Without warning, she shrieked. A painful sensation forced her gaze away from her own reflection. Her mother's lips twitched before deft fingers tugged another willful section of hair tightly into place. "Gods, Mother! That hurt." Her long hair was a weight pulling at every strand upon her scalp.

"It must. I will not have this unruly mess of yours coming undone whilst you turn about the floor."

"Turn about the floor?" Her mouth opened. It took several slow breaths to process her mother's meaning. "I am permitted to dance, then?" Her father always forbade dancing, as was right for a parent with a daughter not yet a woman.

"Yes, I convinced your father. You are nearing womanhood—long overdue I might add." Most girls her age had already bled. She often got the impression her mother resented her for the lateness of it. A girl should be a woman by age fifteen; most girls her age were already married off. "Regardless of your lateness, I see no reason to hold you back. Should you not partake?"

"I...yes." A tingle of excitement seeped into her chest, moving down to the tips of her fingers and toes. "I would like to dance, very much so."

Her mother afforded her a slow, knowing smile, but something about it was off. The gesture was too forced. She ignored it and instead imagined herself turning about the floor, noticed by all, especially Redport's guests of honor. Would her glittering hair and elegant attire disguise her age? She was young after all, just old enough to be selected.

"Do you think the drengr might pick me?" The words were out of her mouth before she thought better of them.

"The drengr, dear? For a dance?"

She hesitated on the brink of a gamble. "No. I mean...do you think they will pick me as a volunteer?"

"Gods, child! I thought your father made his point clear." Lady Redwynn's grip upon her shoulders tightened, almost painfully.

"I thought if I asked you—"

"You thought I might override his decision?" She nodded into the mirror's reflection. "My dear, *foolish* girl—"

"But I want to become a rider! Father knows this, as do you!"

"Nonsense, Tamara." Her mother scoffed. "As soon as you bleed, you will do your duty to your house and marry."

A roaring filled her ears as her pulse quickened. Still, she was desperate. "Mama, please! That is not what I want. I cannot—I cannot do it!"

"You can. You must."

"I do not want to be a *wife*." She spat the word out like rotten greens, spoiled by a winter's mildew. "I do not want to bear another man's children, especially a man who is not of my choosing. Please, mother," she begged, knowing full well her life depended upon it. "Let me volunteer. Let me go to Fort Squall."

Her mother heaved a sigh. "You are too young. They would never select you—"

"I'm old enough. The rules state fifteen—"

"Gods above!" Her mother looked at the ceiling, pleading.

"I will be selected," she said, reassuring herself more than her mother. "I know I will."

She was going to become a rider. She knew it in her very being, the way a spider knew how to weave its web, or a bee knew how to make honey. This was her path.

"These fantasies of yours are only that. Your father will never hear of it. You will watch the spectacle like the rest of us. Tell me, Tamara, do you know what happens to those who are selected?"

"They become riders," she breathed, becoming starry eyed. She could almost picture it, finding a drengr mate, becoming a rider, flying on the back of a dragon. She didn't even care what color— any would do, so long as he had wings and could whisk her away from this place.

Her mother barked a laugh, sweeping away the conjuring. "No Tamara, few of those who get selected will ever have the honor. What happens to the majority who are not so lucky?"

Tamara pursed her lips and shook her head. Silently she chided herself for not knowing the answer. Now she merely looked naive.

Her mother afforded her a pitying look. "Drengr live very long lives. They age at a fraction of the rate we do. A human's lifespan is a small length of time in comparison. A tenth. Few are fortunate enough to become riders. Such a thing is not up to you, no matter how badly you want it to be. It is up to fate and fate alone." Lady

Redwynn paused. "No, what happens to the fort's volunteers is a much sadder story."

Hot anxiety built in her chest, expanding outward. She picked at the gold embroidery upon her heavy skirts. Listening, but fearing the words.

"Those who are selected grow old, Tamara. They grow old, caged within the walls of the fort, riding on dreams of a life that will never come to pass, cooking food and cleaning chamber pots until they die. You were not born to such a life. I would give mine over to save you from such a lowly position."

She opened her mouth to protest, then thought better of it. Nothing she could say would change her mother's opinion. Because in many ways, she was right.

"There now. It is a mother's job to warn her daughter of such things. Reality is rarely to our liking."

A tear freed itself, sliding down Tamara's cheek. Another followed. She knew her battle with Lady Redwynn was lost. There would be no volunteering. How silly she'd been to foster the slightest hope her mother might acquiesce.

Noticing her upset, her mother's face softened. "Dear heart," she said. "You may not see it, but you are luckier than most. Many would gladly trade places with you, especially those volunteering tonight."

She stifled a snort. Her mother didn't seem to notice. She forged on to say, "Those volunteering do not have governor fathers like yours. Yours is the Lord of Redport and all its lands. Tell me, how many governors are there in Dragonwall?"

She ground her teeth together. "Twenty, Mother. There are twenty lord governors in the entirety of Dragonwall, one presiding over each of the twenty dragondoms."

"Precisely. And you are the daughter of one. The hopefuls volunteering for selection do not have duties to fulfill for their family name—*the Redwynn name.* You do." Her mother sighed, patting her head. "There now. Last one." She pinned a broach into place. "You look stunning Tamara. Lord Rhal will be pleased."

"What?!" she sputtered. She placed a hand upon her dresser,

trying to catch her breath. Her corset was too tight. "I do not understand. Lord...Rhal? Why should I care what he thinks?"

But she already knew.

"He is your betrothed."

"My... But how could—?"

"He is an honorable man, Tamara. Governor of Squall's End and its accompanying lands."

"I know who he is—"

"You would do well to see this for what it is and cease your complaints." Lady Redwynn raised her voice to be heard over Tamara's protests. "Few get such an opportunity for an alliance like this one."

Her mouth gaped.Her womanhood was not yet upon her, and already her father had traded her off. It was betrayal at its deepest. Hot, angry fire poured into her chest, welling up. Never had she hated her father so much as she did in this moment.

"Well!" she spat. "I hope the return he gains will be worth the loss of his only daughter."

"Tamara!" Her mother looked as if she might slap her.

"You let him do this, Mother? How could you?"

Color stained Lady Redwynn's cheeks. "I had no say in the matter, daughter."

"But you are his wife—my...my mother! You are supposed to protect me."

It wasn't as if Lord Rhal was bad, per se. She'd heard he was a levelheaded sort of person. His city was prosperous and he was wealthy. None of that mattered.

"This is how life goes in noble families, dear heart. The gods only know, I certainly had no desire to marry your father when your grandfather arranged it."

Tamara bit back her words, momentarily stunned. "But you and father love each other so much. I never..."

Her mother laughed, shaking her head. "Trust me, we did not always. Love develops with time, as many things in life do." As if reading her mind, her mother ended the matter. "Save your words, Tamara. There is nothing more I can do."

She felt numb. All she could do was gaze at her mother's reflection with vague awareness. Was this to be her future? Truly?

"There now. I have a few obligations before the festivities start. Do not be late or your father will be upset," she added.

When Tamara next looked at the looking glass, her mother was gone.

∼

REDPORT's dining hall was the second largest in the region, next to Squall's End. Her father took great pride in that and made sure to tell any newcomer of interest. Hers was an old family, one who ruled the ports of Stormy Bay for many thousands of years. Because she was a Redwynn, for which Redport had been named, she was to do her duty at the bidding of her family, so she found herself seated in her place at the head table on time, just as her mother had instructed.

The food that night was spectacular by the highest standards, fit for a king's table. To her, every bite tasted like gravel and went down like it too. She threw her father a mean look. It was of no use. He did not notice. He sat merrily chatting at the table's center, presiding over the hall. How lovely it must be to enjoy the night at his daughter's expense.

She was glad when the food was finally cleared. Her plate left the table nearly full. Perceptive, Lady Redwynn took note, imparting upon her a look of dismay *and* warning. She pretended not to notice, feigning interest in the new excitement, but she was neither excited nor interested in what came next.

A hush fell upon the room as her father rose from his chair. Lord Redwynn cleared his throat before speaking. "As you all know," his booming voice echoed around the hall, "it is the drengr who keep Dragonwall safe." Many responses of "Aye," and "Yes," broke the silence. Men sat with their cups of ale, while women watched, secretly dreaming of what it might be like to become a drengr's rider. "These protectors and their riders are always in need of volunteers, willing to lay down their lives in support of the forts. Not only that, as our young drengr mature, new riders are needed. That is the reason for this search." His speech was hardly necessary. Everyone knew enough about the search to forgo pretenses.

"Without further words from me, let those who would volunteer themselves for selection step forward." A loud clapping rang out and the hall doors opened. Some of the women rose from benches, but many others less fortunate in birth streamed in through the open hall doors.

It was the first search Tamara was old enough to witness, for none under the age of fifteen were permitted into the hall that night. Just as none under the age of fifteen could volunteer. As she watched, she gripped her chair so tightly, it felt as if her fingers might fall off. It was all she could do to keep from rising to join the line.

A sudden flash of rebelliousness coursed through her. What if she did rise? What if she ran from the head table and placed herself within the group of volunteers. What would her father do? Surely he would refrain from dragging her away—a scene would be embarrassing.

A hand gripped her arm. She looked beside her, to her eldest brother, who afforded her a warning shake of his head before turning his attention back to the volunteers. His hand did not leave her arm. Whether there for comfort or restraint, she did not know.

Taking note of those who shyly presented themselves, she realized that her mother was right. There were none of great nobility present, only those of lesser birth like merchant's daughters, craftsman's sons, servants, and farmers. Each hoped that within the fort they might find a better life working for the drengr.

Several drengr rose from the crowd and began walking along the line of volunteers. Nearly everyone earned a nod. How did they choose? Maybe they had a way of sensing an honest heart. All too soon it was over, and the applauding crowd grew rowdy. She exhaled her pent-up breath. Gods, how she wanted to cry!

In came the minstrels, strumming and plucking away at their instruments. Loud cheers went up as tables were hastily pushed away. It was time to dance—something she had wanted to do for a long time.

Except, dancing no longer held any appeal.

Happy conversations and shrieks of laughter wove themselves together with the loud music. Everyone was having a wonderful time. Everyone *except* her. She scowled, watching the circles of dancers as they changed formation, skipping across the floor.

As the night wore on, she remained seated. Even when Josie beckon her across the room. The head table had emptied long ago. Her brothers were off socializing while her father and mother happily led the dance. She watched them together. Every time she saw her father smile, she grew angrier.

Was her happiness of such little regard to him?

He was everything a good lord governor should be: honorable, just, and kind, except perhaps towards his own daughter. The city of Redport flourished under his meticulous rule. Over the years he'd mastered his title well, just as his father had done before him, and just as his sons would do after. Now, she finally understood her place.

The music ended and her father smiled as he approached a finely dressed young lord near the edge of the crowd. They cordially shook hands and fell into deep discussion. The man smiled and clapped her father on the shoulder. It was only when they both looked her way, catching her gaze, that she realized the subject of their conversation.

Her face flushed and she quickly averted her gaze, feigning interest in a group of gossiping women. So that was Lord Rhal? He certainly wasn't what she'd expected.

The two men quickly parted and Lord Rhal directed his attention upon her, walking directly over. Her heart began to pound. The man's gaze remained fixed upon her as he approached. Her stomach lifted into her throat.

"Good evening, Lady Tamara." He came to a stop before the head table. His voice wasn't unpleasant as she'd hoped it might be. "I have not yet had the privilege of introducing myself. I am Lord Rhal." He dropped into a sweeping bow. A show of respect.

As was proper, she rose and curtsied, but her mouth was frozen shut.

He straightened, eying her, "Forgive me, but might I have the next dance with you?"

Her stomach lurched. "Dance?"

"Yes, my lady. It would be a great honor."

Her stomach heaved. The lord was handsome in his own right. That was not why she felt so unsettled. It was reality, crashing down upon her. "For-forgive me, my lord. I...I think I might be sick." Placing a hand over her mouth, she nimbly stepped around the table. Before the shocked lord could say another word, she dashed away.

"My lady!" he called after her. She could sense him in her wake, following. She did her best to lose him in the crowd. Bodies pressed in around her. There! She could see the door—

She collided with a tall body, causing both of them to stumble. As he jolted forward, he sloshed ale all over the floor. Her next step brought her upon the slippery mess. Both legs flew out from beneath her as she landed hard upon her back.

"Gods be damned!" the man roared just as she looked up at him from the ground. His shock melted into a friendly smile. And... he wasn't a man at all. No, he was much younger. A few years older than her, but no more.

"Apologies, my lady." He held out a hand to help her up. She gladly took it, her upset stomach all but forgotten. A slight tingle passed through her fingers at the touch of his skin, making her blush. Did he feel it too? He gave no notice.

She stood frozen before him, gaping as she made a startling realization. He was one of the drengr! Young though he might be, he was taller and broader in shoulder than a fully grown man.

"You must forgive me," he was saying. "Are you all right? ...My lady? Should I fetch a healer?"

She blinked back at him. For a moment, time had stopped. Now it began again as the events from the evening came crashing down around her. She glanced to the open hall doors, then back at the young drengr. Giving him a single, apologetic glance, she sprinted away.

Once she was through the doors, she did not stop running. She raced across the flagstone entrance, down an empty corridor, and flung open the garden doors, sprinting out into the night.

The openness outside alleviated the building pressure in her chest. So she ran and ran, as if to escape her responsibilities. She ran until she was gasping for air. Hands on her knees, she let her blood rush back to her head until she felt it pounding in her ears.

A familiar red brick wall was before her. She was near the south end of the garden where the large willow tree stood. It was older than Redport, and likely far wiser than the lords within. Underneath its cloak of leaves sat a garden bench—*her* garden bench. Her father had put it there when she was young, when he constantly found her sitting beneath the wispy branches. She went to the bench and plopped down in a very unladylike manner, sighing loudly, as if that would make things better.

Her chest rose and fell in great bursts. Even after running, her emotions were still too pent up. She let out a furious cry, enjoying the way it felt, the way it sounded against the still night air. Then she fell quiet and put her head in her hands.

Gods, she'd been so naive.

The sound of boots scuffed on the stone path nearby. She lifted her face, holding her breath. Had Lord Rhal found her?

"My lady?" The branches of the willow parted and she heaved a sigh of relief. "There you are. I truly am sorry about what happened. I feel responsible for the mishap. I do hope you did not injure yourself or ruin your beautiful gown."

The young drengr's voice was rich and deep. She liked it very much. Instead of answering, she let him talk some more. He seemed eager to fill the silence.

"There was no need to run away as you did. I was not upset." He smiled, taking a step towards her.

Her heart skipped a beat. She took a deep breath and said, "You are not at fault. And I am fine. As it stands, it was I who bumped into you." She paused, then worried at her lower lip. "Can you keep a secret?"

"I can."

"I was in a hurry to leave the party. That's why I bumped into you."

"I...see. But that's hardly worth calling a secret. Who were you running from? Now *that* sort of information would be worthy of a secret."

"A valid point!" She almost considered telling him about Lord Rhal, but decided against it. "It wasn't who I was running from, but *what*."

He tilted his head slightly. "And?"

"I was running from my responsibilities. And hopefully I am free—for now."

He chuckled, amused. It was deep, the sound only a drengr might make. "Gods! I cannot blame you for it."

"You—you have felt the same way?"

"Often. My responsibilities are numerous." She breathed a heavy sigh. "But tell me truly, a lady such as yourself, should you not put your responsibilities aside for a night and enjoy the festivities?" She shook her head. She could not, not when it went hand in hand with what took place within the dining hall. "I see. So you have come out here to be alone and I have disturbed you. For that, you must forgive me."

"Please—" She almost rose to her feet to stop him. "You do not need to leave. Come and join me on my bench." He grinned, then came and sat beside her. She wasn't sure what prompted her boldness, except that she wasn't ready for him to go. "Since you speak of your responsibilities, tell me, have you ever been made to do something against your will? Have you ever had to follow orders simply because others demanded it of you? Even if it meant sacrificing your own happiness?"

He was silent for several long moments. The handsome silhouette of his face made her want to keep staring at him. "Those are heavy thoughts for one so young."

She barked a laugh. "Young? You can't be much older than I am."

"You'd be surprised." There was a sparkle in his eyes. His gaze seemed to penetrate the very depths of her as he studied her, perhaps looking for answers. He sighed. "It does sound like your responsibilities are getting the better of you."

"They are. I simply cannot accept the future others have chosen for me. That is not who I am."

"And who are you?" He gazed at the willow's branches as he asked.

She hesitated. "I suppose I still haven't figured that out yet. But know this, I am not a product of the desires and schemes of others."

"I should hope not," he said, barking a laugh. His agreement felt good—too good. It was all the reassurance she needed. A plan began hatching in her mind, a daring plan that left her shivering with eagerness.

She looked closer at the drengr. His golden hair, his striking features, his fine nose. He turned and his eyes caught her. Blood rushed to her cheeks. "Will you be at Redport long?" she blurted.

"I am afraid not. Matters of importance take me back to Fort Squall immediately."

"Immediately?"

"Aye, I leave after the festivities tonight."

"But...what of the volunteers?" she asked, feigning curiosity.

"Ah. They leave in the morning, just before sunrise. Several of my party will escort them."

She exhaled. Good. That was good.

"Now, my lady, I am afraid I have intruded upon your solitude for long enough. I must return to the festivities."

"Of—of course, sir."

He rose to leave. Just before he parted the veil of the willow, he paused. Then he turned to her and said, "I do apologize once more, for earlier, and for my rude manners. I am afraid I never asked for your name, nor properly introduced myself."

Her name? The beating of her heart quickened. "For earlier, I forgive you. Regarding my name, you may call me...Amber."

"Lady Amber. Well met. I'm Byron." He smiled and held forth his hand to take her forearm, as was common for drengr to do. She reciprocated the gesture, gripping his in return. Through the fabric of his shirt, there was no intimate contact. She was almost sorry for it, for she longed to feel the tingles of his skin again.

All too soon, Byron was gone. She was left to her solitude, but not for long. Amber had work to do if she was to depart before sunrise. So she scurried away like a little mouse, and set about her plans to run away.

CHAPTER 40
TAMING THE BEAST

Kastali Dun

Reyr had never been so displeased with Talon in all his life. Leading up to the trial, he'd held firm to the belief that his king would come to his senses. Unfortunately, Talon's reason had evaporated the moment Claire had presented herself, replaced with an erratic and unpredictable ruler.

He thought back over everything that had happened. What she'd said. Her snark.

"Grinning, are we?" Jovari's question startled him. "Come now, do share. The rest of us could use a laugh."

He shrugged.

"You wish for us to remain sullen, then?" Jovari was never one to give up. Bedelth and Koldis were also there. Verath, smartly, had abandoned Reyr's chambers after their fifth bottle of wine.

"Sullen?" He lifted an eyebrow at Jovari. "After all this drinking?"

Jovari snorted. "As if a bit of drink will fix what happened in there."

"True. And if you must know, that's exactly what I was thinking about. What Claire said to the king."

"Ah-ha! I knew it."

"Quite the ball of fire, that one," Bedelth murmured.

"Ball of fire is an understatement," Koldis said, crossing his arms. "If only you knew what she put us through these past few weeks."

"Believe me, after this morning, my understanding has *vastly* improved. I have never seen someone so thoroughly flay King Talon in front of an audience."

"He deserved it," Jovari said. "He should have listened to us last night. No wonder he's in an uproar."

"Regretting his actions now, I should hope," Koldis murmured, looking into his goblet.

"It is unlike him to behave so irrationally," Bedelth mused. "How long will he remain barricaded within his tower, ignoring us—?"

The door burst open. Their heads whipped around. Jovari reached for the sverak at his side, but it was only Verath. He walked in, and immediately Reyr could sense his worry.

"Ahhh! The high and mighty has returned!" Jovari released the grip on his sword hilt and threw his arms wide, sloshing wine from his goblet. "Not too good for us after all, eh?"

"The king still refuses to see me," Verath grumbled, sitting down to pour more wine into the goblet he'd abandoned.

"Of course he does," Jovari slurred his words. "I would be out of sorts too after that feline's scratches."

"That is not what worries me," Verath growled. He gave Jovari a stern glare, unamused.

"What worries you?" Reyr shifted forward in his seat.

"The guards at King Talon's tower. I do not wish to rekindle our fears from earlier, but perhaps we must do something."

Whatever buzz Reyr had felt, fled. "You do not mean to say..."

"I mean to say that a message was carried from the king's tower to the dungeons. Claire is to be moved. Immediately."

"Moved?" Reyr frowned. "Moved where?"

"Not out of the dungeons, I can promise you of that."

Koldis jumped to his feet. "We've got to do something. He cannot move her to the screamers."

"What?!" Jovari sputtered, blinking. *The screamers,* as in, the torture chambers. "He would not dare! She...she'd never survive that. I thought we decided earlier that it was unlikely he'd go this far."

"Reyr?" Bedelth looked at him. "You can fix this, can you not?"

Koldis abandoned his drink and set about pacing between the table and fireplace.

"I have tried talking to him." Reyr pinched the bridge of his nose. "He has closed his mind to me, refuses to admit me into his tower. What more do I do?"

"You'll have to force your way in," Bedelth insisted. "You alone can make him see reason. You are his favorite, after all."

"I think you mistake me for Cyrus."

"Well Cyrus is no longer here to fix things, is he?" Koldis all but shouted, his temper returned in full. Reyr flinched. No, Cyrus wasn't here to fix things. Not anymore.

"I wish he were here—I wish Cyrus were here," Jovari very nearly whined. "We would not be in this mess otherwise."

"Cyrus *would* be here," Verath said, giving Reyr a loaded glance, "had he heeded Reyr's council."

Reyr's shoulders fell; he aimed a dirty look at Verath for opening his mouth.

There was a pause before Koldis asked, "What council?"

"Reyr tried to talk Cyrus into staying," Verath explained.

"This is my fault," Reyr admitted. "I should have done more."

"Gods above. Really? I already told you. What more could you have done?"

"I should have forced him to stay," Reyr said. "Chained him to a wall, if necessary."

The others merely witnessed this back and forth with stunned expressions, until Koldis managed to say, "You advised him to stay? You did not...I thought we were in agreement with the king's plan? That he should go and retrieve the stones."

"Reyr alone had misgivings, which he voiced. Not that it mattered in the end. We're here, whether we like it or not. All we can do is move forward." Verath eyed them each in turn. "Reyr, you are our best hope. Go to the king. Insist that he see reason. Remind him of what happened the last time your council went unheeded. Fix this."

"And if he refuses to see me again?"

"Then break down his doors."

He sighed. "Fine. I'll go. Just let me get my thoughts together."

WHEN HE REACHED the king's tower, the guards barred his entry. "Begging your pardon, Lord Reyr. We do not like refusing you, but, king's orders."

"You do realize I can easily get past you if I so desire. Save yourself the hurt and let me by."

"If we allow you to pass, the king's wrath will be more severe than yours. We will take our chances."

They were merely following orders.

He sighed. "Very well then, and I *do* apologize." For a moment, his words were met with looks of confusion. He moved faster than they could blink, knocking their heads together. Their helms clanked, echoing down the hall. They fell unconscious. He could have used magic and they would have dropped all the same. This felt more satisfying.

Talon's tower was empty.

His stomach hardened into a knot. He didn't want to consider it, but somehow he knew. He knew where the king would be.

Rushing from the tower, he stormed through the keep. A thousand scenarios played through his mind. What if he was too late? What if he killed her. Worse still, what if he hurt her beyond repair?

He entered the dungeons at a sprint. The guards shouted after him in surprise. He continued down the dark corridors without stopping.

"Please, Lord Reyr," they called in his wake. "None are permitted without the king's permission!"

Their words told him all he needed to know. The king had already been this way. He ignored their protests and their voices faded. They knew better than to chase after him.

The screamers were located on the lowest level at the end of the last corridor. All the doors were cracked open save one. There were no sounds from within, but he did not care to wait for any.

For all he knew, she might already be dead.

"Hinga laesa," he commanded, simultaneously pushing against the heavy door. His hand trembled against the wood. It creaked and swung open.

He blinked, staggering to a stop at the sight before him.

"Talon!" he roared, so furious he was shaking. "What is the meaning of this?!"

Claire was strapped to a rack, gagged and fully restrained. Tears leaked from the corners of her eyes. Talon stood over her, a blade to her throat, looking more crazed than Reyr had ever seen him. In a panic, Reyr's eyes flicked to the lever arms at the ends of the table. The device had not yet been used. His lungs deflated with relief. He was not too late.

"Talon..." His voice held warning.

"If she refuses to talk, I will make her talk." The voice that answered him was not Talon's—it belonged to the snarling beast living inside him.

"Gods, Talon! How can she talk when she's gagged? This is madness! Come into the hall. I must speak with you. Immediately."

"You should not be here, Reyr."

"Come into the hall. I command it of you." Somehow he kept his voice steady.

Talon began to laugh. It was a manic, deranged sound that made his stomach drop to his boots. What if there was no going back? What if Talon had snapped, and all that was left was his dragon? But just as he thought it, the laughing ceased. "You *dare* command me, Reyr?"

He strode across the room and went to the table, eyes meeting Claire's for a brief second. The sight of her green depths calmed him. She was not as scared as he'd believed. She was being very brave. Talon did not remove the dagger from her throat, so he placed his hand gently on the king's arm.

"Talon, *my king*, please come into the hall. Speak with me before you do something you will regret forever." For a moment it appeared as if Talon would defy him. The beast within certainly wanted to. He saw the struggle in Talon's eyes.

Then, the king heaved a frustrated sigh and pulled the blade away.

They entered the corridor. He shut the door to the chamber, keeping his teeth clenched. He wanted so badly to fall into explosive rage, to scream at Talon for being an idiot, to shake him and slam him against the wall. But...Talon was his king. They'd been through too much for him to give up now.

"Talon," he said, keeping his voice controlled, "I cannot bear to think of the outcome had I found you a moment later. Do you think killing Claire will solve anything?"

"You shouldn't have interfered, Reyr. Had anyone else interrupted me, they would be dead." Talon's voice was still very low, very beastly.

"I must interfere! She carries valuable information—information we *need*."

"So you think!"

"So I *know*."

Talon was breathing hard. There was fire in his eyes. "Your mind is too clouded, Reyr, you allowed her to seduce you."

He shook his head. "Talon, you think killing her will bring Cyrus back? That it will *fix* this mess? Is that what you intended? Slit her throat and be done?"

At the mention of Cyrus, Talon's shoulders dropped a measure. He began to look more human. "I admit, it crossed my mind, but no. I do not intend to kill her. Only to scare her."

"Scare her?" Reyr nearly choked. "Good gods, Talon! Of all the insane things you have done in your many lifetimes of years, this is the most reckless and dishonorable." Now was not the time to scold him. Once his dragon finally receded, Talon would feel remorse enough.

"Reyr, she *humiliated* me."

"She gave you no less than you deserved! Like a cat to bait, you threw yourself right back at her. *You are the king*, not the reckless youth of your past! By coming here tonight, you have merely proven correct everything she said against you."

"All that I did was done to protect this kingdom."

"At the expense of your reason! And you have done splendidly until now—until she came along."

"Reason? Bah!"

"I told you she was innocent, Talon. Did we not advise you to forgo the trial? Did we not advise you to speak with her alone as she wished?"

"If you believe she is innocent, that merely confirms my theory. Your mind—"

"I am not under any spell!" he roared, finally losing control. Talon flinched and backed up a step. "She has not bewitched us. You merely fail to see what we see. Do you remember when you asked me to take up my oath as one of your six? I made a promise to you. I vowed that I would be truthful to you, even when the truth was difficult to bear. I told you that I would never hold myself back, even if what you needed to hear might be unpleasant."

Talon's throat bobbed as he swallowed.

"I tell you this now, as your oldest friend. You have made many poor decisions, but this one is both dishonorable and appalling, and perhaps your worst." He waited for a response, hoping Talon might apologize, something. The king remained silent. He continued, "You also made *me* a promise. Do you remember our bargain —or have you forgotten?"

Talon sighed and his shoulders fell. The beast was stepping back into the shadows of his mind. This was a more familiar Talon, the Talon he swore his oath to all those years ago. Reluctant, headstrong, stubborn as an ass, but reasonable. "I promised that if you stood by my side, that if you joined my six, I would grant you one favor, anything within my means to give, at the time of your choosing. But—" Talon hesitated. "You cannot possibly mean to spend your favor now—not on this woman."

"That is what you promised, and yes, I intend to spend it on her. The time has come for you to grant me what was promised. I wish for you to take my side on this matter and adhere to my wishes regarding Claire."

Talon's jaw worked. "I suppose I have no choice in the matter?"

"None whatsoever."

"Fine," he bit out. "What then do you suggest I do, since you are clearly wiser than I am?"

"I *suggest* you go in there and fix this...this *mess* you have created."

Talon huffed. He placed both hands on the back of his head and walked away several paces. His back was visible, but his face was hidden. Good. He was thinking things over.

After several long minutes, Talon faced him. "How do I fix this? Will you go talk to her? Will you go and find out what truly happened?"

"Oh, no!" Reyr backed up several steps. "This is *your* mess, Talon. Besides, she will tell me nothing. It is *you* she requires." He paused to consider Claire's circumstances. She was waiting inside, desperate to tell Talon whatever Cyrus asked of her. The image of her on the rack flashed into his mind and he shuddered. "Gods, Talon. You had her gagged?! She probably would have told you everything you needed to know. You should never punish others for standing up to you like that—especially when *you* deserve it."

"I still do not trust her."

He snorted. "It seems you will never trust her until you talk to her. I will wait out here. If I hear so much as a *yelp* from her, if you so much as harm a hair on her head..." He let the sentence go unfinished.

Talon was far more powerful than he was, but he made the threat anyway. He knew his king would deliver on his end of the bargain. A single favor for a life spent in servitude to his king. Was this favor truly worth it? Gods, he hoped so.

Talon nodded, leaving him to breathe a sigh of relief. "I hope I will not regret this," he muttered, stalking towards the door. His shoulders slumped as he opened it.

"I assure you, my king, you will not."

Without another word, Talon vanished into the depths of the cell.

CHAPTER 41

FULFILLING A PROMISE

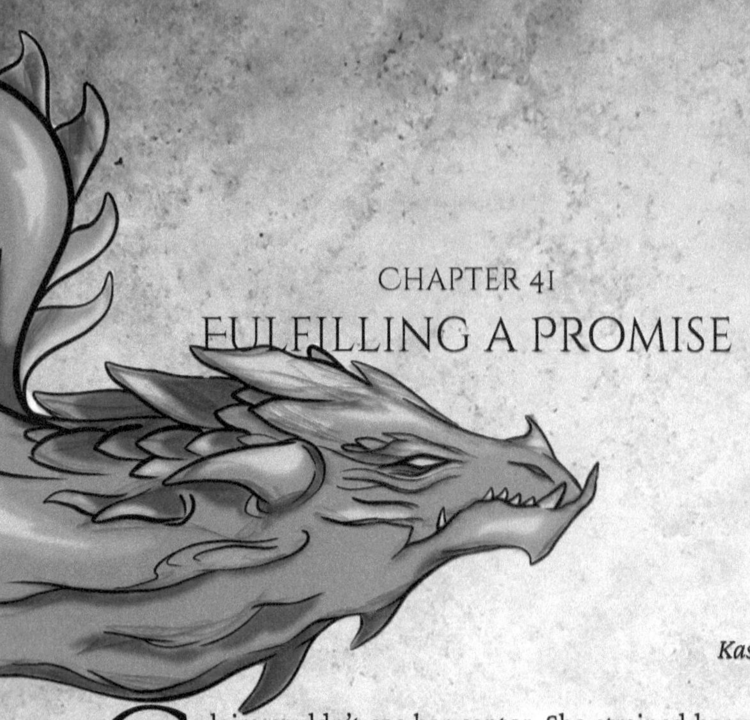

Kastali Dun

Claire couldn't see her captor. She strained her gaze, but King Talon paced just out of sight. Restraints cut into her skin, harsh and insistent, gnawing at her, reminding her that his control was absolute. Her stomach churned, a combination of the smell of death and decay and fear.

All around her, dim torchlight cast an orange glow on the moldering walls, throwing up monstrous shadows from the medieval torture devices. Never in her wildest dreams had she imagined herself in a place like this. She wanted to be brave. She wanted to be strong and fearless. Instead, she could only pretend to be. Cyrus should have chosen better.

A hero is not born, she is made...

Silence fell. The king's pacing had stopped. Her muscles tensed, ready, waiting. She craned her neck and caught movement. He appeared beside her and she flinched.

"Relax. I am going to remove your gag." He no longer sounded like a snarling beast. Actually, he sounded as if none of this had happened, as if his blade had never kissed her throat, as if his guards had never dragged her from her cell. He reached behind her and untied her gag, tossing it aside. Then he stepped out of view.

She rocked her jaw from side to side, trying to relax the muscles—

The sound of metal against the wall made her freeze. A tool perhaps? Something to cause pain? Her breath came faster.

The king reappeared with the vodar short sword, still caked with Cyrus's dried blood. "You are lucky to have Reyr's good grace. I do not think you deserve it, but he gives it nonetheless. Luckier still, I owe him a favor. Since you refused to explain this during your trial, let's start here. Tell me how you came by this sword."

A rogue snort burst from her nose. Now? After all this? He was *finally* ready to talk to her?

So many choice words sat on the tip of her tongue, but the fight in her was gone. "I...I pulled it from Cyrus right before he died."

"And how did it come to *be* there?"

"A group of vodar wraiths stabbed him with it."

"The vodar?" His eyebrows drew together, pulling against the scars on his forehead. "The same wraiths that attacked you on your journey?"

"Yes."

He studied it anew, as if seeing it for the first time. His scowl deepened. "You were wounded during that attack, weren't you? I am told that your skin blackened until you were healed by the sprites."

"That's correct. The same thing happened to Cyrus when he was injured."

"And he died within minutes of being stabbed?" She nodded. "I see. Except, poison does not spread that quickly for a drengr—his magic would have delayed it. I saw his body. His entire upper half was blackened."

She sighed. "Because the vodar attacked twice. The first was seven days prior to the second. If you'd let me explain, instead of trying to find flaws in my answers, we might get somewhere."

"Fine. Start from the beginning," he demanded, setting the sword aside. "And don't even think about lying."

She rolled her eyes.

"I was driving home after a shift at the bar, when a dragon fell from the sky. Cyrus, obviously. I'd never seen one before and—well, that's not important. What is, is that when I found him, he was in human form, bleeding and unconscious."

"You helped him?" There was a flash of something in his expression, there and gone again.

"I am not the villain you believe me to be."

"We will see about that," he scoffed. "What happened after?"

"I saved his life."

"You used magic?"

"No. I can't *do* magic." She told him everything, how she'd stopped the bleeding and stitched him up, how she spent a week caring for him, learning about him, about Dragonwall, and how none of it mattered in the end. The vodar still returned to finish him off, hoping to find the dragonstones—

"The dragonstones?!" King Talon cried. "You *have* them?" He moved faster than she could blink, bending over the rack. His face hovered over hers, too close for comfort. "I promised Reyr that I would not hurt you, but if you do not tell me where the stones are, so help me…"

"They're in my cell," she squeaked, trying to flinch away from him. "Buried in the dirt under my blanket."

He put his back to her and she heard his silent command as he said, *"Reyr, go into Claire's cell. She claims the dragonstones are buried in the dirt under her blanket."*

"The dragonstones?! She…she cannot have them. We asked her." Claire winced at the betrayal in Reyr's voice. It wasn't like she could have told him. Still, she needed to apologize. After a long hesitation, Reyr said, *"I will go and check."*

King Talon faced her and said, "I have sent Reyr to confirm your claim. I hope for your sake that they are there."

"You hope? For my sake?" She huffed a laugh. "You probably hope they aren't, just so that you can finish what you started."

He rounded on her. "Would you like your gag back?"

She gave him a murderous glare.

Minutes passed. Finally, Reyr's voice cut through the others. *"Talon, they are here, just as you said they'd be."*

"Very well." There was relief in the king's voice, but when he next spoke, he gave her only coldness. "It seems you were telling the truth, after all."

She huffed. So much for a thank you. As if protecting them with her life hadn't meant a damned thing.

"I do not know if I should be relieved or furious. You allowed all of us to believe the stones were lost, that we were all doomed—"

"May I finish my story now?"

"Fine! Get on with it."

"Gladly," she muttered, picking up where she'd left off. "Between the two of us, Cyrus and I managed to defeat the vodar, but it was too late. He'd already been stabbed. By then, he knew there'd be no recovering." A tear dropped from the corner of her eye, trailing into her hair. "He didn't think anyone was coming for him. He...he had no one but me."

"So you made an unbreakable promise?"

"His choice, not mine." A dull laugh bubbled up in her chest. "Believe me, I wanted nothing to do with you *or* the stupid dragon-stones. But...but he was dying in my arms." She gasped, sniffling a sob. "He was...he was..." She took a deep breath, trying to regain her composure. "I couldn't deny him his final request. Besides, I owed him a favor...

"As you know, everything started with Saffra's vision. Unfortunately, you sent Cyrus on a mission that was doomed from the start. When he got the stones from the sprites, he was ambushed. That was the plan all along. Why do you think Saffra had that vision?"

King Talon frowned. "The thief manipulated us. He led us to believe the stones were in danger so that we would remove them from the sprite's protection."

"Well done!" Her voice rang of sarcasm.

"What happened when he was ambushed?"

"Kane tried to take the stones. They fought each other and Cyrus broke into his mind."

"Kane?"

"Kane is the Asarlaí who planted the vision," she explained, telling him about Kane's plan to capture all five dragonstones, and how he planned to use them. "He already has three."

"You're certain of this?" he asked. She nodded. The king's jaw flexed, his expression unreadable. "If he already has three, then all he needs are the last two."

"Exactly. And if he had gotten ahold of them, you'd all be stone by now. In other words, screwed. Luckily, Cyrus protected them. *I* protected them."

Talon no longer looked angry. In fact, he looked...diminished.

That didn't matter, because she felt lighter than she'd felt in weeks. The restraining threads of the promise loosened. She was almost there. Almost finished.

"Did Reyr tell you about the wild dragon attack on Belnesse?" she asked.

Talon had started pacing, but he stopped to look at her. "Let me guess, Kane's orders?"

"Yep."

"But wild dragons hate humans, you cannot expect me to believe they would take orders from one."

"Kane isn't human. He's an Asarlaí."

"Yes, but—"

"Oh, and don't forget about the goblins."

"The goblins? We beat them into submission years ago, but... they *have* been popping up in small raiding parties all along the eastern villages." She saw the moment he fully understood. His entire face changed.

"Figured it out, have you? Kane has hordes of them under his command, ready to strike."

"How do you know all of this?"

"Haven't you been paying attention? Cyrus saw it all in his mind."

"But we cannot defeat dragons, goblins, and a sorcerer all at once."

"Don't forget about the vodar. There's a reason they attacked us on our journey here."

"He's trying to do everything in his power to get the last two stones."

"Exactly, and that includes infiltration," she said. Talon's gaze snapped to hers. "How well do you trust your lower council?"

"Everyone on my council has been vetted and deemed trustworthy."

She barked a laugh. "Are you willing to bet your life on it?"

His eyes narrowed. "Tell me what you know."

"I know there's a reason your council demanded my immediate death. There's also a good reason they were so eager to pronounce me guilty."

"They mistrust you, same as I."

"Cute, but no. You've got nasks sitting on your council, right under your very nose."

"Nasks?" He frowned.

"In the days of the Asarlaí, nasks were used to carry out secret business. They were easily possessed, easily manipulated. The Asarlaí used them exclusively to do their dirty work."

"Are you suggesting...no, it cannot be true." His demeanor changed. The same crazed fury she'd seen earlier morphed back into him. This time, she was glad it wasn't directed at her.

His eyes turned into flashing orbs of silver. His jaw clenched. His mouth curled into a sneer. Small black iridescent flecks of dragon scales appeared and disappeared into his skin. Was he holding back the urge to transform? For a moment she forgot to be scared. She forgot to hate him. Instead she watched in fascination.

"Who?" he growled, rounding on her. "Who are they? What are their names?"

"Um..." She blinked up at him. She'd said their names so many times—every morning when she woke and each night before falling asleep, just as she'd promised Cyrus. But now she was momentarily stunned. "Um."

"Well?!"

"Stefan Rosen and...and Euen Doyle."

The promise dissolved. A tingling sensation started at the tip of her nose and ears, working its way down through her fingertips, until it reached her toes. A gasp escaped her lips. She was free! It was done.

The king's breathing had heightened. There were beads of sweat upon his brow. The same strange thing was happening to his skin again. He was going to transform.

The next few moments happened quickly.

King Talon lost control. He opened his mouth and roared. It wasn't the roar of a man, but of a dragon. His body began morphing, enlarging as scales appeared across his skin.

Reyr burst into the room, rushing straight for the king. Simultaneously, he issued a barrage of telepathic commands to Bedelth, Koldis, Jovari, and Verath. The four of them took no time in reaching the chamber. They managed to calm their king before he destroyed half the dungeons with his transformation.

"There now," Reyr said, resting his hand on Talon's shoulder. "Control yourself."

"We have been betrayed," Talon snarled through his heavy breathing.

"Betrayed by whom?" Reyr asked.

"Stefan Rosen and Euen Doyle. Bring them here. Immediately."

His shields blinked in surprise before jumping into action. Reyr stayed, keeping a hand upon the king's shoulder. Koldis was the last to move away. Just as he turned to leave, he spotted her.

His eyes widened and he rushed to her side. "Gods above! Claire?"

"Hi, Koldis," she whispered, giving him a weak smile. He attacked her restraints, undoing the ties on the cuffs, freeing her wrists and ankles. He was gentle as he helped her from the table, rubbing the feeling back into her skin.

She was immediately overcome with emotion. This was the same male who'd tried to kill her. He'd shown nothing but hostility towards her for most of their journey, hating her for a crime she'd never committed. Now he was fretting over her.

She began trembling. The emotions of the past few hours

caught up with her. Even as she tried to stand, she stumbled. Koldis caught her, wrapping his arms around her and tucking her head beneath his chin. "I've got you," he growled.

"Thank you," she whispered, trying to keep her teeth from chattering.

When she regained her balance, he backed away, putting her at arm's length, but keeping a hold of her elbow.

"Koldis, where are you?" Jovari's voice blasted through her mind. *"A little help would be nice!"*

Koldis cleared his throat. "Ahh. It seems I am needed elsewhere. Will you be all right here?"

"Go, I'll be fine."

Before leaving, he gave her a brief smile. Then he slipped through the door and she was left to hold herself together all on her own. She glanced over at Reyr and the king. They spoke in hushed tones, ignoring her completely.

She hugged her stomach, waiting in place, unsure what to do. Her exit might have gone unnoticed, but where would she go with guards everywhere? There was no point in running now.

Several shouts echoed down the hallway. The muttered whispers in the room fell silent. The cries grew louder. The king squared his shoulders and stepped into the shadows, making himself invisible.

Reyr remained motionless for several moments before coming over to her. He was upset with her and it showed. His frown was almost too much to bear. How long would it take him to forgive her for hiding the dragonstones? She wanted to apologize, but now was not the time.

"It might be best if you wait outside," he said, voice flat.

"I—I'd rather stay. Cyrus died in my arms. I held him during his last moments. I may not have known him the way you did, but I deserve justice too."

Reyr's jaw flexed before he nodded and moved away.

Two men were led into the room. She remembered seeing their faces during the trial. They glanced around with wary eyes that had not yet adjusted to the dim light.

"I demand you release us, my lords! I demand it at once!" one of them shouted. "There has been a mistake."

"Wait until the king hears of this!" the other cried.

When their gazes fell upon her, their protests died. Kane must have told them enough about her, about how much she might know. Understanding dawned upon their faces. The king took that moment to step in the light.

"Traitors," King Talon hissed. His voice was low, lethal.

They began to tremble. "Please, Your Grace." One of them fell to his knees. Bedelth and Verath pulled him to his feet, keeping a tight hold of his fleshy arms. "Please—"

"Silence," King Talon hissed. He stepped up to face the man on the left, dressed in fine clothes with a jeweled cloak fastener. "Stefan Rosen. Just weeks ago, you insisted I marry your daughter. You convinced the lower council that my death would leave the kingdom without an heir. You have tried to weasel your way into my castle the same way you weaseled yourself into the politics of this kingdom." The man's gaze widened. "Oh yes, I know all about your start, of how you gained your wife's titles when she died. I never considered it worrisome at the time. That was my mistake."

Stefan Rosen began stuttering. "My—my daughter is innocent, my king. Innocent!"

"You mean to say that she is not a traitorous worm like you?"

"No! No, my king. No! That is to say, I am not, I did not—"

"Not *what*?" the king roared. "Not a traitor?"

"No! No, my king!"

"You would dare lie to me?! You would deny Kane's hold upon you?" At the mention of Kane's name, both men crumbled. "You are both nasks! You both spent your time whispering to the lower council, planting seeds of doubt within their hearts about my rule. Do not think I haven't noticed." Talon let out a ruthless laugh. "No. It all makes sense now."

"Please, Your Grace. Mercy!" Stefan Rosen cried.

The other man gasped. They all turned to look at him. He made a painful, choking noise, like he was suffocating. His face contorted and his eyes glowed bright red.

He began to laugh a sick, twisted cackle.

The hairs on Claires arms rose on end. A shiver raced down her spine. She knew those eyes. The sight of them made her back away.

"Oh, how it pleases me to see you suffer at the hands of my work, King Talon." Euen Doyle's voice was strange and hissing. Like a man possessed. "Give me the stones and I will show your kingdom mercy."

"Kane!" King Talon hissed.

"Yes, yes. You have found me out. My failure to kill Cyrus's little messenger has put a kink in my plans. The vodar paid dearly for that mistake." Euen turned his red eyes directly upon Claire. She froze, ensnared. "Mark my words, you pretty little wretch. You will pay for your interference. You should have stayed in that disgusting little human world you came from."

She swallowed, backing away another step. He couldn't touch her, right? He couldn't hurt her here?

"How *dare* you address her," King Talon roared. "How dare you show yourself here! The stones will never be yours."

Kane began to laugh again. "I do hope you reconsider. I would hate to destroy your precious kingdom. What will I have left to rule after I rip your heart out?"

"You will never succeed," King Talon cried. He thrust a blade into Euen's belly. The man cried out in pain, doubling over. Kane's red eyes disappeared as the king pulled the weapon free. The sound was sickening. Blood poured down to the floor.

Her breaths came faster and faster. Her vision began darkening at the edges—

A new laugh rang out. "I do hope you are prepared for a good fight, dear king. I hope you are prepared to watch your legacy crumble. I will wipe out village after village. I will take numerous lives. There will be nothing left for you to rule. Give. Me. The. Stones!" This time Kane was inside Stefan Rosen's body.

Enraged, King Talon lunged again, stabbing him the same way he'd done with Euen. Kane vanished. Both men were left broken and bleeding, held erect by the king's shields. The king continued his onslaught, now that he had succumbed to his madness. He began slicing his blade across parts of them, drawing blood, giving them agony.

Their cries echoed in Claire's mind. But that wasn't what weakened her now. Kane would continue hunting her! He would make her pay for this.

She couldn't breathe. Her heart raced, blood rushing past her ears. She tried to take deep breaths, fighting her dizziness. Then her vision blackened completely. The last thing she felt was Reyr's hands as he caught her up. Then everything vanished.

CHAPTER 42

A NEW POSITION

Kastali Dun

Claire woke to find herself on a fluffy bed. She rubbed her fingers against the soft linen fabric, sinking in and out of consciousness. When she finally opened her eyes, she saw a white-washed ceiling with dark beams staring back at her. "Where am I?" she croaked.

"You're in the great keep of Kastali Dun," a voice answered.

She recognized it and smiled. "Reyr!" She turned to find him observing her from a nearby chair. Her memories came racing back. The dungeons, her horrible experience with the king, the way Reyr had looked at her after discovering she'd had the dragonstones all along. She'd blacked out. It felt like a lifetime ago. Maybe it *had been* a dream. Why else would she be here instead of her dungeon cell?

"Glad to see you are finally awake," Reyr said.

She struggled to sit up. "How long have I been...?"

"Several hours." His arms were crossed. Still angry, then.

"Reyr, I...I'm sorry! I wanted to tell you. I would have given you the dragonstones when you found me, but Cyrus made me promise. Please! Please don't be angry with me." His expression didn't change. "Please? I can't stomach your disapproval."

He sighed. "I am not angry with you, though I wish to be."

"Wait, you're not?" The tension in her shoulders released.

"You cannot begin to understand how it felt, to believe the stones were lost." His eyebrows scrunched together, as though the mere thought was painful.

"I...I know," she whispered. "Everyone was worried about them and it was all my fault. I was the only one who knew they were safe." That had been one of the hardest aspects of her secret.

"No matter how hard I tried," Reyr said, "I could not understand why the vodar attacked us. Once I got over the shock of seeing them, no explanation was adequate. I did wonder though, I wondered if you had witnessed something you should not have."

"They were after the stones."

"Yes. I know that now." He pulled his chair a little closer.

"I can tell you everything," she offered, hoping to make things better between them.

"I would like that very much. I want to hear the story from *your* side, but tonight we are short on time." His gaze was heavy, serious. "I want to say what I came to say before anything else."

"Oh...okay." She scooted back against the pillows.

"The king told us everything after—well, he told us everything you told him." He ran a hand through his golden hair, pulling at some of the tangles along the way. "The truth is, Claire, I have no right to be upset with you. After what you did for Cyrus, you saved his life without even knowing him. He was a complete stranger, yet you did what you could to help him. He trusted you enough to tell you his secrets. That...that says a lot. Cyrus was not easily trusting. His ability to bend minds showed him things no normal person would ever see."

She swallowed, reminded of the time Cyrus had broken into her mind to see if she could be trusted.

"Ultimately, Claire, Cyrus was mine to save—my responsibility —but I was too late. You got to him first."

Tears sprang to her eyes at the thought of Reyr blaming

himself. "I...I tried to save him, Reyr, I really did. I never wanted him to die. He knew they would come back. I never took it seriously, but he *knew*."

"There was nothing more you could have done. What you have already done, the promise, keeping the dragonstones safe, traveling across an entire kingdom because *he* asked you to—" A depreciating laugh slipped from his lips. "It is nothing short of incredible. I find myself impressed most deeply."

She gave him a shy smile. "Then, you really aren't mad at me?"

His smile came more slowly. "No. I do not think it is possible to be mad at you for more than a few minutes." She exhaled, relieved. "Now, enough of the serious matters. I know talking about Cyrus upsets you, it does me too. Let us address the situation at present."

"The...the situation?" She glanced around the room, only just noticing the finer details of her environment. The chamber was small, about the same size as her cell, but a vast improvement. It was plainer than what she expected to see in a castle. There were no rich tapestries or ornate furnishings. It was simple, yet clean. There was a single chair upon which Reyr sat, a small table in the corner, a wash basin next to that, a window above the bed, a small fireplace with a grate across from her, and the bed itself, upon which she sat. Despite her surroundings, a new question came to mind. "Wait—what happened to those men? The traitors?"

He leaned back in his chair. "After you lost consciousness, the king regained control of himself."

"Did he kill them?"

"No. They were healed, just after you lost consciousness. A quick death is too easy. There will be no mercy for them."

Her stomach tightened. She tried not to think about the barbaric devices in the torture cell. Tried, and failed.

"The king will deal with them later. For now, he has other important matters that require his attention. The heap of information you provided will keep us busy for some time. Anyway, that brings us here." He gestured around the room. "While you were unconscious, the king and I discussed your future—"

"I get to go home now?" She sat up straighter.

Reyr's face fell. "Unfortunately, no."

"But...but I need to!"

It wasn't that she hated this place. Quite the contrary. It was the drengr conversations in her mind; they were becoming too much to bear. Even now, a headache was forming between her eyebrows. She'd thought it was special, being able to hear them. Now, she just wanted the voices to stop.

"I understand where you are coming from, Claire, what it took to leave your old life behind. However, you cannot leave just yet."

"Why?! I did what I came to do. When can I go home?"

"Considering what you know, considering all that has transpired, considering the threat Kane made—he promised to kill you, remember? The king believes the safest place for you is here. I agree with him."

She snorted. "What a glorified way of putting it—I'm still a prisoner."

"Don't think of it that way. You have free reign of the castle—for the most part."

"And what am I supposed to *do*? Sit here all day and wait for the king to kill Kane?"

"Well, that brings us to the next part. For the time being, you will make yourself useful. You will take on duties with some of the servants."

"What?!" she roared. "You're joking, right?"

Reyr flinched, affronted by her yelling. "I am not joking."

"You...you *let* him do this? After everything? You let him condemn me to servitude?"

"Hold on just a moment," Reyr said, taken aback. "You seem to think I have direct control over the king."

"Well, don't you?"

"No, Claire, I do not. Just because I manage to sway him in some matters does not mean I control him in everything. If I am not mistaken, it seems you blame me for this. I had no part in his final decision."

A shield's advice only goes so far. The king is the ultimate decision maker.

Cyrus? she called, fishing into the depths of her mind. It was the first time hearing his voice since the dungeons. She thought he had abandoned her, that he was tied to the unbreakable promise, which had now been fulfilled. It was a relief, a selfish relief, to know he was still with her.

I will always be with you, remember? Always.

She glared at Reyr. "So, putting me here, making me become a servant, that was *his* decision?"

"Aye. I advised him against it." Hearing that made her feel a little guilty. Reyr did a lot for her. If it weren't for him, she would probably be dead. "But, when the king asked if I had a more appropriate suggestion regarding how you might spend your time, a better suggestion of how you might contribute, I came up with nothing."

She threw her hands up in frustration. "I can think of plenty of ways I would rather spend my time, Reyr. None of them include dumping chamber pots. I know more about Kane than pretty much everyone here. I was the one Cyrus confided in. I'm sure my advice can help somewhere. If I'm going to be stuck here, why can't I be on the leading edge of the fight?"

"Firstly, dumping chamber pots will not be part of your job description. That unfortunate duty falls to the chamber maids. And there are few to dump, given that most of the keep has pit toilets." He arched an eyebrow, already driving home the point of how little she really knew. "I think this will be a good opportunity to learn about our way of life. The servants know more about this keep, about its secrets, than anyone." He stood with obvious frustration and placed his hands on the back of the chair, leaning against it. "Besides, it will keep you out of everyone's notice."

She opened her mouth—

"*Secondly,* the war efforts are better left to those of experience in such matters. You may think you know everything about Dragonwall, but there is still a vast deal of knowledge to be gained. That education can begin right here, in the keep. You may not realize it now, but you are getting placed in an excellent position to do so. It is not *ideal,* I agree with you, but make the most of it. I encounter enough stress in my position as it is. Feeling guilty for your disapproval because I could not do more isn't something I can grapple with at the moment."

She exhaled. He was making her sound like a petulant child for complaining. She gritted her teeth to keep from saying anything else. Maybe she *did* need to make the most of it. For starters, it was better than being locked in a dungeon cell. Besides, if anyone was to blame, it was King Talon.

"Fine. I'm sorry I blamed you." She blew out a breath. "So...how long am I stuck like this?"

"I do not know." He pinched the bridge of his nose. "I will do what I can to find a better solution, all right?"

"I...okay." That was better than nothing.

"Now, it is getting late. Tess will have my head if I fail to get you to her before bedtime. Come."

"Tess? Who's Tess?"

"See?" Reyr afforded her a smug grin. "Look how much you have to learn."

"Yeah, yeah," she muttered, "point made."

"Tess is the head woman of the keep. A mother hen, if you will. She's responsible for keeping all her chicks in line. You will like her, I think. Come." He moved towards the door, opening it for her. She followed.

As they moved through the keep, she was captivated. It was as though she was seeing it for the first time, finally seeing it. Reyr did his best to explain various facets before they reached their destination, naming statues and recalling history.

"The cookery," he said, "is located on the east end of the keep. I think you will like it there. It is active all hours of the day, and so is Tess."

When they entered, a wall of delicious smells rose up to meet her. Baking bread, roasting meat, sharp scents of garlic and onions; it all mixed together in a marvelous way. Her stomach rumbled. Then, just as suddenly, she was being hugged. In a flourish of movement, a fleshy body wrapped around hers. It belonged to a woman who smelled like lavender.

"You *poor* child," the woman cried. "You poor, *poor* thing. To go through all you've been through…" She had just a moment to return the woman's hug before she was placed at arm's length for inspection.

"Look at her, Reyr, skin and bones!" The woman rotated her this way and that. "Gods. She is pretty, though. I 'spect behind all this grime she's a right beauty." Tess chuckled, taking her thumb to clear away a smudge of dirt from her face. "My goodness, I'll have a right job keeping everyone's paws off her."

Reyr laughed a nervous laugh. "I suspect you will, dear Tess. Shall I leave her with you?"

"Oh yes, honey! Off with ya. I'll take right good care of this one."

Reyr eyed her. "Goodbye then, Claire. Until next time."

He disappeared before she could say anything.

Tess was generously curved, with a warm round face. She stood tall and husky, with plenty of cushion to her build. This was hidden under her billowing red kirtle. Her face was lit with an enduring radiance when she smiled, and her graying hair was tucked under a bonnet. Only a few flyaways showed. She was, for lack of a better description, perfect.

Claire fought the urge to throw herself at the woman for another hug. Motherly love had a way of healing a person. That was exactly what she needed.

Instead, she blinked and looked around. The cookery was spectacular to behold, bustling with activity best described as organized chaos. There were three cavernous chambers. Tess led her through each one. The inner room held shelves of dishes and wash tubs. Some were piled so high, she wondered how they didn't topple over. At the room's center sat a large well with a pump.

Women in gray and black dresses were positioned at every station. As they worked they sang a lively song, washing to the same speed as their chanting. Each smiled warmly at her, giving friendly bows of their head in greeting.

"Ladies," Tess announced, bringing their music to a short halt.

"This here's Claire. You'll be seeing her 'round these parts from now on."

"Greet'ins miss Claire," some of them said.

"All right!" Tess snapped in a friendly manner, waving around a wooden spoon. "Back to work with ya!" The chanting began anew as they got back to their task. She watched for several moments in fascination.

They moved into the central chamber. This was the biggest room in the cookery. Huge fireplaces and ovens loomed above them, reaching nearly to the ceiling. Delicious smells were coming out of each. Cooks rushed around preparing food.

"We get much of the breakfast meal prepared the night before," Tess explained. "Else we would be up long before the crack of dawn." While the cooks worked, they performed coordinated movements, dancing around the room, never bumping into one another. And like the women in the washroom, many of them hummed or sang aloud with booming voices, lending a buoyant ease to the mood. The friendly atmosphere left her grinning.

Reyr was *right*, she liked it here.

The final chamber, the one she first met Tess in, was for food assembly. Meals were staged before going out. Currently there was no food assembled, as dinner was long over.

"Now, I 'spect you'll be needing some new attire." Tess eyed her clothing with a scrunched nose then took her downstairs to a cellar full of closed doors. The air was crisp and cold and smelled like dirt. It reminded her a little *too* much of the dungeons, and she shivered, fighting back the unease of her memories.

Tess unlocked a small door, leading into a shelved storage room. The shelves were stuffed with folded clothes made of plain fabrics. There were lots of browns, blacks, grays, and whites. "While you serve, you are expected to wear *proper* attire." Tess climbed up on a sliding ladder and pulled out several ordinary white dresses. These looked like nightgowns. They were stiff and scratchy.

"Do I wear these to bed?" she asked, scrunching her face in disgust at the thought.

"Goodness no, child! These smocks are to be worn under your kirtles."

At her confused expression, Tess explained that smocks were used to soak up sweat and odor under the everyday dress. It eliminated the need to wash a gown after each wear. She never realized how complicated archaic fashions were, and she wasn't looking forward to *any* new dresses.

Next Tess gave her a plain, dark gray and black linen kirtle with an apron. "This will be your formal serving attire." Though ugly, it was better than what she had on. Everything she'd brought was now filthy, except for her spriten gown.

Tess gave her a few other items, too. A gown for sleeping, one to be used on special occasions, and an outfit for recreational attire. This consisted of brown pants that buttoned up the front, along with a knee-length tunic.

"There now. All set." Tess climbed down from the tall ladder. "Those'll fit fine," she added, eyeing Claire's figure.

"But..." Tess hadn't given her any underclothes. "What about underwear?"

"I have already given you your smocks, dear."

"Yes, I know, but I mean underwear to wear on, well, you know...?" She gestured at her private parts, unsure of how else to put it without being entirely blunt. The woman would probably have a heart attack if she said the words aloud. Tess put her hands on her hips, regarding her strangely. "You know—*underwear*. Like this." She pulled up on the waistband of the current pair she wore from under her jeans.

"What is that?" Tess balked. So she unbuttoned her pants and showed her a larger portion of what she wore. "Oh, dearie me!" Tess looked faint. She pulled a fan from her apron and began profusely fanning herself. "We certainly do *not* have garments like *that*. Not good for the privates. How ya get any air down there is beyond me..."

"But surely, once a month..."

"Oh! Oh-ho! Of course! Just a moment, dear." She reached into a cubby hole in the back of the cellar and retrieved a stack of thick padded cloths. Each had strings connected to them.

Claire eyed them in horror.

"Here you are." Tess handed them over, and that was the end of that. "Now, there is a washroom with baths down the hall from your new quarters. They are specifically for servant use. There are pit toilets too!" Tess was excited about this marvel. "If ya don't wish to use your chamber pot, that is. But if ya do, there is a waste system in the washroom to dispose of your excrement when you are finished." Claire gawked, astonished, uncertain of how else to respond. "I know! I know! It is amazing that the keep has any plumbing at all. Nowhere else in Dragonwall has such magic."

"Yes." she said emphatically, sarcasm dripping from her voice. "Indeed. It is *truly* amazing."

Tess nodded eagerly.

They made their way back to the cookery. Tess prattled on about the wonders of the keep. "Oh, and I shall have someone bring you a spot of supper tonight, child. I know you're tired, but only just this once. Otherwise, you are to dine with the rest of us, down past the cookery. Take the evening to rest. I will send for ya in the morning."

"Thank you," she said, and felt her eyes turn glossy.

"Are you going to be all right, dearie?" Tess studied her.

"I—I'll be okay," she croaked, though she wasn't certain it was true.

She made her way back to her chambers alone. It was far from easy. Several wrong turns took her through a large, empty corridor. Luckily, the servant quarters and cookery were in the same general area. When she finally found her room, she put her things away and noticed that Reyr had taken the liberty of delivering her other belongings from the dungeons. She would deal with those later.

The prospect of a bath had her rushing to find the washroom.

When she did find it, it was not at *all* what she had expected. There were three giant baths sunken into the rocky ground and filled with steaming hot water, which was delightful. What she was *not* pleased to find was that both males and females used them, simultaneously.

Several men were already bathing. Although they kept to themselves, she had half a mind to run away and forgo the experience entirely. Then she remembered how badly she smelled. How much she missed hot water.

A few women entered. She watched as they removed towels from a shelf near a set of stalls. They entered the stalls and closed the curtains. When they emerged, their towels were wrapped around their naked bodies. They set their clothing down on empty shelving then proceeded to the baths. There they walked down the stairs and into the water. The towels were removed right before they submerged themselves, and placed in a pile on the side of the bath.

The men paid them no attention.

She copied them, selecting the third bath because it was empty. She nearly groaned as she sank below the surface. The hot water did wonders on her tense muscles. It even helped ease her headache.

Her rumbling stomach was the only reason she hurried, eager for the food Tess had promised. She took soap from one of the holders, gave herself a good scrubbing, and worked hard to remove the tangles from her hair. Then she quickly dried and dressed in one of the kirtles, and returned to her room.

Dinner was modest, but delicious. The tray on her little table had boiled chicken covered in dried herbs and gravy, a large chunk of bread with yellow cheese melted atop, and a cluster of grapes. A veritable feast compared to what she'd been eating. She was surprised to see that both ale and water were given to wash it all down.

Contentedly full, she crawled into bed. It was a little lumpy from the stuffing, but far better than the hard ground. Settled in, she blew out her candle and shut her eyes. Then, for the first time in weeks, she drifted off into a peaceful sleep.

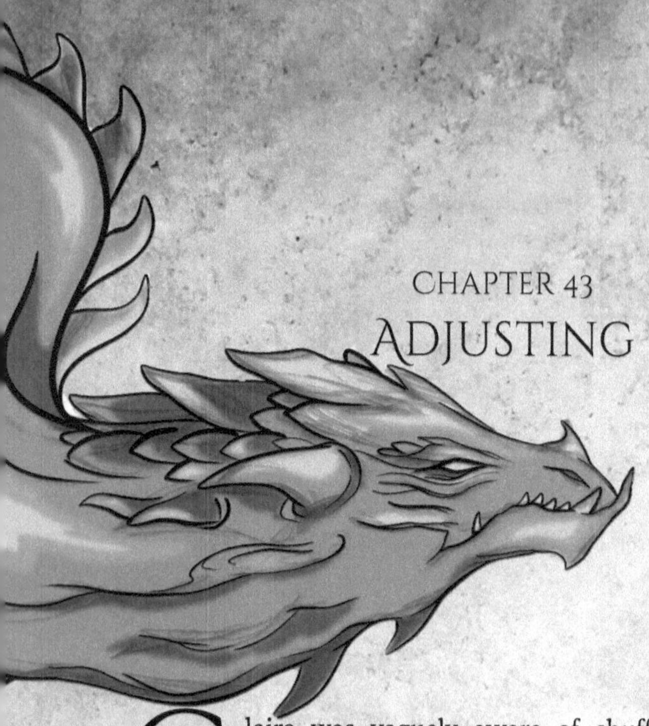

CHAPTER 43

ADJUSTING

Kastali Dun

Claire was vaguely aware of shuffling near her bed. Someone was in her room. A yellow glow seeped beneath her eyelids. She groaned and rolled over.

"Please, Miss Claire!" The voice was insistent. "It's best you wake up."

A dream—this was only a dream. She groaned again and threw the covers over her head. They were ripped from her grasp. Cool air kissed her exposed skin. Her eyes flew open in frustration.

"Miss, Tess will have a fit if we're late," she warned. "Come, dress yourself. We must be going."

Her intruder, a woman not much older than herself, was curvy, with hair and eyes the color of dark chocolate. She had a pleasing, if not a little plain, face, with thick eyebrows and heart shaped lips.

"I'm sorry, but who are you?"

"Oh, do forgive me! I'm Desaree. You will be my charge while you're here."

"Desaree." She said the name out loud to remember it. "It's nice to meet you."

368

"Likewise. Now, if you hurry, we can get some food before we get to work."

The promise of food had her quickly gathering her clothes. Desaree waited by the door. Her lantern cast bright light around the room. The sun wasn't even up yet.

She dressed in the garments Tess had given her, then followed Desaree out of her room. As they walked, Desaree pointed things out. "That's the way to the great dining hall," she explained. "And the guest suites are over here. We'll be seeing a lot of those. Oh, and this leads to the southern wing. That's where the king lives, in a giant tower full of fancy rooms."

They passed carpeted corridors and ornate archways. Walkways lined with statues of armored men, tapestries, and beautiful vases. There were even courtyards with small trees and fountains. Everything was lit by the orange glow of wall sconces and lanterns, still dark, still slumbering.

"Have you ever seen it?" Claire found herself asking. "The king's tower, I mean?"

"Oh, no, I have not. I would love to someday. Only the chamberlain, the lower council, and the king's servants go up there, well, and his shields, obviously. But I *have* heard about it. Rugs woven from the finest yarns, tapestries from the lands beyond the Dragonfire Sea, statues of pure gold..." Desaree's eyes went dreamy and unfocused before she spoke again. "The linen washrooms are that way." She pointed down another corridor, more dimly lit. "You and I will be there later today, I'm afraid."

Claire suppressed a nod, trying to commit everything to memory.

"Oh, and *that* way takes you to the lower courtyard. Someday I will show you the royal garden. We are not supposed to go in there, since we're not nobility, but we all sneak in when no one's looking."

They reached the cookery, too late for breakfast.

"It's all right," Desaree assured her. "We don't usually get much to eat in the mornings, anyway. Besides, if you are smart about it, you can sneak some bread from the ovens. It is better fresh, anyway." The last was spoken conspiratorially in a quiet whisper. From the spark in Desaree's eyes, it was obvious that she did it frequently.

They walked into the cookery. It smelled sweet, spiced bread, warm apples, and roasting ham. She thought of bacon—what she wouldn't give for a few slices of bacon. They washed their hands before Desaree grabbed her and pulled her to the edge of the room. Large steaming loaves of bread were being sliced by a baker.

"Good morning, Thomas." Desaree greeted a balding man who wore a crisp apron over his tunic. "This is Claire—the new girl. You've heard of her, haven't you?" The man turned to them with a wide, crooked smile. He had hazel eyes, and reminded her a lot of her grandpa.

"Certainly. Who hasn't. Pleasure to meet you, Claire. Are you hungry?"

"Starving!"

"Well, now. We can't have that, can we? Both of you have a long day ahead, eh?" He offered them generous slices of buttered bread and sent them on their way.

"If you stay on Thomas's good side, he is always that nice. Not so for some of the others. You will soon learn who to trust." Claire liked the man already. "Only the nobles get fresh butter," Desaree added as they dodged the cooks and made their way to the inner-most chamber. "You had better eat fast. I hear Tess!"

She followed Desaree's advice. The warm bread nearly melted in her mouth. There were little apple chunks scattered throughout the cinnamon swirls. It was absolute heaven.

They found Tess in the dishwashing room. "There you are!" she cried, waving a wooden spoon at them. "You are both *late*! Late, late, late! Not tomorrow, I dare say."

They shook their heads fervently. A rush of heat warmed her cheeks. It was her fault for taking so long to get up. At least Desaree didn't appear bothered by it.

Tess wasted no time going through their duties. First, they would deliver breakfast trays to the nobles who wished to dine in their apartments. "Desaree can show you how it is done," Tess said. Then, before the midday meal, they would clean the ground floor apartments on the western side of the keep. "Each day will be different. Every apartment gets a deep clean once a week." After their meal, they were scheduled to report to the launders in the linen washrooms. "With so many visitors, those poor souls are behind on the washing. I have assigned extra helping hands today, *including* yours."

"Can't we do something else, Tess?" Desaree whined. "The hot water makes my hands crack terribly."

"As it does for everyone!" Tess nipped at her. "But if you do a good job, I may concede. Now, off with you both." She swatted at them again with her spoon. They both giggled and scampered away to the food assembly room.

Much to her surprise, she was excited to help Desaree. In just a short time, she learned more about Dragonwall than she'd bargained for. Perhaps Reyr was right all along. Like it or not, she would make the most of her new position and learn everything there was to know about the great keep. The tidbits of information she gained throughout the day were nothing important, just small details, like the location and purpose for various chambers, rooms, and corridors, the visitation reasons for nobles, the types of business they conducted, and which people and places to steer clear of.

"See that woman over there," Desaree pointed to a finely dressed lady basking in the afternoon sun. She was sitting in one of the many courtyards with several others, chatting and laughing. Her gown must have cost a fortune. It was sunset orange, with streaks of pink woven into the fabric—nothing like the ugly dresses servants wore.

"What about her?" she asked, studying the woman for clues.

"Stay away from her," Desaree warned. "Her name is Lady Caterina. She is an absolute coxcomb."

"A—a *what?*"

"A coxcomb," Desaree giggled, grabbing Claire's arm as they backed away into the shadows. "You know? She is as vain as a cock in a hen house and looks down upon anyone in a lower position."

"So...she's mean?"

"Quite cruel, yes. Best to avoid her."

For most of the day, Claire wrestled with the constant headache caused by the stream of drengr voices bombarding her mind. Sometimes it was a single voice, other times more than one. The contents of these messages were usually cryptic or hard to follow. Still, she had no choice but to hear them. A drengr by the name of Fendrel was meeting his rider, Sasha, in the marketplace. They were going to shop for a new coin purse. Another, named Sarka, was bored. He wanted to know if his rider would go flying with him. It was all so meaningless to her.

Though, she occasionally picked out the shields' voices, and even King Talon's. But, just like the others, nothing important was discussed. Usually just requests to meet, or simple facts and updates.

Time passed quickly. Working on a farm taught her to be diligent. It wasn't as if this kind of labor was anything new.

The most difficult task was helping in the linen washrooms. This series of interconnected chambers had huge tubs with scalding hot water and sticky detergent. Bedding, curtains, table cloths, and clothing were all cleaned here. She and Desaree weren't permitted to touch the beautiful gowns and doublets. Those were left to the experienced workers, with special instructions on how to clean them.

Instead, they were given bedding. The linens were cleaned by plunging them into a tub with a large paddle used to mix everything around. Oftentimes they had to get their hands wet to detangle the cloth. The hot water and harsh soap made her skin burn and itch.

She'd never appreciated washing machines so much as she did now.

The only enjoyable part of working in the washrooms was the singing. Like the women in the cookery, songs were used to make the work lively. It kept the tempo going and increased their productivity. They liked to sing about lost love, young lads chasing tavern wenches, and noble knights courting ladies. After a few hours, she learned some of the lyrics and even found herself singing and laughing along with Desaree.

Most of the servants were humble. They had good spirits and were grateful for their positions within the keep, contrary to what she had expected. Perhaps being a servant wasn't nearly as miserable as she'd believed. Most of the servants knew her identity, but refrained from asking personal questions. She was thankful. The only awkward moments were the curious whispers that followed her.

"They are simply eager to discuss something new," Desaree explained. "Our boring lives never offer much entertainment. The servants enjoy gossip."

Desaree assured her it would die down in a few days.

Supper that night was her favorite part of the day. It took place after the nobles ate their own. A lot of unused food returned from the dining hall, leaving plenty for the servants. She'd worked up a ravenous appetite.

They ate in a large chamber down the hall from the cookery. There were big windows looking out into the cookery's private herb garden. The room was lined with wooden tables and benches, a few tapestries, and a huge fireplace against its far wall. The grate was empty tonight, because of the summer heat.

Buzzing voices permeated the air. Everyone was in a good mood. Jugs of cheap ale were passed around and she indulged. "The nobles get the better stuff," Desaree explained. "They love wine and brandy. Ale is considered a *commoner's* drink."

"That don't keep 'em from drinking it though, does it?" another woman chuckled. Her name was Sarah. She was one of Desaree's closest friends. The three of them sat at the farthest table, near the door.

When the eating ended, someone shouted, "My dear Tess! Give us a song!"

Roars sprang up as everyone began slamming cups on tables

and calling out their requests. To her amazement, Tess climbed atop the bench of her trestle table, billowing kirtle and all. The room fell silent, everyone waiting. She burst into song, her buoyant voice carrying. Just a few words in, everyone picked up on the lyrics, joining in:

Women, women, oh thee women, finer none than ye,
Some be lewd, and all be shrewd, but none be temptin' me,
Some be nice like cluck-house hens, and others be not so,
Women, women, oh thee women, finer none than ye....
A pretty thing so nice to love beneath the kirtle and above,
Some be brown and some be white, but none be temptin' me,
Some be fickle as cluck-house hens, and others be not so,
Women, women, oh thee women, finer none than ye....
A purse or many she may empty if her man's a ninny,
Some be crude, and all be canny, but none be temptin' me,
Some be tame as cluck-house hens, and others be not so,
Women, women, oh thee women, finer none than ye...
A prize to win a prize to hold a woman's hand be plenty
Some be sweet, and all be sharp, but none be temptin' me
Some be shy as cluck-house hens, and others be not so,
Women, women, oh thee women, finer none than ye...

THE SONG CONTINUED IN MUCH the same way, running through repetitive stanzas. The men in the room were especially rowdy as they sang along, laughing at the parts they related to. She didn't know any of the words, so she just watched, fascinated by their antics.

After Tess sat down, she wrapped an arm around the woman beside her and planted a kiss on her lips. The woman only laughed and leaned into Tess. Claire watched, grinning, as Desaree leaned over and whispered, "That's her lover. Hence the song. The nobles wouldn't approve, of course. They'd say it's not *proper*, and then they'd go and do the same thing behind closed doors. The hypocrites! Us servants don't mind a bit."

Claire couldn't help but snort with glee, knowing that.

When it was time for bed, she retired to her room. The light of a single candle cast unfamiliar shadows upon the walls. She lay still, enjoying the flicker, allowing her mind to wander.

The keep was a busy place, full of life and excitement. So much work, so many tasks, not a moment to spare, not a second to think. Now she mulled through the past several days, considering her situation in full.

Without the binding promise, she was free, no longer enslaved to its will, no longer dragged along by invisible strings. Suffocated by its pressure, she was learning to breathe all over again, experiencing Dragonwall with a new perspective, able to appreciate its amazements in full. There was no denying the new pull she felt. She was drawn to this place, enamored by its existence, desperate to know more. It was like being caught up in the middle of a story with an uncertain ending.

She'd spent her whole life traveling through books, captivated by impossible worlds, awed by impactful characters, characters who traveled *with* her through the pages, characters who always endured. The common theme never changed. Whether good or bad, all stories led to an end. From book to book one aspect prevailed. The plot was already laid out upon the pages.

Where was her plot? What was her purpose? Which path was *she* supposed to follow, now that she'd fulfilled her task?

THE NEXT MORNING began the same way, with Desaree pulling off her warm blankets and insisting she get up. This time, she didn't protest. It was easier, and she was even a little excited.

The day after that, it was even easier. She rose without Desaree's assistance. She couldn't help but feel a little proud as she fell into a rhythm within the keep.

With so many tasks, each day began to blend into the next.

On the third day, she noticed Lady Saffra from afar. Their eyes met in silent understanding. They weren't supposed to know each other, so they pretended not to. But Saffra's gaze was encouraging. Her friendship would come in handy, even if they couldn't yet act on it.

She caught sight of the king a few times, too. It left her skin crawling with hatred. Every glimpse brought back uncomfortable memories. Thankfully, each time she saw him he was always deep in conversation, surrounded by a posse of nobles, too busy to notice her, the humble servant. Part of her wanted him to see her, to rush over and apologize for how he'd treated her. The other part of her thought it was a good thing. She couldn't stomach the thought of speaking to him.

His shields, on the other hand, *always* noticed her. Jovari was the first one she encountered in the corridors. He was parading through the keep with several ladies. Like the other nobles, his attire was rich and colorful, nothing compared to the bland travel clothes she remembered. The moment he saw her, he approached and bowed deeply. "My *dearest* Claire." The ladies exchanged looks of surprise, even confusion. She might have been the talk of the keep a few days ago, but in servant's attire, she was already nobody.

"Hi, Jovari. It's nice to see you. This is my friend, Desaree." Jovari, being the suave gentleman that he was, took up Desaree's hand and planted a kiss on her knuckles. Desaree's cheeks turned dark red. Several of the women gasped. If Jovari noticed their surprise, he pretended otherwise. "The ladies and I were just taking a turn about the castle, admiring the beautiful day. Will you join us?" His innocent question earned appalled glares from his companions.

She did her best not to laugh. "I do apologize, Jovari, but I am afraid Desaree and I have many important tasks ahead. This magnificent keep doesn't run itself." As she said it, she looked directly at the ladies.

"Of course. Right." He nodded in agreement. "Another time, perhaps?"

"Sure. Why not."

As the group departed, the ladies began chattering away, glad to be rid of them. Desaree stared after them with wide, unblinking eyes, as if she couldn't quite believe that had happened. It must have been unheard of for a noble like Lord Jovari to approach someone so lowly.

Occasionally she encountered the other shields, too. They greeted her in much the same way, though none of them were as flamboyant as Jovari had been. It seemed he, being the youngest of the five, was often caught up in frivolous pursuits. The others were usually rushing to urgent matters wearing looks of fierce concentration, or frowns of frustration.

On her fourth day, she and Desaree were walking through a courtyard when Desaree pointed towards the sky. "Look at the drengr," she gasped. "What are they doing?"

Above them, a mass of drengr took part in what appeared to be an aerial display of fireworks. They dived and swooped, dodged and ducked, cartwheeled and spiraled, all the while with riders strapped to their backs. Reluctantly, she tried to process the voices intruding into her mind. She'd been doing her best to ignore them over the past few days, not that it helped with her headaches.

She relaxed her mind instead of fighting the voices, and attempted to separate them. The loud buzz died down into perceptible differences.

"*Make sure you dive when I am beneath you, and tuck your wings in.*"

"*I cannot grab you with my talons. Pay attention!*"

"*If you do not take hold of my neck, you have no hope of bringing me down.*"

"*Is this the proper way to grapple with a wild dragon?*"

"Desaree, I think—" She paused to listen again. "I think they are training."

"Training? Above the keep? That's absurd." The sun peeped from behind a cloud. Desaree lifted a hand to shield her gaze.

"*If they attack the keep, we need to be ready.*" Now *this* voice, she recognized. And sure enough, she spotted Reyr's golden glimmer dodging in and out of the wrestling pairs.

"I think they are preparing for an attack on the keep."

"An attack? Who could possibly attack the keep from the sky? Birds?" Desaree's shock was well warranted. She didn't know about the wild dragons. For a moment, Claire considered telling her, then thought better of it.

"I—I don't know. But look, there is Lord Reyr." She pointed him out, steering the conversation in a new direction. She couldn't help but watch him, impressed by his agility. Longing filled her heart. She *loved* flying, all the joy it brought, the freedom. She missed it, and wished she could be up in the sky with him.

"How do you know it's Lord Reyr?" Desaree asked, her eyes following Reyr's descent towards one of the battlements.

"I would recognize his flying anywhere. He carried me across the kingdom, remember?"

"Oh. Oh, yes. Of course." Desaree looked at her. "What was it like? I mean, I know the act is frowned upon—to fly with a drengr that is not your mate. The servants have whispered plenty about it. I certainly do not judge you," she added, making her stance clear. "Was it wonderful?"

"Yes," Claire breathed. "Very few things in life come close."

Desaree spent the remainder of the day peppering her with questions. What did it feel like when a drengr jumped into the air? Did she touch a cloud? Were they soft? How did the ground look from above?

Desaree asked so many questions, she could've written a book on the experience. But it wasn't bothersome. Claire was more than happy to share her excitement.

Reyr didn't visit her until the fifth night. She was so glad to see him, that she went through every detail of the past five days. He was patient, listening intently during the serious parts, laughing when warranted. "It sounds like I was right; you've learned a great deal!"

His praise left her beaming. She was quite proud of herself. "I've learned so much that my head aches!" Her head ached for a different reason, but she kept that a secret. They chatted for several minutes before she excitedly recalled seeing him above the keep. "What were the drengr doing up there?"

"Ah, you saw that, did you? We were training."

"For what?"

He scooted his chair close enough to prop his boots on the bed's frame. "Well, we were training for the possibility of an aerial attack. Just in case wild dragons make it this far south, we need to be ready." His words confirmed her theory. She listened eagerly to him while he explained their plans. Messages had been sent to the other forts, advising them to take the same precautions, just in case wild dragons attacked. In the meantime, the mages were working on new magic to help defeat both dragons and the vodar.

"What about the goblins?" she asked. She'd never seen a goblin, but the description from Cyrus was enough to paint a mental picture. As if on cue, an image flashed into her mind of a green, wrinkly face with large, saucer-like eyes and pointed teeth. She shuddered. Cyrus was pulling something from his memories and sharing it with her. He'd never done that before.

"We cannot be sure *where* they will attack," Reyr said, oblivious to what she'd just seen, "nor when. But the king is devising a plan to increase our troops in the east."

"And the nasks?"

Reyr hesitated. "We have not yet dealt with them in full, but their time will come."

"What if Kane gets to them first? Can he possess them again the way he did before? Will they find a way to escape?"

Ugh, so many questions. She couldn't get them out fast enough. She hated being on the sidelines, hated not knowing, hated having to ask. If they had included her like she'd wanted, she wouldn't have to spend so much time speculating.

Reyr shook his head. "You need not worry. They are heavily chained and under constant surveillance. They will not escape."

"But what about—" A new thought had just occurred, one that left her pulse spiking. "What if he possesses *new* people? What if he turns someone else into his nask? What if they go down into the dungeons and free the traitors?"

Reyr held up his hands to stop her. "Slow down. You certainly have a lot on your mind."

"Well, what do you expect?" She crossed her arms, glaring at him.

"I suppose I should have visited you sooner. Regardless, I will try to come more often. We have a lot of catching up, and you owe me your story, remember?"

She nodded, but her story could wait. More frightening things were on her mind. "Reyr, do you think..." she trailed off, considering all the new people she had met in the past few days. "Do you think we can trust everyone in the keep? Is it safe here? What if there are more nasks plotting to kill me?"

Oh, gods. She would never be able to sleep now.

"That will always be a possibility. You should stay vigilant in all things, never give anyone too much information, be wary of strangers, trust your instincts." As he spoke, his eyes gleamed. "I certainly trust your instincts." At that, she smiled. "The king has taken stringent measures to secure the keep."

"Stringent? How stringent?"

"I suppose that depends. Do you know how a nask is made?"

It had never occurred to her. She shook her head. Reyr explained the process. For initial control, the sorcerer needed to perform the magic in person. It was not something that could be carried out from afar. That meant those possessed would need to enter the keep to cause harm. Everyone currently living within was safe from Kane, assuming the two traitors in the dungeons were the *only* ones.

"The king is no longer allowing newcomers to pass through the gates without intense inspection. This makes it very difficult for those conducting business to come and go, but the measure is necessary. Trust me, Claire, we are on high alert. If you see any strange behavior, anything suspicious, tell me."

Reassured by his answers, she finally put the subject to rest. Their conversation didn't go much further. King Talon called Reyr to a meeting. She heard the telepathic request but pretended not to notice. "I am sorry to depart in such a hurry. I must take my leave. The king has need of my council."

He moved to the door and paused, his hand on the doorknob. "I meant to tell you. It is not yet certain, but I may be taking a journey north in the next few days."

"North?" Her chest deflated. "Can I come?" She already knew the answer, but it didn't hurt to ask. She missed flying. She missed the adventure of traveling across Dragonwall from the sky. Most of all, she would miss Reyr if he left.

He bowed his head. "Alas, I wish you could, but you will be safer here."

"Where will you go?"

"I must pay a proper visit to my brother Davi."

"Oh, Davi. He's the leader of Fort Squall, right? Didn't you just visit him when we came here?"

"Aye. A rushed visit it was. It is not certain yet, but if it becomes so, I will come see you before I go. Until then, farewell, Claire." He departed, closing the door behind him.

She exhaled, sad to see him leave. With him gone, her mind drifted to Kane, thinking about what he was capable of, about what might happen if any of his spies slipped through the gates. Chills left the hairs of her arms on end. Paranoid, she wedged her chair under the door handle, not that it would really do much. Then she blew out her candle and fell into bed. Sleep was a long time coming that night.

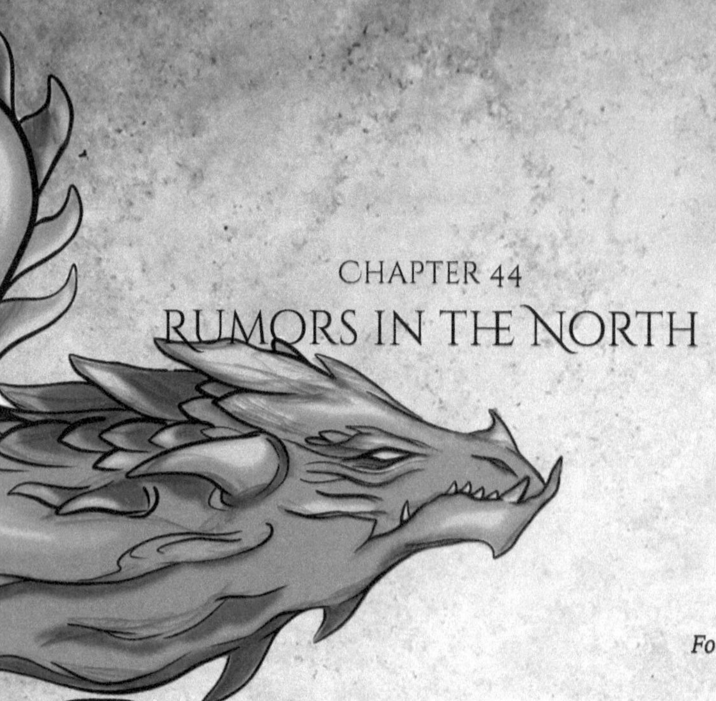

CHAPTER 44
RUMORS IN THE NORTH

Fort Squall

Davi wiped sweat from his brow. Squall's End was blistering hot, today more so than usual, as if the gods were punishing them for the rising turmoil. And the humidity! How he longed for the goddamned season to end.

Returning his attention to a stack of letters, he flipped through the next few. Fear of the dead in Kelnia, corpses rising from their graves, corpses who feared only fire. Rumors of a goag stalking the city of Arkland—he shuddered. Goags were mythical creatures from undirfold, twice as tall as any human, with curving horns and skeletal bodies. He tossed that one away, shaking his head. Impossible. Nonetheless, he took note of the complaint on his list before turning to the next. Vodar wraiths spotted in Brambleton, far north. Now, this one held merit. The next claimed glowing green monsters floated across the marshes near Mistport, dead and undead, simultaneously. Each letter was much the same, warning of strange but impossible occurrences.

The trend was unsettling.

Finishing the last few lines of summarization, he quickly composed a message and folded it into a pocket sized square. He dropped hot wax onto the parchment and pressed his seal to it. The wax proudly displayed a coat of arms unique to his ancient clan, a dragon wielding a sword atop a mountain of iron. The motto beneath the image was minuscule. It read, *Jarnin eflai verus sterk.* Iron makes us stronger. He and Reyr were some of the last traceable descendants from the great Iron Clan.

"Tomah," he called. His page burst into the room, a young drengr not yet fledged. "Deliver this to Marek. You know Marek?"

"I—I think so, my lord."

"Good. He is expecting it. Remind him to make haste. This letter *must* reach Northedge quickly. Hurry, catch him before he goes." The boy took the letter and rushed from his study.

Leaning back in his chair, he inhaled deeply and closed his eyes. His mind was hungry for a moment of peace. A wave of reassurance washed over him, calming his muscles and easing his tension. *"These are worrisome occurrences. You have done well, my love. Averaen is wise."* Emmy's voice in his mind was soothing.

He sighed and said, *"I hope he will have some answers. With the king busy to the south, and Reyr's visit uncertain, I must resort to my own devices."*

He felt Emmy smile as if it were his own. *"That is why you are our leader."* The thought was sent as a whisper, a confirmation, a testament to his abilities. Gods, he appreciated her so much. If there was one true blessing in this world, it was his mate.

Opening a desk drawer, he removed Reyr's letter, looking it over again. The message merely confirmed what Reyr had told him during his short visit. Wild dragons were indeed responsible for the burning of Belnesse. Worse still, they were under the command of an Asarlaí sorcerer by the name of Kane. Could this sorcerer be responsible for the strange missives flooding in?

He read through the list of measures each fort was expected to take, considering the undertakings in earnest. Frustrated, he shook his head. The commands were not stringent enough, not nearly enough. Drengr against drengr combat drills? Doubled patrols? Increased weaponry? None of these addressed the real issue, that of killing a wild dragon.

On a separate sheet of parchment, he began writing his own list of action items, assigning teams to each of the duties by way of brainstorming. If everyone cooperated, tighter measures could be achieved, but it would be a stretch.

A door closed in the main chamber. The sound was muffled, but enough to get his attention. It was fully dark now, which meant he'd missed dinner entirely, but the glorious scent that met his sensitive nose meant Emmy—bless her—had taken care of that for him.

His heart quickened the moment his eyes fell upon her. After two hundred years, she still had that effect on him. Yes, he was a lucky male.

Her eyes sparkled, reading his thoughts. "You may be lucky," she teased, "but you will kill yourself if you do not take care. I cannot bring you dinner every night. Eventually, you will starve."

He sighed. "I would have died a long time ago were it not for you."

She set a plate down beside him and stepped away, but he was too fast for her. Grabbing her arm, he pulled her into his lap. The sound of her giggles left his insides warm. "You best not get distracted, my love. Eat." She tried to stand, but his arm tightened around her hips.

"I can eat just fine *with* your company, thank you." To prove his point, he plucked up a roll from the platter and consumed it.

"Well you had better hurry. The meeting will start in a few minutes. Shall I join you?"

"I would appreciate you there." He spoke through a mouthful as he quickly crammed food down. "Even if the other riders do not choose to attend, your presence would stress the importance of this matter." Riders rarely attended meetings held with his higher ranking drengr. It wasn't necessary, because of their bond. With connected minds, having one present was as good as having the pair.

"All right, I'll attend."

"You *are* the ranking woman of the fort, Lady Emmiline."

When the drengr began filing into his quarters, they set up in the conference room. It was a good thing their riders did not attend, because many of the wing seconds were forced to stand. The fort was two hundred drengr strong, with every wing consisting of twenty pairs. Each wing had a wing leader and two wing seconds, based on the wedge formation in which they flew. He only had sixteen chairs around the massive oak table. Emmy sat at the head. He chose to stand beside her.

The first orders of business were mundane.

"Byron." He turned to the wing second, reminding himself to spare the lad embarrassment by remaining professional. "How fared your search? Have you found enough volunteers?"

Byron nodded, glancing at Fierran, another wing second, before speaking. "Aside from those who have already arrived, thirty-some travel from Redport. They should be here within the week."

The search had kept him away with Fierran for nearly a fortnight, ranging all along the coast of Stormy Bay, and inland as far as Mistport.

"Good. You have done well." He bowed his head, pleased with Byron's efforts. Then again, he was always pleased with Byron. It was a primary reason the young drengr had been promoted to wing second so quickly. The lad was meant to lead, and one day, he would.

"He is hardly a lad anymore, Davi. He's already fledged. You must face his adulthood sooner rather than later." He hated that Emmy was right. He looked fondly at Byron, studying his golden hair and prominent features. Byron looked more and more like him every day. "Besides," Emmy reminded him, *"a day will soon come when he has a mate. Do not let him hear you call him lad then, or he may take offense."*

He grunted but took note.

They caught up on other matters too, discussing the current stores of weaponry and scheduled sweeps for the week. Anything to prolong what was coming, the news he dreaded speaking aloud.

"We cannot be here all night, my love," Emmy reminded him as the hour grew late.

"Right," he said aloud. "Well then. The real reason I called you all here tonight. It has come to our attention that Dragonwall is under attack." He told them first of the wild dragons, and then of Kane. Shocked gasps echoed around the chamber. Hands covered mouths. Eyes darted, catching upon comrades for support. "What's more," he added, "I've been receiving strange letters about creatures better left in stories."

"Byron and I heard similar tidings when we visited Mistport," Fierran said. "I took it as drunken nonsense. Glowing green monsters? Next thing we know, someone will claim that the vodar have brought their souls with them from undirfold."

"Maybe they have," Davi mused.

"And we are to believe this drivel?" Jaheremy asked. He was another wing second. "The vodar, sure. That has been confirmed. But everything else? Goags? Living corpses?"

"Listen, weeks ago, wild dragons were a thing of bedtime stories—bedtime stories we used to scare our children into behaving." Davi shook his head at the thought. "But now, this letter alone,"—he held up Reyr's letter as proof—"confirms their existence."

"So...because of *their* existence, these other terrifying monsters must also be real?" Byron shook his head. "Surely not."

"Aye. It is a possibility," Davi said.

"It's as if we've stumbled into a living nightmare." Byron looked from one drengr to another, willing them to protest the idea.

"Nightmare or not," Davi said, "we have a list of tasks to complete."

"What of the people?" someone asked. He couldn't see who.

"The people do not yet know," Davi said. "The king plans to make the announcement at court in the coming weeks. That leads us to the next matter of importance. We in the north are at greater risk than those in the south. Tomorrow each of you will divide up your wings into groups of five to ride out into Vestur and alert everyone."

"But that will cause mass panic!" Byron jumped to his feet.

"Can you imagine their reactions? And what happens when they begin flocking in droves to Squall's End for protection?"

"Tithes alone will not be enough to support them," another said.

"Yes, the increase could cause serious problems," he agreed. "I will schedule a meeting with Lord Rhal. We will work to devise a plan that would see many of these refugees housed within the city, safely and economically."

There came some grumbling. Not everyone liked that idea. But, what other choice did they have?

"Listen," he said, lifting his hands to silence them. "We cannot leave the people uninformed. At least this way, they might prepare."

"Prepare?" Fierran also stood. "Prepare *how*? How can any one person, or even a number of ill equipped villagers, take down a wild dragon, not to mention one hundred of them. I agree with Byron, it is best if they do not know."

"When they flood into our cities for protection," Byron added, "it will worsen our position. An easy time it will be for wild dragons to target Squall's End directly, targeting a congregated and overpopulated expanse. In one fell swoop, they will remove much of the north."

He looked at Emmy, overcome with helplessness. Their arguments held merit. He'd already considered most of what they said. But it felt wrong. Wrong to leave his people unaware, wrong to withhold truth.

"We shall take a vote." Emmy's voice broke the silence. Nods rippled around the room. That was generally how matters of importance were decided, anyway. The fort leader never held absolute power.

They took a vote by show of hands.

Once tallied, the majority were in favor of keeping silent. He was one of the few to oppose the idea. Instead, they decided a small number of coveys would fly out at dawn, not to inform the people of dragons, but to learn more about the rumors circulating.

"At the least, we must get to the bottom of these stories," he concluded. "They might turn out to be as important as the dragons."

Resulting nods meant his drengr were happy with the idea.

Byron spoke up then. "If I may add, we should also advise the lords to call upon their vassals. Increasing the soldier count in larger settlements will work to our benefit if a direct assault on the fort occurs." Byron's suggestion was met with positivity. His pride for the lad burned deeply within his chest.

"I agree. Sound advice, Byron. We will do that as well." He then took suggestions from each of the other drengr present. The meeting continued late into the night until many of them were drooping with exhaustion. Emmy did her best to scribble notes for each decision until everyone was satisfied. Having a plan of action was a relief, but in no way did he feel better. The road ahead would be difficult.

At last, he and Emmy retired to their private quarters. Too fatigued to speak, she did little more than peck him on the cheek before curling into his arms. He waited for her to fall asleep before considering each of the terrifying possibilities ahead of them.

CHAPTER 45
AVOIDING DISCOVERY

Tamara bit her tongue, careful not to make a sound after her knife had sliced her finger. Gods above! She pulled her hand away before bleeding on anything, and went in search of a bandage. With a cloth strip tightly tied around the wound, she continued. Her pile of diced carrots began cascading down from the top. She picked them up, depositing them into an empty crockery. The others were already full, a product of her labor, many hours, and multiple cuts.

The cook would have sent her away hours ago, had he known of her inexperience. Thankfully, she'd hidden her blunders. Her mind jumped to the chamber pot maids and she shuddered.

When she finished with the last carrot, she paused to admire her work. Not bad for a highborn lady. She stifled a giggle. Her mother would've had a fit, seeing her in such a state. Dirtied face, clothed in homespun fabric, wielding a knife to chop vegetables. It was oddly satisfying as she considered the way her mother might faint at the sight of her.

She placed the large crockeries along the hearth and took up several yellow onions. These were her *least* favorite, for obvious reasons. Why had no one ever told her how they burned, how they made tears fall?

Learning to blend with the servants offered a myriad of challenges, onions being the least of them. The journey alone had been difficult. It had taken over a week to reach the fort on foot. She'd been careful to keep her head down.

Laying eyes upon the city had been worth every blister. She'd gazed upon the magnificent expanse, stretched out before her as their party crested a hill, with tears in her eyes. Just beyond it, she'd spotted the fort.

A rush of hot pride had followed, that she'd done this all on her own, seizing her future in her own hands. And she'd done it without anyone the wiser to her true identity. There'd been no remorse, either. Even looking out over Squall's End, knowing the city could have been hers had she stayed to marry Lord Rhal. No city, not even Kastali Dun with all its rumored splendor, could make up for a stolen life.

"Finished, have you?" The cook's voice startled her. She was staring at her pile of minced onion.

"Oh. Yes, sir."

"Good, gal. Get those into the boiling broth." He pointed his butcher's knife at the largest hearth where a cauldron was bubbling. She followed orders, making several trips to get all the onion into the liquid.

The cook watched her with narrowed eyes, then directed her to a mound of potatoes. There had to be a hundred, at least! "When you finish with those, you may be dismissed."

Eagerly, she began piling potatoes into her apron before unloading them onto the long wooden table. Like the other cuttings, the potatoes were for the stew, a common staple food at Fort Squall. There were many hungry mouths to feed, and with patrol teams coming and going all hours of the day, prepared food was kept on hand. Porridge in the morning, replaced by stew in the afternoon and evening.

The sun was sinking low to the horizon when she completed her tasks. Rising from the bench, she groaned and stretched to relieve her muscles. Her back hurt from hunching, her face was raw from hovering over the fire, and her fingers were nicked everywhere.

Bidding the cook farewell, she departed. Perhaps she'd retire to bed early. It wasn't as if—

She stopped dead in her tracks. Cold dread took root in the pit of her stomach. There was a voice, a velvety smooth voice, deep in conversation. Her mind flashed back to that night, underneath the willow tree's branches. Creeping into the shadows, she tiptoed further down the corridor and peaked around the corner. Byron stood, dressed in beige leggings and a green tunic, his long sverak strapped to his side, chatting with another drengr.

Her heart leapt at the sight of him and she backed further into the shadows. If he spotted her, if he saw her unique eyes, if he realized that she was not among the line of volunteers they'd selected in Redport, he would recognize her for who she truly was. Her fake name would do little to shield her when that happened.

"It's unlike anything I have felt," he was saying, rubbing at his chest. "I can't explain it."

Gods! She needed to run. She needed to get as far from him as possible.

"I felt it in Redport too, stronger than ever. It dissipated when I left, but it has returned."

"And it's been happening all week?" The other drengr tilted his head.

"All week." Byron rubbed his chest again.

"Hmm..."

Holding her breath, she turned on her heel and set off in the opposite direction, keeping her head down. When she arrived at her small quarters, she all but tumbled inside, slamming the door behind her. She leaned against it, panting.

That was close—*too* close.

In the last week, she'd encountered Byron a total of four times. Each time had been much like this one. So far, luck was with her. But with every new day, her dread grew. Eventually, Byron would spot her. If he discovered who she really was, that she was betrothed to Lord Rhal, he would send her away immediately.

She'd come too far to risk it.

She was alone in her room, a small chamber with four cots, each with adjacent shelving. A single washbasin stood near the entryway, and a long looking glass was propped against the back wall.

Three other volunteers shared the space with her. They'd come to the fort for the same reason, with the same dreams, hoping to try their luck at getting near enough to a drengr to discover a mate bond. That was the only way to become a rider.

Lara and Kiviana were in their twenties, beautiful, and everything a rider ought to look like, but they weren't very nice. They'd already made subtle digs at her age, snickering behind her back.

"They're just jealous," Sophie had told her. "Jealous of your beautiful eyes."

Now, Sophie, she loved. She was spirited, smiled frequently, and always optimistic. It was easy to adore someone like that, especially when that someone reminded her of Josie, the only friend she left behind in Redport.

She could not say how long she stood surveying her room before a firm pressure against her back sent her flying forward. Sophie burst into the room looking more frenzied than Tamara had felt after seeing Byron. She was out of breath, her face was flushed, and her eyes were wide. "Amber," she gasped. "You will never believe it!"

"Believe what?"

Oh, gods! Had someone discovered her secret?! Her throat constricted.

"Oh, it's the best news. I can hardly believe it myself." Sophie took her arm and pulled her to the center of the room, eyes sparkling with excitement. "I was on my way here when I heard a peculiar conversation. So, naturally I was curious. I stopped to *politely* inquire—oh, I cannot wait any longer!" she cried. She was bouncing up and down on her toes. "Tomorrow there is to be a touching ceremony. Cannarth's rider, Rene, told me! The fort leader announced it just minutes ago. Something about one of the drengr feeling something strange in his chest ever since the volunteers arrived."

Something strange in his chest...? Oh! She recalled Byron and her eyes widened.

Sophie dramatically threw herself upon her cot, face first, then squealed into the pillow.

"What...what is a touching ceremony?" she managed to squeak. "I certainly do not want anyone touching *me*."

Sophie burst into hysterical laughter, sitting up. "They do not touch *you*, silly. You touch them!"

"Them? I..." Then her eyes widened. "The drengr?!"

Sophie nodded eagerly. "A touching ceremony," she explained, "is a formal ceremony to recognize mates. Tomorrow, all the riderless drengr will assemble on the field between the city and the fort, and we, the hopefuls, will have an opportunity to lay a hand upon their scales. That's how a bond is recognized."

"Truly?" she breathed. Her stomach erupted into flutters. Touching a drengr. Discovering a mate bond. Becoming a rider. "But...how?" she wondered. "How do you know? What happens?"

Sophie took a deep breath. "Haven't you heard the stories?"

"I mean...yes, but they never discussed the mechanics of it."

"*Havadan slatir takenna slakev, tivi gedi gara ein, an hilgar asamat ut ken,*" Sophie chanted.

Gooseflesh prickled Tamara's skin. Such strange words. Sophie struggled as she spoke them, as if the pronunciation did not come naturally for her.

"But...what does it mean?"

"When skin touches scale, two minds become one, the sacred bond is unveiled. It is a translation from the old language," Sophie explained. "You are not meant to understand the old words. I cannot remember the rest of the poem, only that. I have repeated it to myself many times."

"How—how do you know it?"

Sophie smiled proudly. "My great grandmother was a rider. I never knew her. She was one of those here at Fort Squall that died in the battle up north. But she taught her daughter, that would be my grandmother, some words. They were mostly poems and sayings, and a few songs, too."

"Wow," Tamara breathed.

"Anyway, if you touch a drengr tomorrow, you will know, just like it says. Two minds become one."

"But, Sophie, if your great grandmother was a rider, surely you will be too. Drengr blood flows in your veins."

Sophie shook her head. "Her daughter was not so fortunate. My grandmother hoped she'd find a drengr mate, but it never happened. Eventually, she left the fort and fell in love with a human, a minor lord, and had my father." Sophie frowned and shook her head. "If her own daughter could not do it, there is no guarantee that her great granddaughter can. But I must try. I must try."

"I figured all females born to the drengr became riders," Tamara mused, unsettled.

"Not always, Amber. Not if a bond isn't there."

They spent the entire evening engrossed in speculation. Sophie explained that this sort of ceremony only occurred once every few years. That did little to calm her nerves or bolster her confidence. If she failed, she would have to wait a long time to try again. She picked at her supper, unable to eat. While Sophie's excitement was eager, hers was anxious.

Part of her was envious of Sophie with her drengr blood. Surely, despite everything she'd said, it would increase her chances. While she wanted very much for Sophie to succeed, she too wanted to succeed and felt disadvantaged. Moreover, her age had her second guessing her fate.

That night, sleep did not come.

The next day progressed with a sense of growing anxiety. She tried her best to keep her thoughts positive. Her hands shook, and she cut her finger twice because of it. The second time she had to bandage it repeatedly to stop the bleeding. Privy to her struggle, the cook left her to stir the simmering broths, which made her hair frizzy and her face sooty. Increasingly clumsy, she dropped the ladle onto the hot coals then burned her hand when retrieving it. By mid-morning, she accepted that the day would be an absolute disaster.

No drengr could possibly want her.

When the cook's patience was spent, he sent her away to wash windows. "It is normal to be nervous, dear gal," he told her kindly. "But let's keep you from the knife and the fire today."

Washing windows was tedious work, she had to haul buckets of water from the well and back until her arms ached. In fact, more time was spent retrieving water, than scrubbing the glass. She was returning for the umpteenth time when she heard a voice cry out, causing her to slosh water all down her front.

"You, there! Just a moment."

"Oh, gods. Not now," she cried, continuing at a faster pace, as if she hadn't heard him.

"I insist you stop at once!" She did not. Hurried footsteps caught up to hers. A hand grabbed her arm. She was forced to halt.

For a moment, the world tilted on its axis as he pulled her around. She came face to face with Byron. The moment he beheld her blue eyes, his own widened. "I knew it!" he cried, though slightly out of breath. "I knew it was you. *You're* the girl from under the willow tree." Alarmed, she stayed perfectly still. She could not have moved had she wanted to. "I would recognize those eyes anywhere."

She could only blink up at him.

Byron studied her, taking in her dirtied face, the state of her clothing, the water soaking her front. Her hair, messy as it was, fell everywhere. Uninvited he reached forward for a better look, moving a lock of it away from her face. His fingertips brushed her skin. Sensation erupted at the contact. Little tingles spread across her cheekbone.

His brow furrowed. "Interesting. Very interesting..." He studied her with fiery curiosity.

She stepped away from him, confused, and still fearful. Would he send her home? After coming so far, was it all lost?

As she jerked her arm from his grasp, something seemed to

register. He shook himself and regained his composure, taking a large step back, giving her space. The amusement, however, never left his gaze. "Tell me, *Amber*, how is it I find you here in Fort Squall, when I do not recall selecting you from the line of volunteers that night in Redport?"

Stones dropped into the pit of her stomach. "I...you..."

His smile widened, revealing a charming set of brilliant white teeth. They were not pointed and large as they would be in his dragon form, yet they were perfectly even and level.

She tried to stammer through her shock.

He held up his hands in submission. "Calm down, I will keep your secret."

"My—my secret?"

"Oh yes. Clearly you never handled your responsibilities that night. Believe me, if I could run from mine, I would."

"Then...you won't tell anyone?"

He looked thoughtful. "That depends."

"On?"

"I want you to be truthful with me."

She frowned.

"At first I believed your age had you sneaking around, that it kept you from volunteering. But no, you were at the celebration, so you must be at least fifteen—"

"Two weeks from sixteen," she clarified, lifting her chin.

He rubbed the stubble on his jaw. "So, then, what is it that has you sneaking about?" She refused to answer. Even if it looked as though he had already figured things out. "You're the missing daughter, aren't you? The one Lord Redwynn is in an uproar about."

She swallowed. "How—how did you know?"

His eyes swept over her, taking her in anew. How silly she'd been to believe she could pretend to be anyone else.

"I have a duty to report you." His voice was low, almost...grave.

All the blood drained from her face. "You can't."

"And why is that?"

"Because…" Her hands began to tremble. She balled them into fists. "Because he'll force me to marry."

"You are of a marriageable age, are you not?"

Her lips parted, outrage settling over her. "That does not make it right! No one should be allowed to force me to do *anything*!"

"You're right." He sighed, studying her. "The drengr have a different approach to the world than you humans."

"Then…you *won't* send me back?"

His expression turned thoughtful, his brow furrowing as duty warred with conscience. "I won't turn you in."

All the breath left her lungs on a relieved exhale. "Thank…Thank you."

He shrugged. "You're welcome. I'd rather not spend the afternoon explaining to Lord Redwynn that I misplaced his daughter." He smirked and despite herself, she smiled back. "You will attend the ceremony later today?"

"The ceremony? Oh…Right." And just like that, all her nerves came racing back. "Yes. I…I'll be there."

"Excellent. I will see you later, then."

He walked off. *Would* she see him later? And what would happen when she did?

CHAPTER 46

A BOND UNVEILED

Fort Squall

Tamara walked arm in arm with Sophie out to where the ceremony was to be held. They'd both cleaned up well, though she had little more than rags to present. Sophie, however, looked stunning in her burgundy gown.

She wanted to tell Sophie about her encounter with Byron, but that meant telling Sophie that she had lied about her identity.

"Amber? Don't you agree?" Sophie tugged her arm.

"Oh. I...what?"

"I *said*, I hope Lara and Kiviana fail today. They deserve it, after the way they've treated you."

"Oh. Yes. Right. Me too." Except, she didn't really care about the other two girls. She was too distracted by what had happened with Byron. He'd promised not to tell, and he was a drengr, an honorable one at that. Surely things would be...fine?

They traipsed onto a vast, grassy field between the city and the fort. A rush of wind rustled her hair as the sun briefly disappeared behind white, fluffy clouds. It was a gorgeous summer day. There were others, also making their way out onto the field.

A concussion of wing beats sounded. *Drum. Drum. Drum.* There were gasps. She looked skyward and saw why. Nearly a hundred drengr, many with riders, were making their way towards the field. They grew larger as they came closer, then began to descend in lazy spirals, their wings outstretched, heading directly for them.

A few people screamed, moving away from the open area.

Tamara's stomach lurched into her throat, leaving her nauseous. She watched as the drengr landed. Those without riders kept their form. The others became human and walked to the outskirts of the field with their mates.

"I don't think I can do this," she whispered, clutching Sophie's arm. Nearly twenty drengr, took their positions on the field. Their hulking forms were so much bigger up close. Each was a different color, glittering in the daylight. Blues and greens, a few reds, oranges, a purple, a bronze, and even a white.

"Yes, you can," Sophie answered.

Her chest tightened. She took several deep breaths, trying to steady her thoughts. A terrifying realization nearly knocked the wind from her. In the next few minutes, her future would be decided. She'd been naive to believe she had control over her life. That leaving Redport allowed her to chase her destiny. Fate was the making of riders, and no one was capable of commanding fate.

Sophie took her hand and squeezed. "Just keep breathing," Sophie coaxed. "I am nervous too. But we will never know until we try. Remember? We must try!"

"We must," she whispered.

"Come on." Sophie pulled her towards the assembling line. Everyone was silent. The very air was tense. Several hopefuls were permitted forward into the large area where the drengr were waiting in their hulking forms. They stumbled towards those gathered, uncertain and fearful, just like her. With wide eyes, she stood motionless as she watched the event unfold.

The hopefuls walked from one drengr to the next, stopping at each to lay a hand upon their scaly hides. It took about five minutes for the group of four to move through the field. Nothing happened. Realizing their failure, they left with tear-streaked faces, huddled within each other's arms, taking their sobs with them.

She glanced behind her. The line of terrified faces had grown. Many looked more frightened than she felt. That was something, wasn't it? Squaring her shoulders, she pretended she was unafraid, she ignored the mounting tension in her muscles, until a new uneasiness worked its way to her surface, not nearly as potent as her fear of failure, but still viable. One of the drengr on the field was Byron, but which one? If she'd known what color he was, she might have avoided him. Gods!

A joyous cry caught her attention. Sophie squeezed her hand. Out on the field, a drengr transformed. It wasn't Byron. This one had black wavy hair, cropped just above his ears. He was fondly stroking the hair of a woman who gazed adoringly into his eyes. The exultation upon their faces left her speechless.

"They're mates," Sophie breathed. "I can hardly believe it. Look how happy they are."

Cheers split the tense silence.

"All right, the four of you may proceed." The voice could have been leagues away. Caught up in the unfolding scene, she was dimly aware of Sophie's pull on her hand. When Sophie moved away from her, she snapped from her trance and found herself walking out onto the field. She was in a dream. Her legs had a mind of their own, taking her to the nearest drengr. She wanted to turn and run, but she couldn't. Even the hand she extended no longer looked like hers.

The drengr she touched was deep purple.

She sucked in a breath. His glassy scales were incredibly warm, almost enough to burn her hand. She held her palm against him, feeling the hardness beneath her soft skin. The first moment was exhilarating. In truth, she wasn't sure what to expect. Only when his giant head swung around to regard her did she realize she was lingering longer than necessary. This one was not meant for her. Disheartened, she nodded respectfully and moved away.

The next was a dark red with an underbelly that blended to orange. He was beautiful. More hesitantly this time, she laid her hand upon him. Like the rest, he towered over her. She could only reach the mid-part of his belly where his scales changed color. He felt no different than the other. Extremely warm to the touch with scales of glass. Nothing happened. This time she did not need prompting. She withdrew.

Over and again she tried her luck, only to have the sinking feeling in her chest grow stronger. Midway through, a dark blue drengr had a stomach rumble the instant she touched him. She gasped in surprise, thinking *this* was her moment. Then she remembered what Sophie said. Minds become one when a bond is unveiled. Her shoulders sagged with defeat and her throat constricted.

"Don't cry. Don't cry. Don't cry," she whispered under her breath.

There were two candidates left to try when she made her way to the far side of the field. She approached a drengr bigger than most. His scales were ice blue, just like her eyes. She regarded him with curiosity and he did the same, turning his saucer-sized gaze on her.

She stopped beside him, trembling with nerves. His head swung around to better see her, casting her in shadow. Gods, he was huge.

She stood motionless, her hand hovering over his hide. Already she could feel the intense heat radiating from his scales. It warmed her skin. If she never touched him, she wouldn't face defeat. But if she did...

Turning her head, she met his calm gaze, losing herself within the gold of his eyes. Eyes that seemed...almost familiar. Taking a deep breath, she brought her hand down upon him. The world fell away, the ground crumbling beneath her. Nothing existed, not even time. Her mind was wiped free of fear, free of apprehension, free of failure. Then bliss, powerful and penetrating, radiated through her.

Recognition doused her senses, pouring over her like a bottle of perfume. Familiarity seeped into her soul, imprinting itself. It was the kind of familiarity that came from smelling a rose for the thousandth time, or looking upon a face she'd known her entire life. It was an immense understanding that originated from nowhere and everywhere all at once. She exhaled.

A cry sounded. Hers? His? It was impossible to tell.

Flashing pictures that lasted for seconds, thoughts, memories, ideas, all trickled through her mind simultaneously. They were unfamiliar, yet she knew them, these things she had never experienced, faces she had never seen, wonders that were incomprehensible. They weren't hers, but they *were* hers, all at once.

Two minds had become one.

A single existence swam into her consciousness. She knew this drengr, she recognized his heart, she relished in his familiarity. He was a part of her. Everything she felt was echoed within him.

"I have found you at last."

Yelping with surprise, she withdrew her hand. The voice in her mind was Byron's. She opened her eyes, watching the last of Byron's transformation. He faced her in human form, scooping her up into his arms, laughing with delight. He twirled her around until she was dizzy. When he at last set her down, she could scarcely breathe.

Was this...was this really happening?

Her ears rang from the deafening cheers of the crowd. She was hardly aware of it as she gazed at Byron's face in wonder. Two figures descended upon them. She recognized the fort leader and his mate.

"Father!" Byron cried. The two males hugged. "Can you believe it? It was her all along, she was the reason I felt so strange."

"Lord Davi is your father?" she squeaked, taking several astonished steps backwards. How did she miss the connection? They looked nearly identical.

Byron smiled down at her. "Lady Tamara, allow me to introduce my mother and father, Lord Davi and Lady Emmiline, Fort Squall's leaders."

She stammered a greeting, embarrassed by her ignorance, then curtsied.

Lord Davi's eyes narrowed. "Wait a minute. *Lady Tamara?* As in the missing lady who has everyone in an uproar?"

"The one and only." Byron's smile held an edge of guilt.

His father's expression darkened. "Her parents have been very worried, sending out search parties. They've offered a handsome reward for her rescue. Lord Rhal has done the same. I am told she is his betrothed?" Lord Davi looked at her for an answer. "Is that true?"

"I..." She glanced at Byron. His face had hardened with the mention of marriage. Was he recalling their conversation? Of how she was forced into the arrangement—one she had no say in? She wished she could still see what he was thinking, but their minds were no longer connected. Turning back to Lord Davi, she said, "Yes, my lord. Lord Rhal is...*was* my intended, but the match was made against my will."

"Matches usually are where politics are concerned," Emmy sighed, showing clear distaste for the practice.

"This could make things difficult," Davi said, though he did not seem entirely upset. She breathed a little easier.

"Match or not, it hardly matters," Byron growled. "We are fated. The bond has been unveiled. I would not part with her—not unless she rejects me." Byron reached down and took her hand in his—a protective gesture. "You won't, will you?" There was so much hope in his expression. Tingles erupted on her skin. Her face heated, and she was forced to look away from him.

"I won't reject you." Not when she'd hoped for such an outcome. That it was Byron and not some random drengr she'd never met was even better. She'd dreamt of this life. Dreamt of becoming a rider. Was this truly happening?

"We would never rip the two of you apart, dearest." Byron's mother stepped forward, placing a hand upon his arm to calm him. "It would be unthinkable. Fear not, your father will settle the matter." Emmy radiated happiness. "We are so very proud of you. So very proud."

"Thank you, Mother." He dropped Tamara's hand and took Emmy into his arms, hugging her affectionately. When he stepped away, Emmy looked wistful. It was the same look all mothers gave when their sons grew up too fast.

Byron reclaimed her hand before addressing his father. "By your leave, I would like to speak with Tamara alone." Reaching his free arm out to his father, they exchanged a drengr's handshake, forearms grasped.

"Of course." Lord Davi turned to her. "Congratulations, Tamara. It is a proud moment when a father can see his son happily mated. Finding that mate is the hardest part."

Emmy stepped forward, placing a hand on each side of Tamara's face before squeezing lovingly. "I am happy to have a daughter. Congratulations." She was soft spoken, but her words carried immense weight.

Tamara and Byron walked hand in hand back to the fort. At first, she said nothing out of sheer intimidation. The tingles shooting through her skin did not cease. It finally drove her to speak. "Is it always like this?" she breathed. "My skin sparks each time it touches yours."

Byron chuckled. "I feel it too." He rubbed his thumb against her knuckle and the sensation intensified, traveling up through her arm, taking root deep within her. A pleased growl purred within his chest. "In truth, I never expected it to be like this."

Her heart clenched. "How—how did you think it would be?"

"Honestly, there were no expectations. Finding a mate is different for every drengr."

"What do you mean? You do not always feel tingles?" She wanted to know everything.

He laughed and shook his head. "Not always, Tamara. For some it is a pounding in the chest, for others, overwhelming sentiments of love, infatuation, compassion, adoration, anger, irritation. Certain drengr feel it in touch, others in emotion, and some with drastic changes in their mood. Though different, we all experience one commonality when our mate exists in the world."

"What commonality is that?"

"An inexplicable change, a difference, something that offsets our norm." His words sent her imagination wild. Had Byron felt a mysterious change towards her? Had she towards him? Aside from her increasing drive to become a rider, which drove her to run away, she could not discern any deviation.

"The feelings can be subtle at first, especially if you are young," he said. "You're younger than me, so you may not have felt anything before touching my skin. But I did."

"You...you knew?"

He shrugged. "I did not necessarily know it was you. But when I think on it, I felt something different since your birth. I was just a child, then. What I experienced was subtle. It was too early to associate it as a potential bond. Not until it grew."

She stopped and turned to him. "But—what did it feel like?"

"I can hardly say. I, myself, have trouble explaining it. Somehow I knew my mate was out there." He waved an arm. "Waiting for me. That confidence grew. It radiated through me. When I arrived in Redport, when we were closer than ever, I could almost *sense* your presence. Still, I did not make the association, nor recognize you when we met under the willow."

"Shouldn't a drengr always know to interpret this strange deviation as fate?"

He shook his head. "The signs are not always accurate." They began walking again, approaching the fort's walls.

Byron explained in greater detail. Many drengr perceived false signs, leading them to incorrectly believe they had found a mate, only to discover disappointment upon skin touching scale. They might find one whom they loved, take their feelings as a sign, only to fail. "It is so very complicated," she said.

"Indeed. Complicated and unpredictable. It is important to remember, the beast and the human are two different beings. The human may feel one thing, the beast another, and interpretation becomes difficult. In the end, the beast chooses the mate. That is why skin must touch scale."

"Sophie told me that. She chanted something. I could never remember if I wanted to. But something about skin touching scale and two minds becoming one."

"*A Bond Unveiled*. It is an old song."

"Oh."

"Would you like to hear it?"

"I…yes."

Byron broke into a chant.

A DRENGR'S MATE, *a thing of fate,*
Is destined since creation.
To recognize, one must be wise,
Respect this song's advice.
Heed thy heart and tune thy mind,
Prepare thy way and follow.
When skin touches scale, two minds become one,
The sacred bond is unveiled.
Do not falter, one must go further,
Guarantee what is foreordained for thee.
When flesh becomes one, the mind also follows,
Sealed is the bond that should be.

"Wow," she breathed when he finished.

"Every story is different," he explained. "My father told me that when he saw my mother for the first time, his heart warmed from the inside out, fierce like a fire, burning straight through him. Although, we do not feel the true heat of flames."

They entered Fort Squall through the portcullis. Cool air from the stones washed over her as the summer's heat attempted to stifle the world. As they ascended a set of stairs, she breathed deeply. The dark passage let them out along the battlements. There, they stood to watch the remaining ceremony attendees gathered upon the field.

She turned to him. "Earlier today, when we met, did you know that I was your mate?"

"I thought you might be, but I was too afraid to be certain."

She turned her attention back to the field. "That…makes sense. Did your father know? When he saw your mother? When his heart warmed him like fire."

Byron turned to her. "My father traveled halfway across Drag-onwall to find my mother. Like me, he felt something strange. That feeling pulled him in the direction he needed to go. I am sure he had a hunch. But, he did not truly discover the meaning of what he felt until he laid eyes upon her.

"He was not as fortunate as me. His mate did not merely stumble into the fort like mine did." There was a certain smugness in his voice. And pride, too.

"I did not realize that he went in search of her," she murmured, "that he had to find her."

"It is a common occurrence. Like I said, it is different for every drengr. Fate has a way of uniting us. You happened to find your way here. Had you not, I would have come looking for you soon enough. Though, I fear it would have been too late."

Too late...

Oh, gods.

What would have happened if she had been forced to marry before their bond was discovered? She could fully appreciate how close she'd come to a different fate entirely. If she hadn't taken matters into her own hands. If she hadn't run away, things could have turned out very differently indeed.

Byron pulled her from their vantage point so that they could walk along the wall.

A new thought arose. "I thought the touching ceremony was how everyone found mates. I didn't realize they went off on... quests."

Like all the stories she read about maidens trapped in towers.

"The ceremony is nothing more than a formality. Most drengr do as my father did. Fate smiles upon me, it would seem." They stopped again to look out over Squall's End.

"It is not too late, you know. Lord Rhal is a good man. To be the lady of Squall's End is a worthy role. Stealing you away from him, which is how he might see it, will create tension between the fort and the lord governors. My father is right about the difficulty this has created."

"No!" She blinked at him. Where...where was this coming from? Why was he saying this?

"I have no desire to wed Lord Rhal! Besides, if he is a good man, he will understand the importance of our bond."

Byron turned his tender gaze upon her, happy with her refusal. Perhaps he merely needed the affirmation. Needed to know he wasn't taking away any of her choices. That she wouldn't come to regret this. Regret him.

"I am sure you are right. But it is good to hear you say it."

They walked a little further in silence. She had countless questions, but she was also ashamed of how little she knew. "Byron?"

"Hmm?"

"Why can I not see into your mind anymore? When I pulled my hand away, our minds separated. And the poem, it said..." She tried to make sense of the last few lines.

"Only when our bond is sealed, we'll be permanently of one mind, permanently mated."

"I had thought that was why I touched your scales?"

"No." He shook his head. "Skin touching scale merely allowed us to realize the bond, to unveil it. To seal it, we must..." His eyes darted between hers.

"We must, *what*?"

He suddenly looked as if he wished he were anywhere else but here. "I am going to take a wild guess that your womanhood is not yet upon you. That your mother has not yet had this conversation with you." Her face burned and she sputtered with embarrassment. That was a *private* matter. Why...why would he mention it?

She studied the cobblestones at her feet, symmetrically placed with varying shades of gray—

"Tamara..." He gently took her chin in his fingers, lifting so that her eyes met his. "We cannot seal the bond until you have reached womanhood. And even then..." He sighed, looking away.

"That could take ages!" she blurted. "Besides, why should it matter?"

"Gods above." He drew a long breath. "Believe me. It matters. To seal the bond, to become mates, we must *mate*."

"Mate? Like..."

Oh, gods...

Oh, gods!

Blood drained from her face. Realization dawned on her without the need for him to elaborate. But he did it anyway—

"We must make love—"

"Stop! Stop, please. I get it."

"Good. Then you must know that I will not engage in that act until you are ready."

"Oh..." The words died on her lips. She'd never felt so stupid in all her life. So mortified.

Without another word, she turned on her heel and fled.

CHAPTER 47
THE VEREKBLOT

Kastali Dun

Claire wrinkled her nose before stripping away a set of linens. The feather mattress fell back into place with a *poof*, sending up clouds of dust. She tossed the bedding onto the floor then moved away to straighten the furniture in the room. Fresh flowers from her cart replaced dried bouquets, which she threw into a cloth bag for disposal.

She and Desaree were assigned to the third-floor apartments on the west wing. These were some of the best in the keep, with stunning views of the Dragonfire Sea. She glanced out the open window to watch several ships.

"Phew," Desaree uttered with disgust. "Some of these nobles need to bathe more."

She turned and smiled. "Then perhaps they might go sparingly on the perfume."

Claire watched fondly as Desaree laughed and tossed away a dirty chemise. She was a godsend, if Dragonwall's gods were indeed real. The two had become inseparable. Much of it was because of work, but to her surprise, she enjoyed it. It was exhausting, yes, but she was drawn to the busyness of it. The tasks were

410

mindless enough to keep her occupied while allowing plenty of time to think. Although, thinking was increasingly difficult as her headaches worsened.

Twice she'd been confined to bed rest when the headaches turned to migraines and became unbearable. When it had happened, Tess had been there, fawning over her the way her mother would. "Just keep them eyes closed, dearie," she'd say, sponging a damp cloth over her forehead and feeding her broth.

Reyr had visited too, but he never stayed long. It was difficult to converse when her head pounded and words brought stars to her eyes. "I worry about you, Claire," he often said. "Are you sure you will be all right?"

"You frown too much, Reyr. You're going to get wrinkles."

Despite her reassurances, he always left with a grim expression.

Sometimes, when her misery overwhelmed her, Cyrus showed himself. *You must learn to block the voices out,* he'd say. Or, *If you choose which to hear and which to ignore, you will feel better.* The problem was, she didn't *know* how to do any of that. Worse still, his intermittent coaching only increased the pain.

It was during the worst of it that her desire to run away, to leave Dragonwall forever, grew. She could go back to a world where dragons were only found in storybooks and not skies. Where her head belonged completely to herself.

Cyrus hated the idea.

There were good days, too. Some days the voices came less frequently. These timeouts were islands of mercy amidst a treacherous sea.

Wiping the sweat from her forehead, she stood to survey her work. Desaree was finishing up, placing fresh tapers into their holders before declaring the room finished. The two of them moved to the next, and the day flew by like all the others.

That night, Saffra finally came to see her. Three weeks had passed since their first visit in the dungeons. She was climbing into bed when Saffra's knock came.

"Tess told me about your headaches," Saffra said, entering the room. She frowned. "What is the reason for the chair?" She eyed it with suspicion. They both plopped down on the bed.

Claire explained her paranoia and Saffra said, "You are right to be careful. It's hard to know who to trust. Now, tell me, how are things?"

She gave Saffra an abridged version of the past three weeks, but what she really wanted was to tell her about everything before that. She finally had the opportunity to offload what she'd told King Talon, about rescuing Cyrus and their time together before he'd died.

Saffra was crying by the end. "He was like a brother to me," she whispered. "He trained me to interpret my visions, to control them. We spent countless hours together. He was the only person to see into my mind."

"He—he looked into your mind?"

"But of course," Saffra said, as if the knowledge shouldn't have come as a surprise. "He was a mind bender, the only one of his kind. He knew my mind almost as well as I know it myself. It was necessary, so that he could help me interpret my visions."

"Saffra, is there...is there a possibility he saw *me* there?" Saffra's brow scrunched together. "Think about it. If he saw your mind, he saw me."

"Claire, ever since I was a young girl, your face frequented my dreams and visions. You have always been a part of me."

"Everything makes sense now." Claire slapped her palm over her forehead.

"I'm sorry, but what?"

"I always wondered why Cyrus trusted me enough to give me the stones. It was all because of you."

"He trusted you because he had no choice, Claire. It was a life or death situation."

"Perhaps, but I don't buy it. There were some things he said to me, odd things. I thought it was the poison..." No. It was too coincidental, knowing that Cyrus had seen her in Saffra's mind before she'd rescued him, long before he'd dropped into her cornfield.

"What strange things? What do you mean?"

"Cyrus insisted I was the new protector of the stones. That I was an integral part in the story to come."

"What story?"

Claire shrugged. "The story of the stones, I suppose. Or, the story of Dragonwall?" She thought about their time together, dissecting everything Cyrus had told her in a new light, making sure she didn't miss anything. Cyrus's journey had been coming to an end while hers was just beginning. He'd been so eager to give her the stones. *Too* eager. Not only that, he'd known about his death with too much clarity. She'd even gotten mad at him for that —for insisting he was going to die, when the future was not yet determined.

But the future *had been* determined. He'd seen it in Saffra's visions. And since he'd been the one who helped her interpret them, he'd known more than Saffra about what she'd seen. Whatever he did see convinced him that he wasn't meant to be a part of the final picture.

"He knew all along," she whispered, more to herself than to Saffra. "He knew all along and he didn't tell me. Why didn't he tell me?"

Some things are better learned through discovery. You needed to find the answers for yourself. Cyrus sounded sad.

Well...

What other information might he be hiding? What other things had he left for her to discover? She frowned.

"That's...that's almost too hard to believe," Saffra admitted. "But I suppose it makes sense."

Their discussion moved on to other things, like Kane's nasks. Claire told her what had happened in the dungeons, how furious King Talon had been.

"He had every right to be!" Saffra said. "To think, all those times I sat in the lower council meetings, and Kane's puppets were there all along."

"Cyrus said the same thing. He felt pretty guilty about it."

Saffra exhaled, frowning. "All the ways they must have tried to manipulate King Talon. I would've never guessed. But wait..." she gasped, then frowned.

"What? What is it?"

"Well...of course! It makes sense now."

"What?"

"The poison! In my wine—there was poison. I never got the chance...now I know."

"You mean to say—"

"I'm almost certain that Kane's nasks must have been responsible for trying to poison me. Right around the time you arrived in the capital, I got a new bottle of wine. I was eager to try it until I smelled the poison. Kane must have wanted me dead and told them to do it."

Claire huffed. "Well, looks like I'm not the *only* one he wants dead," she said, attempting humor.

"I suppose not. We had better be careful."

They chatted a bit more until Saffra said, "Oh, silly me! All this talking when you've got a headache. That is why I came—to give you this." Saffra procured a large velvet drawstring pouch from a hidden pocket within her gown. The contents smelled of flowers and peppermint. "Our ancestors called it *aegan*. It translates to *bliss-flower*. To create the medicinal solution, a very special process exists, a combination of aegan flower petals, pure oils like peppermint, and quite a bit of complicated magic. The contents of the brew must be dried over the course of a year, starting on the summer solstice and ending there as well. Only then can it be used. This is all that remains of last year's batch."

Claire inhaled again, this time more deeply. "It smells wonderful!"

"Besides myself, there is one other mage in Kastali Dun capable of making it, and mine is the best, the most potent." Saffra's grin widened. "I also add a few tricks of my own." There was a wicked gleam in her eyes. "Most do not know it, but I often provide aegan to the king when he has trouble sleeping—which is often. Although...I do not believe he utilizes it enough."

"But…what does it do?" Claire asked, already beginning to infer the substance's purpose.

"It will dampen your headaches, take away pain, relax your body, open your mind…"

"All those things?" She tightened her fingers around the pouch protectively.

Saffra laughed. "Well, not all at once. Somehow aegan knows what ails you most. When you consume it, it selects its target."

She grabbed a candle and held it close to the bag's contents to have a better look. It looked like loose-leaf tea.

"Take a pinch, *only* a pinch," Saffra warned, "and grind it between your fingers. Then sprinkle it into your drink." She rose and took Claire's cup from the table, still full of water, and reached into the pouch doing just as she advised. Then she handed it over. The aegan dust was glowing blue and bubbles rose to the surface creating snakes of smoke.

She looked back into the cup. "But it's all gone now. All the pieces have disappeared."

"Of course they did." Saffra eyed her. "The magic I embossed within the substance allows it to dissolve in any liquid. One of my finer touches I might add."

"Wow," she breathed.

"Just a small pouch of aegan costs a fortune, ten gold dragons, sometimes more," Saffra added. "I make plenty of money in my position, but I also enjoy selling my wares when I can. Whatever profits I make, I donate to the orphanages."

"That's…that's really nice." She swirled around the contents and took a big gulp of the aegan water, then another, and then she finished the whole cup. "It tastes like peppermint. Like *Christmas*."

Saffra snickered. "It is wonderful, is it not? But…a word of caution. Aegan should not be used in excess. It could become addictive."

"It is. Thank you—for everything. I'll be careful."

They said their goodbyes and Saffra left.

～

With aegan, Claire's headaches disappeared entirely. She attacked her duties with new fervor. Desaree noticed, pleased. "I am over-joyed by this change in you! What has prompted it? The Verekblot, perhaps?"

They were cleaning suites on the second floor of the western wing. Claire stopped her sweeping to look at Desaree. "The...Verek-*what*?"

"The *Verekblot*!" Desaree said, hesitating. "Oh...you did not know." She bit at the skin on her lower lip. "I am so sorry. Please don't be angry with me."

"Angry with you for what?" Claire set her broom down and plopped down into an overstuffed chair. She sighed and melted into it.

"Well, you have been rather...*indisposed* as of late. I forgot to tell you. Verekblot is tonight."

"All right. But, considering that I don't even know what Verek-blot is, and it's impossible to be angry with you over anything, no harm done."

"Right! Of course you don't," Desaree said, as if realizing for the first time that Claire was an outsider. It was flattering, at least. "It is a feast to honor the god of blessings. A commoner's celebration. We hope to earn favor with Verek, so that the fortunes of those *less* fortunate might one day improve."

"Oh. That sounds...fun."

Verek was responsible for judging a person's actions. If that person did well, they would be rewarded; if they acted poorly, they would be punished. Verek brought about changes in the lives of others, whether good or bad. While the nobles recog-nized and worshiped Verek, Verekblot wasn't generally cele-brated amongst their ranks. Those of higher birth were already plenty fortunate, what did they care for others beneath them? "Few besides commoners care for commoners," Desaree explained.

The feast was set to begin later than their usual evening meal, allowing the servants time to dress up. "We always wear our finest garments," Desaree said. "You can borrow one of my gowns. The one Tess gave you is deplorable." Desaree wrinkled her nose in disgust then whispered, "Do *not* tell Tess I said that."

The cooks were busier than usual. They were preparing special dishes not meant for the nobles. "We aren't eating leftovers?" she wondered, dishing gravy from a pot.

"Not tonight!" Desaree's eyes were wide with delight. "We get a feast of our own during Verekblot."

"You mean, all of this is...is ours?" Claire eyed succulent dishes sitting off to the side of the cookery. Carved turkey and ham dripping in juices, tureens of mashed potatoes sprinkled with fresh rosemary, honey glazed carrots with thyme in delicate slices, and giant loaves of brown oat bread with bowls of fresh honey, all sat steaming over little fires.

"Of course, it is! All ours!"

"But...*how*? Who paid for all this?" It was a fortune's worth of food.

"The king of course!"

Her jaw dropped. "The *king*?"

Desaree grinned. "The king always pulls from his private coffers for Verekblot, just as he does for the other commoner celebrations. So that we servants might dine in splendor. Is he not generous? Wait until you see how he has decorated our dining room."

Claire sputtered, refusing to believe it. The *king*—decorating? "Don't you mean he sent servants to decorate for him?"

Desaree smiled, shaking her head. "No. I saw him in the dining room down the hall earlier, with Lord Reyr and a few other shields. Oh, wait until you see it! But that is for later. Come!" Desaree grabbed her hand, pulling her away from the cookery. She still couldn't believe it, but she left without protesting.

With their duties finished for the day, Desaree was eager to get dressed up. Admittedly, she, too, was brimming with anticipation.

After Desaree finished getting ready, she stopped by Claire's room to help. Claire couldn't stop looking at her. Desaree's thick chocolate colored tresses were pulled into a fancy braid down her back with little white flowers woven into the strands. It was positively divine. Her gown was pretty too, a pleasant lavender color with a corset that accentuated all her curves. It was such a difference to how she usually looked.

"You're beautiful, Des!" Desaree smiled brightly before handing her a gown. This one was varying shades of crimson and gold, with little pink flowers embroidered across the corset. It was simple like Desaree's, nothing like the gowns noble women wore, but so much better than the unshapely kirtles.

Better still, the gown was adjustable. Ties were hidden everywhere to remove the sleeves, separate the skirts, and hold the petticoats beneath. "You pull the ties here and here," Desaree explained, "if you want it tighter. And these will adjust the length —and these, the arms."

It was genius, allowing women of different sizes to fit within the same dress.

Desaree also offered to do her hair, pinning it back with gold pins until most of it was trussed atop her head. Little wisps hung about her face. "Look how stunning you are!" Desaree cried, picking up a small polished mirror.

She was nearly unrecognizable. There were her green eyes staring back at her, but her face was leaner than before, accentuating her cheekbones. Naturally, her hair stole the show. "I don't think I've felt this pretty in a long time," she sighed. "Have you always been good with hair?"

Desaree blushed. "My mother taught me because we had hoped... Well, never mind. We are already late."

They raced through the corridors, hand in hand, giggling from exertion while their slippers pattered on the stone and their skirts swished about their ankles. A shadowed figure appeared at the end of the corridor. Desaree reacted first, pulling her to an abrupt halt. Her skin started to crawl. Coming towards them with long, unhurried strides was the King of Dragonwall.

Claire glanced around. There was no one else in the corridor. Nowhere else to hide.

Heat flushed her cheeks. Her fists clenched together, nails

biting into her skin. What was he doing here, in this part of the castle?

Desaree, being all properness, fell to one knee saying, "Your Grace," with downturned eyes.

She refused to bow. She stood frozen, staring at him as a mixture of fear and hatred churned in her gut. For a second, the memory of him looming over her, knife to her throat, flashed into her mind—

Take control of yourself before your emotions take control of you!

It was rare for Cyrus to scold her, but his biting remark helped. Schooling her features, she gave a graceful curtsey. "Your Grace," she said, greeting him with an overly sweet voice. Desaree had not yet risen; she had not been invited to. That was the correct way servants ought to greet their king. But Talon was not her king.

"Good evening, Claire, Desaree," he said, nodding at each of them. She blinked. He took in the sight of them, waiting for her to speak. She studied him, too. He stood at ease, one hand placed upon the hilt of his sverak, the other at his side. He held something in his fist, but she couldn't tell what.

She ground her teeth together. "To what do we owe the singular pleasure of your appearance, Your Grace? Surely you must be lost. This is the servants wing. We will happily point you in the correct direction."

"You think I do not know my own castle?" he drawled, offering her a glare. "I know exactly where I am. I *thought* you would be resting."

"Resting? Whatever for?"

"For your headaches," he said. "And why is it that no one told me of these episodes before?"

"Oh," she professed. "I suppose I ought to take better care of myself. I can hardly bear the thought of worrying you. Tonight is the Verekblot. I am a servant, so it is well within my rights to celebrate, and I intend to." She paused. "Thanks you for your concern, though."

His expression darkened. "Fine. If you insist on go—"

"Have you something for me?" she asked sweetly, looking

down at the pouch clenched in his fist. "And Desaree!" she whispered, nudging her friend, "for goodness sake, *stand up*!"

The king wasn't used to being interrupted because he cleared his throat and said, "I—yes. I brought this for your headaches. It is difficult to come by." He held it out to her, but she made no move to take it.

She disguised her snort with a cough and said, "How very kind of you to think of me. What is it?"

When she didn't reach for the object, he dropped his arm. "It's medicine. *Aegan*. Lady Saffra makes it better than anyone."

"Oh, that! Thank you, but I already have plenty."

"Did Reyr give it to you?" he bit out, his face clouding with something she couldn't quite interpret.

"No, no. Lady Saffra."

"Lady—Lady Saffra?" His muscles tightened. "And how is it that you know her?"

"Oh." She gave a false laugh. "I don't. She merely heard of my headaches and kindly stopped by to tend to me."

"Gods above!" he swore, his composure slipping briefly. "Does everyone know of your suffering before I do? I had to hear about it from Reyr. It seems even *he* was late in telling me."

"How unfortunate."

"Indeed." He scoffed. "Well, clearly you have no need of me." He pocketed the pouch. "Next time, do tell me if you suffer. I do not appreciate getting information secondhand."

"Of course, Your Grace. I will *surely* inform you in the future. Now, I do not wish to take any more of your time. It is too precious, and we are late, so we must be going."

"Right. Do enjoy yourselves." He stepped aside, letting them pass. Grabbing Desaree's hand, she rushed off. Neither of them said a word until they were good and far from the corridor. Then they burst into a fit of laughter.

"Bless the Gods, Claire. You are brave! Never in my life..." Desaree gasped, trying to breathe. "The way you spoke to him!"

"It was no less than he deserved after the way he treated me."

They arrived at the servants dining room just in time. Others were already filing in ahead of them, everyone dressed better than she would have guessed. When it was their turn to enter, she sucked in a breath of astonishment. The room was transformed, gloriously transformed. "It's unrecognizable," she gasped.

The tables were there, but everything else was different. All along the whitewashed ceiling, garlands were draped and hung, dangling down over the tables, attaching to the walls. It reminded her of the forest. Fresh flowers were woven through the leaves, and little glowing lights twinkled within the depths of the thick strands. Petals of different colors covered the tables and floor. It smelled *divine*.

"Glows," Desaree whispered, pointing at the little lights. "It takes magic to create them, lots of magic. I bet the king did them himself," she supposed. Claire did not want to think about the king, or that he could do anything nice for anyone besides himself. She pushed the thoughts from her mind, intent on having a good time.

Dinner was exuberant. The great platters she'd seen earlier were brought forth and passed around. It was delicious beyond imagining. She went back for thirds before reaching a near catatonic state.

"Save some room for dessert!" Desaree warned.

"Dessert? I might need you to loosen my corset," she breathed, feeling a little faint. She reached for the hidden strings on her skirt to free her waistband.

"I will not loosen anything! You will get sick if I allow you to eat yourself silly. Besides, you can dance it off to make room!"

Dancing?! She'd forgotten about the dancing. How did people in Dragonwall dance?

As if on cue, several musicians entered the room. They were dressed well, better than the servants who wore their finest attire. "The king's own minstrels," Desaree all but squealed, clapping her hands together, jumping to her feet along with everyone else. The musicians set up on the far side of the dining room, pulling out their instruments. They weren't so different from what she might expect. Old fashioned, sure, but they sounded lovely.

The buzzing voices magnified along with the commotion as tables and benches were pushed aside. People began lining up to face each other in two long lines.

"Desaree," she gasped, grabbing her hand. "I don't know how to dance like that!"

"Oh, you will catch on fine!" Desaree laughed, leading her to a spot. "Here, be my partner for the first round. Follow my lead."

Seeing that they were assembled, the musicians fell quiet. A drum was struck, beating out a tune before the other instruments joined in. At the same moment, the room turned to an excited frenzy as everyone began the dance. She couldn't help but laugh hysterically, doing her best to copy Desaree's moves. Others laughed too, smiling with exhilaration.

It was a line dance, with lots of skipping and hopping. They often switched places until she grew dizzy. Many in the crowded room shouted and whooped in unison when this happened, excited to place themselves in front of new partners. It was loud and rambunctious. When the song ended, she had to double over just to breathe.

Desaree and Sarah were clinging to each other in fits of laughter, their faces glowing with happiness. Everyone clapped loudly, shouting out requests for the next dances. She cleared off to the side of the room, hoping to catch her breath.

Just as she did, Thomas, the baker, came over and requested a dance. "It would be a true honor, Miss Claire. The ladies say I'm a *fine* partner!"

"How could I refuse?" she cried. She grabbed his hand and found the floor again. The next song was much like the last, with lots of drum beating and hornpipes.

As promised, Thomas was a good partner. For being so old, he never missed a step. That only made the dance more fun.

After a few more, each with different partners, her face hurt from smiling. She'd expected the dances to be more formal, waltzes and such. But they were far from it, making the affair a rowdy one. She mentioned this to Desaree.

"Oh, that kind of dancing is for stuffy nobles. We *here* like to have fun."

She, Desaree, and Sarah made their way to the side of the room for dessert. She was just reaching for a sweet square of frosted cake when the room fell silent. She froze, glancing over her shoulder. The dancing had come to an unexpected halt. Everyone turned toward the doorway. There stood Reyr, elaborately dressed, with a long golden cloak the same color as his scales. It fell in elegant ripples to the floor. Whispers echoed down the dance line as he entered.

The servants weren't used to seeing a lord at Verekblot.

"May I join you?" he asked. His gaze circled the room until it fell upon her.

The already drunken crowd merely cheered at his arrival. The music resumed. Reyr made his way over. At the same time, Desaree and Sarah suspiciously disappeared from her side.

"I hope you are not bothered by my intrusion," Reyr said, taking up a vantage point beside her. "I could hardly foster the idea of you having so much fun without me." There was a wicked gleam in his eyes.

"It isn't a bother," she assured him, a sudden thought coming to mind. "Did the king send you here to keep an eye on me?"

"Now, now, what makes you think that?"

"Oh, I don't know. Maybe the strange visit I received on my way here, thanks to *your* telling him about my headaches." She crossed her arms and frowned at him.

"Ah, yes. Funny you should mention that. You certainly had an effect on him. He came to me a short while ago with his feathers all ruffled, perturbed by how you'd acted, still angry with me for not telling him sooner." He reached behind her for a little dainty square of cake and popped it into his mouth. "Mmmm. Delicious. Anyway, it is not as if I had anything to do with how you spoke to him. What in the name of the gods did you say?"

She shrugged, then offered him an evil grin. "Nothing...impolite. Besides, I'm sure his upset feelings were merely meant to make you feel bad for not telling him sooner."

"I see." Reyr frowned.

"And since when does the king care about my ailments anyway?"

"My thoughts exactly." A couple swept past them, laughing. "Your surprise is as great as mine on the matter. As soon as I told him about your headaches, he insisted on paying you a visit. Immediately."

"Ugh. Thanks for that. I certainly enjoyed seeing him. Not. You know how I feel about him, after what he…" She exhaled, stopping herself.

"I do apologize for the sudden surprise of it. It was never my intention for that to happen."

"I just can't understand why he would care in the first place. Why bother, after everything?"

"Perhaps he feels guilty."

"Ha! Him? *Guilt*? He was literally about to kill me in the torture chambers before you stopped him."

"He was not."

"Um." She grabbed a fistful of his tunic and marched him out of the dining room. The music was too loud for a conversation like this. "Maybe I'm mistaken, Reyr. But you saw the blade he held against my throat. He was seconds from slitting it."

"I saw it, Claire. But know that he never intended to kill you, only to scare you. He told me so himself."

"To—to *scare* me?" She blinked back at him. "You're joking, right? That's *worse*! What kind of monster resorts to that?"

Reyr sighed. "I do not like the idea any more than you. Nor would I condone that kind of behavior."

"Yeah? Well then, maybe *you* should be king, and *not* him."

"Claire!" his face changed. Instant fury. It was the deadliest she'd ever seen him. "Your words are treasonous. You forget that I am his *shield*. That he is my brother, and I love him." Reyr took several heavy breaths before continuing. "Besides, I could never do half as well as he has. You have no idea what you are saying, none at all, no idea the things King Talon has accomplished during his reign, no idea of the struggles he has faced."

Her stomach bottomed out. He was hurt by her words because she'd been careless with them. She'd forgotten that he was a shield first, and her friend second. "I—I'm sorry, Reyr. That was thoughtless of me."

"Thoughtless, indeed. That tongue of yours will get you in serious trouble someday. See here, I understand your contempt for King Talon. He treated you ill, behaving in ways no king should. But never would I so much as utter such an insulting idea. Guard your thoughts more wisely next time."

She nodded, blinking back tears of shame and anger. Reyr's scolding hurt. She deserved it, but that didn't make her feel any less poorly over the matter.

He sighed and leaned his shoulder up against the wall of the corridor, watching her until she felt awkward. "I'm sorry," she repeated. "I didn't mean to insult you—or him."

"We are his brothers, Claire. His guards. His *family*. We support him in all things, no matter how good or bad. We swore an oath. We have given him our lives. Any insult to our king is an insult to us. I hope you can understand that?"

"I—yes. I understand," she mumbled.

"Good. Now that I have thoroughly ruined your night, which mind you, was not my intention, I do hope it is not too late to ask you for a dance."

Her heart thudded several times, not because of any feelings for him she might have, he was just a friend after all, but because she hoped this meant she was forgiven. "You aren't too mad to dance with me?"

"No. Not when your gown suits you so well. Not when your hair looks so grand."

She opened her mouth, then paused. Was he...*flirting*? "You are...too kind, Reyr."

He bowed his head. "I hope that by dancing with you, I might salvage what is left of this night I have ruined."

She nodded, happy to leave their argument in the past. He took her hand, placing it about the crook of his arm, and guided her back into the dining room just as the next boisterous tune began to play.

Reyr danced far better than she did. It was almost embarrassing to have a partner who outdid her so well, but his quick footedness did keep her on her toes—literally. They danced every song together until the end of the evening. By then, she hoped their argument was forgotten.

Exhausted, she said goodnight to all her new friends, and Reyr escorted her back to her room. "I do hope you can forgive me for being so harsh with you earlier. I took no joy in it."

She wished he wouldn't bring it up again. "I forgive you. Just as you said, dancing was an adequate way to salvage my evening. It is all but forgotten. Though, I have learned a valuable lesson, and I will try to be better about my rotten tongue."

The side of his mouth twitched into a small smile. "I do enjoy your witty cynicism, Claire, your smart remarks, and your honesty. But yes, where the king is concerned, that rotten tongue of yours may get you into trouble. Guard it wisely."

They stopped before her door. "You never answered my question earlier. Did the king send you?"

"If I say that he did, does it diminish our night together?"

She shrugged. "I would have rather you come simply to spend time with me." As she said it, she hoped her words did not give him the wrong idea about her feelings, especially after his surprising compliments.

"Well then, I am pleased to tell you that the king *did* suggest I go to Verekblot, if only to make sure you were well enough to dance. But the choice was mine. I was happy to take the opportunity." The look he gave her, soft and gentle as it was, left her worried. Was he developing feelings for her? No, surely not.

"Very well. Good night, Reyr. Thank you for your company."

"Good night, Claire." He lifted her hand to his mouth, kissing her knuckles a little longer than he should have. Then he disappeared down the corridor humming the last tune they had danced to. She was left to watch his retreat down the corridor until he disappeared into the darkness.

CHAPTER 48
BATS AND BLOOD SPIDERS

Somewhere in Dragonwall's Wilderness

Kane watched sets of jagged peaks slide beneath him, so sharp they would skewer any man unlucky enough to topple upon them. The air was thin, the kind that needed deep breathing but never really filled you. He stretched his lungs wide. Wrath's wings labored beneath his weight, flapping powerfully before extending his pinions to catch the wind.

"I do not appreciate carting you around as if I'm some kind of pack animal," Wrath had scornfully told him when they'd set out. *"It is beneath me."*

"You act as if I won't reward you."

Like some sprites, the asarlaí possessed the unique ability to communicate with dragons. A handy tool. One that made all of this possible.

They descended towards a set of caves. This was where he planned to hide his first dragonstone. He reached beneath his cloak to stroke its glassy surface. It responded to his touch, radiating scalding heat, feeding from his energy, swallowing up all that he gave it. His greed, his desires, his malice.

"Set me at the mouth of the cave—there."

Wrath merely grumbled a response before landing. He slid down the dragon's scaly hide and set out to explore the depths of the mountain. It was a dark place, with bats that liked eating flesh, and red blood spiders larger than his hand. They'd make perfect critters for his experiments.

Moving carefully, he made his way to the lowest part of the cavern. There was a lake, perfect for concealing a small blue stone like the one he carried. He set about the magical wards that would deter curious eyes from coming near the body of water. Thrice he walked the lake's perimeter muttering incantations. He walked until he felt the invisible strands of his magic take form.

Wards were useful forms of magic. Unless a person knew the stone was there, unless they were intent on finding it, the wards would send explorers away, tricking their mind and rewriting their curiosity. They'd suddenly find themselves very far from where they had originally intended.

He did the same to the stone, placing protections over it. Fish in dark places were often hungry enough to eat stones. He put wards around himself too, because getting eaten would not be pleasant. Then he swam out into the lake, diving deep, deep, deeper still, until he reached the bottom. There he placed the stone upon a rocky surface. With his mind, he commanded it to stay put, and it would, for magical objects listened to him when he bade them.

The flight back to Shadowkeep was longer than he wished. Wrath was heavier now, carrying cages he had conjured to house some of the unique beasties from the cave. The spiders would give him potent venom for poisons, but it was the bats that most excited him. Oh yes, they would come in handy. He could allow them to multiply and grow with magic until they were giant winged creatures. They would make great weapons in the war to come. How sweet it would be to see one gobble up the king's soldiers whole. He bared his teeth in a strained smile—if one could call it that.

Since King Talon's interference with his nasks, his mood was foul at best, and today was no exception. Even though one stone was successfully hidden, even though he carried dangerous critters that would be *ever so fun* to use against his enemies, even though he should have been happy for the destruction to come, his mind writhed with hatred and anger.

When he'd begun his efforts, the idea of ruling had ensnared him. How powerful, how formidable he could be. With control of the kingdom, he would send humans of nonmagical blood through the gates and fulfill the destiny his forefathers had intended. The desire had imprinted upon his heart, rooting deep within. But now, something sounded remarkably more alluring: punishment, revenge, pain.

Had it been *any* other king, he might have let the matter rest, he might have carried out his initial plans with no deviation. But this was not any king. This was King Talon. He hated King Talon—hated him fiercely. Why was that?

Was it because Talon had interfered? No, any king would have done the same—any king would punish traitors. He looked down at the spires below, now flying past at great haste. Why King Talon? Why was he repulsed merely *thinking* about him?

King Talon was not especially liked by his subjects, not the way some kings had been. Yet neither was he disliked. Dreaded, certainly. His subjects whispered monstrous stories about his scarred face that twisted into their own horrors. Talon was respected, to be sure, by those old and wise enough to know some of his deeds.

So why, then? He dug deep into himself before dragging forth the true reason, ripping it free of the blackened monster that was his soul. The true reason he wanted to see him suffer was *fear*. He feared Talon. This king, unlike many before him, was capable of much more than he'd ever imagined; that scared him, it angered him, it even *mortified* him. How dare any, be it the highest mage or the lowest serf, be greater than he?

Shadowkeep loomed into view, placating some of his worry.

Wrath's dragons flitted and fluttered around the mountainous hold. He watched them as he approached. The dragons were almost beautiful. *Almost.* It was no wonder The Five had been eager to create them. If only they had taken the time to read their futures.

If only...

The sun was sinking towards the horizon when he made his way to the dark caverns beneath Shadowkeep. Along the way he deposited his prizes, placing the spiders in their cages within his room of horrors. It was the antechamber to a more harrowing one, stocked with bottles of strange liquids and vials of dangerous contents. Strychnine, hemlock, curare, arsenic, and nightshade were mild compared to some of his own creations. Yet they were all there, a bit of every poison within Dragonwall, housed within *Agony's Library*, innocently posed upon their shelves waiting to inflict screams. Yes, this was his most prized achievement, a lifetime of work capable of inflicting the worst migraines, the ugliest coughs, the hottest fevers, and the most painful deaths. He shut the door, bidding the spiders goodnight.

The bats he took elsewhere, to a cavernous room overtaken by stalactites and stalagmites. At the opening he placed a magical barrier to keep his little creatures contained. They would like it here, so long as there was enough human flesh to feed them.

They took to the ceiling, wrapping their leathery wings about their bodies to hang. "Are you hungry, my sweets?" Several of his prisoners were procured from the cells below, sent unknowingly into the room. "Your freedom awaits within," he coaxed, watching the hope flare up upon their gaunt faces. They went eagerly at first, until the bats scented them. One after another, they sniffed deeply, until the creatures launched themselves from the roof.

He stayed to watch, just beyond the opening's magical barrier. Their shrieks lifted in pitch, and they began running towards the opening, only to be thrown backwards into the bats' clutches. It was over in minutes, but their anguished screams would keep him entertained for hours. Happily fed, his little bat children returned to their positions.

~

STANDING BEFORE HIS MAGICAL WATERFALL, he called forth a place he frequented, located in the small town of Sutton, just outside the Vallahurst Forest. *The Filthy Pigeon* swam into view. The tavern was already packed with guests, their attention turned to the front of the room. They did not notice him lurking behind the watery barrier.

An orator stood upon a trestle table, passionately speaking to his audience. "If the drengr don't act, we must take matters into our own hands. I say we march to Fort Squall and demand protection."

"Aye!" Mugs of ale slammed down upon the table tops.

"Rumors of dragons are one thing. But the dead? My cousin saw them claw their way from the grave, saw them *plain as day*," the orator shouted. Whispers and speculation coursed through the room.

One man claimed his daughter had found a dead corpse standing over her bed. It'd tried to strangle her in her sleep. A woman swore she saw a group of them sneak into her barn and eat her youngest goat. "By morning," she cried, "there was naught left but bones."

Kane smiled. Yes, things were going very well. Soon the developing unrest would create a great deal of problems for the drengr. With people flocking to their nearest forts, his plan would play out exactly as he intended it to.

Taking a vial from his pocket, he filled it with the icy water from the fall. Then he stepped through the cold sheet. No one noticed his appearance.

The orator was speaking again. "We ain't safe here anymore."

"But what're we supposed to do?" someone shrieked.

He kept his voice steady, lowering it as he said, "I say we pack everyone up and march for the fort. Demand their protection. Isn't it written in the laws? According to the charters, we are considered refugees if the land is under attack from outside forces. That includes the dead."

"Here, here," several voices called. No one bothered looking towards him, but if they had, they would have seen a cloaked man whose face was shadowed beneath a hood.

"Let the drengr do somethin' for once," someone else cried. "We pay 'em enough tithes as it is."

He spoke again, making his voice echo panic and fear. "My daughter was dragged from our cottage just the other night. I barely got her away alive. I'll be damned if I sit and wait for another attack." Shocked whispers broke out beside him.

"Aye! Well said!" a few shouted.

"So, it's settled, then?" The orator lifted his hands to silence the audience. "Tomorrow we pack. Those willing will depart for the fort, ready the wains for the old folk, and take only what you can carry. Shall we take a vote?"

"Yes!" Affirmations echoed around the room. "A vote must be taken," someone else cried.

A vote was indeed taken. He made sure to lift his hand with the others. It was hardly necessary. The decision was unanimous.

He crept away, moving through the shadows and exiting the tavern. He traveled to the town's edge before removing his vial of enchanted water. Facing a stone wall, he pulled the stopper off and splashed it against the wall, envisioning what he wanted. A wavering surface appeared as the waterfall materialized. Behind it, he saw the cave's walls and the dancing torchlight beckoning him home. Stepping forward, he walked through the icy sheet and reappeared in his waterfall room.

One after another he visited familiar taverns and alehouses adding more fuel to his fires. When the night was over, he toppled into his waterfall room for the last time, exhausted from the toll of his magic. The sheet of water may have been the means for transportation, but it took a great deal of energy to withstand its forces.

"*Wrath,*" he called.

"*Yes, my lord. What is it now?*" He ignored the sarcasm in the dragon's voice.

"*Your time has come again. At dawn, take your clan to the locations we discussed. Burn what you want and eat whomever you like. Return to me at dusk with as many live humans as you can carry. I've got hungry bats to feed."*

"We shall make our enemies wish they'd never been born." Wrath's pleased snarl echoed in his mind.

A smile crept to his face, crinkling the skin around his eyes. He had a promise to fulfill. He had already afforded the king ample opportunity to give up the remaining dragonstones. King Talon had failed to do so. A promise was a promise, and this was only the beginning.

CHAPTER 49
REDCOTE THE FOX

Northern Barrier Range

Mikkin heard Jamie's surprised cry before his eyes opened. When the lad shook him awake with whispered curses, his own eyes widened and his breath caught in his chest. Shadows passed overhead, blotting out the sun in spurts. He jumped to his feet, pulling Jamie to the nearest tree. The forest offered some camouflage, but dragons would surely have keen eyesight and keener sense of smell.

"Don't breathe, lad," he whispered, holding Jamie by the collar of his tunic. He too held his breath but was soon forced to abandon the advice.

When the last of them passed over, he sank to the ground, gasping. "We're safe. For now."

"I never wanted to believe you." Jamie's voice trembled. "Now that I've seen them... Mikkin, where...where are they going?"

He looked up, tracing his gaze along the traveled path. The dragons had passed overhead traveling south east, a route that would take them out of the mountains and into Dragonwall's northern territories.

"Hunting, most likely. Nothin' to worry yourself over." Even he didn't believe his own lie. His posture was hunched. His hands began to shake as he recalled flames hot enough to melt metal. Anguished cries still echoed in his ears. His heart withered with failure and wept for his family. Vengeance was all he had left.

"When you say *hunting*,"—Jamie dropped his voice to a whisper even though the threat had already passed—"do you mean hunting game or hunting humans?"

"Let's hope the former." He shut his eyes, trying to see the backs of his lids. Instead, flames danced. He could feel the heat of them; he could feel their destruction.

"We must warn them! My mother...my father..." Jamie sank to his knees. "I should have never come. Gods! What have I done?"

He stared at the lad for several moments before speaking. "If the dragons target your village, Landow is finished. You're safer with me." He thought of Belnesse, of the bell that never tolled, of his friend Renard, fighting to reach it and sound the alarm before being swallowed up whole.

"Your words make me sick," Jamie hissed, turning to retch what little his stomach had to give.

"Tynen is smart. He will protect your mother."

"Can we not warn them? Is there no way?" The lad wiped his mouth on his sleeve, crinkling his nose in disgust.

"Dragons have wings. So, no."

"Don't remind me of what they have." Jamie scooted away from his mess and put his head in his hands.

Nothing he could say would help. He leaned his head against the pine's trunk, closing his eyes to think. One thing was certain. He was going in the correct direction.

When Jamie next spoke, he sounded a little more like himself. "What do we do now?"

"When you're ready, pack our things. We will continue north west, in the direction from whence they came."

They walked for several hours until the sun was high in the sky. He used his bow to shoot some fowl from the trees, which he tied to his pack for later. It was a strenuous trek, working their way towards higher ground. He wanted a good view of the mountain peaks, and perhaps a better view of the dragons' return.

When he located a rocky outcropping in the distance, they stopped for their midday meal before tackling it. They'd skipped breakfast, and ravenously devoured the birds he'd shot. They'd need the fuel for their climb.

Continuing their journey, he chatted about the forest, offering beneficial tips, talking of ways to track game and find water. Anything to keep Jamie distracted from his fear and from thinking about what the dragons might do to Landow. The advice he gave was the same he had hoped to give to his own sons.

His heart constricted as he thought of them, thought of the adventures they might have had, trekking through the forests, hunting, gathering around a campfire in the evenings. They'd always loved hearing stories at night; he would have told them many during these times.

Now...he'd never get the chance.

"Tell me, Jamie," he said, breaking the silence. "Have you heard the story of Redcote the Fox?"

They made their way around a cluster of boulders.

"I know it," Jamie answered, breathless from their hike. "It was a favorite growing up. My father used to tell it." Mikkin used his sleeve to wipe the sweat beading his brow. Jamie glanced back at him. "You can tell it now, if you like."

"You are not too old for children's stories?" he asked, teasing. Jamie only shook his head. "Good. There are always lessons to be learned even in the most childish of tales."

They began a downward descent that would soon continue upward at the base of their vantage point. It was a long slope with sharp rocks and few trees. At the top, clusters of boulders were scattered to offer hiding places.

It would do nicely for a look-out.

He launched into his story, eager to tell it the way he would have with his sons. "There was once a just and fair king named King Noble. He presided over all the animals of the forest, for he was a lion. Every year, King Noble held an assembly for the forest animals—great and small—to discuss matters of importance. Here, they would bring forth grievances and deal justice should such a thing be necessary." He sidestepped a sharp rock, pausing momentarily to regain his footing.

"On one particular occasion during these yearly gatherings, all the animals of the forest were present. All except—"

"Redcote the Fox," Jamie said, keeping his gaze focused ahead.

"Aye." Mikkin nodded. "When it came time to report grievances, the absence of the fox was noted, for many brought accusations against him. In fact, nearly every beast in attendance testified to some crime or dark deed for which the fox was responsible—everyone except Grímnir the Badger, who was ever steadfast towards the poorly accused fox.

"The chief of these accounts was from Wendal the Wolf. Wendal claimed that Redcote had cruelly mistreated his children and shamed his wife. No sooner had the wolf ended his allegations than a new one was brought forth by Rakki the Dog. He pitifully described how he once found a small scrap of meat in a thicket and the fox unfeelingly purloined it. He explained that the fox had no concern at all for his poor, famished state.

"Amongst others to come forth was Thomas the Cat, Herald the Hare, and Morgan the Grazer. When all the animals finished their complaints, Grímnir stepped forward. Already King Noble was distraught, but he patiently listened to the badger's defense of Redcote. The badger had a way with words you see, such that soon the tables were turned upon the animals.

"Grímnir explained how Wendal the Wolf entered into a dishonest partnership with Redcote. This he did to obtain some fish from a traveler's merchant cart. As a ploy, Redcote pretended to be dead in the road, whereupon the traveler picked him up and tossed him into the wagon, greedy for his fur. In the back of the wain, Redcote began tossing fish out one by one. Rather than collect them, the greedy Wendal started eating each fish upon the road until there was nothing left! When the fox jumped from the wagon to claim his share, there was naught but bones to give."

Jamie chuckled at this part. "Poor Redcote! *So* misunderstood."

"Indeed!" He let the lad have his laugh, taking a moment for a breather before continuing. "After the story of the wolf and the fox, the badger set forth to bring accusations against each of the other animals in turn, who had claimed ill of the fox. Upon finishing, he turned to look at them, happy to see their shock. Flattered by his eloquence, he then took matters further. He claimed that ever since King Noble decreed peace, the fox had taken up a holy life in penance to the gods, hoping Verek would one day bless him. Thus, the complaints were almost dismissed.

"At that very moment, Kockle the Rooster appeared, followed by his two sons. They bore the mangled remains of a poor hen. Kockle claimed that when the proclamation for peace was declared, Redcote had come forth dressed as a hermit carrying the parchment from the king himself. Redcote claimed that he wished to share the message with the hens and handed forth the parchment. Overjoyed by the news, Kockle invited his family into the open. The hens proceeded unprotected into the forest where Redcote lay in wait. The fox then proceeded to attack all but five of his brood and devour them, except for this one, which still died anyway. Kockle laid the remains of the hen's body at the feet of King Noble, as was custom in matters of death.

"The king was most disturbed. He called forth his strongest guard, Blackjack the Bear. He bid Blackjack to summon Redcote from his home and bring him forth to the forest council, where he would undergo trial for his crimes. The bear agreed and set upon his long journey. When he arrived at the fox's den, he was tired and hungry. Many times did he pound upon the door to no avail, for the fox was inside devising a plan.

"After a time, the fox leaned out of his window and shouted to the bear, apologizing for taking his time. He explained that the reason for the delay was because he was indisposed from poor digestion. You see, he'd had all this honey, nasty, sticky, and sweet, but it did a number on his bowels.

"The bear, a lover of honey, became distracted by the mention of it. So when Redcote invited Blackjack in to help relieve him of what remained, the bear was happy to oblige. Redcote explained that his stores were rather low, which was most unfortunate, and that he would need Blackjack to help him obtain more. He assured the bear that he knew exactly where to find it.

"Blackjack forgot all about the summons and happily agreed. The two of them set off across the river to a peasant's yard where a half-split tree-trunk sat. Redcote explained to his companion that he need only thrust his nose into the hollow and feed his fill on the honey supply. Blackjack happily agreed and inserted not only his muzzle, but his paws too. At this point, the tricky fox cleverly removed the wedges of the trunk such that the tree snapped together, leaving the poor bear prisoner."

Again Jamie laughed, bursting into a fit. "I can see him now," he cried. "Oh how he must have felt, stuck in that tree covered in sticky honey!"

Mikkin smiled and nodded, then continued his tale. "The sound of Blackjack's howls brought the peasant and many helpers too, all in possession of various weapons to kill the bear, but Blackjack succeeded in wrenching himself free. Angered, he returned to King Noble and submitted his grievance against the fox.

"And so for a second time, the fox was summoned." He looked at Jamie, catching the lad's eye. The story was working. Unlike most, he told his version a little differently, embellishing some of his own ideas, and the lad seemed to like that. They were almost to the top of the outcropping now, and a few times he had to reach down to the steep slope for balance while climbing.

Continuing his rendition—though it left him rather out of breath—he started again. "After the second summons for Redcote, it was Thomas the Cat who agreed to go forth and fetch the fox. When Thomas arrived, Redcote was gracious. He told the cat of a wondrous barn where there were mice aplenty. Distracted by the mention of mice, Thomas commanded Redcote to lead the way. Redcote showed Thomas the small hole which the cat could *easily* squeeze through. Redcote knew that the farmer's son had set many traps the day before to catch any trespassers. Thus, the cat was ensnared.

"When King Noble found out, he was infuriated. King Noble

declared that he would give the fox one last summons before his guards were sent to kill him. Grímnir the badger agreed to go forth, for he knew the fox would not try to tempt him. After all, they were friends.

"When he arrived, he explained to Redcote the situation, and Redcote begrudgingly agreed to set forth. And so the two of them made their way to the forest to treat with the king.

"When the fox met with the king, he fell to his knees pitifully. He argued that all of his misdeeds were done because of the insurmountable fortune he discovered. He explained that he had found chests of gold, and that it had turned him wicked.

"King Noble perked up at the mention of gold, for lions are fond of riches. The lion listened to the fox's pleading. Redcote explained that he knew he was wrong, apologizing profusely. He told the king that if His Majesty could only take the gold off of his hands, his life would return to normal. He promised that if the king should do such a thing, he would never again disobey. Instead, he would make a pilgrimage in honor of the gods to the sacred temples in Kengr.

"The king was very enticed by this, so he agreed. He told the fox that if the location of the gold was given, the fox might indeed depart upon his pilgrimage. Overjoyed, the fox quickly explained the location of the treasure. He even drew the mighty king a map. Happy and elated by the hunt, the king bid the fox safe travels then dismissed him. Gathering together his household, the lion set forth in search of the treasure, but when he arrived at the destination, there was no gold to be had.

"Angered by the trickery, he hurried back to his home where he dispatched guards to search for the fox. Far and wide they looked, but they never found old Redcote. And thus the fox settled in a new kingdom far to the north, beyond the Northern Barrier Range, where he repeated his wickedness all over again, for the fox was smart. He knew that greed was a powerful ploy, and one need only play upon the greed of another to make gains. In doing so, brain would always win over brawn."

Jamie applauded just as they crested the rocky outcropping. He was covered in sweat as the sun beat down upon them. "Your retelling is favorable to my father's," the lad admitted. "Though, if we ever see him again, keep that to yourself."

"I certainly will." He took deep breaths, allowing his breathing to slow.

"Shall I climb that rock there and see what I see?" Jamie offered.

"Let's both go."

The two of them selected a particularly large boulder atop the outcropping, using the rock's uneven surface to climb their way to the top. The view was spectacular. Already the sun was dropping to the horizon creating an orange glow on their world. He looked first to the north, studying the mountainous backdrop. Somewhere there, a dragon's lair was hiding. Then he turned and saw Jamie's face. The lad was motionless. He'd gone pale.

He followed his gaze and saw something he never wished to. His stomach sank. Smoke, just visible on the horizon, was rising in tendrils as it snaked towards the sky. The dragons had burned today, they had killed today, and they would not stop.

"If I ever find them," Jamie whispered, fury rising in his voice. "I'll kill them."

He clenched his fists, vengeance flaring up within him. "We will kill them together."

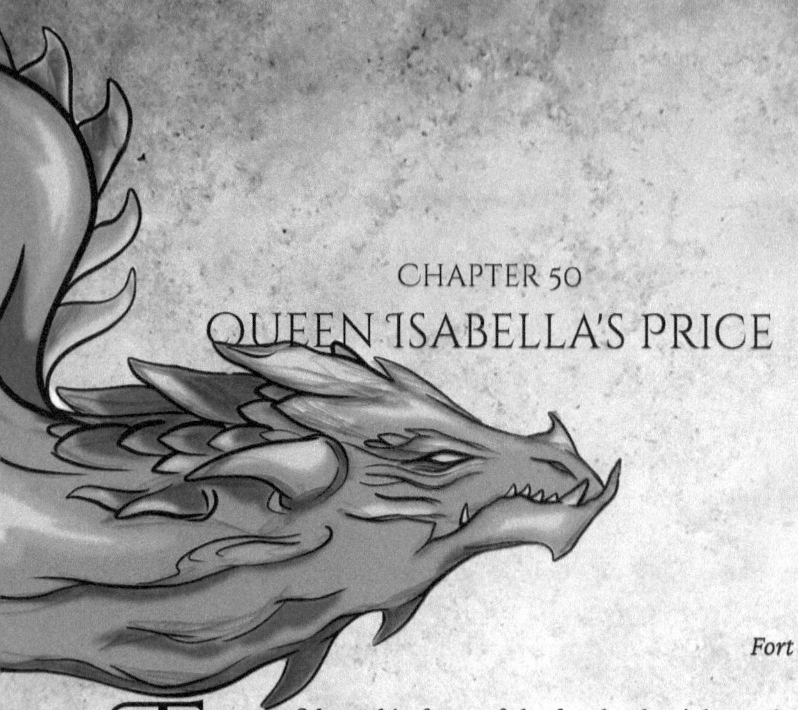

CHAPTER 50

QUEEN ISABELLA'S PRICE

Fort Squall

Tamara fidgeted in front of the fort leaders' door. She lifted her hand several times before conjuring enough courage to knock. "You may enter," a muffled voice called from within. Taking a deep breath, she opened the door.

Emmy greeted her with a warm smile. "Follow me, dear." She was ushered through several rooms to a large oak table. They both took a seat at the end, with Emmy at the head.

The fort leader's mate folded her delicate hands. She wore a plain silver band on her right forefinger. Upon her left wrist was a pattern of vines, etched into her skin like scars. Tamara had seen this before on other riders—

"This is Fort Squall's council chamber. You will come to know it well. Davi conducts all his formal affairs here. I thought it would be adequate for our lessons."

She looked around the room. It was fairly plain—not ornate like the council chambers at Redport. There were large windows along the west-facing wall. She saw the sea, sparkling with its dark blue waters. Ships traveled to and from the port at Squall's End, their sails unfurled. A few drengr swooped back and forth through

442

the air, training with their riders. She suppressed a pang of jealousy and looked away.

Her circumstances were unusual. When mates were recognized, a ceremony was held and their bond solidified. Following this, formal lessons commenced, training the rider in areas of magic, politics, combat, and flying.

"I know your situation is…unique," Emmy said, as if reading her thoughts. "Davi and I have agreed that until you are ready, you will receive lessons from me exclusively. You and I will discuss politics, history, the structure of the monarchy, and anything else that may benefit you. I encourage you to ask questions and learn as much as you can."

"No magic?"

Emmy's smile was kind. "Not yet, dear. A rider's ability to do magic comes from being mated to a drengr. You are not yet mated."

"I wish we could be. I am sure my womanhood will come soon."

Emmy sighed. "Young people are always so eager to grow up. Enjoy this time while you have it. Once your womanhood is upon you, I assure you, you will not be so eager for it. And believe me, you will be stuck with it for a while."

"A while?" She made it sound like a plague, like some kind of unfortunate sickness.

"You must contend with it until you bear a child. After that, it will depart, and you will be glad of it."

Her eyes widened. Bearing children was hardly something she wanted to consider at present. So she said, "It simply leaves? After childbirth?"

"Well yes, because you will only bear one child."

She blinked in confusion. "My mother had my brothers *and* me."

"Your mother was not a rider. You can thank Queen Isabella if you like. She paid the price for her misjudgment."

"I do not understand?"

"Come now, surely you have heard the story? Queen Isabella's

Price?" Tamara's cheeks flushed. She shook her head and turned her face towards the table. "Gods, girl! Did your kenna teach you nothing?"

She looked up and stuttered, "Well—she—she taught me to sew. My needlework. To sing. To draw. Sometimes I played instruments—"

"Yes, yes. The marks of a *true* lady," Emmy muttered, waving a hand to whisk away the nonsense. "I am all too familiar with stories like yours. Rest assured, what we teach in the fort is far more useful."

"If...if you would not mind, I would very much like to know the story."

"Good. I was hoping you would ask. Let us consider it your first lesson." Emmy's eyes brightened. "Now, as I am sure you know, Queen Isabella made the drengr race for a single purpose. Do you remember?"

"To unite the peoples of Dragonwall against the common enemy."

"Good." The side of Emmy's mouth twitched in approval. "All is not lost." Tamara sagged with relief, happy to produce a correct answer. "Queen Isabella—being a typical sprite—worried that the Drengr might become the new enemy. She feared her creation would overpopulate our world and outnumber the rightful owners of the land. Thus, she implanted a failsafe."

"Only one child?"

"Correct. With her magic, she ensured that mated pairs would not overpopulate Dragonwall. She combined this into the price she promised the drengr race, a price all drengr would pay on behalf of her bestowed favor."

Emmy adjusted her skirts before continuing. "Now, here is where this story takes a turn. The sprites are great fortune tellers. Queen Isabella herself saw the drengr coming before she decided to make them. But she never bothered predicting her own future once they were created."

"She didn't?"

"No. She was destined to become a rider—a mate—and she

never knew it. Vigilance loved her, his dragon loved her, long before she changed him. Somehow that imprint of feelings, that undying love, rewrote the spellwork of the world."

"Vigilance?" Tamara asked.

"The stories *you* are familiar with call him King Eymar, founder of Kastali Dun. But he was born with a dragon's name."

"Oh..."

Everyone knew of King Eymar. He was the most famous drengr, responsible for vanquishing Rage and his evil clan. As a child she'd often begged for the story until she was old enough to read it herself.

"Anyway, perhaps the gods intended for Queen Isabella to become King Eymar's mate. Perhaps they wanted to punish her for her wicked trick." Emmy's lips pressed into a thin line. "Permitting a single child when humans can have as many as they please! It is ridiculous—selfish! After all, we mothers are not so different from humans. You, Tamara, are human until you mate."

Her cheeks colored with heat. Mating with Byron. She pushed the notion away, considering what it would be like to outlive everyone in her family. Her parents. Her brothers. She pushed that notion away, too, and said, "What happened to Queen Isabella?"

"Queen Isabella tried to run from the bond, but her love for Vigilance was too strong. By then he was already calling himself King Eymar. The two of them mated, becoming King and Queen of Dragonwall, retiring to the south where they built Kastali Dun. And then the queen bore a baby girl."

"Princess Irelia..." Tamara whispered.

"That is correct. Irelia was the jewel of the kingdom, the first of the world to be born with both sprite and drengr blood. She was destined to do great things. Do you know what happened to her?"

She swallowed, recalling the tragedy. "Irelia died at a young age," she whispered. "But I do not believe it."

Emmy scowled, taken aback. "You do not?"

She shook her head. "Her body was never found."

"Indeed. At the age of thirteen she disappeared. Drengr were sent far and wide to search for her. And not just the drengr. Many dragons still remained in the world. They too searched. King Eymar's own clan, the Iron Clan, the clan your future mate descended from, searched the kingdom, never to find her. At last, her death was accepted."

"But they never found her."

"Thirteen year olds do not simply vanish." Perhaps Emmy was right. "Queen Isabella was devastated. She was grief stricken. She retreated into Kastali Dun, working hard to finish the great citadel that now adorns the city's center. The great keep, they call it." Her gaze took on a dreamy, faraway look. "Queen Isabella used the remainder of her magic to finish its construction. It is the only great castle to be built in the length of a human's lifespan, and far more marvelous than any to come after it, or any that will ever come again."

"It's all so sad," Tamara whispered, her heart aching. "I have heard that the sprites are meant to live for thousands of years, far longer than any drengr."

"They do. They're immortal. But as you can imagine, Queen Isabella paid more than one price. With her daughter gone, she could never have another child, for she was mated. She was subjected to her own curse. Perhaps another child might have given her a new purpose to live." Lady Emmy sighed and shrugged. "I suppose we will never truly know. But consider this. Sprites never do well away from their forest. By all accounts, the sprite queen could have lived for thousands of years. After all, Queen Jade is said to be twenty thousand years old, perhaps more."

Queen Jade was supposedly Isabella's niece. The daughter of Isabella's sister, who'd taken over rule after Isabella became mated to Eymar.

"So...Isabella died?"

"Yes, she died when King Eymar was only six hundred years old. The grief of losing both his daughter and his mate was too much for him. He followed them to the grave shortly thereafter."

"It's so *tragic*." Tears slipped down her cheek and dropped onto her folded hands.

"A sad story, indeed. And now you know. Queen Isabella paid

the price of her own making, as terrible as it is. We riders have one child. This ensures that our race will never outnumber those we protect."

She hardly knew what to say. For several long minutes, they sat in silence. Emmy's face showed plainly the pain she felt by the limitation. She'd seen a similar expression when she discovered her bond with Byron. It was the look of a mother who knew her child would not be a child forever.

"Wait!" A realization hit her. "What about Davi? Is he not brothers with Lord Reyr?"

"Ah!" Emmy's face lit up. "It seems you have discovered the loophole."

Her brow scrunched together. "Loophole? How?"

"Well, Davi and Reyr are identical twins. Moreover, they are not the first. It is rare, rarer in fact than the birth of a female child, which we all know is rare."

"So, it has happened before?" Her curiosity was rising. It appeared that there was a great deal she did not yet understand about the drengr.

"Indeed, it has happened a number of times." Emmy began to tick off the names of those throughout history to be born as identical twins. She found it hard to follow, especially because her head was spinning with information. "It seems," Emmy concluded, "that there is one set with every generation. Davi and Reyr were this generation's." There was pride in her voice.

"And what about females?" Tamara asked, thinking of Sophie, who'd not been successful in finding a mate. "Sophie said that her great grandmother was born a female to a drengr-rider pair. She has drengr blood."

"Yes, I know whom you speak of." Emmy sighed. "There is a great deal we will never understand about Queen Isabella. But know this, she is far more selfish than most will ever know."

Tamara cocked her head. "Because of the one child rule?"

"Her deceit goes much deeper than that. Tell me, what do you think happened to all the dragons after the drengr came to be?"

Her eyes widened. "She killed them?"

"No, dear. No. But she certainly wasn't kind to us. Queen Isabella was a sprite, through and through. Her race walked this world long before the dragons, longer still before the asarlaí."

"Truly?"

"Do you think the sprites were happy when the asarlaí made the dragons? Of course not! And then, in desperation, Queen Isabella created a new super race to defeat those dragons. In her mind, she was solving one problem by creating another, and she couldn't settle for that."

"I never thought of it that way..."

"Queen Isabella, in all her infinite wisdom, was cunning. She understood something most did not. See, the dragons secretly coveted humanity's fragility. They longed to fit in. They envied the human race."

Tamara's jaw dropped.

"Behind Vigilance's back—and keep in mind this was long before they were mated—Queen Isabella devised a plan of her own. When he went away to war, there were plenty of good dragons who did not partake in the final battle. Thousands of them, in fact. Queen Isabella went from clan to clan, secretly offering them humanity. They took it eagerly."

"I can hardly believe it!"

"When Vigilance returned from battle, he returned victorious. He also returned to find thousands of drengr in the world."

"I always believed that the drengr merely grew in population. That she only changed a few of Vigilance's friends, and together, they grew their race over time."

Emmy shook her head. "No, sweet girl. Queen Isabella knew that the fastest way to rid the world of dragons was to offer them something fleeting. They would still live a long life, but they would be condemned to one child, which they did not know at the time of their blessing."

"So she intended to defeat both dragons and drengr, stretched out over a long time scale?" Tamara's heart hammered as the atrocity sank in. "The drengr race is *dying*?! You said there were thousands when Vigilance returned. But now... Now each fort has a mere two hundred. And...there are only four forts."

"There are currently five-hundred-twenty-four drengr alive today, split between the four forts. In another fifty-thousand years, twice the length of time since their creation, the drengr will be fully extinct."

"But...can't we do something? We can go to the sprites! Beg them to reverse the curse."

Emmy laughed outright. "The sprites do not care for our race. Nor have they ever. Besides, it was Isabella's curse. I suspect that only her blood can reverse it, and as you know, her only child died."

"Why didn't she reverse it after Irelia's death when she had the chance?"

Emmy shrugged. "Who can say? Stubbornness? Grief? Perhaps she was too weak when the essence of the forest began leaking from her soul."

"So...we will all die?" She felt sick to her stomach. Queen Isabella was someone she'd grown to revere, admiring the great sprite queen for her creation.

"You will not die, dear. Neither will your child. But over time, with every female born, with every drengr who fails to find a mate, or simply chooses not to, those who fail to conceive, those who die in war, or any other manner of things, our race dwindles."

It felt as though they were running out of time. The world had gone unchanged for thousands of years. Nearly fifty generations of drengr had come and gone since Isabella's creation. It was difficult to stomach their evanescence. Dragonwall was in its Third Age, the age of the drengr. The Fourth Age—what would that look like?

She swallowed. "Emmy? How—how often are females born?"

Emmy turned her gaze towards the windows to watch the training pairs. "It differs, but we see a few each generation."

"Are they hated?"

Emmy turned to her in surprise. "Hated?"

"Yes. I mean, if every female birth adds to the dwindling of the race, shouldn't they be hated?"

"Gods, no! Every child born to a pair is precious. If anything, the females are *more* precious. Think of Princess Lena."

Princess Lena had been born a female into the drengr monarchy six generations after Queen Isabella's death. Princess Lena and Prince Gallant were a popular romance story. She'd grown up with the novel on a shelf above her bed.

"Princess Lena's parents loved her fiercely, did they not?" Lady Emmy asked.

"They did."

"Very well, then. I think that is enough history for one day, especially on such a depressing subject."

"Emmy?"

"Yes, dear?"

"What are those markings on your wrist?"

"Ah." She lifted her wrist and pulled back the sleeve of her gown to expose it. "This is the symbol of my bond with Davi. Every rider has one, though it does not always look identical. You will also bear this mark when you become mated."

"Does it...hurt?"

Emmy smiled. "I doubt you will notice. Other things will capture your attention when it takes form."

"Oh." She could guess the other things. Her face heated. "What is it like—being mated? Is it true that your mind is forever linked to Davi's? I hear it is like having another person's head connected to yours..." She trailed off. "Emmy?"

Emmy's face had gone pale and her eyelids fluttered, blinking rapidly.

"Emmy? Are you—?"

Emmy shot to her feet. "No! It cannot be!" she hissed. Her eyes were far away and unseeing. Worry crept into Tamara's stomach. "Plase, tell me it isn't true." Her voice was so quiet, Tamara barely heard it. She walked over to the back wall and sank helplessly to the floor.

A wailing cry erupted outside. The hairs on the back of Tamara's neck rose on end. Something was very, very wrong.

The keening grew louder, reverberating through the walls, up through the floor, digging into her very bones. Tears began flowing down her cheeks. More keening joined the first, until the voices of a hundred drengr permeated the air.

She raced to the window, clutching the sill with tight fingers. What she saw, she would remember for the rest of her life. Every drengr within the fort had taken to the sky, most without their riders. Byron's icy blue form was among them; her heart jolted at the sight.

The drengr beat their wings, allowing them to hover in midair. But it was the way they held themselves, their necks elongated, their faces upturned towards the heavens, their jaws wide open. The harrowing sound continued to pour forth from their maws. It could only mean one thing. Death. Death had come again to Dragonwall.

CHAPTER 51
COUNCIL MEETINGS

Kastali Dun

Talon shifted in his seat, scowling at the two empty chairs in his council chamber. They'd belonged to Stefan Rosen and Euen Doyle. This was their third council meeting since Claire's trial. It was proceeding as poorly as the first two.

They'd discussed the kingdom's traitors. They'd discussed Kane. They'd even discussed the wild dragons.

Now, they were discussing Claire.

"How are we supposed to trust an outsider within our walls?" Lord Raffe demanded, looking about the table for support. "We know nothing about her!"

Talon fiddled with a coin, polishing the golden surface with his thumb. A gold dragon—the first ever minted. It had been gifted from his father, passed down generation after generation.

Lord Karney harrumphed. "You're worried about a silly little girl? When we have dragons on our borders?"

"He has a right to be worried!" Lord Wyndham slammed his palm against the table's surface. "Just because she isn't in league with our enemies, doesn't mean she's harmless. We've no idea what sorts of corruption she brings from the other world. Things we cannot possibly understand."

A quiet snort drew Talon's eyes to Saffra. She alone sat silently, too good for the likes of *this* lot. No one seemed to notice her.

"You sound as if Claire's going to poison the minds of our wives," Lord Morad scoffed. "What? Do you think she plans to preach her own foreign ideals in our city streets? Start a cult and recruit members? Lead a rebellion against our current laws? Gods above, man! Don't you think you're giving her a little too much credit? She's just a girl. And Karney is right. We've bigger things to deal with."

"I say we send her back," Lord Glover demanded. "Whether she's harmless or not, better to avoid the risk entirely. She's not from here. Doesn't belong here. Send her home and be done with it."

"We cannot send her back, Lord Glover," Talon growled. Though, he wished it were possible. He'd allowed them to bicker long enough. "As I have already said, Claire is to remain within the keep under *my* protection. Outsider she may be, but she is under a death threat from Kane. Moreover, she possesses information that should not wander freely. She stays."

"But, how can you trust her?" Lord Wyndham cried, rising from his seat. "How can you trust anything she says?"

He forced his features to remain blank and said, "She has already proven herself. Now, *sit down*." Wyndham sat down in a huff.

"If the king trusts her," the steward broke in, "we should not question him. If he wishes to keep her here, we ought to respect his decision."

"Thank you, Mathis. That is the best thing you've said all day." He turned from the steward to face his council. "Tell me, what is it about this woman that truly bothers you? Is it really her lack of pedigree and where she comes from?" He lifted an eyebrow in challenge. When they did not answer, he said, "Or, is it because it frustrates you that Claire has done more to save this kingdom than any of you have?"

His statement was met with open mouths and shocked gazes. Except for Saffra. A small, wicked smirk played at the corners of her lips. Their eyes met, only briefly, and he saw approval in her gaze.

"Perhaps our king has the best of it." Lord Rosk broke the stunned silence. "After all, this girl is merely a servant with no rank. No bother to us, eh? Let us lay down our arguments and accept the king's decision with dignity."

Not *everyone* on the council was useless. Some of them *did* contribute good ideas to the ruling of the kingdom. But, he had no say in who sat in those seats. "The king chooses his shields and the people choose theirs," his father had once told him. Each of the twenty council members were selected by the twenty lord governors along with their people, to represent the dragondoms at court. Except Saffra, who was a default for Galadhal, as the kingdom's seer.

"No bother, Lord Rosk?" Lord Glover refused to let the subject drop. "Just the other day, my wife and some of her ladies took a walk with Lord Jovari. After coming home, she went on and on about how Jovari greeted this servant as if she were royalty. He even invited her to join them on their walk! A servant, invited to walk with the ladies!"

"Lord Glover!" Talon slammed his fist on the table. "Do you question the actions of my shields?"

"No. No, Your Grace. I merely—"

"You merely intend to pass judgment?" The color drained from Lord Glover's face. "I can assure you, my lord, that no harm has come to your wife by way of Jovari's actions, no matter how appalled she may be. Furthermore, I suggest you go home tonight and explain that it is the servants who bring her food, the servants who clean up after her, and you may finish by telling her that it is the servants who contribute far more to this keep than she ever has or will."

The room fell completely silent. No further protests followed, thank the gods. He breathed a sigh of relief.

Putting Claire in a position of servitude had been done deliberately. His council believed she was merely there because she was of no consequence. It was what he *wanted* them to think.

He could have treated Claire like the hero that she was—although *that* matter still irritated him, because *he* should have been the savior of his own kingdom—but he didn't want to draw attention to her. She would be far safer unnoticed, especially if Kane's servants were looking for her.

His gaze flicked around the table, landing on his steward. "Mathis, now that Lord Glover better understands me, what other matters of import remain?" The chronicler's quill paused above the parchment, where he'd been taking notes. "I'd like to get this meeting moving again." If only to get Claire out of his head.

"Of course, Your Grace. The Council wishes to hear an update regarding Lor—regarding Stefan Rosen and Euen Doyle."

He'd spent the better part of the week in the dungeons with Doyle and Rosen, and quickly found they were useless. Verath had no answers regarding the ruin of their minds, only that Kane must have tampered with them. Nonetheless, the effects on his temperament had been miraculous. He almost felt like himself again... almost.

"They are of no further consequence. Schedule the execution."

"Done." The chronicler's quill began again.

"If that is all, let us conclude today's meeting." He placed his hands on his chair, preparing to stand—

"Just a moment more, Your Grace. There is one more matter on our agenda." Mathis circled something on his parchment, then looked up. "We have yet to discuss the matter of you finding a wife."

"A wife," he repeated.

"Yes, my king. I hope the duration of time allotted was sufficient to think the matter over."

"You wish for me to marry the daughter of a traitor?" He kept his voice low and controlled, allowing an edge of ice to seep in.

"No! No, Your Grace," Mathis cried. "Any lady will do. Any lady. The people need reassurance. They could use a positive diversion amidst the chaos beset upon us."

"So, then, any wife I choose? That would please them, would it?" Never mind that only a mated female could bear the child of a drengr. They always seemed to forget that.

"Of course, Your Grace." Mathis bobbed his head.

"I see. And would dying gruesome deaths while they sleep also please the people?" Shocked gasps echoed around the room. "Last I checked, Mathis, it was the people's safety to which I look. They would rather I go gallivanting off in search of a wife, than see to the more immediate threats? Lest we not forget, Kane with his wild dragon horde to the north, goblins to the east, vodar wraiths wandering about the kingdom, and pirates raiding the shores."

"Certainly, my king. Certainly. When you put it that way..." His council members were squirming in their seats. "Finding a wife can—"

"I've an urgent message, Talon." Reyr's voice filled his mind. *"May I enter the chamber? I would rather deliver the news in person."*

"Yes. Come and save me from this headache."

Reyr stormed in.

"Lord Reyr," Mathis cried, jumping to his feet. The council members around the table rose in unison.

"Good afternoon. I apologize for the interruption." Reyr nodded to each of them until his gaze settled last upon Talon.

"You look as though you have seen a ghost," Talon said, his stomach hardening with worry.

"There has been another attack—in the north. A string of them, actually."

"Attacks?" several lords cried in unison.

Talon's stomach flipped over on itself. While they'd been in here bickering about Claire, his kingdom had been under attack. He wanted to rage against the uselessness of the day. Against the last two hours he'd wasted, stuffed in this room.

"Give me the worst of it," he commanded.

Reyr opened a letter. "This reached me five minutes ago, from Fort Squall. From Davi. The date is three days prior. Dragon attacks in the north. Ravaging and burning, beginning with Landow. If you remember correctly, that was the village where I found our witness—Mikkin."

"Aye. I remember." He slumped back in his chair.

"There is more."

"Gods. There cannot be more," Lord Rosk breathed.

"Indeed. Five drengr and their riders—dead. A small covey in the area was intercepted by the dragon horde. They managed to send a few panicked messages to another covey nearby before they were eaten alive."

A few people in the room shrieked. He did not hear the remainder of their surprised remarks. Couldn't hear a thing past the roaring that filled his ears.

The way he'd felt when Cyrus died was still too sharp. It resurfaced with this new loss. Too many lives, and all because of his leadership, his failure. His heart constricted. He needed fresh air—needed to get out of here. Without another word, he stood and fled the room.

CHAPTER 52
SHARING A SECRET

Kastali Dun

Claire's eyes flew open. Panting and covered in sweat, she pushed her blankets away. Tonight marked the fourth night this week. She got up and lit a candle then sat cross-legged upon her cot to think.

The dream was the same as before, bits and pieces, like riding on the back of a red dragon, a dark cave with a lake, a blue dragonstone, images she hardly comprehended, except one—a single picture that was unforgettable. Kane's glowing red eyes were burned into her mind, staring back at her through the reflection of the lake water. Those eyes had haunted her for days.

Ever since she'd started drinking aegan.

Unable to fight it, she got up, and made another draught. If she didn't, the consequences would be far worse. *You must learn to control the voices,* Cyrus prompted. *Aegan weakens your mind when you sleep.*

She knew he was right, that she had to find a way to control it without potions. But what did Cyrus mean about the aegan weakening her mind? Was Kane toying with her from afar?

At last, she sighed. She needed help. This wasn't a problem that would fix itself.

The next morning, she woke more exhausted than ever. More than a week had passed since she'd started the aegan. She was beginning to fear it, hate it, love it. Perhaps sleep was a small price to pay in exchange for headaches.

She and Desaree spent the day working in the gardens outside the servant's dining room. The private cookery's garden had become her favorite place. Its sun drenched greenery sat just within the keep's outer wall. She could hear the city, reminding her that a whole world existed beyond the keep.

Within its garden, raised planter boxes were arranged in neat rows. They held every herb imaginable. Oregano, parsley, rosemary, sage, and thyme, just to name a few. Their scents mixed with the sea breeze, combining to create a divine aroma.

In many ways, the garden reminded her that Dragonwall was not so different from her own world. And yet, this world was lost somewhere in time. Instead of technology, like on Earth, there was magic. Somehow, that ability to conjure cures and speak powerful words, had eliminated the people's desire to advance into what she considered *modern times*.

Wasn't that the beauty of it?

"Claire?" Desaree's voice filtered into her thoughts. They were on their hands and knees, pulling weeds. "Whatever is the matter with you today?"

"What?" Her head chose that moment to pulse with discomfort, as several drengr voices pounded against the magic of the aegan. She'd have to take a stronger dosage tomorrow.

"I asked what you thought of the king's news?"

"Oh. Right." The morning before last, a royal proclamation had been made. "I think the king was right to tell everyone about the dragons. Our people need to know. We need to be prepared." She hesitated, surprised by her words. Did she consider herself a part of Dragonwall already? She frowned, reaching for another cluster of weeds.

"Perhaps it was the correct thing to do," Desaree said, "but *dragons?* No one believes it, least of all me."

She sat back on the heels of her feet and looked at Desaree. "Why ever not? The king wouldn't lie."

"Well, because..." Desaree paused. "Because dragons are extinct. I know you do not understand much of our history—no offense. Dragonwall rid itself of dragons tens of thousands of years ago. They cannot simply spring back into existence."

Desaree wasn't the only one struggling to believe the news. The keep was rife with speculation. The worst of it was that the king had lost his mind. Easier to believe that, than the alternative.

"You're right," Claire said. "I may not be from here, but I do believe the king. If dragons are back, then we all have a right to know. Furthermore, we've got to do something about it."Desaree pursed her lips and returned to her work. "Des, there's a lot I haven't told you about why I came here, and what I was involved in. A lot I *can't* tell you because it would put you in danger, just knowing. But I can tell you this, the dragons are real and—"

The groan of hinges interrupted her. Tess materialized. Claire blinked at her sudden appearance. Had she just...?!

"Oh, dearie me!" The head woman turned a deep shade of red. She glanced back at the secret door in the garden wall, now shrouded by ivy. "I didn't think you gals would be out here in the heat of day!" She held a basket in the crook of her arm, filled with fabrics, a couple of books, and bottles that suspiciously looked like liquor.

"You need not mind us, Tess," Desaree said. "We won't tell a soul."

Tess hesitated, then gave them a curt nod and went inside.

"Des?" she said, voice filled with suspicion. "Where does that door lead?"

It was so well disguised, there was no way to tell it was there.

"Oh, that's one of Tess's big secrets." Desaree's laugh was a little too high. "It allows her to go to the market when she pleases without having to deal with the guards. The keep has been under intense scrutiny as of late. A bit inconvenient if you ask me."

"Does anyone else know about it?"

"Of course not. Why do you think she was so surprised to see us? I only know about it because, well, the woman practically raised me."

She hoped Desaree was right. Secret access to the keep was not a good thing. In the wrong hands, that door could be dangerous.

After finishing in the garden, she snuck away and scribbled a message to Reyr. She bribed a serving boy to push it under his door. He'd been absent a full week since the dragon attack in the north. There were things she wanted to discuss with him. Well, one thing especially.

Just as she was preparing for bed, there came a knock at her door. "You have need of me my lady?" Reyr said as she let him in. He carried a small cloth sack. He handed it over and she took a peek inside.

"Reyr!" she gasped. "Candy?"

"Consider it an apology for my behavior during Verekblot. I often forget that you are not familiar with our customs. Sometimes I judge you too harshly."

"I deserved it. Besides, I've forgiven you. Plus,"—she was grinning widely now—"this makes it so worth it!"

There were all sorts of colorfully wrapped goodies, a rainbow of sugary delights. Her mouth began watering.

Reyr knew all about her sweet tooth. He'd made fun of her at the start of their journey after discovering her sugar stash, which she'd demolished in a few days. That he'd remembered made her heart swell with warmth.

"I should have gotten this sooner, but you know how busy I have been." She smiled and set the bag on the table, grabbing a handful of toffees. Then she sat cross-legged on her cot to enjoy them. Reyr sat opposite her. "I take it you've heard the news?"

"I have. And is it any surprise? Kane promised that he would attack if we didn't give up the stones. He's making good on that promise."

Reyr's eyes closed. "Indeed. He warned us. That blood is on our hands."

"Can you tell me more about what happened?"

"I suppose there is no point in withholding information from you."

"There isn't. Plus, I hate not knowing what's going on." Maybe it was petty to narrow her eyes at him, to make him feel guilty at all, but she hadn't seen him for a week, and felt like he'd forgotten all about her. Weren't they supposed to be friends?

"I know. I know." He gave her a rueful smile. They spent a while talking about the attack, getting lost in the details. A total of four settlements had been burned, countless lives lost, even some of the drengr and riders had died.

"Dragons like to eat their prey," Reyr explained.

"That's barbaric—!"

"*Reyr, where are you? I've got an idea.*" King Talon's voice intruded into her mind.

"*Shall I come to the tower?*"

"*Yes. I've summoned the others to join us. They will be here shortly.*"

"It seems I must go," Reyr said. He stood to leave. "I apologize for the abruptness of my departure."

"Wait," she cried, jumping to her feet. Her heart began to pound.

"What is it?" His head tilted, concern lining his features. It should have worried her, but she was too worried for other reasons.

"Reyr, I...I know the king wants you to join him—in the tower, I mean." Reyr frowned, not quite comprehending. She couldn't back out now. This was why she'd called him here, wasn't it? Because she couldn't do this alone anymore?

"I can hear the drengr speaking to each other. Their conversations. I hear everything. I heard what the king just said to you, that he got an idea, that he's summoned the others, that he wants you to go to his tower."

"You...you're being serious?" He stood frozen.

"Yes. Please. I need your help."

"You can hear the drengr speaking telepathically." He said it as if it wasn't a question. As if he didn't believe her.

She swallowed. "I can."

"*What you claim is impossible. No one can hear all the Drengr.*"

"It's not impossible. I can hear everything. Even that."

His eyes widened. He opened his mouth and then shut it again. After studying the abandoned chair, he returned to watching her. "For how long?" he finally asked.

"Since the beginning," she whispered.

His face reddened, but his expression quickly changed into something else. Anger? Betrayal? Disappointment?

Oh, no. What if he told the king? What if she'd made a huge mistake?!

"You've heard us all this time and never mentioned it? Why? Why would you keep something like this from me?"

"I—I wanted to tell you." Her heart squeezed. "But after everything you guys said about me, about how I was guilty, how I deserved to die, what the king said, what Koldis and Jovari said to you when you found me. I just...I couldn't bring myself to it."

"Gods above! You heard all of that?" He slouched back against his chair.

"I heard everything everyone said about me." She shrugged. "Look, I'm not trying to make you feel bad for what was said. I just...I just want your help."

"How? How is it even possible?"

"I—I don't know. Maybe there's something wrong with me. I...I can't make it stop."

"Nothing is wrong with you, Claire. I know that much." His eyes widened. "Your headaches!"

She nodded. "Cyrus said..."

Reyr sat up straight. "What did Cyrus say?"

"Nothing." Guilt needled her chest. "What I meant was, if I don't learn to block it out, the headaches will ruin me. I need to learn. There must be a way."

He studied her. "There is a way, I think, to mute the voices. We drengr can block each other out if we choose. Sometimes the king blocks me out when he is upset. I am sure the technique would be the same. Hold on a moment. Can you talk back?"

"Talk—talk back?" She swallowed. "What do you mean *talk back*?"

"I mean, can you reply to my thoughts?"

Her eyebrows drew together. "I...don't think so. Or at least, I've never tried."

"Let's try now. Say something to me with your mind."

"I don't think it works that way, Reyr."

"You will never know unless you try."

She focused on him, on his voice. *"What do you want me to say?"* It was merely a thought, no different than if she had spoken it to herself, except she thought of Reyr while she said it.

"Unbelievable!" he gasped. "You *can* talk back!"

She smiled, pleased with her instant success. *"I can only imagine the all things my rotten tongue will do with this newfound ability. Now you'll never be rid of my snide comments."* She almost hoped her words would fail to reach him, but they didn't.

He grinned. *"That rotten tongue of yours is going to get you into trouble someday."*

She laughed.

"Reyr!" The king's booming voice interrupted them. *"I thought you were coming. Where are you?"*

She flinched.

"Give me a moment. I will be along shortly." Reyr stood and looked at her. "I take it you heard that?"

"Yep. You—you won't tell Talon will you? Please don't!"

He stared at her. "You wish for me to lie to my king?"

"If he finds out, he'll kill me."

"I very much doubt that."

"Please!"

"I will not lie to my king," he said, his voice turning hard. "You know what I am. You know the oath I am under."

"I know," she said. "But you don't have to outright tell him. If he doesn't ask, then it isn't lying, right?"

He scrubbed a hand over his face. "Fine. I won't mention it. But you should tell him. Sooner rather than later."

"I...I will." The lie rolled offer her tongue too easily.

At last he nodded. "Very well. I must go. Will you be all right here?"

She rolled her eyes at him. "I'm not some fragile thing. I've been through worse."

"All right. When I next return, we will see to your training. There is a way to help you, I think. Can you sit tight for a few days?"

She grinned. "I'll be fine. Go."

"Good. We will see each other again soon." With that he left the room, closing the door behind him.

She exhaled. It could have been worse. So much worse.

Reyr's voice filled her mind. *"Thank you for sharing your secret with me. I cannot take back the things that were said about you. But I will try to make this right, somehow."*

"Thank you for understanding. And...I know." She smiled and buried herself under the covers, extinguishing her candle.

CHAPTER 53

THE IMPOSSIBLE

Kastali Dun

Saffra freed an arrow from her bow. It struck a dummy's chest, but not its heart. She scowled. Three points were awarded for striking the head or heart, two for the chest or neck, and one for the abdomen, arms, or legs. With the fall tournament approaching, she had every intention of defending her title.

She walked over to the dummy, some sixty feet away, and recovered her arrows. Even at midday, the sun's harshness was diminishing as summer came to a close. But, it was still hot.

She was alone at the longbow range. No one heard her swear in frustration as she wiped her brow. Most archers preferred the shorter range. It was unheard of for a female of her stature—riders excluded—to possess the strength needed to pull the weight of the longbow. But, she was not merely a human. Magic made her strong.

She found her position again, nocking another arrow. She exhaled. Just as she released, her vision blackened at the edges. The bowstring twanged, and everything vanished.

. . .

SHE BLINKED at the sight of the mountain fortress. Shadowkeep's ramparts were like shards of broken glass decaying into the crumbling heaps of rock that settled around its base. She whooshed forward until she stood before a man, red eyed and menacing. Kane. He wasn't looking at her. He was watching someone else. A woman.

Saffra's breath caught in her chest. She whirled to find Claire. Rocks tumbled into the pit of her stomach. Claire looked...different. Changed. She stood cloaked in black velvet, radiating strength and confidence.

Her expression was fierce, unyielding as she looked out over the landscape.

Kane laughed, making Claire jump and glance around. Her eyes widened right as he lunged, shooting forward as he called out words in the old language. A ball of magical energy manifested between his fingers, growing into an orb with blackened veins. It expanded outward like a bubble.

Saffra screamed, trying to warn Claire. A human would never stand a chance against an asarlaí like Kane. Try as she might, not a single word escaped her.

Claire was going to die.

Claire moved with surprising speed. A staff materialized in her right hand and Cyrus's sverak in her left. She crossed them like a shield. She began speaking, but Saffra failed to understand her words. There was a song in Claire's voice.

The orb of dark magic shattered against an invisible barrier. A deafening crack split the silence. Saffra gasped as an explosion of power surged through her, searing like fire—

∾

Her eyes flew open.

"Lady Saffra?! Oh, thank the gods. You're awake." She was tucked into familiar arms, against a solid chest. Her lips pulled into a pleased smile. She opened her eyes to find warm brown ones upon her.

"Commander Daxton," she croaked.

"I am here." He kept his voice low, cradling her. Her brow scrunched in confusion before he bent to kiss it tenderly, as if attempting to smooth away her worry. At the touch of his lips, warmth spread through her insides.

She tried turning her head but it hurt. The sun was glaring down upon them. Despite its warmth, she was still freezing cold. "What...what happened?"

"You fell. You were here with your bow." He lifted it from the grass. "I was training some new recruits. As soon as I saw you, I came straight over." He helped her sit up.

The movement brought her vision flooding back. She stiffened. Claire and Kane fighting each other? How was it possible? How could a human defend themselves against a sorcerer?

She groaned, blinking against her watering eyes.

She needed to record the vision before it faded away.

"Another vision?" Daxton asked.

She nodded and closed her eyes, trying to focus—

"Will you be well? Should I call for a healer?"

"I'll be fine," she muttered. "Thank you for rescuing me, Commander." She afforded him a small smile. He was her knight in shining armor, or in this case, knight with a sweaty chest, not that she minded. "I hope I didn't frighten you."

"You did." He nuzzled against her. She blinked back her surprise at his open show of affection. What if someone saw them?!

She cleared her throat. "I ought to return to my room and record what I've seen."

"And what *did* you see?" he asked, curiosity forming lines on his brow.

A frown pulled at her lips. "I...I hardly know. Without Cyrus, I cannot seem to understand what I see."

He exhaled. "Cyrus was your crutch. There was once a time when he was mine, too." It was Cyrus who had trained Commander Daxton. Cyrus taught him everything he knew about fighting. "But, Saffra, you are still the king's prophetess. You must learn regardless. I know you can do this—you were *meant* to do this."

She gave him a weak smile. "I will try."

"Very well then, little dove." He helped her to her feet, handing over her things. Then he walked her to the edge of the practice yard. She turned to leave just as he said, "Uhm...Saffra? May I come by your chambers later this evening?"

"You wish to visit me? Are you not worried someone might find out?"

"I do wish it. I promise that I will use the utmost discretion. You have my word." He placed a hand over his heart and bowed his head.

Her heart melted and she smiled. "Then of course you may come."

"Excellent." His wide grin crinkled his eyes until they were narrow slits of happiness.

"See you tonight." She turned to leave. Suddenly a hand grasped her arm. Dax pulled her back to him. The force of it left her breathless. He cupped her cheek in his hand and bent to kiss her gently. She could hardly take in air.

"Commander!" she scolded, pulling away from him, glancing around to see if anyone had seen.

"There, now," he said. "That is a proper goodbye." His grin left her heart racing.

"What are you playing at?" she whispered, worried.

"Do not fret, my lady." He afforded her a quick wink before walking back to his students.

She was still flustered when she returned to her chambers. Dax never showed his affection in public, and for good reason. They both worried over how the king would react. Neither knew if their relationship was permitted. She was the king's seer, after all.

She rummaged for her journal, grabbing a quill and bottle of ink before scribbling down notes. She had seen Kane and Claire. Seeing them together in a single vision was peculiar. Alarming, even.

Claire had been holding something, too. A sword, perhaps? A staff? What *was* it? She ground her teeth together in frustration.

Closing her eyes, she allowed her mind to wander over the scene. The staff was strange, made of dark wood with a single gem glittering on top. There were spriten markings etched into it. She wondered about the gem before shaking her head. It was a shame she no longer remembered the color. And the sword; she knew the sword.

"It cannot be possible!" she muttered, jotting down more notes, trying to draw little sketches of what she'd seen—

"My lady?" Jocelyn's voice sounded from the bathing room. "You wished for a bath upon your return. Your gown is laid out and ready, too." Jocelyn took one look at her and rushed over. "My lady? Is everything all right?"

"I...I hardly know." She turned back to her scribbling.

"Do you wish to speak of it?"

She shook her head and pursed her lips. "Not now. My head aches terribly. Get some of my aegan, will you?" She had given Claire nearly everything except a very small amount, leftover from two years ago.

"Will you go to the king again?" Jocelyn sounded hesitant. "I know how he flusters you."

"I..." *Should* she take this to him? "No. I do not know enough about this vision to waste his time. Perhaps when I learn more..." *Would* she learn more? Would more visions like this one visit her?

After dinner, she found Claire in her room, albeit surprised by the unexpected visit.

Claire quickly ushered her inside. "Would you like one?" she asked, offering up a toffee. "They're from Reyr. He brought me a whole bag yesterday."

"Sure. Thank you." She took one of the brightly wrapped candies and popped it in her mouth. After savoring it, she pushed it into her cheek and explained the reason for her visit.

"Let me get this straight," Claire said, frowning. "You saw me battling Kane, and somehow I defended myself against him?"

"I warned you it was strange. Claire, the asarlaí are an ancient race, powerful and terrible. No human is capable of doing what you did, defending yourself against him." She hesitated. "This might sound unbelievable but, I do not think you are human. You cannot be. I thought all of my visions foreshadowed your coming here. Now I believe there is something more."

An expression flashed across Claire's face. Her lower lip caught between her teeth before she said, "Maybe I'm *not* entirely human. I... There's something I should tell you." Saffra sat up straighter. "I was hesitant to tell anyone, but last night I finally came clean to Reyr. I suppose you deserve the truth, too."

Her heart quickened. "What did you tell Reyr?"

"I can hear all the drengr talking to each other."

Saffra opened her mouth. "The...the drengr? Like, through telepathy? Explain."

"I heard them before Cyrus died," Claire said, going on to detail her strange ability to hear all the conversations exchanged between drengr kind. She described the way she'd felt when Jovari, Koldis, and Reyr talked secretly about her, and the way she cried when she heard the king's voice saying mean things.

"But...no one can hear *all* the Drengr, Claire. No one. Not when they do not wish to be heard."

"I know," Claire muttered, her expression darkening.

Everything she'd seen in her vision was suddenly a possibility. She cleared her throat. "Can you think of any reason why you were holding Cyrus's sword in my vision?"

Claire's face turned deep red. "Uhm...I...I don't know."

"Are you sure?"

She began biting her lower lip. "I think Cyrus and I are connected."

"Connected, how?"

"I know it sounds weird, but I can hear his voice in my head sometimes. Like...talking to me."

Saffra's stomach swooped. "His voice? But how?!"

"I don't know! Believe me, I really don't."

"Unbelievable. You are full of mysteries." They talked about it for a few minutes more, trying to discover the reason for it. But nothing made sense.

When she finally left Claire's chamber, she left with more questions than when she had arrived. Explaining her vision was challenging enough, but coming up with an explanation for Cyrus's voice was an entirely new obstacle. This day had been full of impossibilities.

A tiny pang of jealousy pierced her heart. She missed Cyrus so much that it hurt to think of him. To know that Claire had the ability to converse with him when *she* was the one who needed his help with her visions, felt unfair. But none of this was Claire's fault.

She planted herself upon her sofa within her chambers. All she could do was stare at the fire in the grate. "Is the Commander still coming by tonight?" Jocelyn's voice roused her from her daze.

She jumped from the couch. "Commander Daxton. Good gods! I forgot. Hurry, help me with my gown." She had already unlaced it after returning, so Jocelyn helped before dismissing herself.

Moments later, there came a knock.

"Good evening, my lady." Daxton greeted her as she opened the door. He was dressed in a fine tunic and freshly shined boots. Such a contrast to the training clothes he usually wore.

She stepped aside, offering him a shy smile. He didn't move. Instead, he pulled a bouquet of wildflowers—bluebells and orange poppies—from behind his back. Her face flushed. "Those are for me?" she stupidly whispered, flattered.

"You like them?" His words were hesitant. "I picked them before dinner, just outside the city." Bits of color rose on his cheeks. Not like his usual brash manner. He was rarely shy.

"They are positively beautiful!" She inhaled deeply, eyelids fluttering. "Will you come in?"

He followed her inside.

After putting the flowers in a vase, she poured them goblets of wine. Then she sat upon the sofa just close enough that their thighs nearly touched. He immediately scooted a cushion's length away and angled himself to face her. She almost giggled. "You are behaving rather oddly tonight," she said. His face drained of color and he fidgeted.

"Saffra..." His throat bobbed. "Do you love me?"

"I..." Her brow furrowed. "You know I love you. I've told you so many times over. I love you more than anything."

"And I, you," he finished, saying nothing more as he fussed with his hands. He wouldn't even look at her.

"Is everything all right?" she asked.

"Yes." He exhaled. "Do you remember when we met?"

She smiled down at her wine. "Aye. I remember it well." She had been a nervous child at that time, in possession of an incurable fondness for him, though he never knew it until they were much older.

"I, too, remember it like yesterday. You were just a child to me then." He frowned. "When I came back from the goblin war, that was no longer the case. You caught my eye immediately. I saw you that day at the target range. Do you remember?"

She thought back to his return, the day she had laid eyes on him after so many years. "I do. You came over to me. I believe you told me my archery progress impressed you."

He chuckled. "And it did, but it was far more than that which caught my attention. The moment I laid eyes on you I longed for you. I may have not said so, and obviously I did not express as much. I can be...overconfident at times, even I admit to that."

She barked a laugh. *At times*? Still, she had come to love him. Especially his swaggering personality.

"You may not know it, Saffra, but I was not honest with you initially. I hid my true feelings from the outset. I knew I wanted you even then, but I also knew you were a lady of the court. Not just any lady, but the king's own prophetess, and I, a lowly soldier in his army. It occurred to me that if I was ever to win you, I would have to make you want me first." He shook his head, perhaps ashamed of his behavior. "I believe my tactics—no matter how conniving—worked?"

His grin turned devilish.

"You self righteous, boastful, wretch!" she cried, reaching over and slapping his chest as hard as she could with each word. He grabbed her arm and encircled her waist, dragging her across the sofa so that her back sat flush against his chest. Her wine nearly spilled from its goblet. Now atop his lap, he wrapped his arms around her so that she could no longer fight him. All the while, she giggled.

Removing the goblet from her grasp, he drank the remainder in one gulp, and then tossed the empty cup away. "I knew I had to make you mine," he whispered into her ear. His touch sent warm tingles down her spine. Her laughter stopped. "Do you wish to be mine, Saffra?" he asked.

"Yes!" she whispered, breathless. He turned her in his lap so that he could look at her. The relief in his expression surprised her. Had he actually doubted her? For years, it was she who'd doubted him. It was an unexpected turn of events.

"If that is true," he said, "if you would have me, then I would make it official. I would ask for your hand, to make you my wife."

She opened and closed her mouth several times, stunned. "You—you want me forever?" she asked, incredulous.

"I never wish to share you with another. You are mine—forever—if you would have me." His request was no small feat. She had magic, powerful magic, and that would age her more slowly. She would be forced to watch Daxton grow old. Who could tell how much longer she would outlive him? Yet, her love trumped everything.

"I would have you forever and ever, Dax," she whispered. "You have always held my heart. Surely you know that." Her words left him smiling.

"Aye, I know, but I wanted to hear you say it." He bent down and kissed her. Then he nuzzled his nose against hers and happily sighed.

"Since you will have me, we can be married as soon as you wish."

She pulled away from him in alarm. "But the king! What if he is against it?"

"Not to fear, little dove, not to fear." He sounded far too calm. "I spoke with him early this morning and he has graciously given his consent."

"What?" she shrieked, pulling away to slap his chest, yet again. "You never told me!"

"Of course I didn't," he admitted. "I wanted to be sure of where we stood before asking you. But I wanted the king's consent before that." Again he took her in his arms. "It was all a process. I have also spoken with your father if you must know, quite some time ago. He too gave me his happy consent."

"My...my father?"

Gods! How long had he been planning this? A rush of overwhelming happiness flooded her as she finally allowed herself to imagine a future with him. She pictured their lives together, the memories they might share, the children they might have, the experiences they would live through.

She burst into tears and laughter all at once. Dax squeezed her tighter. This man—one whom she'd met under unlikely circumstances—wanted to marry her. When she was ten, she'd never imagined such a thing could be possible.

"As I said, whenever you are ready, we may be wed."

Could one die from too much happiness? If so, she might have dropped dead then and there! Yet she did not. Rather, she relished in the moment, enjoying the safety and assurance his arms afforded her. After she composed herself and wiped the tears from her eyes, she reached for his head and met his lips. It was the sweetest kiss they had ever shared.

CHAPTER 54

SURPRISING MAGIC

Kastali Dun

Desaree deposited a stack of empty trays in the washroom, sighing once she'd rid herself of the weight. With breakfast done, she departed in search of Claire. Tess stepped in front of her, brandishing her spoon. "You take extra care today with Lady Crafton's chambers," she said. "I'll not have that woman chasing me down again."

"I'll clean it till it sparkles," Desaree grumbled, stepping around Tess's imposing frame. She left the cookery, pushing Lady Crafton out of her mind, occupying it with something far more pleasant.

Daydreaming of Lord Verath had become something of a guilty pleasure. Crafting scenarios where he rescued her from kidnappers, confessing his love, before gathering her up into his arms. In her conjurings, it never mattered that he was a king's shield and she was a mere servant—

"Desaree?" She froze in her tracks. "Over here!" An arm reached out from the shadows, grabbing her hand and pulling her into darkness.

She gasped. "Lord Verath?"

He chuckled. They stood in a shadowy nook. He leaned with comfortable ease against the stone wall to regard her. "I saw you passing and thought to hide myself and surprise you."

"Whatever for?" Her mind jumped to the daydream she'd just been having, and her cheeks flushed hotter. It had started a lot like this.

"I thought I might speak with you in private. When I saw you walking... Anyway, I would like to have dinner with you tonight, if that is favorable? I know your duties keep you from eating early. Perhaps when you have finished for the night?"

"Oh..." Her her heart leapt. "What of the suspicion that will create? Others might wonder..."

"No one will question my ordering dinner late," he said.

She chewed on her bottom lip and his eyes darted downward at the motion. She released her lip and said, "Very well. I accept."

"Perfect. See you later."

She watched his retreating figure, completely mystified.

Shortly thereafter, she found Claire in the west wing of the castle. "Something has you in a good mood," Claire said. "Are we friends enough to share secrets?"

"I...I am afraid to say for fear of jinxing it."

"Oh come on, tell me!"

"Fine," she said, grinning, "but you must promise not to say a word."

"Cross my heart and hope to die."

Desaree lifted an eyebrow at the strange expression. She was used to them now. Then she said, "Verath asked me to have dinner with him tonight. He cornered me in the corridor. Pulled me into the shadows. It was..." She sighed, feeling dreamy.

"Lord Verath?" Claire gasped in delighted surprise. "You? And Lord Verath?"

"Why are you surprised?" she asked, suddenly defensive. "We are only friends, at least I think we are friends. I should like to be his friend..."

"Don't get me wrong, Des. He's handsome. They all are. It's just —" Claire bit her lower lip.

"*Just* what?"

"He's so reserved compared to the others. I guess I never would have guessed he would be interested in *anyone*. But clearly, he is! Why else would he single you out?"

For all her dreaming, Desaree had spent an equal amount of time doubting. How could Verath feel anything beyond friendship for her? But Claire's words left her hopeful. "You...you really think he cares for me?"

Claire tutted. "Desaree! He coerced you into a dark hallway to ask you to *dine* with him. I think he has more than friendship on the brain."

Her face flushed. "I hope you are right. It would make me happy beyond imagining. But it would also be very bad."

"Why? How can it ever be bad?"

"Because he's a shield." When Claire didn't appear to understand, she took a moment to explain why someone like him, sworn to protect the king, should not engage in relationships of love.

"So they can't take riders. What's the big deal?" Claire merely shrugged, belittling the matter. "It doesn't mean they can't enjoy love every now and then."

"If we fall in love, Claire, he'll have to watch me grow old and die." Considering how much longer the Drengr lived compared to humans, the thought was appalling. She didn't mean to sound so negative. It was her doubt talking, clawing at her.

"Gods, Desaree!" Claire sputtered. She almost laughed because that was surely the first time Claire had ever used the word *gods*. "Quit being so extreme. It's just dinner. And if it leads to more, then go with the flow. Have you ever been in love before?" She closed her mouth and shook her head. Of course she hadn't! "Okay then, allow yourself to experience it. Who knows when you'll get another chance like this one? He's a shield, for crying out loud."

"But—but what about all the heartbreak I'll feel?"

"What about it?" Claire shrugged. "That's all part of falling in love, Des. There will always be the risk of heartbreak." She sighed and her brow pulled together. "Listen, if you let your fear control your choices, you'll never experience one of the most powerful emotions in existence."

"Maybe you're right." Desaree exhaled. If she didn't stop over-thinking her relationship with Verath, or lack thereof, everything she wanted to experience would pass right by her.

~

TRUE TO HIS WORD, Verath submitted a late request for dinner. Just as she was finishing up her duties, a serving boy rushed into the cookery. She watched as he breathlessly blurted out the request to Tess. Simultaneously, she and Claire exchanged a knowing look.

Tess rounded on her. "It seems Lord Verath has requested you to deliver his dinner tonight. Again." The woman eyed her suspiciously. "He has taken on quite a liking to you, Desaree."

She merely shrugged before gathering food from various platters, arranging it neatly upon a tray.

"My, my, that looks like a lot of food for just one." Tess missed nothing. Yet despite her keen observation, there was no judgement in her voice.

"Lord Verath is a drengr, Tess. He will be quite hungry, I suspect." She noticed the twitch of Tess's lips before she turned and left. Meanwhile, Claire's malicious grin was contagious. She felt her own materialize.

Just as she was lifting the tray, Claire passed by her and whispered, "I can't wait to hear all the details. Good luck!"

Before she reached his room, she took a moment to adjust her clothes, tidy her hair, and pinch her cheeks, then she picked up the tray and continued. When she knocked at the door, Verath pulled it open almost immediately, affording her a pleased smile. "Thank gods you're finally here!" he growled. "I am so hungry, I could eat three grazers." Her eyes widened. He chuckled. "All right, fair enough. I suppose this meal will do just fine."

She walked in and he closed the door behind her. "Do the drengr truly eat that much?"

"They do when they're as hungry as I am."

She set the tray upon the table and began unloading it. Verath's hand swiftly closed around her wrist. She expected his hold to be harsh, but it was gentle and lingered before he pulled it away. "You sit. I will serve." His warm touch left her skin burning in an unfamiliar way. He pulled out a chair for her. She sank into it.

He began removing items from the tray and dishing out food for them both. What a wonder it was to be served. "There. Eat."

She did exactly as ordered. For a time, they were quiet. She enjoyed the silence. It allowed her to steal glances at him.

His hair was messier than usual today, and longer too. That she knew his preferred length was a clear sign that she was overly obsessed. She almost choked on her mashed potatoes at the thought. Verath's dark locks swept down to his eyebrows. Every so often, he absentmindedly pushed his hands through his hair to move it away from his eyes—

"You look amused," he said. She shrugged and returned to her food. "Come now, I wouldn't mind a bit of amusement."

She glanced up at him. "I was merely thinking to myself."

"Come now, do share."

"You truly wish to know?" She set her fork down, hoping he would decline. When he nodded, she said, "Well, I was just thinking that you are in desperate need of a haircut."

He threw his head back and roared with laughter. "Indeed! I was thinking so myself just the other day. I've been so busy, I've neglected my own hair. Are you good with shears?"

"Me?" Her eyes grew round. "I certainly hope you are joking. Can't you do it yourself?"

"Oh, I can, but wouldn't it be more fun for *you* to do it?"

"Uhm...I..." Butterflies settled in the pit of her stomach. She yearned to say yes, but her mind begged against it. So, she merely shrugged.

"How about after dinner?"

"All right," she managed to croak.

After that, their conversation flowed freely. He was mostly curious about how she spent her spare time. "I enjoy reading," she said. "On the rare occasion that I can sneak into the royal library to borrow books."

"Which are your favorite?"

"Everything," she breathed, growing excited. "Truthfully, anything I can get my hands on."

"I see." He rose and went to his bookshelf. It was an impressive personal collection. "I have several here you might like." He began pulling books. Minutes later, he had a towering stack. He set them on the table with a thud. "There. Take these with you when you go, and keep them as long as you like. Though, I wouldn't mind hearing your thoughts when you finish."

She closed her mouth, stunned. The prospect of discussing books with Lord Verath thrilled her. She promised to give him a thorough assessment of each.

They moved on to dessert while he told her about *his* favorite books. Truthfully, she found it difficult to follow his conversation. Too often she was caught up in watching him speak, the way his eyes twinkled when he grew passionate, and how animated he became with his hands.

When they finished dinner, he stood and said, "Time for my haircut."

Butterflies settled in the pit of her stomach. To Verath, the simple act was nothing. To her, it felt intimate. But...recalling Claire's advice, she was determined to go with the flow of things, so she took the proffered scissors.

It was just a haircut, she tried to tell herself—

He casually shed his tunic, tossing it upon the sofa. She swallowed down the lump in her throat and gaped at him. Verath was standing before her—shirtless. Oh, gods. What was... But, of course, otherwise it would get covered in clippings. She blinked, trying to gather her scattered thoughts.

When he caught her staring at his sinewy chest and broad shoulders, his eyes glowed with satisfaction. He didn't say anything about it, thank the gods. Instead, he positioned his chair in the middle of the room and sat down, waiting for her.

She shook herself, then moved forward and began trimming

away the pieces that had grown too long. "I hope to keep the ends even," she said as she went, slowly working her way around. She hardly knew what she was doing. She'd watched the servants assist each other with haircuts. Most often she trimmed her own hair if the ends became too tangled. But this was different.

Her fingers brushed his skin. Her stomach clenched, sending tingles straight to her toes. She took advantage of the opportunity, allowing her fingertips to linger against his scalp for longer than necessary. He hummed. The sound was low and masculine.

Once she finished, she took the liberty of rustling his hair with her fingers. It was so soft! He let out a guttural growl deep in his chest, . Her heart skipped at the sound of it.

Reluctantly, she stepped away to review her work. She'd done well enough. His hair looked as it usually did. All was back to normal in her *Verath-centered* world. She was rather pleased with herself, though she would not admit it. Instead, she grimaced and shook her head. "Gods! I'm so sorry. It's absolutely terrible! You never should have trusted me."

His mouth opened and closed. "Is that so."

"Yes, I fear you may need to hide away from the public or suffer their laughter."

He chuckled. "It is only hair, Desaree." The way he said her name made her toes curl in her slippers. "It will grow back. Perhaps next time you'll do better."

Next time.

She bit her lip. "I was only kidding. Your hair looks fine."

He rose and went to examine himself in the mirror, running his fingers through it. "Indeed! A fine job."

She fixed her gaze on him as he threw his tunic over his head and came to stand before her. In height, she reached his shoulder, forcing her to tilt head back. This was the closest they had ever been. She could feel a dragon's fiery warmth radiating from him. She could feel his breath upon her brow. She could see the stubble growing upon his jaw. *And* she could smell the scent of wood and smoke upon his skin.

His fingers brushed against her cheek. "Thank you, Desaree.

I've kept you long enough. Take your books and go, but don't stay up too late, eh?"

She nodded and scrambled away, collecting the book pile before bidding him goodnight.

The following day, she struggled to pull herself from her bed. She'd done exactly the opposite of what Lord Verath had advised. It was the only way to keep her mind off the feel of his hair in her hands.

Claire attacked her for details the moment they saw each other. They delivered breakfast trays, accomplishing bits of discussion in between each delivery. "He let you cut his hair?!" Claire gasped. "Oh. My. God! Desaree, tell me everything."

Her cheeks blushed merely thinking of the encounter. But she revealed everything, except the last part, where he'd caressed her cheek, gazing into her eyes. That belonged to her.

Throughout the day, Claire brought up snippets, over-analyzing the details down to each word. Desaree didn't mind. It was fun to share her excitement with a friend.

They walked from the west wing to the cookery, giddy with speculation.

"I think when he said—"

Lady Caterina came into view, followed by her entourage. Claire stopped short, letting the rest of her thought go unfinished.

Desaree's blood turned to ice. The ladies were coming straight for them. As was proper, she pulled Claire to the side of the walkway and stood, waiting for them to pass. The serving class was required to allow any of higher rank to pass by, undisturbed. Claire followed suit, albeit after protesting.

"Look, ladies. It is the scum of the keep." Caterina sneered at them in passing.

Ignoring insults might have been second nature for Desaree, but not for Claire. "Excuse me?" she said, stepping out into the corridor. Desaree tensed, grabbing her hand, attempting to pull her back, but Claire ripped her arm away. "I asked you a question, Caterina?" Claire called after their retreating forms.

Caterina stopped and turned to face them. "I called you scum, for that is what you are. Look at you, dressed in rags. You are worth *nothing*."

"How dare you!" Claire's expression turned to outrage. "How dare you judge us when your father betrayed the king!"

Caterina's face turned paper white.

Desaree gasped. She'd only heard rumors, but she had no idea that they were true. That Lord Stefan Rosen had betrayed the king.

"I don't know what you're talking about." Caterina turned back to her ladies. "Never trust a servant. They lie about everything."

But the damage was done.

"I think you know exactly what I'm talking about." Claire cried. "You see, I am the one who turned your father in. I am the one who gave his name to the king." Claire stepped towards Caterina, holding her ground. "And from now on, stay away from Desaree. Don't you so much as *look* at her, or I'll make sure you follow your father to the dungeons."

"Oh, gods," Desaree gasped, covering her mouth in shock.

Caterina's movements were slow. She turned back to face them, her face contorted. "You?! It was you?! I will kill you for that!" She lunged at Claire, but Claire was too fast, quickly side stepping out of the way.

Desaree tried to move, but stood frozen in shock. Everything was going so, *so* wrong! How could Claire do this? Draw attention to them like this?

An audience gathered to witness the spectacle.

Caterina screeched, rounding on them again. Desaree's scalp erupted in pain as Caterina reached out and grabbed a fistful of her long hair. She cried out, struggling to get away, but Caterina was too strong. Little stars erupted in her vision as Caterina shoved her into the ground. She tried to pull away—

"Don't you *dare* touch her!" Claire screamed.

Caterina was ripped away and flung up towards the ceiling of the corridor. Gasps echoed down the walkway as her body slammed against the stone. As if she'd been thrown by an invisible force. She dropped to the ground in a heap of fabric, silent and unmoving.

Desaree rushed to her feet, trembling, speechless. She looked with wide eyes from Caterina to Claire. Then she turned and noticed the gathered crowd.

"What's going on here?" A voice cut through the silence. Lord Reyr came to a stop before them, assessing the scene. Claire's face was bloodless. "I will ask again. What happened here?"

One of the bystanders, another servant, pointed at Claire. "She used magic! That one there, Lord Reyr! She hurled Lady Caterina into the ceiling. With magic!"

Lady Caterina's ladies were crouching over her now in hysterics, fussing. Reyr strode over to the wretched woman, pushing the two ladies aside. He felt her neck for a pulse, then stood. "Only unconscious," he announced. There was no relief in his voice. "You two," he called to the guards who had arrived. "Carry her to her room. Ladies? You can follow. See that she's all right."

He then turned to face them. "Claire? You're coming with me." He took ahold of her arm and ushered her away. Just before she melted into the crowd, Desaree saw her glance back over her shoulder with an apologetic look. The onlookers dissipated thereafter, until Desaree was left standing alone.

She blinked several times. What had just happened? Everything had moved so fast she could hardly make sense of it. Somehow—and she could not explain it—Claire had used magic. But that was not what had stunned her. All the rumors she'd heard were true. Caterina's father, Stefan Rosen—a man who had once been her own stepfather—had been imprisoned.

CHAPTER 55

THE GIFT

Kastali Dun

Claire allowed Reyr to drag her through the keep's corridors towards what was undoubtedly the south wing. She might have fought him, but instead, she could only blink numbly at the corridors they passed through.

She'd done...*magic*?

She'd done magic!

One moment, she'd been rushing to save Desaree, the next, she'd flung Caterina through the air without even touching her. She might have argued against it. But she'd felt it, too. Felt the explosive rush that came from her body. Felt the wave of exhaustion that followed. Like exercising a muscle for the first time.

"Reyr..." She finally managed to get his name out. They climbed a set of stairs that took them into a wide corridor. "I swear, I didn't mean to hurt her like that. I don't understand how it happened."

She blinked at the sight of plush carpet and beautiful vases. The south wing. She pulled against Reyr's hold but he didn't release her. "Whether you understand it or not, it happened. You performed magic."

"But...I..." She fumbled for words. "Can't we stop for a moment to talk about this? Please! There's no need to take this to the king."

She managed to stop him. For a moment, they stood gazing at each other. Then his face softened. "Unfortunately, it is too late for that. You of all people know how quickly thoughts travel. You must have been too flustered to hear his command. He wants you in his tower, immediately."

"Oh..." Aegan had dulled the potency of voices within her mind. But he was right—she'd been too flustered. "It was only an accident, Reyr," she whispered, taking a step backwards. "You know how he's going to react. He'll make this more than what it is."

"And what *is* it? How do you explain what happened? How do you explain the fact that you *just did magic*?!"

"I..."

"Come, let's not leave him waiting." He placed a hand firmly on her lower back.

This time her reluctant feet moved slowly, each step heavier than the last.

Reyr led her down a carpeted hall and a sense of dread settled over her shoulders. She glanced around for an escape route.

Opulent paintings lined the walls, enshrined within finely carved wooden frames painted with gold leaf. Each showed a large dragon and a crowned woman. She passed several before—

"Oh, gods, Reyr!" She gulped in air, trying to breathe. "You're not going to tell him about...about my ability, are you? You're not going to tell him that I have telepathy?"

He sighed but did not answer. They'd come to a door. The keep's soldiers stood guard, parting their spears.

Blood rushed past her ears.

Every interaction she'd ever had with the king had gone poorly. This one would be no different. She steeled her nerves.

She and Reyr stepped into a lavish entry that led directly into a circular sitting room. A large couch arrangement was set around a tall fireplace. For a moment, she simply blinked, taking in the magnificence of it.

Then, her eyes zeroed in on the statuesque draconic male

standing with one arm propped upon the fireplace mantle, staring into its dying embers. The sight of him completely stole her breath. Talon's gaze snapped to hers. The hairs on her skin reached outward, as if trying to flee her body. Apprehension sank into the pit of her stomach. His face was stone, but his silver eyes danced with suppressed anger.

Reyr deposited her in front of an armchair that faced the king, then strode away, leaving her to fend for herself, the traitor. "Sit." Talon's cold, clipped command had her scrambling for the chair. Today he wore a dark blue velvet tunic with a silver dragon head embroidered just above his left breast. His black pants were accented with shiny black boots. Strapped at his side, was his Sverak. He wore the same crown she'd seen on his head during her trial.

The other shields were there too, already sitting about the fireplace. Her eyes flicked to each of them before finding Talon again. She wouldn't dare let him out of her sight.

"Explain yourself," he demanded, voice low and unyielding.

She opened her mouth and croaked. Mortified, she swallowed. "I don't know what happened."

"How can you not know?" His gaze narrowed. "Did you or did you not render a lady of the court unconscious?"

"I...I did—"

"What lady?" Jovari interrupted.

"Lady Caterina," Reyr said. "There was a skirmish between them in the corridors."

"*Lady Caterina?*" Koldis sat forward in his seat. "*That* is the reason for this emergency? Sounds like you've done us all a favor." He moved to stand, as though this meeting was a complete waste of his time.

"Sit," the king barked. Koldis had the audacity to roll his eyes before collapsing back onto the sofa. "We are not here to discuss who, but how. Now—" He turned his attention upon her once more, waiting.

"I told you, I don't know how it happened. One moment, Caterina was hurting Desaree, and the next, she was flying through the air."

"Desaree?" Verath startled, sitting forward.

"Yes, Lord Verath," she snapped, losing patience. "Caterina attacked Desaree. If I hadn't... I was just so *angry*—"

"I do not need the background story," Talon drawled. "What bothers me, is that you lied to us."

"No..." She shook her head. "I didn't know. This is the first—"

"How old are you?" he demanded.

"Twenty-two."

"People do not simply live out twenty-two years of life and suddenly perform magic." He exhaled, pinching the bridge of his nose. "How can we trust you after this?"

"Everything I ever told you was true!" she cried, raising her voice.

"Perhaps this is an opportune moment to reveal your little secret." Reyr locked eyes with her, lifting an eyebrow.

She gave him a small shake of her head. She couldn't. Not now. Not yet. Not like this.

You must tell him about me, Cyrus said. *It is time.*

All the air left her chest. "Wait," she said. "There was something I might have forgotten to mention."

"Excellent," the king said, unamused. "The truth comes out at last."

"I never lied," she snapped back at him. "But..." Her fingertips went to her lips. Talon's eyes narrowed following the motion. "Before Cyrus died...he...he kissed me."

There was a long, long silence in which Talon frowned. It was a rare moment, seeing him let his guard down. The rest of her audience gaped at her. They thought she was crazy, didn't they?

"I never mentioned it because it seemed harmless. A simple act to ease his passing." She blinked to clear her vision.

"A kiss is hardly important to us," Jovari scoffed.

"But...don't you see?" She looked from one of them to the next.

"I fail to see what this has to do with anything." Talon had schooled his features once again.

She sighed. "Just before Cyrus died, he asked me to do something—one last thing to ease his suffering. I thought…" She shook her head. "He asked me to kiss him. I believed that he was merely lonely. Something must have happened when our lips touched." She knew exactly what had happened. Somehow, Cyrus's voice had embedded itself within her mind. "Now all of a sudden I can do magic. Not only that, sometimes he talks to me. Tells me things. That's how he told me about the laws, the charters, during my trial—"

"The gift." Verath's voice was filled with disbelief. "Is it…is it even possible?" He looked at Talon. "It would explain her magic and the presence of his voice in her mind."

She swallowed. "What is it?"

"That's impossible," Talon scoffed.

"Not necessarily, Your Majesty. Think about it. Cyrus knew what was coming. He knew of Kane's plans. He knew Claire's promise would be difficult for her. An outsider with no knowledge of Dragonwall could hardly hope to achieve what she has. Against many odds, she succeeded. You heard her, he was feeding her information from inside her *mind*."

She listened, wide-eyed, to Verath's explanation, because not only was he fighting for her, but everything he said made so much sense.

"Wait a moment!" Jovari burst out. "The vodar attack! She fought against them as if she were Cyrus himself."

"Jovari's right," Koldis said. "She fought just like him."

"In his final moments Cyrus knew—somehow he knew," Jovari said, eyes wide. "His gift was his final act. It was all he could do to help us."

"It's rather incredible." Bedelth spoke for the first time.

"I suppose it *is* plausible," Talon mused.

They all began speaking at once—

"Excuse me," she shouted, interrupting them. "But is anyone going to tell me what this gift-thing *is*? I'm sure you'd all love to discuss me indefinitely, and by all means, continue after I have left.

But right now, I just want to know what the hell is happening to me?!"

Verath said, "Apologies, Claire. The gift is a rare and ancient magic. Very little is known about it. How many documented cases have there been?" He looked about the room. "Three, perhaps? I am shocked that Cyrus knew enough about it to succeed. Then again, he was always well read." He paused. "The gift is a blessing...of sorts. Cyrus used an act of intimacy to pass his soul to you. In so doing, everything that was bound to him—his magic, his ability to bend minds, his memories—all passed to you."

"What?" She deflated against the sofa, horrorstruck. "How... how is that a *gift*?"

"I suppose the term is a bit ironic."

"You think? So, I've got to live with all this...this stuff *inside* me now?"

"It is not a plague," Talon sneered, affronted. "Cyrus is not some disease you must be subjected to for the remainder of your life. He made a selfless sacrifice, giving up his soul's opportunity to pass into the world beyond."

She stared at him in disbelief.

"If what you say is true, Verath, then Cyrus is not with Leeana." Reyr sounded sad. He was the only other shield to have once had a mate, so he understood the implication. "Cyrus has sacrificed his eternity of happiness for us, so that his soul might remain here longer than it ought."

"I can hardly believe it," Koldis whispered. "Cyrus has truly returned to us."

Reyr stood and came over to her, going down on one knee. He took her hand in his. "All this time," he whispered, studying her face with utter disbelief. Staring at her as if she were someone else entirely. "All this time and you were right here with us."

Her eyebrows scrunched together. Okay, this was getting... weird. She looked up from Reyr and saw that the others were looking at her similarly. She pulled her hand from Reyr's grip. "It's still me in here, you know. I'm still the outsider you all hate so much. I don't think you can simply talk to me as if I'm Cyrus now. It doesn't work that way."

"Perhaps not." Reyr's expression didn't change. "But now we know he's a part of you." He stood and turned to face the king. "You know what this means, Talon."

Talon's face was unreadable. Maybe he regretted the way he'd treated her, knowing Cyrus's soul dwelled in her. That what he'd done was like hurting Cyrus, too.

Talon sighed, his shoulders dropping. "It means a great deal. Claire must be trained. Her abilities will strengthen our odds in the war to come." When his silver eyes fell upon her, they weren't angry anymore. They were hopeful.

"And what of her position?" Koldis came to stand behind her. He placed a hand upon her shoulder. The simple act comforted her.

"She can be a servant no longer." Talon ran his fingers along the mantle. "My attempt to hide her away was going to fail anyway."

She frowned. Hide her away? *That* was his intention?

"The people will resist her," Reyr said. "They will be reluctant to accept an outsider."

"Yes, their reluctance will be severe. There is only one way to mitigate it. I must change her status officially within the court."

Reyr opened and closed his mouth. "Let me be certain I understand you. You would take responsibility for her?" He paused to allow for Talon's interjection, but it did not come. "I admit, I am surprised."

Talon shrugged. "Be surprised, if you must. It is the best way to proceed. I must declare her my ward. The people will have no choice but to accept her. From now on, she will be my responsibility, under the protection of the crown."

Her jaw dropped. "I am not a child to be looked after!" she hissed. "How is this any better than—"

"Claire, you misunderstand," Reyr interrupted. "Becoming King Talon's ward does not peg you as a child. You are a woman grown, after all."

"Then what does it mean?"

"It means that you will be elevated in status, elevated higher than everyone but King Talon himself."

Her eyes widened. "But—"

"It means," Talon cut in, "that you will be royal."

"Royal..." she repeated, allowing the sound to tumble off her tongue like a foreign word. She frowned. *Royal...?!* She burst into hysterical laughter, doubling over in her chair. After everything King Talon had put her through, treating her like a traitor, throwing her in a cell, trying her in court before the elite of the kingdom, forcing her into a torture chamber, subjecting her to servitude, this was the most outlandish thing she could have imagined.

It was simply too much.

Her psychotic laughter died down and she looked up. The others gazed back at her with perplexed expressions. "Excuse me a moment," she said, "I'm just thinking about how lucky I am to become the responsibility of someone who tried to *kill* me."

Her words hit their mark. King Talon turned a dark shade of red. She'd never seen him flustered. Never. He quickly honed his expression. "Accept it," he snapped. "You can start by acting like a lady. That includes watching your tongue when you address your king."

She schooled her features. Was *this* what it would be like? Scolded and rebuked at every turn. "I take it I have no choice in the matter?"

"None whatsoever."

She clenched her jaw and held her tongue, not because the king told her to be lady-like, but because she knew if she opened her mouth now, she was going to get herself into trouble.

"Both of you ought to relax," Reyr said, lifting his hands to diffuse the situation. "Let's all get along. We are not your enemies, Claire."

She flashed Talon an angry glare before turning to Reyr. "So what happens now?"

"Well, the king will announce the changes, but until then you should lay low."

She opened her mouth—

"She will need to begin her training soon," Verath said. "The sooner she learns to control her magic, the better for everyone."

"Agreed," Bedelth said.

"And she ought to be given a better room," Jovari added, crossing his arms, eying her with what looked like mischief.

"And something better to wear." Koldis grinned down at her.

They erupted into a flood of comments and suggestions, each expressing concern over the future and the role she would play. She felt a little lightheaded listening to it. She wasn't certain *how* the king's announcement of her status would go over, but one thing was certain. Everything was about to change.

CHAPTER 56
A CURIOUS PAST

Kastali Dun

Desaree collapsed into an armchair—the only one she owned—her head still spinning from the fight with Caterina. She sat, staring unblinkingly at her chamber's bare wall. What would happen to Claire? Would she be punished for harming someone above her status? And Lord Stefan Rosen, esteemed lower council member, a man who'd once been her stepfather. What of him?

She squeezed her eyes shut, thinking very hard on the affair. The mysterious pieces fit together perfectly. She was familiar with the rumors of his treason, but before today, she had struggled to believe them. He had been missing a fortnight from court—never seen during dinner in the great hall, or passing through the corridors with his lovely daughter dangling on his arm.

She had no choice but to accept the news, that Stefan Rosen had betrayed the king—

There was a knock at her door.

"Desaree, are you in there?" Sarah called. She didn't answer. "Desaree, I know you're there. What is the matter? Tess says you should be helping with dinner."

She cleared her throat. "I...I cannot come. I have taken ill."

"Have you, truly?"

"Indeed. I should not be near the food. Tess will manage without me." She waited for several long breaths. After a long silence, she exhaled, relaxing her shoulders. She pulled her legs up and clutched her knees to her chest, pressing her forehead against them and closing her eyes—

A heavy fist pounded at her door, making her jump.

"I told you!" she shouted. "I have taken ill—!"

"Desaree? Are you in there?"

She jumped to her feet, gasping as she backed away towards the farthest wall. "Lord...Lord Verath?"

"May I come in?"

"Oh, gods!" she whispered, glancing about her chamber. Hot embarrassment flushed her cheeks at the thought of him in her tiny little room.

"Please," he added.

She took a deep breath, settling herself, then opened the door a crack. He stood in the hallway, breathing heavily.

"Gods above," he swore, the moment his eyes landed on her face. He took hold of the door and pushed it open. "Did she do that to you?"

"Uhm...who?"

"Caterina! Gods, woman, who do you think?" Grabbing her hand, he guided her back to the armchair and pressed her into the seat.

She watched him with wide eyes. "What has gotten into you?"

"You're hurt," he snapped. "What do you think?"

"It is nothing more than scratches and wounded pride."

Certainly nothing he needed to rile himself over.

He scowled, taking further liberties with her. His fingers ran down the nail marks, trailing along her neck until he was forced to stop at her neckline. Her skin heated beneath his touch and shivers raced down her back.

His gentleness was unexpected. She turned her face away. This was too much—today had been too much.

"May I?" he asked.

She blinked at him. "May you *what*?"

"Heal them. I can, if you let me."

She shook her head. They would heal just fine on their own. Verath's frown deepened. "Never mind your wishes, I will heal them anyway."

She opened her mouth—

He began muttering, his palm warm against her neck. His eyes were focused. She pressed her lips together as a strange tingling sensation spread over her skin.

"There." He stood and stepped back.

She went to her mirror. "They're gone..." She placed her fingers over her perfectly unmarred skin.

"Why are you frowning?" he rasped. "Are you hurt elsewhere?"

"I'm fine," she said. "You need not fuss over me."

He snatched a small wooden chair from her table, turning it backwards to sit. She tried not to look at the flex of his arms as he placed them atop the chair's back. There were bits of stubble growing on his jaw. She tried not to look at that, too. Tried not to look at every part of him. Sitting here. In her *room*.

"Why does Caterina hate you so much?"

She blinked. "Oh. She has always hated me."

"Explain."

She inhaled. "I would rather not explain anything."

"I insist."

She snorted, rolling her eyes. Of *course* he insisted—

"Did you just—"

"No." Her cheeks colored.

"You did. You rolled your eyes at me."

"You're teasing me. It won't work. I don't want to talk about Caterina."

"Well, that's too godsdamned bad," he growled. "Talk."

She stared at him, at his hard expression. He wasn't going to relent, so she sat down on her cot, within reach of him. "Fine. Caterina and I have history."

"What kind of history?"

She flexed her jaw. "I wasn't always a servant. I used to be a noble." Verath's brow furrowed. He quickly schooled his features. "I do not expect it, but perhaps you have heard the surname Kendall?"

"Kendall…" He hesitated, then blinked. "I have. A line of wealthy merchants, no?"

"That's…yes. I'm what's left of that line."

"You?"

"My father died when I was young—four years old—leaving my mother a dowager."

There was very little to be recalled from that time. Just a single memory of her sobbing in the street, holding her mother's hand while her father's body was ferried away to the cryptons for burial preparations. She told Verath what had happened after that, of how her mother had fallen in love again. How she'd come to her, excited to announce that she would have a father again, and a big sister, too.

"Caterina?"

"Yes." She sniffed. "Before they married I met Caterina. She was two years my senior, just shy of nine. Oh, she was all smiles, all feigned politeness. Everyone loved little Cat. It was an act I learned too late. My mother was married."

Verath's expression softened.

Caterina had been awful. Pulling her hair when no one was looking. Destroying her toys and blaming things on her.

"What happened?"

She shrugged, lifting a shoulder as if to minimize the outcome. "Two years later, my mother fell ill and died."

"She was still young, was she not?" His brows knitted together.

"Thirty-six. A young age to fall ill and die within the span of half a day. The healers hardly had time to see her before her chest was heaving, her mouth frothing, and her eyes rolling."

"That is heavily suspicious, Desaree. Was no mage called for a cure? Did the healer doubt the situation?"

"How was I to know?" she cried, suddenly agitated. "I asked

those same questions that day, and for many days—for many *years* after I left."

"You left? Is that how you came to be here at the keep?"

"No. I did not leave immediately. I was the heir to the Kendall fortune, or so I'd thought."

She'd been nine at the time. She'd known very little of politics, and less still of the cruelness of others, though Caterina had given her a taste. Stefan Rosen's cruelness came after her mother died. She felt tears pooling in her eyes, as words poured out of her mouth.

"Once my mother died, Sir Stefan Rosen, who is now Lord Stefan Rosen, shunned me. He turned a blind eye to Caterina's nastiness. Within months of her death, I was shoved away in the attic, forced to sleep in moldy bedding, forced to wear rags, afforded scraps of old food. If I complained, if I came down into the house, Caterina dragged me away by my hair. Or beat me. One day —" She took a deep breath, struggling to control her tears. "One day, I worked up the courage to demand my inheritance. I was going to leave, but not without it. They could keep the gods-damned house if they wanted. But I? I wanted the rest." A hollow sound dragged from her chest. "I will never forget how he laughed."

"It was taken from you..." Understanding lined Verath's features, but it quickly turned to fury.

"Yes. My wretched stepfather had my mother sign away her fortune and titles to him shortly before she died. I cannot think of what excuse he used to win it."

"So you got nothing."

"Nothing. It was ripped from me—everything was ripped from me." Tears rolled down her cheeks now, but she kept going. "I was not bound to the Rosens, so I left, though I had nowhere to go. I happened upon Tess in the market. Gods! She looked like an angel, showering everyone with smiles, walking along with her basket swinging, skirts billowing, humming a happy tune. She saw me and hastened over, wrapping me in a cloak, offering me food from her basket."

It had been one of the best days in her wretched memory after her mother's death. Tess became something of a mother to her after that. She'd filled that gaping hole.

"Gods." Verath ran a hand through his hair. "Remind me to thank her next time I see her."

She swallowed, then nodded. He reached out to wipe a tear from her cheek, and she shivered at his touch. His hand dropped.

"I thought I would be happy within the keep," she admitted. "I hoped for it. I did not mind servitude. Better that than homelessness. But Caterina could not afford me so much as that. She followed me here."

"Caterina's mage training brought her here. I remember it now. Caterina's father came along too." His nose crinkled in disgust. "I was always surprised by the speed at which Stefan earned his seat in the lower council. I never questioned it then. Seventeen is old for a person to discover magical abilities. Saffra discovered hers at the age of eight. I wonder…"

She frowned. "What?"

"Nothing." He stood and began pacing. "Those two have caused you enough grief, Desaree. You need not fret any longer over their doings."

"Please, Verath. Do sit down. Tell me—what of Lord Stefan Rosen? I have shared my secrets with you. You know of my right to the information. What has happened?"

He sat and reached for her hand, a gesture that surprised her. Taking her fingers, he laced them with his. It calmed her, but she reclaimed her hand; she would not have him avoid the truth.

"There are some things that are better left undiscussed."

"It is true then? He betrayed the king?"

"Aye. He and another. I will not utter that man's name, either. You may consider your previous stepfather as good as dead."

Her eyes grew wide. "What did he do?"

Verath gazed at her for the span of several breaths, studying her face with his keen eyes. "Perhaps it is unfair to hide the truth. If anyone deserves to hear it, you have earned that right." He shifted in his seat. "You have heard about the new threat to the north, yes? The wild dragons?"

She nodded, though she still struggled to believe it.

"The dragons are under the control of a sorcerer named Kane. He's powerful. So powerful that he turned Stefan Rosen into a puppet to do his bidding. He has been pulling Rosen's strings for some time—who knows how long. Perhaps the man was already under his control before he moved into the keep. Or—"

"Or perhaps the sorcerer offered Caterina magical powers as a means to get them into the keep," she gasped, covering her mouth in shock. A theory took form in her mind. "What if—what if he somehow granted her magical abilities as a payment for her father's loyalty?" Blood rushed past her ears as her heart raced. "You did say it was strange that she discovered her abilities at the late age of seventeen."

Verath was very, very quiet. She waited for him to say something. In her mind she began sifting through her memories. What would this sorcerer look like? Had she seen a strange man visit the home while she was with the Rosens? It was difficult to recall.

"You catch on fast." His fingers drummed on the chair's back. "I cannot say if the theory is correct. But...it certainly holds merit."

"If it is true," she said, "then Caterina is as guilty as her father."

"Aye. She would be considered a traitor. The king hates her, to be sure. But he had not planned to take action against her."

"Why not?"

Verath sighed. "It would be a sad world if children were punished for the crimes of their parents."

"I suppose you're right."

"However,"—Verath held up a finger to emphasize his point—"if we can prove your theory correct, if Caterina indeed came by her abilities through Kane's doing, then it would be enough to convict her. At this moment, she remains a mage in training."

"You cannot take her into custody now? Ask questions later?"

Verath grunted. "Can you imagine what the people would think? Remember, Caterina is favored among the court. Many wished for her to marry King Talon, even."

"But you could tell them—you could explain that she was working with Kane." Her frustration was growing. It was not in her nature to be vindictive, but she wasn't doing this for revenge over her mistreatment. She was doing this to protect the kingdom. "Besides, you took Claire into custody, pronouncing her guilty before knowing her story."

"That is different. Claire was an outsider. The king was not in his right mind."

She deflated and shook her head. "I apologize. I know the king and his shields—you—will get to the bottom of this, hopefully quickly. I hate to think of the chaos a woman like Caterina might cause."

"Indeed. Now that I understand her history, I can take action." Once more, he took her hand in both of his. This time, she let him. Her heart thumped as she gazed into his eyes.

Her emotions deepened as the silence settled between them. She tried to make sense of her feelings. Make sense of what she felt. Was it gladness, to know that a man she hated would finally receive his just desserts? Anger, over the possibility of Caterina's crimes? Relief, that the secrets of her past were now known by someone she admired? It took several fresh tears sliding down her cheeks before she realized what it was. It was all of those things.

Verath scooped her into his arms, sitting down with her upon the cot, holding her against him, rocking her back and forth. His efforts made her shed more tears. It felt good to cry—good to release everything burning within her.

Verath brushed his fingers through her hair. "There now," said he, pulling away to look at her face. "Feel better?"

"Yes," she sighed, snuggling deeper into his arms. Gods, it felt good. He tucked her head under his chin. For once, she ignored everything in her mind about who he was, his titles, his position.

Claire would be so proud—

She stiffened. Fresh panic filled her. "Verath, what is going to happen to Claire?"

"You needn't worry about her. She'll be fine." His voice was ever so calm—*too* calm.

"You mean, she will not suffer punishment?"

"Not at all." She exhaled. "Moreover, you need not fear Caterina any longer, Desaree. No matter what happens, she will never hurt you again. This I promise."

Her shoulders relaxed. The thought of never suffering from Caterina's treatment again, was almost too difficult to fathom. She was tempted to question it. But she reminded herself that Verath was a shield. She trusted him. So she squeezed her eyes shut, vaguely aware of the smile pulling at her lips. Despite the darkness behind her eyelids, the world appeared much brighter than it had in a very, very long time.

CHAPTER 57
BLOCKING THE VOICES

Kastali Dun

Claire watched Reyr pace back and forth. She didn't stop him. She was too enamored with her surroundings. The main room of her new suite was an opulent sitting and dining room stuffed with plush couches, oversized arm chairs, little end tables topped with flower vases, a dining table, and a marble fireplace. The far wall was made of glass windows and doors that opened outward to a terraced balcony overlooking the sea.

A second chamber was located through a wide set of double doors; this housed her sleeping accommodations. A massive four-poster bed with cream and gold fabric—to match the upholstery in the main room—and end tables. There was also a large walk-in closet, currently empty, but capable of holding more gowns than she could possibly count.

At the back of the bedroom, another set of double doors led to the final chamber. A bathroom of marble and pearlescent tile. Not only was there a private pit toilet, but her own bathing pool. It was heated like all the other bathing pools in the keep, with water that circulated, pushing out the dirty and pulling in the clean.

A knock brought Reyr's pacing to a halt. She stood, but he beat her to the door, motioning for her to sit. Scowling, she followed orders.

"Claire's dinner, m'lord," came a servant's voice. Her shoulders fell when it wasn't Desaree's. She'd wanted to visit her, to make sure she was okay, but Reyr had forbidden it.

Reyr took the tray with the contents of their dinner to the table. "I imagine you're hungry?" he asked.

"Famished," she said, in the time it took her to reach his side. After serving herself and scarfing down a few bites, she added, "I want to go see Desaree tonight. I want to go check on her."

"We've been through this. The king wants you out of sight for the next few days until this whole debacle blows over, until he can inform the council and court of your new position."

She ground her teeth together. "I don't like being a prisoner, Reyr."

"A prisoner? Gods, Claire. You have one of the largest accommodations in the keep. You'll manage for a couple of days." She glared at him and he sighed. "You're worried about Desaree, I get that. Verath has already informed me that she is fine. Shaken up, but fine." He lifted his goblet and leaned back to watch her, his food untouched. "Besides, I thought you wanted to spend tonight practicing to block the drengr voices, do you not?"

"You're mad that I didn't tell the king about my ability, aren't you?"

The creases in his forehead immediately disappeared. "What makes you think that?"

She rolled her eyes. "I know you. And besides, I told you that I would tell him, just not yet." She set her fork down. "Look, I *do* want to practice tonight, if you're willing to help me."

"Good. Finish your food and we will get started."

"You know, you've gotten pretty bossy lately." She crossed her arms and glared at him. "Like, this whole not letting me leave my room business."

He dragged a hand over his eyes. "I am only following orders. I know you do not like being bossed around, especially by King Talon. Please do not treat me like the enemy."

She exhaled, feeling immediately guilty. "Sorry," she mumbled, lifting her fork to push at the remainder of her food. "It's been a really long day."

"Yes, it has, hasn't it? You have gone from outsider to servant to royal. From believing yourself ordinary to discovering you are extraordinary."

Extraordinary. Her stomach swooped at the sound of that word. At what it might mean.

"Now, finish up. I am going to run to my room and retrieve something. Then we can get started."

Reyr was back a few minutes later with a small leather book, which he plopped down on the table before her. She studied it, picking it up and flipping through its pages.

"It looks like a journal of some sort," she said. The scrolling handwriting was archaic, but legible.

"Correct. It took me a few days to find that, and quite a lot of convincing to borrow it."

"Whose is it?"

"It belongs to Marcel, but it was once the property of Grand Mage Orin's."

"And who was *he*?"

"The first grand mage. His fascination with the drengr, a newly created race, led him to conduct extensive research about their existence. He specifically focused on their telepathic abilities because the idea of telepathy during the early years of the drengr was foreign to anyone of non-draconic origins. Even new riders found it utterly perplexing that they could converse with their mates."

"Huh." She scowled down at the book.

"Many in the society were envious of our propensity for communication. Still are. It is a useful capability."

She snorted. "Useful unless you can hear all of them and are rewarded with headaches because of it."

"It is said," Reyr added, "that many of the asarlaí sorcerers possessed the ability. So did some of the sprites."

"Like Queen Isabella?" She perked up.

"Ah, yes. Queen Isabella *could* communicate with those of draconic blood, but not like you. You are...unique."

Unique...

"Because I can hear all of them even when they don't intend for it?"

"Exactly." Reyr sat and watched her with curious eyes, like he was still trying to figure her out—something he'd been doing since their first meeting. Knowing what Cyrus had done, and that Cyrus did everything with intention, hinted that she was meant for some unknown purpose. He appeared desperate to discover it.

"So, do you think there is a chance I might block the voices out? Will this journal help?"

He blinked, then exhaled. "I had hoped it would, but the explanations are vague. I imagine Orin never succeeded in his quest for telepathy."

She glanced through its pages, but there didn't appear to be a miraculous solution. Most of Orin's interviews with various drengr said that the ability was innate and intuitive. At last, she set it aside and decided the best way to tackle this was to simply practice. So, Reyr set about sending her thoughts while she did what was *supposed* to be instinctive—block him out. Except, it never worked, and she only grew frustrated.

"Maybe we are going about this all wrong," she exhaled, long after darkness had fallen, when the candles burned lower in their holders.

"How so?"

"Well, when you try to explain how to block the drengr, you can't, because instincts aren't something that can be explained."

Instinct requires no thought, Cyrus said, speaking for the first time. *You must simply believe you can do it.*

Her mouth fell open.

Reyr scowled at her. "What?"

"Cyrus! He said...but, of course! Why didn't I think of it before?"

"Cyrus?" Reyr perked up, leaning forward in his chair. The eagerness in his expression broke her heart.

"Cyrus said that I shouldn't overthink this. That it requires no thought. That I must simply believe I can do it." Reyr grunted. The wheels of her mind were spinning. "Whenever I do it, I'm always *trying* to do it. Probably trying *too* hard."

Reyr blew out a breath. "I am so envious of your ability to converse with him." He slumped back in his chair. Her heart tightened and she felt an urge to give him a hug, but instead, she stayed seated. "Anyway, his advice does not really explain how to do it."

"What Cyrus meant—I think—is that I must *believe* I can do it. It's a confidence thing, don't you see? Because it's instinctual to be able to do it, you take it for granted."

She worried at her lower lip. There were plenty of things innate in nature—reactions to stimuli that happened outside of thoughtful control.

"Like, when you do it, you simply choose to ignore the voices and your body knows *how* to do it. You don't have to think about it. You don't force it. You just do it because you know you can."

Her heart began beating a little faster. The voices had plagued her so often. Was there ever a time that she simply relaxed and accepted them? No, she fought them at every turn. The aegan helped relax her, and that dialed the noise down to an ebb.

Reyr watched her but said nothing.

Preparing for another attempt, she rolled her shoulders and rotated her neck, easing her tense muscles. *Cyrus, I'm going to need your help on this one,* she said, hoping he listened, but mostly because she was offering up a prayer to him the way one would the gods. Taking a deep breath, she focused on her breathing as if she were meditating. Closing her eyes, she let the darkness comfort her. She could do this because Cyrus was there. He was a drengr, and all drengr knew how to block telepathic voices. If he could do it, and his soul was truly with her, then she could do it too.

"Okay, I'm ready," she whispered. She kept her eyes closed. Keeping her mind relaxed, she waited. She could *do* this. She knew she could. So she sat there, confidently waiting. "Whenever you're ready," she added, peeling open an eye to glare at him.

Reyr's forehead furrowed. *"You did not hear the thought I sent?"*

"I heard that one."

"But the first?" he asked.

"What first?" She sat up straighter. "What did you say? Wait—it worked?!" she shrieked.

A grin stole across his face. "It must have. You did not hear my comment about the time—about it getting late?"

She shook her head. "No. Do it again. Say something else."

They practiced several more times. Just like before, she didn't force it. She accepted that her desire to block voices was intrinsic, that if she wanted it, it would happen. Each time he failed to say something in her mind, a little brightness, a little more hope, seeped back into her.

"It's working!" she gasped after their fourth success. It was hard to tell how much of her victory came from Cyrus and how much came from herself. Did it even matter? The fragments of his existence were with her now, and she had better get used to it.

"I think we have made good progress for tonight," he said, finally calling an end to it. It was well past midnight. "I admit I had not expected such rapid results. Then again, you never cease to amaze me." His voice was soft.

"Do you think Cyrus helped me?" she asked.

"Who can say?" The side of his mouth twitched. "But I like to think he's in there helping you."

He stood and made his way towards the door, but she was too excited to sleep yet. "Reyr? Do you think you could stay a little longer?"

"You ought to get some sleep. As should I. Tomorrow we execute Rosen and Doyle. It will be a long day." She gave him a hard stare. "Very well," he relented. Refilling his goblet, he left her for the balcony.

She followed after him, inhaling the salty sea breeze. The darkness below was lit with tiny dots from the ships coming and going. They gazed out into the night, silent.

Tomorrow, the kingdom's traitors would die. Her throat went dry. It was difficult to put into words the way she felt. She'd *loved* Cyrus. He'd been taken from the world way too early, so unfairly. The men involved with Kane deserved their punishment. Still, she never liked death. Knowing that she was responsible for sending them to theirs was a strange responsibility to bear.

She blinked away her thoughts, letting the presence of the ocean calm her. The breeze whispered over the cliffs below, and beyond that, she could discern the faint ringing of bells at the dockyards. Even now, there were ships coming and going, unloading and loading their goods.

The empty void beyond her hid the complexity of Dragonwall's world, disguising the inevitable future that awaited it, a future she was now bound to through Cyrus. The subtle sounds and smells were a facade for the chaos that was sure to come. She sighed, taking it all in.

"Considering what awaits us," she said to Reyr, "sometimes I feel like running away." He turned to her. Even in the darkness, she could see his surprise. "Sometimes I am tempted to slip away in secret, cowardly as it is. Going back home seems easier than what we must confront."

"You are not alone, Claire. You have us. You have Cyrus. Nor are you to believe that the future's burdens are yours to bear. We are all in this together."

She shrugged. "What if I'm not supposed to be involved at all? Dragonwall isn't my home."

His brows lifted. "Isn't it?"

She opened her mouth but stopped. Was it? Despite all the challenges she had faced, something about this place felt...right. "Maybe you're correct," she admitted at last. "Maybe this is more my home than I realized."

That both scared and thrilled her.

"From the moment I met you, Claire, I have noticed strange things about you, a few of them easily explained by the gift. But what about your ability to hear the drengr? That was no result of

Cyrus. You heard my voice before he breathed his last. That alone means the gods have given you a purpose. Did Cyrus know of your destiny? Did he see your importance? I like to think that he did. And then," he added, "what about the Gable Forest?"

Her mind was suddenly filled with longing as it swept back to Esterpine. "I miss it," she breathed. "I want to go back. I never wanted to leave."

"See? Don't you find that strange? You alone located the spriten stronghold. Perhaps Jovari and Koldis did not question it, but I did."

"What are you saying?" She feared his answer.

"Cyrus knew something we did not. The bonds of this world are tied tightly around you, perhaps tighter than any of us realize."

With that, they both fell silent.

She placed her forearms against the terrace and leaned over it until her hair hung down. It stretched towards the white foam created by the collision of saltwater against rock. That's how she felt, she realized, watching the sea spray.

What did Cyrus know that she didn't? What had he seen in Saffra's mind? Saffra believed she was meant to defeat Kane based on a mere vision. The training necessary to get to that level of magic seemed impossible. Not to mention frightening. Kane was the only person who scared her more than Talon did.

"It isn't going to be easy, is it?" she said at last.

"Life is always difficult before it is easy, Claire." Reyr turned. He took her hand and kissed her knuckles before dropping it. "But, it is life's challenges that allow us to grow."

He retreated back into her chambers. She snorted before following after him. He stood near the door.

"You're starting to sound like Cyrus, you know."

The side of his mouth twitched. "I am afraid I must leave you now." His hand was on the doorknob.

"Thank you for staying with me today, and for keeping my secret. I know it goes against what you are, your honor, all that. I hope you know I appreciate it, and your willingness to help me."

Reyr had become her rock.

He nodded. "You're welcome, Claire. Good night." And with that, he disappeared out into the corridor, quietly closing the door behind him.

CHAPTER 58
A NEW PROMISE

Kastali Dun

Claire greeted the day with a groggy groan. The morning was already half over when she rose. After sleepily stumbling through her apartments, she found breakfast waiting on her dining table. Out of curiosity she checked her chamber door.

Locked.

Reyr must have been by. This was his way of ensuring she did not disobey orders. She exhaled. He knew her too well.

She shrugged it off and went about eating, then bathing, all the while deep in thought.

It was the morning of the execution and the weather matched the mood. Overcast and gloomy. Maybe it was good that she wasn't allowed out of her chambers. She glanced at the door, frowning. Perhaps King Talon had sequestered her in here for more than one reason.

Part of her *wanted* to see the traitors beheaded. They deserved it, after all. But their deaths wouldn't bring her closure.

She wandered around her suite, studying it in detail, examining the trinkets on the mantle, looking over the titles on the book-

513

shelves. She went out on her terrace balcony, gazing out over the water. Then her restless feet carried her to her bed. She plopped down with her legs crossed, trying to think, to better understand what she was supposed to do with herself, with her new life, with the gift Cyrus had given her.

Closing her eyes, she said, *Cyrus? I need to speak with you.* His presence was always unpredictable. There was no guarantee he'd answer. *Cyrus,* she tried again. *You said you would always be with me. I need you now. Like, I really, really need you.*

Something tightened in her chest. She swallowed down the lump rising in her throat. It was a miracle she'd held together this long. That she hadn't broken down *once* since yesterday's discovery.

Her foundations had been shaken. There was something more to her, something deeper that made her question everything about herself, about the person she thought she knew. Sure, she was still stubborn, spunky, and headstrong. What about beyond that?

Of its own volition, her mind swept back to her beloved porch swing, back to the day she and Cyrus sat sipping tea together. He was showing her something. A small smile crept to her lips as she watched the memory.

Who were you then? Cyrus asked.

"I was naive," she whispered, snorting. "A silly, overwhelmed girl with wanderlust for a place that seemed impossible. A place *you* called Dragonwall."

But you were also brave and noble, he added. *Why else did you choose to rescue the beast that fell from the sky? To save my life?*

The scene continued to unfold. They swung back and forth. Cyrus spoke to her, his pain evident in his expression, his fear evident in his eyes. He knew he wouldn't live long. She recognized it now. Why hadn't she seen it then?

You needed me to become the new protector, she observed, *but I was too scared to acknowledge that responsibility. Too afraid to admit you might actually die.*

Yes, responsibility is difficult for everyone, he said. *Even when it's staring them right in the face.* He sounded both understanding and regretful, but that didn't change the sting of his words. *The only way to discover who you truly are, is to stay here and figure it out.*

Does figuring it out have something to do with the vision Saffra saw of me defeating Kane?

Ahh... he said, chuckling. *You want to know if I saw your future in Saffra's mind.*

Of course I want to know. She got up from her bed, opening the doors that led to her terrace. The sea breeze swept across her skin. She gazed out over the open ocean. Dragonwall was beautiful, but no matter how much everyone claimed she belonged, she missed her old home, her parents, her friends.

Will you tell me? she asked at last. *I deserve the truth, don't you think?*

Truth never makes things easier, but I will tell you anyway. I never saw your future. I only saw your potential, your heart, your goodness, and your importance. It was enough.

Her chest tightened and her hands dropped to her sides. She'd been convinced that some inescapable destiny awaited her, and that Cyrus had seen it all. That he'd chosen her because of it. A tiny laugh bubbled up from her chest.

Your old life awaits you, he told her. *If you so choose, you may go back. But Dragonwall would be a lesser place without you, in so many ways. Would you leave it to its fate?*

The possibility of returning home vanished like a sinking boat. Pressure returned to her chest, as if she were on it as it dragged her down. She looked upward and saw nothing but water, with only a glint of sunshine. It was too far for her to swim to the surface.

She wasn't the only one drowning.

A tear freed itself, falling down her cheek. She angrily wiped it away. Cyrus had given her the gift of his soul when he could have passed peacefully into the other realm. Now he was stuck with her, and if she went back home, she'd be taking him out of the world he'd known his entire life.

Do not worry about me, he told her. *Worry about yourself. Discover who you are and the secrets of your ancient blood.* Chills spread across her skin. *Together, you and I will defeat Kane. But only if you understand yourself and what you can truly do.*

She blinked, stunned.

Cyrus, what...what are you saying? Panic seeped into her. But he didn't need to make it any clearer. She struggled to breathe. Cyrus poured strength and understanding into her.

Claire, no one is ever ready to do what fate asks of them. We do not get to choose our destiny. It finds us, just like I found you. Do you ever wonder why it was your cornfield I fell into? Why it was you who rescued me when anyone else could have been watching?

Of course she'd wondered! Not a day went by when she wasn't asking, "*Why me?*"

Destiny gives us purpose, Cyrus added. *Destiny gives us a place in the world. It gives us an existence. Your destiny is simply more monumental than others. You cannot ignore it. That would be a travesty.*

So...I have no choice? she asked.

There is always a choice. One way or another, you must face the obstacles placed before you. That is how you come to know your true self. Only then will you truly answer the heaviest questions upon your heart.

"And in so doing, I will discover who I am, " she whispered aloud. As she spoke, she heard the faint sounds of a cheering crowd.

You wanted answers about your identity. All that remains is your decision. Will you chase your destiny and discover your true self? Or will you return home, never knowing if you might have saved a dying kingdom? There is always a choice.

She took a deep, unsteady breath. There might have been a choice, but she had already made hers. "If this is my destiny, then I accept it."

And therein lies the reason this is your *destiny and not another's. Although you have decided, fate knew your answer long before you gave it. And I knew it too, else I never would have made you promise.*

The promise.

She scoffed. Everything always came back to it. She shook her head, incredulous to how this had played out, how it had circled back around. Her new life had started with a promise. It would finish with one too.

Her mouth felt dry, but she knew what she had to do. Taking a deep breath, she said to the wind and the sea, "I, Claire Evans, make a new unbreakable promise. I promise to avenge Cyrus's death. I promise to kill the sorcerer who calls himself Kane. In so doing, I will see the kingdom restored to its full glory. I promise this with all my heart. I will fulfill this task with the power entrusted to me, or die trying."

The moment she closed her mouth, her body began to tingle. It recognized the magic she'd called upon, that Cyrus had helped her weave again. At that same instant, the world around her gave witness. The seagulls squawked as they flew past the cliffs. The sea crashed upon the rocks beneath her. The wind picked up frantically, whistling past her ears. The world responded. It spoke to her, saying, *It is done; you have promised, and the fate of Dragonwall goes with you.*

CHAPTER 59
THE EXECUTION

Kastali Dun

Reyr stood as motionless and unmovable as stone, hands clasped behind his back. His fellow shields stood upon the platform beside him, and before them, King Talon. Everything was ready: the high block, the axe, the executioner, and the crowd. All that remained was the spectacle.

He turned his gaze to the threatening sky before bringing it down upon the gathered crowd. Hundreds stood waiting. The rich and the poor. It didn't matter who they were, they were here. Though, it should have. There were some people who probably shouldn't witness a gruesome thing like this. Especially the children. Even *they* appeared eager for entertainment.

Cries from the peddlers of, "Buns for sale! Three steelies each! Cheap ale, too!" rang through the air. Beheadings were good for business, at least.

He thought of Claire in the keep, glad she wasn't here to see this. He'd locked her door, knowing how stubborn she was. What if that hadn't been enough? He glanced through the sea of faces, looking for her green eyes and blond hair. Then he snorted at his

518

paranoia. He'd used more than a key to ensure her door would not open.

Gemma would have approved. *Gods*! She'd been on his mind more than usual as of late. Hundreds of years had allowed her name to sink into the depths of his soul. Claire's sudden appearance had unburied it—

"Make way!" A gruff, commanding voice lifted above the rest. Captain Jon Henry appeared. He was an older fellow, not that his age hindered him. He was well seasoned, having lived through the goblin wars, and commanded the keep's guard with honor.

"In the name of the king—I say—make way!" He led his guards forward through the crowd as if in battle. Their shields and spears pressed and pushed, vying for space. At last the onlookers fell back and an aisle formed. The traitors were led through. These weren't the first traitors Captain Henry led to the chopping block, but they might have been the worst.

While their faces were covered with black sacks, their bodies were naked, illustrating their shame.

He clenched his jaw. The *true* shame was, Doyle and Rosen could not appreciate the gravity of the situation. They would not despair. They would not weep during their last moments. They would not pay a fair price for their deceit. There wasn't enough of them left.

As they passed through the crowd, the gathered masses screamed gleefully. They pointed. They laughed. They snarled and called. Little good it did.

He wanted this done and over.

Guards filed on to the platform. The noise rose to new heights as the naked, faceless men were presented to the crowd. Still, he did not move. King Talon stepped forward, lifting his hands. A hush fell upon the crowd. "Citizens of the crown," he cried, his voice echoing. The city's square—where all public executions took place—was surrounded by buildings on all sides. "There are *traitors* in our midst!"

Disgusted echoes of, "Traitor!" and, "Kill them!" followed his pronouncement.

"These men have betrayed us, and in so doing, betrayed the gods. What is the just punishment for their crimes?"

"Death!" a loud voice cried. "Death!" others repeated, taking up the chant.

King Talon allowed them to continue, turning instead to the executioner. He gave Sir Boris Patrice a nod. The gnarled man stepped forward, positioning himself beside the high block. Patrice had seen enough fighting for a lifetime, earning his position fairly. Reasonable men turned down the opportunity to kill. Not Patrice. He *enjoyed* killing, even enjoyed torturing when the need came. Perhaps the king liked him more for it, and for the eyepatch disguising the empty socket where his left eye once was, and for his missing left ear, and for his missing forefinger.

With a simple flick of a wrist, Euen Doyle was brought forward. The guards positioned him before the block. "Kneel," came the command. Doyle did not respond. "I said, *kneel.*" The guard did not wait for a response this time. He put his boot into Doyle's knees, forcing the man down, positioning Doyle's head over the block.

"A traitor deserves no last words," King Talon said.

The chant of *Death!* continued.

The king looked at Patrice, affording him a brief nod. The executioner reached forward and removed the sack upon Doyle's head. Then he heaved his axe high in the air, disguising its weight with an effortless, practiced movement. In a single, sweeping stroke, the axe came down. The thud of Doyle's head went unheard as it fell and rolled the wooden planks. The cheers of the crowd were too loud. Doyle's head rolled forward once, and then twice, before coming to a stop. His unseeing eyes held no shock.

And so ended the life of the first traitor.

As quickly as before, Rosen was brought forth. "Kneel," commanded the guard. Perhaps Rosen was more coherent. He followed the order. The guard pushed his body forward positioning him upon the block. Patrice took his position once more. A hush fell over the crowd for a second time. Even the pigeons could no longer be heard—

"Mercy!" An anguished cry drew everyone's attention. "Mercy, my king. Mercy!" Reyr gazed out over the crowd, his brow furrowed. Whispers followed as a woman staggered forward, pushing her way through to the front. Lady Caterina.

"Mercy, Your Majesty," she cried again as she ascended the steps of the platform and stumbled up them like a drunkard, tripping upon her gown. Her face was streaked with tears. King Talon did not move. Perhaps he was too shocked.

"Please!" Caterina threw herself down before the king, sobbing into his boot. "Please, Your Majesty. Spare him. Give him mercy!"

The king's face hardened. He turned and motioned towards the guards. Two rushed forward, dragging Caterina to her feet. She continued to weep. King Talon then addressed her. "Do you not see, Lady Caterina? What I offer your father *is* mercy."

"No!" she said, still crying silent tears as the guards kept her upright. "Have you no room in your heart to hear my plea? Have you no affection for me whatsoever? I beg of you, mercy!"

Reyr snorted under his breath.

"Affection? Hardly. Now, stand down." With a second nod, the guards dragged her backwards. She was forced to watch.

"Father!" She cried out desperately. Rosen recognized her voice, somehow, despite his lost mind. He straightened, lifting his chest to look around, unseeing.

"Get back down, you!" Rosen's guard pushed his chest back into place. The king gave the order. Patrice pulled the sack away then lifted his massive axe high in the air. He brought it down, hard. Caterina's piercing shriek was hardly audible. The screams of the crowd weighed more. The moment her father's head struck the wooden platform, the guards released her. She fell into a heap of fabric upon the planks of the platform, her gown fluffed around her. There she sobbed, ignored by all...her lowest moment yet.

He frowned. A daughter should never see her father's death, no matter the reason, no matter how well deserved. His heart did not break for her, but his honor did. Those around him began to dispense. He went to her, helping her to her feet. Then he looked up. "You there," he said, motioning for two guards to assist him.

"Take this lady back to her chambers. See that she has what she needs."

When he turned, he noticed Verath's intent gaze upon him. His fellow shield stood scowling. "What? Was I wrong to take pity upon her?"

"Your pity is earned all too easily," Verath said, "especially for her." With that, Verath turned and walked off. He was left to puzzle out the meaning, frowning.

He blinked, then quickly escaped the platform to catch up. "What have you learned, then?"

Verath shrugged. "Something that disturbs me. I will bring it to the king's attention."

"And must I wait until you do?"

"Aye. I would like to do a little digging of my own first." Verath increased his pace to leave Reyr behind.

Well, then.

When he returned to the keep, he went straight to the cookery. "Tess, where might I find Desaree?"

"My Lord Reyr, do I look like a homing pigeon to you?"

He smirked. "Hardly, my dear Tess. You are far too beautiful."

Tess crossed her arms, pretended to be mad for only a moment, and then smiled her famous, radiant smile. "Oh, very well. She is assigned to the north wing. You will find her there."

"Excellent. I hope you do not mind if I borrow her for the afternoon. Also, might I get a tray of food? Whatever you have on hand. I think Claire might be hungry."

"You are full of requests today, My Lord," she said. The woman might as well have been a noble. Everyone within the keep knew not to cross her. "But I'm feeling generous today, given the circumstances." She bustled off, assembling a generous portion of cold pork, buns, cheese, and honey.

"You are too good to me, Tess." As he took the tray, he kissed each of her cheeks affectionately, then departed.

He found Desaree and informed her of his intentions. Together, they departed for Claire's chambers. "She has been begging to see you," he said. "I disallowed it yesterday, but I believe she would be glad to have your company today."

"Indeed, I had hoped to see her. I found her room empty yesterday, emptied of all its belongings. Lord Verath assured me she would be fine, but I still worried she was taken away. Taken…"

"Lord Verath came to see you, did he?" His question left her skin a deep shade of red. "Come now, you need not fret. And yes, Claire is fine. A little shaken up, I imagine. But I will let her tell you what happened."

They stopped before Claire's door and he offered Desaree the tray. After muttering words of magic, he lifted its guard. Then he procured a key from his pocket and unlocked the knob. "We had better knock first," he said, lifting his fist. Then he took back the tray.

Claire greeted them moments later. Her eyes fell upon him first, and then Desaree. She rushed into the hall and gave the serving woman a long hug. "Oh, Des! I was so worried!"

Affording them space, he went to her dining table and deposited the tray. Then he collected the one from that morning. Claire entered with Desaree, pulling her into the room. "I have so much to tell you," she said. Desaree's eyes were wide as her gaze circled Claire's new accommodations.

He cleared his throat, not minding in the slightest that they ignored him. "I have brought you your midday meal. I will leave the two of you alone. Remember, Claire, do not leave this room until the king has removed your restriction."

"You're not going to stay and eat with us?"

"No, not today. This afternoon's court begins shortly."

"Can't you skip today?" she asked. It was a half-hearted request. Clearly she wanted Desaree's company to herself.

"Not today." He turned and left, closing the door behind him. The sounds of their giggles followed him down the hall. He couldn't have stayed even had he wanted to.

CHAPTER 60
A BEAUTIFUL DISTRACTION

Kastali Dun

Talon drummed his fingers upon the armrest of Dragonwall's throne. Its white marble was smooth under his skin, its finish as glossy as the day he'd taken up his rule. The throne was the pinnacle of the great keep. Dragonwall's kings would come and go, but it would *never* change.

If only he could say the same about his current circumstances.

Mathis shuffled in front of the crowd, calling for silence. An eager hush fell. "There will be no petitions today," he announced, unrolling a scroll to read from. "By order of King Talon, the outsider known as Claire Evans, who has demonstrated *unquestionable* magical abilities, is to become his royal ward."

The cries were immediate. Not just from the crowd. Lord Layton Raffe jumped to his feet. "Magic, you say? Bah! I oppose this decree!"

Talon clenched his teeth. Raffe had *always* opposed her. Remnants of the seeds planted by Doyle and Rosen, no doubt.

"Lord Raffe," the steward sputtered, "the topic is not yet open for discussion! You are speaking out of turn—"

"Out of turn?" Raffe cut in, raising his voice, "There is no discussion! I'll not have it! Not while I sit upon the council."

More muttering from the courtiers.

Reyr stood, calmly facing Raffe with his stony expression. "*Raffe*, the steward has not yet opened the discussion. You are indeed out of turn. If you cannot uphold court rules, then yes, you are indeed welcome to step down from the council. In case you have forgotten, two positions are currently open. Why not make it three?"

Raffe turned a deep shade of purple and sank back into his chair with a huff. Reyr turned to the other council members, sitting in both boxes to the sides of the dais. "Any further protests? Good." He held his hand out for Mathis to continue.

"Thank you, Lord Reyr. As I was saying..." He cleared his throat. "As the king's ward, *Lady* Claire will undergo magical training by the mages. She will assimilate into our way of life. She will no longer be an outsider, but a citizen of Dragonwall. She is to be respected and treated as such." With that, he rolled up his scroll.

The hall was deathly silent.

He paused before saying, "Lords and ladies, the floor is now open for discussion. Those wishing to voice concerns may bring forth *constructive* arguments." He directed a glare towards Raffe. "Once all voices have been heard, the king will make his final decision."

Final decision. Talon snorted under his breath.

Lord Ashton Wyndham was the first to stand. "I would like to argue against this decree, Your Majesty." Talon did not answer. "I have not seen the evidence of Claire's magic. Have any of you?" He looked around the throne room, at the courtiers. They afforded him the courtesy of shaking their heads. "I thought not. Your Majesty, rumors spurred by yesterday's events between the serving girl, Claire, and Lady Caterina, are mere embellishments, surely. Surely we are not basing this decree on a mere squabble."

Talon looked at Wyndham and calmly said, "Thank you for your *dignified* argument, Lord Wyndham. While rumors can easily be misconstrued, I am completely certain that magic was indeed performed."

The lord swallowed. "Forgive me, Your Majesty, but did you *see* her perform magic? With your own eyes? Did your shields? No lord or lady that I know, aside from Lady Caterina, can lay claim to such." He paused briefly. "The servants that gathered in the corridors...well...we know how servants like to talk." A number of hearty chuckles followed his comment.

Talon sighed. "No, Lord Wyndham. I did not see any magic. Your point is taken. However, it was Lord Reyr who ought to speak on the matter, for he arrived shortly after it happened."

Reyr stood. "I did not see Claire perform any magic, Lord Wyndham. I arrived too late. Regardless of this, we have unequivocal evidence. Claire is indeed in possession of magic, though untrained."

"Very well." Lord Wyndham respectfully took his seat.

Other council members presented their arguments. Claire was an outsider, how could she possibly deserve an elevated position? Jealousy. She was ignorant of Dragonwall's ways, how could she honor such a position? Ignorance could be corrected. She was out of control, look how she'd reacted when provoked? But magical control could be learned.

Each argument received a just explanation, and he found himself growing bored.

When Lord Glover stood, he braced himself, and his daydreams of flying faded. Gods, how he detested Glover. "Your Majesty, I have heard every argument and my stance remains unchanged. You argue that Claire has the makings of a mage. Mere hearsay will not do! I demand solid proof—"

"You wish me to bring her here, Lord Glover? You wish me to force her to perform for you like a circus animal? Is it a show you seek?" He'd not forgotten their previous quarrel over Glover's ungrateful wife.

Glover sputtered. "Not...*necessarily*, Your Majesty. If Claire indeed possesses these abilities, perhaps someone of magical expertise ought to attest to your claim before we go and turn her into royalty?"

"Aye!" came a few echoes of agreement.

"Of course. How could your king's word *possibly* be enough?" Talon said, his gaze narrowed—

"I can attest to her abilities." A throaty, feminine voice silenced the room. Lady Saffra, who for some reason was *not* sitting with her fellow council members, pushed her way to the front of the crowd. She was disguised beneath the hood of a cloak, which she removed as she came forward. Realization of her identity swept the room. The grand mage trailed behind her.

"Steward," Saffra said. "May I speak?"

"Of course, Lady Saffra."

She nodded and said, "I have seen Claire's magical abilities in my visions. Perhaps that may not be enough for *you*, Lord Glover, but my visions have proved true in the past. Remember the goblin wars?" She lifted her eyebrows in challenge. "Besides that, I think most here will agree that I possess significant magical expertise. I am, after all, the king's royal prophetess."

Talon huffed, pleased but also...curious. "What magic have you seen in your visions, Lady Saffra?"

She squared her shoulders, lifting her chin to address him. "I have seen Claire use magic to defeat our enemies." Before her words had the time to sink in, she turned to the courtiers. "I have seen Claire use advanced magic far beyond the abilities of most mages. If that is not reason enough to earn your trust, then you are all lost."

Silence fell.

Without another word, Saffra lifted her hood and turned, melting back into the crowd.

The steward snapped out of his surprise and cleared his throat. "Grand Mage Marcel, have you anything further to add?"

Marcel looked just as shocked, opening and closing his mouth before he recovered. "I do indeed, Steward." He took two steps forward, looking at the lower council. "I merely wish to say that in my *expert* opinion, Lord Glover, Lady Claire possesses extensive magical potential."

Marcel knew all about the gift, but only as of yesterday. He'd been sworn to secrecy, like everyone else who knew. Talon couldn't have people running around shouting that Cyrus lived on in some human outsider.

Lord Glover wrinkled his nose, displeased, but was resigned to sit. The steward thanked Marcel and sent him away. One last opportunity was given for arguments, but it seemed everyone was now too scared to speak up. Saffra's words had hit their mark.

"Very well," the steward said. "Your Grace, the time has come for your decision. Do you stand by your decree?"

He sat forward. "I do."

"Then it is final." The steward looked over to the chronicler and nodded. The hunched little man scribbled something upon his parchment. Court was dismissed. Those in attendance scattered, retreating from the vast hall. He remained seated, deep in thought.

"Do you think it's true?" Reyr asked, climbing the steps of the dais. "Claire will defeat our enemies with magic?"

"I hardly know."

"If it is," Verath said, "Claire has suddenly become a valuable weapon."

"It would seem so." His brow furrowed.

"Shall I go and inform her of the outcome?" Reyr asked, lifting an eyebrow to inquire.

He almost nodded. Almost. "No. I will do it."

Reyr's mouth fell open, but he said nothing.

Talon left the hall. The closer he came to Claire's chambers, the slower his footfalls became. When he arrived, he heard voices, laughter, coming from within. His jaw clenched tight when he knocked. Without waiting for permission, he opened it. Claire was sitting beside a serving girl—Desaree. Their faces were alight with mirth. He paused briefly, taken aback by the way her happiness had transformed her beatifically. The moment she laid eyes on him, however, the smile slid from her face.

He squirmed under her gaze.

Desaree jumped to her feet. "Your Majesty!" She fell to one knee.

"Please stand, Desaree," he said. She followed orders, glancing at the open door behind him, as if she were desperate to escape his presence. "Yes, yes. You may go." She scurried away like a frightened animal. He was used to it.

He shut the door and took a seat across the table from Claire. She gazed at him like someone ready to argue, despite the lack of any accusation. After the silence stretched on, her eyebrows pulled together. He watched her, hoping to spur intimidation.

Instead, *he* was the one who felt deeper unease as the moments ticked on.

He tapped his fingers against his knee before saying, "It may please you to know that the court has been informed of my decision to elevate your position. I am removing the ban I have placed upon you. You may roam the keep as you wish."

He'd expected...*something*, but she remained silent. Discomfited, he filled the air with more words. "From this day forth you are officially my ward—my responsibility. I expect you to behave appropriately, to acclimate into society. Reyr will see to the matter of...your attire."

Her kirtle was stained in several places. He wouldn't have it said that he took poor care of her. But that wasn't why he cared for her appearance. The *real* reason was, he wanted to prove everyone wrong.

Claire would be worth their time *and* their respect.

He wished she would speak. Instead, she pierced him with her gaze, making him all but squirm. He cleared his throat. "Saffra came to your aid today. You ought to thank her next time you see her."

Her eyebrows pulled together. "Saffra?"

There.

"Indeed. She presented an interesting theory. Apparently, she has seen you aid us in battle—defeat our enemies."

Claire's lips parted. "She *told* you about that? She told the court?"

"You knew?" His voice was flat.

"Of course I knew, Talon. The vision was about *me*, not you."

"You will address me as, Your Majesty, Your Grace, or King Talon. I understand that our society is different than yours, but if you are to blend in, then you must learn some propriety."

Her cheeks reddened. She looked about ready to protest. He dared her to. But instead, she pursed her lips.

"Tell me," he said. "Did you know of Lady Saffra's vision before or after your little magical display?"

"Before." She crossed her arms.

"Had you come to me, or even Reyr, we might have avoided yesterday's fiasco."

She laughed, making him shift in his seat. "Right! Come to you. Forgive me, *Your Grace*, but you're delusional. After everything, you expect me to trust *you*?" Her eyes narrowed. "Trust is earned. I'm sure you know that."

He growled, caring little that it made her flinch. "You hate me. I understand that. Very well. Go on hating me. But if we are going to outwit Kane and whatever enemies you're supposed to defeat, we must cooperate."

Her chest deflated and she schooled her features. Her eyes took on a far away look that had him leaning forward curiously. "Cyrus said you're right, and that I ought to be more respectful. That you're just trying to do your job."

His chest tightened painfully and all the fight went out of him. "He really talks to you?" A flood of desire washed over him. And jealousy.

She shrugged. "Sometimes. Like when he doesn't think I'm behaving appropriately, or if he wants to offer advice. Other times he's just my biggest cheerleader."

"Cheerleader?"

"Yes, cheerleader. You know...oh, gods, never mind." She slumped back against the sofa.

"And do you agree with him?"

Her exhale was overly dramatic. "Yes. We can't save Drag-onwall if we're fighting each other. But that doesn't mean I have to like you. I'll cooperate as best as I can—I suppose—as long as you don't keep acting like a complete and total ass."

"A donkey?"

"Ugh!" She threw up her hands. "This is ridiculous! An ass. A jerk. A horrid person. However you want to interpret it."

His mouth dropped open. She was...*insulting* him?! He almost fired back, then thought better of it.

"Do we have a deal?" she asked, narrowing her gaze.

"Fine. Deal," he barked, desperate to escape. He jumped to his feet and left without another word.

Gods, he could hardly stand another moment in the same room with her. When he reached his tower, his skin was flushed and his irritation soaring. Who did she think she was? He'd given her an elevated position, and this was how she acted about it?

He growled, going immediately to his terraced balcony. There, he shed his skin the way one discarded clothing. The dragon within him was itching to break free, clawing at him, sharp talons and all. He let it.

Leaping from the balcony, he spread his massive wings. Today, he would head north. He would leave the city far behind. He flew out over the sea before angling his left wing downward. His body swept around towards the keep. A glint of gold caught his eye. He descended.

Claire stood out on her balcony, gazing up at him.

Dropping lower, he edged closer to the castle's edifice until his wingtips nearly grazed the stone. Just as he came upon her, he caught sight of her surprise. He opened his maw and roared, shooting flames. She yelped, jumping backward.

There! Let her know his frustration. Perhaps now she would fear him like the rest. He pumped his wings once, twice, three times, in powerful downward strokes. The keep disappeared beneath him. Hopefully Claire would, too.

The last thing he wanted were thoughts of *her* intruding into his time in the sky. This sacred ritual was entirely his. Rolling over, diving down, then pulling up again, he savored the wind as it whistled past him. Still, no matter how hard he tried, he couldn't seem to get the godsdamned woman out of his head.

A chuckle rumbled deep in his belly. Her shocked expression just now had been priceless. He would pay a hundred gold dragons to see that look again. Satisfied, he beat his wings onward in the direction of Eigaden's plains. His stomach growled. The grazers would be out this evening.

As he neared the vast expanse of wilderness, thoughts of Claire continued to plague him. The way her happiness had died when he'd walked into the room earlier. The way her eyes glittered with hate when she looked at him. He couldn't blame her.

He *had* handled the entire matter of her arrival into the capital terribly. She'd tried to warn him from the start. He'd been too blind to see her real purpose—Cyrus's purpose.

She never should have gone into a dungeon cell. The trial had been absolutely unnecessary, but the way he'd behaved afterward? That was the real reason she hated him.

A flush of hot shame spread through him. She would never forgive him—not for that. He snorted. What did it matter, anyway? He did not need her forgiveness, merely her cooperation.

Aggressively, he snatched up a plump grazer and ripped it apart, feasting on its body. The poor beast did not deserve his punishment, but emotion beat him down like hammer blows. When he finished feasting, he rose into the air and claimed another. By the third, he could take no more. His stomach was stuffed. He felt his hide stretching, his scales pulling apart to accommodate.

If only Claire could see him like this, caught up in the frenzy of feeding. Perhaps *then* she would truly call him a beast. He would never—could never—forget her words. Nor could he forget how she'd unhinged him.

What *was* it about her that made him fearful?

He lifted into the air. Beneath him, only bones remained. He began his flight home. As usual, he was reluctant to return, especially knowing *she* was there.

Her presence felt like a danger to him.

He beat his wings harder, hoping the exertion would steady his mind. He dug down deep, searching himself until an answer formed. Claire felt dangerous because of the way she made *him* feel. A woman like her could only hurt him if he allowed himself to know her. He didn't need that kind of pain.

The city's lights came into view long before he reached its walls. He circled lazily towards the lowest courtyard, ignoring the light he saw from Claire's window. The way it made his pulse jump with curiosity.

He'd given up intimacy a long time ago, and for good reason. With his scars, most couldn't stomach his appearance. There were some, like Lady Caterina, capable of looking past his face for the pure sake of having the crown.

But Claire? She *looked* at him. She actually *looked* at him. There was never disgust or fear in her gaze, only hate, and that was not something created by his appearance. He'd done that all on his own.

He transformed midair, landing on his feet. Several of his guards rushed forward to greet him. "Welcome back, King Talon."

"Thank you." He nodded and strode away.

Claire hated him, yes, but not more than he hated himself. Perhaps it was better this way. After all, her kindness would do nothing more than remind him of what he could never have. No one could possibly love someone like him. Not her. Not now. Not ever.

~+~+~+~+

THE DRAGONWALL SERIES **continues in book 2: Reyr the Gold which can be found here: Reyr the Gold**

If you enjoyed this book, please consider supporting me by leaving a review or rating on Amazon and Goodreads. These help get my book noticed which is important for indie authors like me.

If you would like to stay up to date with book news, new releases, spoilers, and bonus content, sign up for my newsletter mailing list at https://www.authormelissamitchell.com/newsletter signup

ABOUT THE AUTHOR

Melissa Mitchell is a fantasy romance author and creator of the seven-book *Dragonwall* series. Her love of fantasy began with *The Dragonriders of Pern*, and she now writes stories full of dragons, magic, hidden royalty, and slow-burn romance. She holds a PhD in physics and lives in Atlanta, Georgia with her husband, a husky, and four very spoiled bunnies. When she's not writing, she enjoys baking cookies, bullet journaling, and figure skating—usually while plotting her next book.

Visit her online at: authormelissamitchell.com

Also by Melissa Mitchell

The Arcane Artifacts

Bound by the Blood Ruby

The Dragonwall Series

Talon the Black

Reyr the Gold

Verath the Red

Koldis the Green

Bedelth the Orange

Jovari the Blue

Dallin the Violet

The Lady Witch Series

Wielder's Prize

Wielder's Bond

Wielder's Might

Witch's Ruin

Witch's Heart

Witch's Crown

Royals of Dragonwall Series

For the Crown

Stand Alone Titles

Blood and Ballet